INTERSTELLAR
MAGE

BOOK ONE
OF THE RED FALCON TRILOGY

This edition published in 2018 by:
Faolan's Pen Publishing Inc.
22 King St. S, Suite 300
Waterloo, Ontario
N2J 1N8 Canada

ISBN-13: 978-1-988035-63-5 (print)
A record of this book is available from Library and Archives Canada.
Printed in the United States of America
1 2 3 4 5 6 7 8 9 10

First edition
First printing: November 2017

Illustration © 2017 Jeff Brown Graphics

Faolan's Pen Publishing logo is a trademark of Faolan's Pen Publishing Inc.

Read more books from Glynn Stewart at faolanspen.com

STARSHIP'S
MAGE

INTERSTELLAR
MAGE

BOOK ONE
OF THE RED FALCON TRILOGY

GLYNN STEWART

FAOLAN'S PEN
PUBLISHING
faolanspen.com

CHAPTER 1

MARIA ISABELLA SOPRANO had been taught a wide variety of magical techniques while in the service of the Mage-King of Mars. Among other tricks, the ring she wore would heat against her skin if the spell carved into the silver runes on its surface detected drugs or poison in her drink.

Her "date", however, was so bad at trying to slip the drug into her drink discreetly that it was all she could do not to laugh in his face.

Once that urge had passed, however, the tall and dark-haired ex-Navy officer slid her chair back from the table in the bar and glared at the somewhat pudgy man she'd met for drinks.

"What the fuck was that?" she said sweetly. "Did you just put something in my drink?"

She hadn't even realized she was fingering the gold medallion she wore on her throat, the one that marked her as a fully trained member of the Mage Guild of the Protectorate. It carried the three stars of a jump mage and the crossed swords of a combat mage—the standard symbols of the Mage officer of the Royal Martian Navy she'd once been.

Her date was staring at the medallion as he flushed and half-stumbled out of his chair.

"I didn't... I was just..."

"You just tried to drug me," Maria observed, shaking her head. *Idiot.* She wasn't quite hard up enough to need to sleep with him for a place to stay tonight, but she'd been planning on doing so. Until he'd tried to drug her.

She rose, towering over the man and intentionally using her magic to add new shadows to her loom.

"Get away from me," she continued conversationally. "Xu?"

The bartender was a massive man with a shaved head, heavyset facial features, and a pronounced fold to his eyes. At her call, he calmly produced a police-issue stungun from under the bar and laid it on top of the smooth plastic surface.

"You're paying your bill and leaving now," the big Asian man told Maria's date calmly. He didn't exactly *approve* of her habits, but being the one bar with magical gravity in the zero-gee section of Tau Ceti *f*'s main orbital station was worth a lot—and Maria was cheaper than any other Mage he could get to run his gravity runes.

"I didn't even—"

"Pay and leave." Xu picked up the stungun. Its SmartDarts were intelligent enough that the man was in no long-term danger if the bartender shot him, but it still wouldn't be a pleasant experience.

Flushing, the man tapped his wrist personal computer on the table's reader, paying the bill, and almost evaporated out of the bar.

Shaking her head, Maria took her date's drink and stepped over to the bar.

"Thanks, Xu," she told the big man.

"Warned you you were going to run out of even half-decent men for your game," Xu replied. "You're going to end up in trouble. Again."

She took a sip of the beer silently. There was no point arguing with Alexis Xu. His cousin, Sagacity Xu, had been the Martian Marine commander on her last ship, and she'd almost dragged Sagacity Xu's career down with her own.

"I got more cousins," Xu noted after a moment. "Keri works with the Jump Mage Guild. She can get you onto a ship. You're *ex-Navy*, for crying out loud. Any jump-ship in the system will fall over themselves to hire you."

"I'm one step above dishonorably discharged," Maria reminded him softly, staring into her beer. No pension. No right to the uniform.

Nothing. That was what happened when you screwed up, but not quite badly enough to get an actual dishonorable discharge.

"Half of the ships in the system won't *care*," the bartender told her. "Not for a trained Navy Commander, regardless of her current status."

"Leave it be, Alexis," she said. "I'm not going back to space."

The stipend paid to every unemployed Mage in human space would keep her fed. Her "game", as Xu called it, helped her put more aside.

Maybe someday, she'd even go home. There wasn't much appeal to the thought of the little Brazilian town she'd come from. She could follow in her father's footsteps and drink herself to death on the beach.

Or she could do the same thing here in Tau Ceti. What was the point in paying for a starship ticket when the result wasn't going to change?

Xu sighed and slid another beer across the bar.

"This one's on *your* tab," he said dryly. "And I remind you, again, that we do have a spare room back in the half-grav rings. If Sagacity finds out how you're sleeping, he might just kill me."

"My problem, Alexis," Maria told him as she took the beer. The night crowd would be wandering in in another hour or so, shipyard workers and ship's crew. She'd find someone willing to take her home in that group.

She wasn't particularly interested in using any of her *skills* at this point, but fortunately, she was still beautiful.

Maria was making carefully calibrated eye contact with a young man in a merchant uniform, waiting for his companions to talk him into approaching the older woman, when someone sat down at the bar next to her.

The newcomer cut off her eye contact with her mark, and she barely managed not to glare at him as she processed who was sitting next to her.

He was an older gentleman, likely in his late sixties or early seventies, but still clearly trim and fit. His hair had gone pure white, but he had a full head of it cropped close to his skull. He wore a plain black suit and white shirt without a tie, and was smiling knowingly at her as he shook his head.

"You know, Mage-Commander," he greeted her calmly, "when I'm sent to look for an officer who I'm told is drinking and whoring themselves to death, I expect something somewhat different."

Her irritation flashed to anger and she felt warmth flare around her fists as her magic unconsciously responded.

"I don't see how it's any of your fucking business," she said bluntly. "If you'll excuse me."

She began to rise, only for a liver-spotted-but-still-iron grip to lock onto her shoulder and pin her to her chair.

"I apologize," he replied. "That was rude, but...it was a point that needed to be made, Mage-Commander Soprano."

"I am not a Mage-Commander anymore," Maria hissed. "If you have a clue who I am, you know that."

"True enough." The iron grip didn't move. "I am Brent Alois, and I am a friend."

"Bullshit. I don't have friends anymore. Who's friends with the disgraced?"

"Mr. Xu over there might object to that comment," Alois told her. "I didn't say you were my friend, Commander. Only that I was yours."

"Did the Xus send you?" she demanded. "Are you another goddamn cousin?"

Alois laughed, a cheerful noise that flashed pure white teeth.

"No," he told her. "Though I did interview Lieutenant Sagacity Xu before I came to see you."

Maria winced. *Lieutenant* Sagacity Xu had been *Captain* Sagacity Xu before she'd dragged him into her damn fool crusade. He'd been demoted. She'd been kicked out.

Disobedience to orders could be forgiven if the results proved out the actions. Hers...hers hadn't done anything close.

"What do you want?" she finally asked.

"Ten minutes of your time. Maybe twenty," Alois replied. "I have a proposal for you, Commander."

"I'm not a Commander anymore," she reminded him.

He smiled.

"I know. And I know why. I'm also quite certain that Navigator Jamieson behind me won't disappear in the next half hour, so if you *aren't* interested, you can go right back to seducing the poor kid with your eyes and cleavage."

"You're not my type," she snapped.

"No, I presume not," he agreed cheerfully. "But I was on the other side of this conversation once, long ago. Please, Miss Soprano. Twenty minutes of your time. That's all."

She glanced over at Xu. It wouldn't be obvious to most people that he was giving her and the strange older man space, but she'd been half-living out of this bar for six months. Xu might not know who Alois was, but he was a good judge of character—and the space he was giving meant he thought the man was worth hearing out.

"Ten minutes," she said shortly. "Then you can go fuck yourself."

The iron grip relaxed and Alois smiled at her.

"My wife would *hate* it if I did that. Come on, Mage Soprano. I have an office booked nearby."

Outside the runes that Maria had installed for Xu's bar, they were in the steady-state, zero-gravity portion of Tau Ceti *f*'s Armstrong Station, the main orbital for civilian shipping above one of the two worlds in humanity's first colony.

Like the hundred or so colonies that had followed it, Tau Ceti paid allegiance to the Mage-King of Mars in exchange for his protection and the services of the Mage Guild in providing the jump mages that tied humanity's far-flung worlds together.

Science had never given humanity the keys to the stars. Mages like Maria Soprano, however, had—even if the price for their existence was enough to give those who researched it nightmares.

Alois handled the switch to zero gravity with the assured aplomb of an experienced spacer, another piece of a puzzle that Maria was beginning to see the outline of. She wasn't quite sure what the solution to the puzzle was, but she could tell it was there.

The office he led her to also had gravity runes, an unusual expense but a requirement to have an office space in the zero-gravity section of Armstrong. There were six small rooms off a central hub, all with gravity, and all empty. It was late in the night by the time of the far-distant Olympus Mons, the standard time the Protectorate's space installations ran on.

"Rental offices are handy things," the older man told her as he pulled a chair out for her. "They give you a key, don't care if you come in after hours, and don't ask too many questions."

"I can't imagine one with gravity runes is cheap," Maria observed. She suspected he'd rented the office just to meet with her, too, and she wasn't sure just what she had agreed to.

"It's not," he confirmed. He took a seat and gestured her to the other one. "I'd offer you a drink, but all they have in the fridge is water, and the coffeepot hasn't been run. It's slow and would cut into my ten minutes."

"So is your babbling," she replied crisply.

Alois grinned at her and tapped a key on his wrist-comp. The wall behind him dissolved into a screen showing the Royal Martian Navy service record for Mage-Commander Maria Isabella Soprano.

"You," he said unnecessarily. "Earth native. Mage by Blood, descended from MGS-276, AKA Megan Grayson. Neither of your younger siblings pinged, though," he noted. "One of those unfortunate flukes that come along."

Mages by Blood were linked back to the survivors of Project Olympus, their families forming a pseudo-aristocracy for the Protectorate. They were confirmed by the testing every child of the Protectorate underwent, unlike Mages by Right, the uncommon flukes the tests existed to catch.

"Excelled in school, excelled at the Lunar Academy, top efficiency reports from your midshipwoman cruise," he continued. "Service with distinction for ten years in His Majesty's Navy."

"I know all of this," she pointed out. "And how it ended."

"Indeed." Alois shook his head. "Unilaterally assuming command of your destroyer while the skipper was on shore leave, and rushing off to tangle with pirates. You misestimated the enemy, and *Swords at Dawn* was badly damaged, leaving now-Lieutenant Xu trapped aboard the pirate station until Commodore Cor arrived in the actually planned counter-operation and saved everyone under your command."

"I know what I did," she snapped. "If all you're going to do is rehash history, I think we're done here."

She began to rise, but Alois chuckled.

"The door won't open for you," he said quietly. "The office landlord would be quite displeased if he found out what I've done to it, but I'll fix it before I give it back. We're also inside a white-noise privacy generator, if you were wondering what the buzzing was."

"Let. Me. Go." Power flared around Maria as she turned on the strange little man, but he just smiled and shook his head.

"You said ten minutes, Miss Soprano, and I'm afraid I must insist."

"How do you plan on stopping me?" she demanded.

"Honestly? I have no way to stop you," Alois said with a small smile. "But I am the only person willing to offer you what you need. What you've been looking for since the Navy kicked you out."

"And what's that?"

"A cause," he told her softly. "You charged to the rescue. It was foolish and careless, but it was for all the right reasons. There are many people in this galaxy who will do what they think is the right thing when it doesn't endanger them.

"There aren't many with the courage to put their entire life's ambition at risk to do what they think is the right thing. You were wrong and you failed, but that doesn't change what you did or why you did it."

"Who are you?" Maria asked.

"Major Brent Alois, Martian Interstellar Security Service," he said simply. "The Agency. We are the shadows in the dark, Mage Soprano, who watch for the knives aimed at the Protectorate's back. Like the Royal Martian Navy, we serve His Majesty, Desmond Michael Alexander the Third, but we are not the public face of his sword."

That fit with the puzzle.

"Ex-Marine," she concluded, slotting the last piece into place.

He chuckled again and nodded.

"I was a Marine Captain once, yes," he agreed. "Like your Xu, I followed a Navy officer into the wrong place for the right reasons. In my case, the officer in question ended up dead," he concluded sadly, "so I took the fall. Dishonorable discharge for mutiny in peacetime.

"Then someone came into the bar I was drinking myself to death in and gave me an offer, just like I did for you. MISS has been my life for thirty-five years, Mage Soprano. Guarding the shadows behind the Protectorate's back." He smiled. "It's a cause worth fighting for. Worth *living* for."

He was certainly passionate enough, twinging the same nerves that had resulted in Maria being damned stupid back aboard *Swords at Dawn*.

"*If* I were interested," she said slowly, "what would you want me to do?"

"You were a Navy Mage-Commander," Alois replied. "Every merchant ship in this system would love to snap you up—and we'd like you to be snapped up by a specific ship.

"The crew has been in and out of a lot of trouble and the Protectorate owes them a debt—but they've also got a target painted on their backs.

"We want you to protect them," he noted. "But...we also want to use them as bait.

"With you as the first jaw of the trap."

CHAPTER 2

LIKE ANY MERCHANT CAPTAIN of the twenty-fifth century, David Rice was familiar with a vast variety of paperwork. Contracts for carriage. Permits, authorizations, licenses and ownerships for starships and space shuttles. Contracts for employment.

The form on the screen in front of him was brutally straightforward and utterly terrifying.

It authorized him to carry an arsenal of no more than one hundred antimatter-fueled and -armed missiles, ten five-gigawatt battle lasers and twenty-five five-hundred-megawatt rapid-fire laser anti-missile turrets.

The ship hovering just outside his window had been a Royal Martian Navy armed auxiliary once, with enough firepower to make certain that no pirate dared threaten her. The magazines for her ten missile launchers could carry four times as many weapons as the Navy was allowing him to own, but his "normal" paperwork included the authorization for as many fusion-drive kinetic missiles as he could fit aboard the ship.

RFLAM turrets were normal, if not usually in this quantity. His last ship, *Blue Jay*, had carried two. Defensive battle lasers and missile launchers loaded with fusion-drive missiles were uncommon, but licensed through normal procedures.

Normally, a vessel like *Red Falcon* would have been stripped of her original guns. New, civilian-grade missile launchers would have been installed. Indeed, David had acquired all of the permits necessary to do such *before* the document on his screen had arrived.

The content of the document was terrifying enough, but the plain signature at the bottom still almost refused to register.

Captain David Rice of the merchant ship *Red Falcon* was authorized to keep the ship's service weaponry under a personal writ from Mage-King Desmond Michael Alexander himself.

The ship was a payment of debts owed. Royal Martian Navy warships had destroyed his *Blue Jay* after her Ship's Mage had made some theoretically impossible and unquestionably illegal changes to the rune matrix that allowed the ship to jump.

Red Falcon was a replacement, signed off on by the Hand of the Mage-King, one of Mars's roving warrior-judges, who'd drafted said Ship's Mage a year ago now. David didn't know exactly what Damien Montgomery was up to now, but apparently it was enough to make the Mage-King think the debt extended to allowing David an armed merchant ship.

He tapped a button on his wrist PC, linking to his ever-loyal executive officer.

"Jenna, can you meet me in my office?" he asked softly.

"We need to meet with Commodore Burns in just over an hour, boss," Jenna Campbell replied. "Can it wait?"

"No," he decided after a moment. "Get up here, Jenna. You need to know what we've got into *before* we meet with Burns."

David's long-time friend, comrade and subordinate was a broad-shouldered, noticeably overweight blonde woman of his own indeterminate "forties-ish" age. Jenna Campbell had been merchant ship crew her entire adult life, without his own stint in the Royal Martian Navy, working her way up from cargo handler to executive officer, as high as a non-Mage could go without owning the ship themselves.

Currently, technically, she was no more an XO than David was a Captain—*Red Falcon* wasn't yet an active ship, though ownership had been transferred. If they weren't doing much to the weapons systems now, he'd have his ship soon enough.

He wordlessly pointed her to the wallscreen where he'd thrown up the authorization form. Campbell took a few seconds to skim it.

"Holy shit," she exclaimed after a moment, then paused to consider. "That accelerates the fitting-out process significantly if we don't have to rip out and replace the guns."

"And leaves us with almost three times as many launchers, turrets and beams as I was planning on having added to the girl," he agreed. "I wonder if Burns knew this was coming. He was certainly dragging his feet on when they were going to get around to disarming her."

Red Falcon wasn't the absolute last of her kind in the Royal Martian Navy, but the Martians had decided a while back that, since the limiter on *strategic* speed was how many Mages a ship had, they were better served by purchasing regular ships and stuffing them with Navy Mages than having custom ships.

The Armed Auxiliary Fast Heavy Freighter program had been shut down, but the Navy had found themselves with twenty-odd ships that could accelerate alongside cruisers, fight alongside destroyers, and carry as much cargo as a large civilian ship.

The cost of the AAFHF ships like *Red Falcon* had to be part of why they'd stopped building them, but David was surprised at how quickly they'd been phased out of service. It seemed to him that having dedicated ships that could carry Navy cargo and keep up with Navy task forces was worth keeping some around.

But he didn't run the Navy. Just his one no-longer-little ship.

"What about the deposits on the weapons we had booked?" Jenna asked.

He sighed.

"I'm going to confirm with Burns before I do anything, and we'll still be stocking up on fusion missiles regardless—the Navy launchers can fire both, and I think we can fit two of the kinetic-kill birds in where we'd have one AM weapon—but I'm pretty sure I'm out the deposits," he admitted.

Which was painful. While he wasn't complaining about what the Protectorate was giving him in trade for *Blue Jay*, he was starting to feel the pinch on his cash reserves from sitting still for a year and hanging on to his best officers along the way.

Falcon was also going to require over four times *Jay's* crew, especially with the gunners he'd need if the Navy were leaving her full weapons systems intact.

"It's going to be an interesting few days," he told Campbell. "Once we meet with Burns, I think tonight may be the last free time you have for a few days, XO."

"A few days, boss?" She laughed at him. "If we're getting the keys, we need to hire four hundred hands, at least half of them with real Navy experience, ASAP. That bird is going to take *tons* of antimatter to operate, and she won't be making us a dime sitting in dock."

"That she won't," he agreed. "I want to be in space fifteen days after they hand her over, Jenna. We've still got Kellers as chief engineer, but we'll need new Mages, pilots... Once we've got the officers, I'll leave the rest to you and them while I find us a cargo."

"Sure, take the *easy* job!"

"If you'd rather switch," David replied, "I'm sure I can find ex-Navy gunners in one of the Mage-King's biggest Fleet bases more easily than I can find *twenty million tons of cargo*."

Commodore Rasputin Burns's office was in the main command center for the Tau Ceti shipyards. The center was attached to the zero-gravity section of the main station, an armed and armored spike that stood sentinel over the heart of the yards.

It was outside the sections of the station that spun to provide the closest thing to technological artificial gravity humanity's technology could provide, but the Mages who had given humanity interstellar travel had also discovered a way to provide artificial gravity.

David Rice didn't pretend to understand how Mages did *any* of what they did, but there were certain sets of runes he'd learned to recognize: the jump runes that allowed starships to travel between worlds, and the gravity runes that allowed him to walk safely.

Few ships could afford the latter outside the Navy, mostly because they required weekly renewal by a Mage. Navy ships had more Mages aboard than did civilian ships, for multiple reasons, and hence could afford the time and energy.

A shipboard facility like the command center was easier to justify, David supposed, though much of the center would still be zero-gee. Only the main thoroughfares and offices had magical gravity, but as a civilian he'd never see anything else.

He and Campbell were met by Royal Martian Marines when they entered the station, a smiling pair of young men who cheerfully saw them through the plain corridors to where Commodore Burns was waiting for them.

The sharp-featured and dark-haired Commodore greeted them with a broad smile as they stepped into his office.

"Captain Rice, Miss Campbell. It's a pleasure as always. Coffee? Tea?"

"Coffee, please," David told him.

"Tea," Campbell added.

They took their indicated seats while the Commodore's aide poured the drinks. Burns's office was the same standard Naval administrator office David had seen in four different postings in three star systems during his service. The desk, the chair, the computer screens and filing cabinets were all identical to those offices, courtesy of the Mage-King's military logistics pipeline.

Burns, however, had decorated his walls with models of the current generations of destroyers and cruisers of the Royal Martian Navy, vessels that would have been built in these yards under his supervision.

One of the models caught David's eye. It was the almost unique tall mushroom of the AAFHFs like *Red Falcon*. A forward dome shielded the cargo and habitation spaces from radiation, and a rotating ring was tucked under the shield to provide living quarters and work space for the crew. A long, narrow stem extended back from there, providing the base for an array of struts that cargo containers could link to, with a massive cylindrical pod at the end of the core to contain the engines and fuel tanks.

"We built two of the AAFHFs after I got this office," Burns said, seeing where David's gaze had gone. "The last two ever built, so far as I know. Hulls twenty-four and twenty-five. Twenty-four entered service for a year before decommissioning." He laughed, somewhat bitterly.

"Hull twenty-five went straight from space trials to mothballs," he admitted. "And that's the one His Majesty is giving you, Captain Rice. *Red Falcon*."

"His Majesty's generosity continues to amaze me," David told him. "Even if the timeline hasn't been what I'd hoped for."

"I understand," the Commodore agreed. "Much of that was politics." He waved his hand dismissively. "The politicians involved may have worn uniforms, but that doesn't change the nature of the problem.

"*Red Falcon* was fully worked up, with all of her weapons systems checked out, but she only ever made two jumps. We haven't had a lot of time to go over her systems over the last eight months, and, frankly, some of the people who should have been making sure it happened weren't comfortable handing that ship over to a civilian."

"I see their concerns," David conceded, "but I understand that His Majesty has made his opinion very clear."

Burns smirked.

"Hand Stealey told me what this was in payment of," he told the merchant captain. "Mikhail Azure's death seems enough to me, even if I get the feeling that the Lady Hand wasn't telling me everything."

David managed to keep his smile. There were aspects of the situation that Hand Alaura Stealey, the Mage-King's personal troubleshooter who had drafted his old Ship's Mage, had told him were going to remain secret. *Red Falcon* was the payment for keeping their mouths shut.

"I was also waiting on the writ that arrived from Sol this morning," Burns noted. "I was honestly expecting it three months ago; that's why I didn't push any of my idiots."

"I see," David admitted. "So, do I get my ship?"

He felt a bit rude putting it so bluntly, but he'd been cooling his heels in Tau Ceti for almost an entire year. He was a *spacer*. He wanted stars under his feet again.

"The last I'd heard, all of her systems were back online and everything *should* be working," the Commodore replied. "I gave the orders to start fueling her up an hour ago, but filling the hydrogen and antimatter tanks on a ship of her scale from nothing to full takes a while.

"We also need to load your hundred missiles," he continued. "His Majesty made clear that those were coming from our stocks."

"His generosity continues to amaze," David repeated.

"I can tell there's more going on than I was being told," Burns said. "But I'm a military officer. I know when to shut up and soldier on, Captain. You'll have *Red Falcon* in three days. Will you have crew for her?"

"I have some personnel from my old ship, Jenna here and my old Chief Engineer," he replied. "We'll be recruiting once we have her in hand."

"Of course," the Commodore agreed. He tapped his wrist PC and ejected a chip. "Certain...mutual friends told me to pass this on to you. It's contact information for a Mage who is uniquely qualified for your needs."

David eyed the datachip warily.

"How uniquely qualified are we talking?"

"She was a Navy Mage-Commander until a few months ago," Burns told her. "She's *good*, Captain Rice, and if you can, I'd snap her up before someone else does."

"If she's so good, why is she available?"

Burns shrugged expressively.

"Well, she *was* discharged for disobeying orders," he said delicately. "Some people prefer not to hire those who have creative interpretations of the rules. Your reputation, however..."

GLYNN STEWART

"Precedes me, I see," David agreed with amusement of his own. "I'll interview her, Commodore. Tell your 'mutual friends' I don't promise more than that."

CHAPTER 3

THE ELEVATOR PODS that moved people from the zero-gravity, mostly motionless core of Armstrong Station to the spinning rings with their three quarters of a gravity, clearly labeled what direction gravity was going to be upon arrival.

David had ridden hundreds, if not thousands, of similar pods over his life, and it was inevitable that someone in the vehicle didn't pay enough attention. A burly gentleman in a simple suit, almost certainly a planetsider of some kind, missed the flashing arrows and came crashing down as the pod accelerated up to the speed of the rings.

As was typical, the big man crashed down across a pair of teenage girls with the lanky builds of the spaceborn. They'd oriented themselves perfectly and had been lost in conversation with each other and several other people on their wrist-comps.

The businessman was starting to splutter angrily at the two shocked kids he'd landed on when David and Campbell materialized. David Rice wasn't a tall man, but he was heavily built with broad shoulders and an imposing physical presence.

Campbell's own bulk was less intimidating, but it also made her motherly enough that the two girls almost instinctively tucked in behind her as David *politely* offered his hand to the fallen businessman.

"You should watch the signs," he told the stranger. "Falling like that can hurt yourself and others."

He turned to the girls. "Are you two okay?"

"Yeah," the taller teen responded after visually checking over her more shocked friend. "Thanks, Captain."

The burly stranger took David's hand and carefully came to his feet, swallowing his irritation and embarrassment, as it was clear no one around him was going to side with him over the girls.

"Thank you, Captain," he echoed the teenager finally, then inclined his head to the children still half-hiding behind Campbell. "My apologies, ladies. This is my first time in space and I didn't know where to look."

The self-effacing humor was forced and stilted, but it was better than the tongue-lashing he'd clearly been planning on giving them. A token effort made, the stranger half-stalked away into the small crowd in the pod.

David watched him for a moment to make sure the crisis was defused, and spotted another man who was standing on the edge of the crowd with a wry grin. He was a tall, dark-haired man with shoulders almost as broad as David's and looked like he'd been about to wade into the mess himself.

Despite his plain shipsuit, something about the man screamed *soldier*—but he simply gave David a respectful nod before disappearing into the crowd himself.

"Black hole," the outspoken teenager hissed after the departing businessman once the crowd had closed behind him. "Always some planet-sucker without *eyes*."

"Always," David agreed cheerfully. "You should keep your own eyes peeled for them."

The quiet girl giggled and poked her friend, who sighed and nodded.

"Fair enough, Captain." The two girls gave him grateful nods of their own. "Thanks again."

Leaving the pod, David and Campbell passed into the rapidly shifting crowds of Armstrong Station Ring One's main concourse. The designers had put a massive public gallery next to the main arrival station for the transfer pods, and their successors had happily installed everything from a public water feature—a combination pool, fountain and quarter-million-liter water reserve for the station—to a shifting holographic mural—this week a hand-rendered scene of Paris on Earth—to dozens of restaurants, shops and market stalls.

It was the retail heart of Ring One and constantly packed. Armstrong Security officers were scattered through the crowd in stand-out pale-blue uniforms. While David knew from the bitter experience of a misspent youth that the security guards carried stunguns, they kept them out of sight.

Here, at least, they were glorified mall cops.

"Any chance to go shopping?" Campbell asked with a laugh.

"We've been here for months," he pointed out. "Anything you've needed, I'm sure you found by now."

"Yes, but I've been living out of a cheap short-term rental for those months," she replied reasonably. "Now I know we're going to have a home in a few days."

He chuckled.

"The Navy built her," he pointed out. "I wouldn't count on your quarters being big enough for much of anything. Their priority was cargo space, speed and guns—in that order, so far as I can tell. Comfortable quarters weren't in there at all."

"It can't be *that* bad."

David Rice, who had once been a junior petty officer in His Majesty's Navy, just shook his head. His XO had *no* idea just what the Navy could cram into a berthing compartment.

"You'll learn," he warned ominously. "The innocent always learn."

Before Campbell could respond, however, someone stepped up between them and put a hand on David's shoulder. It was the big observer he'd seen on the pod, the man who'd registered as a soldier.

"Captain Rice, you are in danger," he murmured in a soft baritone. "There are three men following you. They're good but not good enough."

"Who are you?" David snapped, though he was willing to extend enough trust not to look for their pursuers.

"A friend," the soldier murmured. "Also, a job applicant. My resume is buried somewhere in your stack for Chief of Security."

"So you're stalking us?" Campbell said.

"Nah, I just recognized you in the pod and then spotted your tails," he told them. "Turn left here."

Here was a side corridor that led them past a curry restaurant and out of the main gallery. The soldier guided them away from the concourse into quieter corridors.

"Are you armed?"

"No," David replied. "This is Armstrong Station!"

"Apparently, some of your enemies have a long reach," their new friend told them, glancing back over his shoulder. "Here."

He pulled a familiar Martian-built caseless pistol from the pockets of the unmarked shipsuit. "I only have one spare, so whichever one of you is the better shot..."

David took the gun, checking the safety and ammunition level. The Martian Armaments Caseless Six-Millimeter was a familiar old friend, but he'd never expected to need a gun here. The only enemy he'd had with this long an arm had died a year earlier, in the same incident the Navy was giving him *Red Falcon* to make up for.

"Shouldn't we still be moving?" Campbell asked.

"Won't do you any good," the man said grimly. "If they picked up our side trip here, they'll follow you anywhere. They've got you dialed in, probably through station security."

"You've given me a gun," David pointed out. "You may as well give me a name."

Especially if the man was applying for a job on *Red Falcon*. David found the mess suspicious, but something about the man suggested he could be trusted—which left David suspecting *why* he'd been around to see the hunters rather than his intent.

"Skavar," the man told them. "Ivan Skavar, once a Sergeant in the Royal Martian Marines. Currently retired."

"Indeed," David accepted calmly. "So, tell me, Ivan, who's paying you to watch my back?"

Skavar didn't even blink.

"Don't know," he admitted. "Ask came down through my old captain; he begged a favor and said it was from the highest of high mucks."

That was almost certainly Hand Alaura Stealey.

David shook his head, but before he could say more, gunfire echoed in the cramped corridor. A gray-clad figure stepped around a corner and opened fire with a submachine gun before any of them could react.

Skavar slammed into David, flinging the starship captain to the deck as bullets ricocheted down the corridor. Rolling off of a winded David, the Marine opened fire with a weapon the captain hadn't seen him draw.

His weapon was almost identical to the one their attacker was using, but Skavar was kneeling on one knee with his SMG in perfect firing stance. Their attacker had emptied most of a magazine down the hallway and hadn't hit either man.

Skavar took him down with two three-round bursts to the chest.

"Check your friend," he snapped at David before firing again, another three-round burst dropping a second attacker before they could do anything.

That was when David realized the Marine had only knocked him down. Campbell was hit.

Leaving the shooting to the expert, he knelt by his old friend, checking over her injuries. She'd taken several solid hits across her arm and upper torso, and while they weren't instantly fatal, none of them looked good.

The bubbling red froth on her lips told him the first concern. She had one lung untouched, but the other was a classic sucking chest wound. The medical supplies he had on him were limited, but they should be enough to keep her alive.

David barely heard the continued exchange of gunfire as he focused his will on keeping Jenna Campbell alive. She'd lost consciousness from blood loss *far* too quickly for his peace of mind as he taped a bandage over the hole in her chest, leaving a corner open to "breathe", and then worked over her other injuries.

Skavar reappeared from somewhere, pressing a Marine emergency personal medkit into his hand. The kit was a rough-and-ready thing, designed to allow someone conscious but injured to keep themselves alive until help arrived—but it was more than he'd had.

Bandages went onto wounds. A shot of adrenaline went into Campbell's neck while the Marine held her still. The two men stayed focused on her for long enough that David didn't think either of them realized one of Armstrong Station's emergency medical carts had arrived, a pair of EMTs dismounting to take over the task.

Letting them take care of his friend, David collapsed against the wall, breathing heavily as he looked back up the corridor. Four bodies were sprawled on the ground where they'd met Ivan Skavar's gunfire.

"You were looking for a job, huh?" he asked softly.

"Like I said, my resume is in the stack for your new Chief of Security," Skavar confirmed. The ex-Marine was breathing heavily, but the only blood on him was Campbell's. None of their attackers had even managed to hit him.

"You're hired."

"Oh, good," the big man replied. "Explaining this mess to Armstrong Security is going to suck regardless, but now I can dump most of that on you...boss."

CHAPTER 4

DAVID AND SKAVAR were left to wait in an office at the nearest Armstrong Security office for several hours while the police went through the scene and tried to work out just what had happened in that secluded back corridor.

Eventually, a middle-aged woman with a perpetual frown and wrinkle lines clomped into the office and offered them both a perfunctory handshake.

"Detective Olivia Constantine," she said briskly. "Congratulations, gentlemen, you've stacked up more corpses in an afternoon than my district usually sees in six months."

"It wasn't exactly our choice," David told her.

"No," Constantine agreed. "I've already reviewed the footage. There's no question who fired first, though Mr. Skavar here seemed quite certain an attack was coming."

"I was trained in VIP protection as a Marine noncom," Skavar replied. "I can recognize a tail setting up to start a fight."

She glared at the ex-Marine for several seconds but then nodded.

"I'm familiar with the program in question," she said with a sigh. "Like I said, it's a pretty open-and-shut case of self-defense, and a bug has already been put in my ear that barring evidence to the contrary, we won't be pursuing that further."

"Thank you, Detective," David said. "Do you know who tried to kill me?"

"Good news and bad news on that front," the cop told them. "Bad news is they aren't known to Armstrong Security or the Tau Ceti security forces in general. Didn't flag on Protectorate databases, either.

"Good news is that we traced them back pretty easily, for all that," she continued. "Your foursome arrived together on a passenger liner a week ago. We're checking to see if we can link them to anybody else, but it looks like they came here looking for you in particular, Captain Rice."

"Wonderful," David said flatly. And now Campbell was in intensive care. Either he had enemies he didn't know about, or someone was looking for revenge for Mikhail Azure.

"We'll coordinate with the Martian Investigation Service," she told him. "They'll likely take over the case now that it looks to be interstellar in nature."

The MIS were the Protectorate-wide investigators, the people with the multi-system jurisdiction whose job it was to make sure that criminals couldn't just flee one star system and be safe.

"I appreciate your help, Detective," David said. "This wasn't where I expected my day to end up."

"It's never where anyone expects their day to end," the detective agreed. "If anything comes up to give you an idea of who tried to gun you down, I'll let you know. Otherwise, I'd ask that you not leave Armstrong Station for a week or two while we get things sorted out."

"I'm supposed to take possession of a new ship in a few days," he warned her, "but it'll be a week or so before we're ready to ship out."

"That should be fine," Constantine admitted. "I'll let you know if there's a problem before then, Captain."

A light blinked on her wrist-comp and she checked her message. A ghost of a relieved smile crossed her face.

"That was from the district hospital," she told them. "Your officer is out of surgery and looks like she's going to pull through. I can have a cart brought up to take you over?"

"I'd appreciate that," David repeated. "And thank you for all your help."

"I didn't do anything yet," the woman replied grimly. "Thank me if I manage to trace the shooters back to the hand that set them in motion. And, Captain?"

"Yes?"

"Until we find that hand, watch your damned back."

The small electric cart delivered them to the district hospital with aplomb, though David carefully didn't note that their driver wore the shoulder flashes of Armstrong Security's tactical team.

The two guns that Skavar had produced earlier had disappeared into the labyrinthine confines of Armstrong Security's evidence lockers and attached bureaucracy, though David suspected that the dark-haired ex-Marine was far from unarmed.

The last former Marine he'd commanded had been a pilot, not a ground-pounder, and it had *still* been impossible to make sure the man was ever unarmed. He'd have been surprised if Skavar didn't have at least one more gun, let alone anything else.

At first glance, the district hospital didn't stand out significantly from any other collection of rooms attached to the main thoroughfares of Armstrong Station. Unlike most, however, it had a set of glowing green crosses on the doors, projecting out into the hallway to make sure the hospital was as obvious as possible.

The Protectorate Charter, the deal the system governments made for the Mage-King's protection and access to the Jump Mages of the Mage Guild, required a minimum level of healthcare for all citizens. Hospitals like this, funded by a mix of Protectorate, private and system funds, were the main delivery vector for that care.

"This is where I leave you," the cop told them. "Here, take this."

He slipped David a red data disk.

"That contains the direct alert code for the AST teams," he continued. "Flash that through your wrist-comp and we'll have a dozen armed cops on the scene inside ten minutes, anywhere on the station."

"Thank you," David told him. "I hope I won't need it."

"Someone tried to hunt you down and shoot you on our station, Captain Rice." The cop smiled grimly. "Armstrong Security Tactical takes that...*personally.*"

"I'll keep it on hand," David promised.

They were met in the front reception of the hospital by a tall dark-skinned doctor in a white lab coat and matching white turban. He flagged them down before they even reached the main desk, crossing to them briskly with a wide smile and an outreached hand.

"Captain Rice! You're looking for Miss Campbell?" he asked.

"I am," David replied. "I think you have the advantage of me."

"Dr. Abdullah Singh," the physician introduced himself. "I'm the third-shift trauma surgeon here. Detective Constantine told me you were on your way."

"How is my XO, Doctor?" David asked.

"Come this way," Singh instructed. "We're better off discussing this in private."

He led the way into a side office and gestured the two men to seats. "This is the young man who intervened to help?" he asked, eyeing Skavar.

"He is," David confirmed. "And now my Chief of Security, once I have a ship again."

"From what I've heard, it would have made a solid job interview," Singh agreed. "Miss Campbell will live," he continued. "But...it will be some time before she is fully up to speed again.

"Her right shoulder blade and upper arm bone were both shattered," he said calmly. "She also took two bullets through her right lung and had her air pipe clipped by another round. You were the one providing first aid on the scene?"

"I was," David said, shivering at the calm litany of injuries.

"You saved her life," Singh stated. "Without proper care for the chest wound, she would have died before the EMTs reached her. She will live because you acted quickly and appropriately."

"What kind of recovery is she looking at?"

"I'll want to keep her in intensive care for at least a week," the doctor replied. "After that, if you have a decent ship's doctor, I could see releasing her to their care aboard ship, but she would need to be restricted to very light duty, no more than a few hours a shift, for at least a month."

"We can do that," David promised. Hiring a doctor had just moved significantly up his priority list.

"Good. She should be awake shortly if you want to wait around to talk to her," Singh told him. "But you will need to take it *very* carefully with her, today and in future. She's going to be in bad shape for a while."

"I owe Jenna Campbell my life a few times over," David said quietly. "Whatever it takes, we'll make sure it happens."

"That's what she needs," the doctor replied. "She almost died today, Captain. That takes some coming back from."

"I know. She'll get what she needs."

"You should probably go get some rest yourself," David told Skavar. "I'll be here for a bit and I shouldn't need security."

"All right," the ex-Marine replied. "You said we don't have a ship yet, but is there an office I should be checking out for security and safety?"

"Yeah." David reeled off the address. "The yards say we're going to get *Red Falcon* in a few days, so we don't have to worry about the rental office for too much longer. I'll decide if we're going to keep it for interviews, well, after I've checked on Jenna."

"Good call," Skavar agreed softly. "See you on the flip side, Captain."

"Git," David ordered.

The Marine obeyed and David stepped into the room where Campbell was resting. Slumped back in the bed unconscious, she looked astonishingly frail and vulnerable. Several cuffs around her arms and legs were connected to various scanners and bags of fluid, and he winced at the bandages across her torso.

He'd hoped that this kind of trouble was over for him and his crew. The Blue Star Syndicate had hated his guts, but after Damien Montgomery had been done, they'd been a headless mess.

David missed the earnest young man who'd been his Ship's Mage. He did *not* miss the young Mage's ability to be a trouble magnet. He'd lost too many crew running across the galaxy with Montgomery, though he'd freely admit half of that had been *his* fault.

He took the seat next to the bed and sighed. To his surprise, his XO slowly opened her eyes at the noise.

"I didn't mean to wake you," he said softly.

"Wasn't asleep," she whispered. "Just resting."

"They tell me you're staying in here for a bit," he told her. "And you're going to listen to them and do what they say, is that clear, XO?"

Campbell laughed, then coughed and winced.

"Clear, skipper."

"Does it hurt?"

"Nah, I'm too drugged up to hurt much," she admitted. "They do good work, from where I'm sitting. I'm going to be fine."

"So they assure me, and the doctor seemed trustworthy."

"Reminds me of Narveer," Campbell told him. "I've met Sikh men who weren't honest bastions of good, but they do seem to be the exception, don't they?"

"True enough," he agreed. "You didn't have to get shot to get out of the interviews, you know. If you'd told me it was *this* much of a problem..."

Even in the dimly lit hospital room, he could see her roll her eyes.

"Wheel my hospital bed in and I'll do your damned interviews for you," she told him. "You ain't that helpless!"

"No, I'm not," David said. "And you are doing *nothing* except healing for the next week. *Red Falcon* won't ship out for a week to ten days at least. You can let the doctors put you back together."

She exhaled heavily and nodded slightly.

"Can't argue there," she murmured, her eyes half-closing.

"Rest, Jenna," he ordered. "I'm not going anywhere. I'll be here when you wake up."

CHAPTER 5

MARIA STOPPED OUTSIDE the office she'd been given the address for, facing a matched pair of male and female guards from a very familiar mold. They wore plain, unmarked shipsuits, but their body language told her everything she needed to know: Captain Rice's security were ex-Marines.

And based off her own situation, she suspected there might be less *ex* about them than the good Captain thought. The young man on the left, for example, *might* have completed his training and a single five-year tour.

Maybe.

She turned an executive officer's level gaze on them.

"I'm here to meet with Captain Rice," she told them. "I have an appointment."

The female Marine was far closer to what Maria expected of retired ex-Marines, clearly into her thirties with short-cropped hair and the lines around the eyes of someone who'd seen real action. She had a holographic screen projected from her wrist-comp and checked it.

"Commander Soprano?" she asked respectfully.

"Just Ms. Soprano now," Maria replied, "but yes."

"Of course." Both Marines saluted regardless. "Corporal Lisa Ambrose, *Red Falcon* security. You're expected."

"I'm meeting with Captain Rice and Officer Campbell, correct?"

"Officer Campbell is in the hospital," Ambrose replied. "She'll recover, but you're just meeting with the Captain today."

"What happened?" Maria asked. From her conversation with Alois, she could guess. It seemed that the good Captain's past was already catching up with him. The ex-Marines were less decorative than she'd thought, then.

"Not my place to say," the guard said crisply. "We got hired after; don't know the details anyway. Skipper is waiting for you in the office. Good luck, ma'am."

"Thank you, Corporal."

Past the guards, the rental office was a small space. A tiny reception area with a drink station, a meeting room and four offices. The reception desk was occupied by a tall, dark-haired man with his feet up—and a standard Royal Martian Marine Corps nine-millimeter battle rifle lying on the desk next to him.

"Captain Rice is in the third office," the man told her. "You're the senior Ship's Mage candidate? Soprano, right?"

"I am," she said. "And you are?"

"Ivan Skavar, the new Chief of Security. Recently of His Majesty's Corps."

"I'm shocked," Maria replied dryly. "You and the two outside couldn't scream 'Marine' more obviously if you had big flashing signs."

Skavar grinned.

"I was going for 'threatening'," he admitted, "but I'm not going to blink at people picking up on where the new hires came from. The Captain gave me a generous salary and a generous budget—and is a damned good man, from what I see."

The cheerful grin evaporated instantly and black eyes focused on Maria like a tracking gun turret. She'd seen warmer eyes on the JAG prosecutor who'd cashiered her.

"And I know your story, Commander Soprano," he said levelly. "And the mess you've made of yourself the last year or so. If you're looking for an easy ride, I suggest you keep walking."

Well, if Skavar *was* someone's plant, he at least didn't seem to be Alois's plant.

Maria took a deep breath and summoned her best officer's glare, focusing on the ex-noncom with a level look as she pinned him to the wall with her eyes.

"That isn't your call, *Chief*," she said. "But for your information, I'm here because someone dragged me *out* of the damned bottle and sent me on my way. Clawing upwards is all we got from here, but I'll remind you that if the Captain hires me, *you* will answer to *me*."

Skavar blinked and the gun turret was gone, the smile returning with a disarming warmth.

"All right, boss lady," he told her. "Last I checked, as Chief of Security, I'll report to the Captain, but if he hires you, we'll work together. Just... fuck over Rice or fuck me over and there'll be hell to pay."

Her medallion with its Combat Mage swords didn't seem to faze him.

"Third office, you said?" she asked sweetly, trading firm, understanding nods with the Marine.

"That one," Skavar replied, pointing helpfully.

The office was just as plain as the reception area or the door. While Rice clearly had resources—he wouldn't be a starship captain if he didn't!—he clearly wasn't splurging them on his space for meeting with people.

The man himself was equally plain, a stocky broad-shouldered man with graying mild brown hair who reminded her of any of a dozen Chief Petty Officers she'd worked with over her career. David Rice seemed calm, inoffensive—nothing special enough to warrant the effort the Martian Interstellar Security Service had gone through to make sure she ended up as his Mage.

And then he looked up and she met his gaze. There was no pressure, no flatness. None of the forceful aggression her "officer's glare" contained. And yet...there was no question in that instant which of them was in charge.

"Captain Rice," she greeted him, offering her hand across the table. "I am Mage Maria Soprano."

He shook her hand firmly and warmly, gesturing her to a seat.

"Welcome, Mage Soprano," he said. "You come surprisingly highly recommended by His Majesty's Navy for someone they cashiered."

She sighed.

"It was not a dishonorable discharge," she pointed out.

"But it was also not a voluntary one," Rice replied. "And yet your contact info was given to me—along with your full Navy file, if you were wondering—by Commodore Burns. I find that an interesting contradiction, don't you?"

"I was discharged without prejudice for disobedience to orders," Maria said woodenly. She'd hoped to not have to face this today, but she'd expected it regardless. "Regardless of that, however, I *am* a skilled and decorated Ship's Mage from His Majesty's Service.

"I am a trained Jump Mage, an experienced department administrator, and a fully trained Combat Mage," she continued. "I was executive officer of my last ship."

"I did you the courtesy of not reading the portion of the file related to your discharge," Rice told her. "Explain it to me."

"That's...quite the ask," Maria admitted, trying to marshal her thoughts.

"As Ship's Mage, you would be my first officer, above even my XO," he replied. "I have read your record, the citations for your decorations, the details of a decade of distinguished service. I have every faith in the skills and experience of the woman those files and your resume describe.

"What I do not know and *must*, Mage Soprano, understand is the quality of that woman's judgment. I must understand what that decorated and distinguished officer did to earn a 'discharge without prejudice'—and I must understand *why*.

"The cut-and-dried reports of a court-martial won't tell me that," he concluded. "Only you can. So...Mage Soprano. Explain it to me."

She swallowed hard, her thoughts and memories mostly corralled into line, and met Rice's gaze again.

"I was executive officer aboard the destroyer *Swords at Dawn*," she began. "We were docked at the New Berlin system when a damaged starship limped into the system. They'd been part of a convoy that had been ambushed on the way to the Ardennes System.

"New Berlin has a Runic Transceiver Array, and my captain was down on the planet. He reported in and touched base with Ardennes. We were closest to the incident, but with only one destroyer, the decision was made to have Commodore Cor carry out the counter-operation with her cruisers."

Maria shook her head, keeping her face a mask.

"The distances and times were wrong," she admitted. "We were close, and too many people had been captured. The extra few days until Cor could intervene would leave civilians to die.

"Captain Janson told me the situation was under control and returned to his shore leave. I and the other senior officers, however, had spoken to the crew of the freighter that escaped. We—*I* felt that something had to be done."

Regardless of what she'd told the court-martial, it hadn't been entirely her idea. She suspected JAG had known that too but had let her throw herself on her sword for the bridge officers.

"We abandoned Captain Janson and took off back along the route to where the pirates had ambushed the convoy. They'd left a ship behind to try and take out anyone who came in to do search and rescue, but she was an under-gunned pinnace—handful of fusion missiles and a laser, no match for a Navy destroyer."

"I'm familiar with the type," Rice said dryly, gesturing for her to continue.

"We disabled her and boarded her, interrogating her Captain to learn where the pirate home base was." She sighed. "If we'd stopped there and waited for Commodore Cor to arrive, the results would have justified our actions."

"But you didn't."

"No."

"What *did* you do?" Rice asked.

"We discovered they were based out of an old mining station in the outer asteroid belt of New Berlin, one of the ones that was abandoned when they realized the outer belt was too far to be practical," Maria told him. "It had been right under our nose and we missed them, and I think we all took it personally."

"Isn't New Berlin's outer belt half a light-month away from the star?" the Captain asked dryly.

"Yes. There was no way we would have known they were there, but still...we felt responsible. And we didn't take the pirates' warning of how powerful their 'mighty flotilla' was seriously.

"So, we went after them. One destroyer. One company of Marines." Maria shook her head. "*Dios mío*, we were arrogant."

"What happened?"

"We punched out their flotilla of cheap armed jump-ships, got half-wrecked in the process, and inserted our Marines. It was a shit-show in progress, but our Marines were holding their own...and then their *other* hunting flotilla arrived.

"We were out of ammo, mostly crippled and entirely unfit for a fight. We had to withdraw, abandoning our Marines to try and hold what they'd taken of the station."

She shivered. She could still remember Xu telling her to run, that a suicide stand would be pointless.

"It turned out that Commodores Cor and O'Reilly had been hunting this particular pirate group for months as the bastards moved from system to system. They'd all but nailed down the base, and the freighter that had limped into Ardennes shortly before the one that reached New Berlin told them exactly where they needed to be.

"Their carefully planned operation with full details on the enemy fired off about twelve hours after our half-cocked assault," she said quietly. "The flotilla I couldn't fight with my stolen, half-wrecked destroyer didn't stand a chance against four cruisers with full escort. They landed an entire brigade of Marines to extract Xu and the prisoners.

"Everything had been in hand, but we hadn't had need-to-know and thought too highly of ourselves," Maria concluded. "We probably saved a few prisoners who might have been killed or raped in those intervening hours. We *definitely* got forty-three Marines and sixty-one Navy personnel killed...but on the other hand, we killed nine pirate ships that otherwise might have got away."

"But they might not have, either," Rice said quietly.

"No. Which is why I took the fall for my crew and got kicked out of the Navy," she told him. "The final call was mine at each step of the way. I was responsible, and I got a hundred people killed who didn't need to die."

"Wrong thing, sorta right reasons," he concluded. "Would you do it again?"

Maria hesitated. "I don't know. I think I'd ask for more details on what *was* being done, in the same situation, rather than firing off with half a brain. But...without knowing that the relief force was on the way and knowing the pirates had prisoners?"

She hadn't really thought about it.

"I might," she admitted. "But I'd like to think I'd find out if I needed to, first."

"We all make mistakes," Rice told her. "I once found out I had a cargo of containers full of cryo-frozen sex slaves. It's what we do after that that matters."

"I haven't done much since," she admitted.

"You protected your crew. You accepted your punishment. Now you're trying to still make something of yourself," he pointed out. "So, what would *you* do if you found slaves aboard the ship?"

The question surprised her, but it was also clear that it was something he needed to know.

Maria met his gaze and smiled grimly.

"You'd have about forty-five seconds to convince me you didn't know either before you'd be breathing vacuum and I'd be taking over," she admitted. "There damn well wouldn't be any delivery going on."

Rice nodded with a grim laugh.

"Good enough."

"Good enough?" she asked.

"You're hired. We take possession of *Red Falcon* in thirty-six hours, and my XO isn't out of the hospital for five more days. Congratulations, you're the new first officer, and that means you're helping me interview everyone else."

Rice grinned.

"Get ready for a grueling two weeks, Ship's Mage. I plan to be underway in fifteen days, and I have no idea what quirks we're going to find aboard *Falcon*."

"I served aboard *Scarlett* for a year early in my career," Maria told him. "The AAFHF ships are pretty quirky birds, all things considered."

"I know, on both counts," her new Captain confirmed. "But I still wasn't going to hire you until I was sure I knew how you ticked."

CHAPTER 6

RED FALCON hung in space, suspended against the starry sky by a series of fueling umbilicals and support gantries. The Navy shuttle that arced David and his newly reinforced senior officers around their ship flew slowly, allowing them to take it in as Commodore Burns pointed out features.

"Unlike the *Venice* class that you're most familiar with, all of the crew compartments and working spaces are concentrated at the front of the ship, under the radiation cap," the yardmaster pointed out, gesturing to the thickest part of the "stem", with a rotating ring wrapped around it but still inside the "mushroom cap".

"While most civilian vessels are looking to maximize cubage, and the rib design is useful for that, the designers of the AAFHF type were mostly warship designers," he admitted. "They had enough civilian input to install the centripetal gravity ring in the first place, but these ships were intended for a high-threat environment."

Burns pointed out a quartet of pods that hung between the thick inner core of the ship and the rotating ring.

"Those are emergency engines," he said. "Not as powerful as the main drives by a long shot, but they're not designed to move the whole ship. They're designed to move the forward crew components after you've abandoned the cargo."

"That wouldn't work with the jump matrix," Soprano objected. David was amused by the Commodore following the usual pattern of men interacting with his new Ship's Mage—his gaze turned to her, flicked down to her chest and then immediately refocused on her face.

"The simulacrum needs to be at the center of the ship," the Mage continued. "If you were to chop off two thirds of the length, you'd lose the simulacrum chamber."

"You would," Burns agreed. "It's an emergency measure and, well... the same process that would eject the rear portion of the ship would bring the simulacrum chamber forward. It's a destructive process," he concluded, "and one I wouldn't recommend you try. The ship won't be reparable afterwards."

"That sounds more expensive than I want to have as my headache," David agreed. "Why did we even leave the pods installed?"

"I was told to give you the ship with *all* of its gear fully intact," Burns replied. "Guns, quirks, missiles, engines—the works."

"Speaking of guns," Skavar noted as they approached the edge of the radiation cap.

"This is where we're back to 'the designers were used to building warships'," the Commodore said. "Most of our warships are optimized for pursuit. A freighter, logically, shouldn't have the same optimization, but..."

"They didn't think of it?" David asked.

"So far as I can tell," Burns agreed. "All of your missile launchers and beams are in the front cap. You have RFLAM turrets space along the length of the spine to cover the cargo, but your offensive weapons are mounted in the radiation cap, which is also far more heavily armored than the rest of the hull."

"So, we have an armed freighter built like a battering ram?" said freighter's new Captain observed.

"Yes," the Commodore said. "You've got the engines to pull ten gravities at full load, but most of the ship's gravity runes were grounded and discharged." He shrugged apologetically at Soprano. "It'll be up to you and your Ship's Mages whether you want to recharge any of them, or how many."

"The runes were left throughout the ship?" Soprano asked.

"Everywhere except the gravity ring," the Navy officer confirmed. "Same as a Navy vessel. The AAFHFs were built to *be* Navy vessels."

"Every trick and gear intact," David echoed, studying the ship the Mage-King had given him. "This is one *hell* of a compensation package, Commodore."

"I'm not entirely certain just what you did for His Majesty, Captain Rice, but this is what he ordered me to give you in return," the Commodore said. "Everything we can do has been done. She's been fueled and cleaned. We did first-run checks of her systems, but she's been in mothballs for four years, Captain."

"We're going to find problems," David agreed. "Some of them won't show up until we're six jumps from anywhere and it's all down to our crew and engineers. James?"

The fifth, so-far-silent occupant of the shuttle grinned brightly at him, his teeth shockingly white against skin the color of a starless night.

"Then you'll be glad you have me," James Kellers, David's old chief engineer replied. "Because I'm pretty sure I can fix whatever you break, Captain."

"You always have," David said. "You always have."

"That's the outside tour," Burns told him. "Shall I have the pilot bring us in?"

The shuttle carefully maneuvered onto the floor of *Red Falcon*'s shuttle bay, magnetic feet locking the spacecraft in place.

To David's surprise, however, she wasn't the only shuttle in the bay. *Red Falcon* had three shuttle bays—two in the main working section at the front, just behind the gravitational ring, and one at the back by the engines—and each had twice as much capacity as the one bay aboard his old *Blue Jay*.

He'd been budgeting for filling them as best he could, but he'd been planning to operate with roughly a third of the heavy-lift shuttles a ship of *Red Falcon*'s immense size needed.

Shuttle Bay Alpha, however, already contained neatly locked-down rows of shuttles. Eight heavy-lift shuttles, four personnel shuttles and four repair pods were lined up in the bay, and David sneaked a suspicious glance at Burns.

"Every trick and gear intact," he echoed again. "How many shuttles are you leaving aboard?"

"Her full complement," Burns told him calmly as he drifted competently through the zero gee. "Though you'll note that there are two slots in each bay for assault shuttles that we've left empty. You are getting twenty-four heavy-lift shuttles, twelve personnel shuttles and twelve short-range repair craft.

"Is that going to be a problem?"

"Every time I turn around, Commodore Burns, you're making me rewrite my crew budget," David told him in mock complaint. He was starting to look for another shoe.

"Make no mistakes, Captain, this ship is far from perfect," the Commodore said softly as he led the way out of the shuttle bay. "But she is about the best thing we could possibly hand over to a civilian, and my orders were to make sure she was fully stocked. Shuttle bays. Food lockers. Armories.

"Everything that we would have equipped this ship with for Navy service is aboard, except we've only provided a one-quarter load for the missile magazines and haven't included exosuit armor or assault shuttles."

"I can live with that," David replied. "His Majesty is generous. And so are you."

There were a hundred or more ways that Commodore Burns could have fulfilled the letter of his orders without going this far out of his way.

"His Majesty's intentions were quite clear," Burns told him. "I am not one to honor the letter and not the spirit of my orders, Captain. I imagine the Protectorate would be pleased to have you consider yourself to owe us a favor or six for this, but my understanding is that the Mage-King feels he owes you a significant debt—*and* a replacement ship."

"This is a bit more than a replacement," David said, looking around as Burns led them to the bridge.

"Honestly, Captain, I'm worried we're handing you a white elephant," the Commodore told him. "She's a big ship with immense operating costs. The kind of cargoes she can carry are usually hauled by big ships belonging to big lines. An independent big ship..."

"I have my connections," David admitted. "I think we'll be fine."

"I trust you on that," the other man replied. "But if you find yourself between work, the Navy will happily hire you for our needs. His Majesty thinks he owes you, and that means His Majesty's *Navy* owes you.

"You get me, Captain?"

"I get you."

"Good. Here's your new bridge."

It was hard to come to a full stop in zero gravity, but *Red Falcon* had enough straps and handholds scattered around that there was one easily to hand. David latched on and slowed himself to a halt, allowing himself to survey his new domain.

Red Falcon's bridge was significantly larger than any merchant bridge he'd ever served on before, though most of his career prior to owning his own ship had been on vessels much the same size as his *Blue Jay*. For all of its size, however, there was very little space left to waste.

The space had been designed to function under either acceleration or magical gravity, with all of the stations mounted on one "floor" aligned with the ship's engines. Some thought had been put into using the bridge in zero gravity, however, and long railings were bolted into each of the walls to allow crew to move hand over hand between sections—or just stop themselves where they needed to be.

Most freighter bridges only had stations for the Captain, sensors and navigation, with maybe a repeater for engineering. *Falcon* had all of those, with a full station for an engineering liaison officer, plus consoles for backups.

The main addition was a tactical section that wouldn't have looked out of place on the bridge of a destroyer. Three consoles were linked together around a secondary display a good fraction of the main screen's size. The section was farther from the Captain than it would have been aboard a warship, but the hope was that *Red Falcon* would make far less use of her weapons than a warship would.

The main difference between here and an actual warship's bridge was that it wasn't also the simulacrum chamber that linked to the ship's rune matrix. A civilian ship carried a jump matrix, capable of allowing a Mage to teleport a full light-year.

A warship carried an amplifier matrix, which applied a similar scaling effect to any spell the Mage cast. Since the amplifier was the ship's single most powerful weapon, the simulacrum chamber was also the bridge, allowing the Mage who commanded a Navy warship to control its most powerful weapon herself.

David took a minute to survey it all and then launched himself for the Captain's chair. A perfectly positioned handhold allowed him to slide easily into the seat, and automatic straps slid out to gently hold him in.

Systems lit up around him, giving him the status of every part of the ship. The seat was Navy-style with multiple repeater screens, he noted, rather than the single display he'd grown used to.

"Fuel at one hundred percent," he said aloud. "Both hydrogen and antimatter tanks full and stable. Munitions at exactly one hundred." He shook his head. "All bays report their shuttles loads as promised, all self-checks are green."

He carefully turned to look at Burns as the Commodore drifted in next to him.

"Everything looks aboveboard to me," he concluded. "Thank you, Commodore."

"Final transfers were made over to you as of this morning," the Navy officer said. "If you run into any problems before you leave, feel free to let me know. We'll probably have to charge you at this point, but we'll give you a good rate."

From the Commodore's broad grin, he knew that David knew just how much money had been sunk into this ship.

"I'm also instructed to let you know there's a personal message waiting for you in the Captain's office," he concluded. "With that, however, my part in this is done. I have a few people standing by to give your senior officers tours of their sections as they want, but I need to get back to my regular job!"

"I appreciate everything you've done, Commodore," David said, shaking the man's hand carefully. "I don't see a need to keep you further."

Burns somehow managed to click his heels and bow slightly in midair before drifting back out of the bridge, allowing David to look over his officers in private.

"All right, people," he said. "This girl is ours now, which means we want to go over her from stem to stern. Don't hesitate to use the Commodore's people, even if we end up going into what they'll need to charge us for. I have no problem giving the Navy anything they ask for right now, for some reason," he concluded dryly.

"I'll want to check out the simulacrum chamber and do a first-cut sweep of the matrix," Soprano said calmly. "I trust the Navy's check-up, but I want my own eyes on the most sensitive parts."

"And that's about how I feel about power plants and engines," Kellers agreed.

"Don't forget you still need to fill out the rest of your departments," David warned. "We don't have long before I want to space out, and we don't have Jenna to lean on right now.

"Go play, but keep an eye on your schedules," he ordered.

The tools and systems available for *Red Falcon*'s Captain were going to take David days to just find the full extent of, let alone get used to. He toyed with the repeater screens in his chair for a few minutes after his staff scattered to the corners of the ship, and then decided to go see just what the message waiting for him was.

Even in zero gravity, getting to the captain's office was relatively straightforward. This section of the ship would have gravity only if he had Soprano recharge the gravity runes—they were already there, after all, the silver whirls and lines of the Martian Runic script etched into the deck beneath him—or if the ship was under acceleration.

The captain's office, however, was even more set up to function under gravity than the bridge was. Burns's people had clearly put some thought into making it work without magical gravity—installing the same auto-restraining type of chair he'd seen on the bridge, for example—but it was still a standard-enough office to have problems in zero gee.

The chair was enough for now, however. If Soprano got her hands on enough junior Mages, David probably was going to get the runes restored—having a chunk of the ship that would be the same gravity no matter what acceleration they were under was handy.

He strapped himself into the chair and linked his com into the desk console, bringing up the screen and checking into *Red Falcon*'s systems.

The computers asked a bunch of validating questions as he convinced it to accept his wrist-comp as the Captain's comp, with attendant authority, and then linked in into the full computer network layered through *Red Falcon*'s hull.

He couldn't fly the ship from his office, but it had a better interface into the ship's automatic reporting than *Blue Jay* had had. From here, he could see how much fuel he had left, what the overall cargo mass was, how many missiles they had in the magazines...everything he could see from the bridge.

It was an impressive setup.

There was also, as he'd been promised, a blinking icon of a waiting message that instantly added itself to his inbox. There was no sender tagged onto it this time, but he was pretty certain he knew who it was from.

He was unsurprised when the screen dissolved into the image of Alaura Stealey, Hand of the Mage-King of Mars. She was a graying middle-aged woman, still athletically built but going soft around the edges in a way that David was all too familiar with himself.

"Captain Rice," the recording greeted him. "This message should be waiting for you when Burns leaves you aboard your new ship, and if you're the man I know you to be, you're wondering if the good yard-master went further than we wanted him to.

"He didn't," she said flatly. "You have no concept of what a prize you delivered to us with Damien Montgomery—not merely in his skills and gifts, but in the honor and integrity I was not certain would have survived months on the run.

"I credit you with the survival of his soul, Captain Rice," Stealey told David. "And where I give credit, so does His Majesty. If our instructions have been followed—and I know Rasputin Burns of old—you now possess one of the last fully functional Armed Auxiliary Fast Heavy Freighters still in existence."

The image shook her head.

"So, now I will tell you a secret: the records will show that your ship was partially disarmed before she was handed over to you. According to all official records, *Red Falcon* kept only half of her defensive armament and two lasers. Nothing more."

David nodded slowly. That bit of misinformation would come in handy, though anyone who interacted with his crew for long wouldn't be fooled.

"Now, I'll be honest and admit that this all wasn't entirely done as a favor," the Hand noted. "You and Damien killed Mikhail Azure, but the Blue Star Syndicate is dying more slowly—and messily. We're aware of at least four functioning fragments of the organization, each large enough to be a major crime syndicate in their own right.

"I believe at least one is going to come after you, David Rice," Stealey warned. "So, I have turned you into a trap. With all that we owe you, I feel a bit guilty about that, but..."

She shrugged.

"I have a job to do and I will use every weapon I have to hand for that job," she reminded him. "But remember as well, Captain Rice, that you have established an account of some depth with the Protectorate. We will use you as both bait and trap for our enemies, but we have no intention of leaving you hanging.

"If Azure's remnants come hunting for you, remember that His Majesty's Protectorate extends over you. Call and we will answer," she promised, then smiled wryly. "If for no other reason, Captain Rice, than because experience suggests that I need to keep an eye on you!"

CHAPTER 7

DAVID WAS BACK in the office on Armstrong Station, going through page after page of resumes for junior officers, when one of Skavar's security officers pinged him. They had yet to hire anyone resembling a secretary, which meant Skavar's slowly growing force of predominantly ex-Marines was doing all of the greeting and screening.

If that scared anyone off, well, they probably wouldn't be interested in serving on a ship the Protectorate seemed determined to make a stalking horse to bait their enemies.

"What is it, Corporal Ambrose?" he asked.

"I've got a group of people here who say you know them," the security woman told him. "Names don't mean much to me, but they say they're from *Blue Jay*."

David sat up. He'd held onto Campbell and Kellers, but that was all he'd been able to justify keeping on salary while sitting in port. He'd sent the rest of his junior officers on with glowing letters of recommendation and his best wishes.

They'd all been hired, so if any of them were showing up now...

"Send them in," he told Angler. "But keep an eye on the panic button. I wouldn't put it past someone to *pretend* to be my old crew."

The corporal nodded with a more serious expression than David's comment deserved.

"Wilco, Skipper."

After the incident in the concourse, David no longer went unarmed. He slid the drawer in his cheap rented desk open, leaving the caseless automatic inside it easily within reach.

The petitely attractive purple-haired young woman who came through the door first, however, put his worries to rest and he smiled broadly.

"LaMonte," he greeted her. "And Kelzin!"

The young man who followed her through had grown his hair out since David had last seen him and apparently bulked up, gaining at least twenty pounds of muscle since Mike Kelzin had been the replacement First Pilot aboard *Blue Jay*.

Kelly LaMonte had been one of Kellers's junior engineers aboard the same ship. She'd also been Damien Montgomery's lover and the first of David's officers to disappear into the ether after they'd returned to civilized space after *Blue Jay*'s destruction.

The second man was less familiar to David, a sandy-haired older man who'd worked as Campbell's assistant and proved his worth mostly by never coming to the Captain's attention. He gave a slightly less casual salute than the two younger officers.

"Bran Wiltshire, sir," he introduced himself, apparently concerned that David would have forgotten him.

"I didn't forget you, Bran," David told the man with a smile. "What brings the three of you to my office, and in a group, too?"

Kelzin and Wiltshire both instinctively deferred to LaMonte, he noted. The young woman with the long purple hair glanced back at both men and visibly swallowed a sigh.

"We were all on the same ship," she began. "*Dreams of Excessive Profit*. Gods, the name should have been a clue but, well..." She shrugged. "When I signed on, I wanted a million light-years between me and anyone who'd remind me of Damien.

"*This* pair," she gestured at Wiltshire and Kelzin, "took my presence as a recommendation."

"I take it that didn't work out well," David said mildly.

"Could have been worse," LaMonte replied, an ugly expression flashing across her face. "Almost *was* worse, but Captain Melbourne very distinctly had his limits. Cut corners to save costs? Totally okay. Sexually harass the new junior engineer? You're finding dirt under your feet before you realize what hit you."

"I'm sorry to hear about that," David said. LaMonte was young and pretty, and on *his* ship, he'd made damn sure Kellers was keeping a careful eye out to nip that kind of issue in the bud. It shouldn't have been allowed to *get* far enough to require beaching someone.

"Could have been worse," she echoed. "But *Dreams* is an unpleasant ride. If a corner can be cut, it gets cut. If a customer can be squeezed for a few extra bucks, the customer gets squeezed. She's a ten-million-ton freighter I half-expect to fall out of the damn sky."

There were few harsher condemnations from engineers, in David's experience.

"So, you're looking to switch berths?" he asked. That could give him a headache but would be worth it for Kelzin and LaMonte—and he had no qualms taking on the fight for Wiltshire on pure stubborn loyalty grounds.

"We already told Melbourne where he could stick his death trap," the older man said crisply. "He took it better than the kids were expecting—I don't think it's the first time an engineer has talked their friends off his boat."

LaMonte wasn't even fazed at being called "the kids." Clearly, she'd grown at least somewhat used to Wiltshire.

"So, we're jobless but heard you were looking and figured we'd check in," she concluded. "Talked four more crew—two engineering techs, a shuttle pilot and a junior ship's mage—into jumping ship with us. If you want them, I can talk them into signing on."

"You'd recommend them?" David asked. No one in the room was pretending he wasn't hiring on his old crew.

"In a heartbeat," LaMonte confirmed. "Xi Wu is no Damien, but she's no slouch as a Mage, either. I wouldn't want to fly with her as the *only* Mage, but..."

"*Red Falcon* is going to have four," he told her. "Assuming Soprano can find them, anyway. Have your friends get in touch. You three are hired, if you had any doubts," he concluded with a grin.

"Wiltshire, Campbell's in hospital. You'd be the security team's hero if you'd take over running the front desk," he continued. "LaMonte, Kellers is back on the ship making sure everything is in order. Once you've pinged your friends, move your crap aboard and help him out."

Finally, he turned his gaze on Kelzin.

"I don't have a First Pilot yet," he told the younger man, "but..."

"I wasn't First on *Dreams* and, hell, Skipper, I *saw* the specifications for *Falcon*'s boat bays," Kelzin replied cheerfully. "I won't be offended if you bring in someone above me."

That was another giant check mark in David's mental book for the pilot, and made up at least part of the decision.

"You'll be Bravo flight leader," he decided instantly. "That makes Shuttle Bay Bravo your territory, under the First's orders once I've hired them. Work for you?"

"If you'll trust me with it," Kelzin said carefully after a quick glance at LaMonte.

David concealed a smile. It didn't look like the pilot had replaced Montgomery in the young engineer's affections yet, but he certainly seemed to be applying for the position as hard as he could!

"Screw it up and I'll bump you down to cargo hauler," he half-jokingly warned. "Until then, yeah, you've proven you can handle a boat bay to me. All of you, get moving. I've got a list of interviews to schedule as long as my arm!"

"Pass that my way," Wiltshire told him. "I'll take care of it. I always did for Jenna."

If any member of *Red Falcon*'s new and rapidly growing crew didn't need an escort, Maria was quite certain it was her. Chief Skavar, however, had been at least a little spooked by his dramatic "job interview" and was insisting that the senior officers be escorted by at least one guard everywhere they went.

So, when Maria headed to the hospital to meet Jenna Campbell, she brought Corporal Sylvana Spiros and Trooper Vishal Akkerman with her. The two wore newly issued uniforms with semi-covert armored vests and *Red Falcon* shoulder flashes to go with their station-authorized SmartDart stunguns and only-arguably-legal concealed handguns.

Maria wore a similar uniform with the same flashes, though hers didn't have the body armor and she'd unzipped the suit low enough to show a carefully calculated amount of distracting cleavage. Where Spiros and Akkerman had security and rank insignia pinned to the lapels of their shipsuits, Maria simply wore her gold Mage medallion.

Once *Red Falcon* had more Mages, she would add the silver dot of a senior Ship's Mage to her own lapels, but for now she would revel in living without insignia for the first time in her life.

Well, the first time while doing a real job, anyway.

Dr. Singh was waiting for her in the front of the hospital when she and her guards arrived, the physician completely unbothered by her obvious escort.

"Miss Campbell is resting comfortably and should be fine to move aboard ship tomorrow, presuming you have hired a physician by then," he told Maria crisply. "You should be fine to meet with her for about thirty minutes, but I do ask you to pay attention to her energy levels. If she is flagging or otherwise appears ill, please cut things short.

"She was quite severely injured and there may be medium-term consequences we've missed so far."

"Everyone tells me you've done a fantastic job, Doctor," Maria replied. "The Captain is interviewing doctors today; we should have a ship's physician aboard by tomorrow. There's a lot of work to be done, though, and I don't want us to rush through it without Officer Campbell's opinion."

Maria had pages and pages of reports to go over with Campbell if the woman had the energy, though that was hardly the point of this meeting. The point was to make it clear that she respected Campbell's position and authority.

The balance between the Ship's Mage, a civilian ship's first officer and the one who took command if something happened to the Captain, and the executive officer who ran the ship on a day-to-day basis, was always a careful one.

"She's in room seventeen. I'll walk you down."

Maria stepped into the hospital room on her own, leaving the doctor and her escort outside and closing the door behind her as she met Campbell's questioning gaze.

"New uniforms?" the XO asked. "I like the flashes."

"I'd hope so," Maria said with a smile. "David said you designed them."

She pulled a chair up next to Campbell's bed.

"I'm Maria," she introduced herself. "I believe the Captain told you he'd hired me?"

"The ex-Navy Ship's Mage," the other woman agreed. "I'd welcome you aboard *Red Falcon*, except *I* haven't been aboard her yet."

"Tomorrow, Dr. Singh tells me," Maria promised. "We're trying to keep you in the loop, but it's being a hectic mess."

"Given how fast the boss wants to turn this ship around, I'm not surprised. Do we have a cargo yet?"

"Not yet. The Captain is still working on getting a crew together. We're still short a tactical officer and a surgeon for senior officers."

Campbell shook her head.

"Can't believe I'm going to be on a ship with a *tactical* officer," the merchant officer replied. "It's a weird thought."

"*Red Falcon* is a weird ship. Half-Navy, half-civilian, all-expensive. Running her is going to suck."

"The boss will find a way," Campbell said. "Did you get the reports I asked for?"

"I did," Maria told her. "And then did you one better." She tapped her wrist-comp against Campbell's. "You now have a live encrypted link to the ship's computers. That should help you pull any data you need to get up to date before tomorrow."

"Thanks. Not even tempted to keep me half-out?" the XO asked dryly.

"Hell, no," Maria denied with a smile. "If we don't have a good XO, *I* have to do way too much work. Everything I've seen tells me you're damn good—only a few other reasons why Captain Rice might have kept you around for a year, after all."

She couldn't keep herself from arching a questioning eyebrow at Campbell. The woman wasn't particularly attractive, but that would hardly be a barrier to a romantic matchup between Captain and XO who basically lived in each other's pockets. They wouldn't be the first pair to run a ship like that, either.

Campbell laughed aloud, then stopped and coughed painfully.

"You're asking if I'm sleeping with Rice?" she asked. "No. Never. Not each other's type, and neither of us would be inclined to screw up the ship like that. Plus, he's got a girl on Amber, and much as I *like* her, she's fucking terrifying."

Maria smiled apologetically.

"I had to know what I was getting into," she said. "You and I and the Captain have to work together no matter what, and I haven't had a chance to see you two interact yet. That's a minefield I needed to know if it was there."

"Fair enough. No, *our* job is going to be keeping the boss out of trouble. He's got a soft streak a light-second wide, and it leads us into a lot of causes we're better off avoiding."

That fit with why Alois had drafted Maria to be Rice's Ship's Mage, as well as the way everyone aboard seemed hyper-protective of the captain. It wasn't like Maria wasn't familiar enough with her *own* soft streak, though.

"Well, with two stubborn old biddies like us to keep him on the straight and narrow, we should be fine," she told Campbell.

"That we should," the XO agreed with a grin. "Now, those reports, Ship's Mage Soprano?"

CHAPTER 8

BY NOON, David had interviewed three doctors, four potential First Pilots, and one candidate for tactical officer who had left him wanting to wash his hands. A *lot.*

It was hard for him to say just what had set him off about the little man, but he'd managed to set David's teeth on edge the moment he'd walked into the office, and fifteen minutes of conversation with him had allowed the Captain to realize two things about the man:

First, he was exactly as competent, knowledgeable and skilled with shipboard weapons as his resume indicated—and secondly, he had acquired *none* of that knowledge aboard the Royal Navy ships said resume said he'd served on.

David was grimly certain he'd just interviewed a pirate, but he had nothing solid to give law enforcement to prove it. He sighed and shook his head, consigning the resume to the virtual garbage bin and studying the three doctors.

Any of them would do, if he was being honest, which made choosing between the three difficult. Normally, he'd run them all by Campbell and get his XO's opinion—he would have, in fact, had her in the interviews.

As it was...

His wrist-comp chimed.

"Rice," he answered crisply, glad for the distraction.

"Boss, it's Wiltshire," the administrator greeted him. "I just got a request for an appointment with you on an 'as soon as possible' basis. I have your schedule in front of me and you're blocked off for review and lunch, but if you want, I can get him in maybe fifteen."

"That depends on who it is," David admitted.

"Trade Factor Harvey Nguyen of Cinnamon," Wiltshire reeled off instantly. "He's the senior representative of their off-planet office here. Cinnamon is—"

"A primarily agricultural MidWorld thirty-six light-years from here," David concluded. The various worlds of the Protectorate didn't, technically, have embassies or consulates on other planets. They had "trade offices" and "investment factors" that served much the same purposes for worlds that shared a national identity but remained days or weeks apart by ship.

The senior trade factor for Cinnamon there was basically the planet's ambassador to Tau Ceti, in itself the third-largest system economy in the Protectorate. Sol was wealthier. Legatus was wealthier—the decision of the first of the "UnArcana Worlds" to ban Mages on the planet meant the system had built an entirely independent industrial empire to fulfill many of its needs.

Cinnamon probably didn't have a trade office on Legatus, so after their Councilor and trade factors in Sol, that made Harvey Nguyen one of the most important off-planet officials the system had. If he wanted to meet with a freighter captain, that made David smell profit.

Which certainly ranked above trying to pick between doctors in his books!

"Let Mr. Nguyen know I am available at his convenience," he finally told Wiltshire. "Let me know when he gets here."

In the meantime, he turned back to the screen on his console with the three resumes, smiled to himself, and then sent all three over to Maria Soprano, asking her opinion.

If he had his Mage first officer around, after all, he may as well make use of her!

Factor Nguyen was a pudgy little man in a perfectly tailored black suit and bowler cap, the height of current fashion on Cinnamon, according to David's quick research in the fifteen minutes it took the man to show up.

That research had also warned him that his initial impression had, if anything, underestimated Nguyen's influence. The man was not only the representative of the Cinnamon system government but *also* the primary agent for Cinnamon's largest syndicate of importers.

He wasn't particularly wealthy in his own right, but a message from the fussy little man in David's office could send millions—if not billions—of dollars into motion.

"Please, Mr. Nguyen, sit down," David greeted the man respectfully. "Can I get you something to drink? A snack?"

"No, thank you," the Factor replied. "I have quite strict dietary requirements for my health; it is difficult for others to meet my needs." He forced a wan smile. "It is easier simply not to try, Captain Rice."

"I see," David said, leaning back in his chair and studying the Cinnamon man across the table. "Then how can I be of assistance to the government of Cinnamon today, Factor?"

"I find myself in a somewhat awkward situation, Captain," Nguyen admitted. "An...embarrassment of riches, I suppose.

"While the government I represent and the syndicate I work with are capable of mobilizing a great deal of capital, that kind of capital must be carefully distributed across the interstellar banking network. Cinnamon lacks a Rune Transceiver Array, so all of our banking must be done with inevitable time delays which require careful management."

David nodded his understanding, waiting for Nguyen to get to the point. Every ship that traveled between systems did with a heavily encrypted postal "lock box" of data, mostly news and financial information. The RTA's were fantastic for allowing interstellar communication, but since they only projected the voice of the Mage using it, they were useless for data transfer.

Since those lock boxes were the primary means of transferring money around, it meant that each portion of someone's money effectively had a physical location. Cinnamon might have, say, ten billion in available cash and credit—but if they'd only assigned fifty million to Tau Ceti right now, that was all Nguyen had to work with.

"My homeworld, like all MidWorlds, is self-sufficient, but our industry lags behind most developed planets," the trade factor continued. "Most of our heavy industrial equipment and power systems are manufactured off-world, and making certain that our supply of such is sufficient to our needs is a major portion of my job."

"I see." David was still waiting for the point.

"An opportunity has crossed my path to acquire the inventory of a near-bankrupt manufacturer of such systems on Tau Ceti *f*," Nguyen explained. "Said inventory would fill your ship, twenty million tons of robotic manufacturing systems, power plants, several container surface ships, the like."

And David finally saw the point.

"And you don't have enough money," he said quietly.

"I negotiated the price, believing that I would be able to readily access credit here in Tau Ceti," Nguyen admitted. "I have had difficulties doing so quickly enough. I have no concerns about my ability to do so in the long term, but there are other players and this deal has a limited time.

"Basically, Captain, if I do not deliver the funds within the next seventy-two hours, the company I am dealing with will have to declare bankruptcy and their inventory will be tied up in those legal proceedings," the little man told him. "If, however, I *make* that payment, I will have a twenty-million-ton cargo to send home, and a company I have done solid business with for twenty years will be able to make their bond payment, avoid bankruptcy, and acquire new inventory to continue operating."

It was a cute sob story, David had to admit. It might even be true, though the "warm fuzzies" of saving a company and the attendant livelihood of its employees had to be secondary in the cold calculus of a starship captain.

"You need a partner," he said calmly.

"I need a partner," Nguyen agreed.

"What's your offer?" David asked. With the money he'd clawed back from not having to replace *Red Falcon*'s weapons and his other resources, he'd been considering buying a largely speculative cargo in any case—though he'd be far happier carrying someone else's cargo and holding that money against future problems and operating costs.

"I will pay half of your normal contracted shipping rate in advance, and my government will pay half upon arrival in Cinnamon," the factor began. "And I will offer you a thirty-percent stake in the cargo for one hundred fifty million Martian dollars."

Red Falcon's Captain winced. He'd dealt in that kind of money before—*Red Falcon*, for example, was valued at around thirty-two billion dollars—but that was a lot of money, even for a starship captain.

He simply didn't have it right now. He could *get* it—it wouldn't be the first time he'd put a mortgage against a starship, and it would be easy to get a one-hundred-and-fifty-million-dollar loan with a thirty-billion-dollar ship for collateral, but...

"Fifty percent," he said calmly. "For me to find a hundred and fifty million dollars in three days? I need a fifty-percent stake in the cargo."

"The cargo costs far more than three hundred million, Captain!" Nguyen objected.

"And will be completely lost if someone doesn't come up with the missing money, won't it?" David asked.

"You rob me, Captain!"

"Please. You're paying, what, four, five hundred for the cargo, all in?" David said. "Fifty percent is a premium for my contribution, yes, but if you're getting a deal, you're expecting a twofold return on sale in Cinnamon at least. And without my money and my ship, you don't have a deal at all, do you?"

From the way the trade factor coughed, David was close to the mark.

"Forty-five percent," Nguyen said firmly. "Anything more and both my government and my financiers will have my head!"

"Good enough," *Red Falcon*'s Captain replied genially, offering his hand. "Get a contract to my man up front as soon as you can and I'll have you the money in forty-eight hours."

"We have a deal, Captain."

CHAPTER 9

SOMEHOW, despite everything going on, the following week passed in surprising calm. David kept waiting for the next batch of assassins to emerge from the station crowds, or for the deal with Nguyen's contact to fall through, or...

None of his worries had materialized and things had run smoothly until the moment finally came for them to detach from Armstrong Station and dare the meteor swarms Tau Ceti was famous for.

Tau Ceti had been one of the first systems scouted when humanity had first reached out for the stars under the Mage-King of Mars. The second actually colonized as part of what many still regarded as the biggest bribe ever paid in human history.

When the Eugenics Wars of the twenty-second and twenty-third centuries ended, the first Mage-King had found himself unwillingly in control of the entire human race. Since he and his fellow Mages were a product of the Eugenicists' bloody Project Olympus, he had no more love for his creators than the rest of humanity—but refused to allow his people to be slaves again.

He'd offered the Compact: in exchange for a number of privileges and guarantees, Mages would put their considerable powers to the service of mankind instead of its mastery. The first service they'd offered had been the jump-ships, carrying humanity's diaspora outward.

Now, two hundred years later, Tau Ceti's two habitable worlds were the anchor for one of the richest systems in the Protectorate. Both planets had been pounded by once-a-century meteor storms before humanity's arrival, keeping their biospheres primitive and unchallenging to human settlers.

A massive space station orbited ahead of Tau Ceti *f*, visible on David's screens and scanners as a distant, slightly brighter star. The chilly but heavily populated *f* itself occupied almost half of his view as *Red Falcon* slowly came fully and entirely alive around him.

"All systems are online," LaMonte reported from the engineering repeater station. The young woman had many talents, but she was also one of the best programmers David had ever met. She could do most of her engineering job from anywhere on the ship, so having her as the liaison made sense.

Not that Kellers or LaMonte had asked his opinion.

"Fusion One, Two, Three, Four and Five are fully operational and clearing one hundred percent on draw stress tests," she continued. "Stepping down to regular power needs. Engine nozzles have been swept for FOD and are ready to ignite.

"Engineering reports ready for flight, sir."

"Anybody else got problems?" David asked. Two of Soprano's new junior Mages had run through the core of the ship during the last week, reactivating all of the gravity runes. His shiny new ship could actually use her engines' full capacity without crushing the crew, which was a strange thought for a freighter captain.

"My board is green," Jenna Campbell reported from the executive officer's navigation station. "Armstrong reports they're ready to pull umbilicals and reminds us not to activate main engines within ten thousand kilometers of the station."

She paused.

"They're repeating that and requesting confirmation," she observed with a smile. "I wonder why?"

"Because nothing in space short of a battleship has bigger engines than we do," David replied. "And they're not used to big antimatter rockets on a civilian ship. Let Armstrong know their signal is received and I intend to observe a *fifteen*-thousand-kilometer safety radius on the antimatter engines."

"I'm sure they'll appreciate that," his old friend said. She still looked pale and weak, but she was moving under her own power again, and their new doctor, Jaidev Gupta, had cleared her for this much duty.

"Umbilicals withdrawing," Campbell reported after a moment. "Docking clamps released. We are floating free."

"Has Tau Ceti f Control given us a flight path?"

"They have."

"Take us out, secondary thrusters only."

Fully loaded and fueled, *Red Falcon* massed somewhere in the region of thirty million tons: six million tons of starship wrapped around twenty million tons of cargo and four million tons of fuel. Her massive anti-matter-fueled main engines could fling that around like a toy with surprising efficiency—but they would melt Armstrong Station's hull with equal efficiency.

Instead, a suite of several hundred ion thrusters, fundamentally unchanged in principle for half a millennium, lit up and began to move *Falcon* away from the massive bulk of the space station. It wasn't much acceleration, but it added up quickly.

At two meters per second squared, however, it would still take over an hour for David's ship to clear the safety zone he'd specified. On the other hand, once he opened up *Red Falcon*'s main engines at ten gravities, he'd reach flat-enough space for Soprano to jump them in just over five hours.

The trade-off seemed fair.

"Mage Soprano." He opened a channel to the simulacrum chamber in the middle of the ship. "Any concerns?"

"None," the ex-Navy officer replied cheerfully. "The rune matrix checks out. All tests I can run, both magical and visual, are done. We'll be clear to jump once we're far enough out."

"I'm currently estimating six and a half hours," he told her. "There isn't much point to you and your people hanging out in the simulacrum chamber until then. I'll make sure we let you know half an hour before jump."

Soprano's lips pursed.

"Right, one-light-minute jump radius," she said, somewhat sourly. "I forgot about that."

Navy ships' full amplifiers meant they could jump far closer in to gravity wells than a civilian ship's jump matrix. She would be used to the ten-gee acceleration but not the full eighteen-million-kilometer safety radius for the jump.

"You'll get used to it," he promised.

He had, after all, grown used to having the ability to jump from farther in himself, and the fact that *Blue Jay* had been modified to have an amplifier was why his old ship had needed to be destroyed.

While it was certainly possible to provide magical gravity for the simulacrum chamber at the heart of a starship—it was done on every Navy vessel—Maria had decided to instead provide magical *zero* gravity. No matter what maneuvers or acceleration *Red Falcon* underwent, the core of the ship would remain untouched.

As they approached jump time, she floated against the wall of the chamber, surveying her domain with careful eyes. Every part of the outside of the chamber was covered in screens and silver runes. The screens showed the feed from hundreds of cameras across *Red Falcon*'s surface, allowing someone at the heart of the ship to see as the ship saw.

The runes linked into the matrices of runes that wove throughout the starship's entire hull, feeding and channeling power into the liquid-silver model at the exact center of the chamber and the exact center of the starship.

That liquid silver model would change and flow to match any adjustment to the ship around it. It currently showed the rows upon rows of ten-thousand-cubic-meter cargo containers that made up *Red Falcon*'s cargo in perfect detail. The only difference between the model and the ship it represented were the runes swarming across its surface in glowing colors, two clear spaces on the model marking where the jump mage would put their hands to interface with the spell.

The young Asian woman floating next to the simulacrum looked nervous, but Maria gave her a reassuring smile. She was perfectly confident in Xi Wu's ability to make *Red Falcon*'s first jump. If it hadn't been the very first jump they were ever going to make, she wouldn't even have been supervising the younger jump Mage.

"I make it ten minutes," a voice she wasn't expecting said from behind her.

Maria turned in the air to level a calm glare on *Red Falcon*'s third officer, their newly hired tactical officer. Iovis Acconcio was an olive-skinned heavyset man she'd served with before, and he gave her a careful zero-gravity bow as she turned.

"Shouldn't you be on the bridge?" she asked.

"Captain stood everyone down," Acconcio replied. "I wanted to watch the jump, if you're okay with that?"

"You were a Navy Warrant Officer," Maria pointed out. "You have to have seen what, five hundred of these?"

Chief Warrant Officer (Gunnery) Iovis Acconcio had been Mage-Lieutenant-Commander Soprano's strong right hand when she'd been second-in-command of the tactical department aboard the cruiser *Righteous Declaration of Justice*. He wasn't much older than she, but that extra five years of experience had been enough for him to earn a non-com's warrant as an alternative to a commission. He'd taken her under his wing then, and so, when he'd applied for the job on *Red Falcon*, she'd recommended him to Rice as highly as she could.

It hadn't been needed. There had been very little legitimate competition for the role.

"Never been on the bridge, for one," he admitted. "My place was missile control." He shrugged and smiled. "And now my place is on the bridge, but the bridge isn't the simulacrum chamber. I'll leave if I'm a distraction, but I want to watch."

Maria shook her head at her old friend and looked over at Xi Wu.

"Xi, you're jumping us this time," she told her subordinate. "Your call."

If Wu wasn't comfortable, she could let Acconcio watch the next jump, in two hours. That one would be Maria herself. Then her other two subordinates would each take one, after which Wu would have had the eight hours' rest required between jumps and would take the next one.

Four mages would allow *Red Falcon* to move twelve light-years in a day. In addition to her sheer size and defensibility, the big AAFHF was also incredibly fast.

"Won't be a problem," the young woman replied, the extra distraction apparently evening her confidence out. An audience could do that.

Xi Wu wasn't a Navy Mage, but she was an entirely acceptable civilian Jump Mage. If Maria had managed to recruit ex-Navy Mages, *Falcon* would have been even faster—civilian Jump Mages had to be able to jump every eight hours, which was also the standard the Guild set for the most they were *allowed* to do.

Navy Mages had to be able to jump every *six*. With four Navy Mages aboard, *Falcon* would have moved sixteen light-years a day and been able to keep up with Martian warships and task groups—which was, of course, the point in her design.

"If the jumping Mage says you're okay, you're okay," Maria told Acconcio. "Distract her for one second, though, and you're out."

Acconcio managed another zero-gravity bow.

"Of course, my dearest Ship's Mage," he promised. Living up to his promise, he promptly settled against one wall of the simulacrum chamber to watch Maria and Wu work.

"Mage Soprano." Rice's voice echoed through the chamber as an intercom window popped up on the screen. He paused as the return image came up, then the Captain bowed his head in apology.

"*And* Mage Wu," he greeted the junior Mage as well. "Ship's scanners report all gravimetric interference at low enough for jump. Do you have our course plotted for the Cinnamon system?"

"We do," Maria confirmed. Xi Wu might be making the first jump, but the young woman was doing it with figures and distances that Maria had calculated for her. She was confident in her junior Mages, but there were limits to what she could risk.

"Then the ship is in your hands," Rice told them. "We are cutting engines to zero and standing by for jump."

With the zero-gravity field in place, there was no way to feel that the engines had halted. The bright white flare of *Red Falcon*'s antimatter engines slowly faded off the camera views, however, and the ship ceased accelerating.

She was still moving through space at a measurable percentage of lightspeed. That was something Maria had included in her calculations, but was also something that Wu would have to adjust for.

Rather than explicitly watching over the younger woman's shoulder, she'd mirrored the display from the simulacrum platform to her own wrist-comp, checking her subordinate's calculations in real time.

"Adjusted calculations for current velocity," Wu said in a soft voice. "Stand by to jump."

She waited for long enough that Maria could have interjected if something *had* gone wrong in the calculations, and then closed her hands onto the simulacrum, linking her magic into the multi-megaton bulk of the starship.

Then reality *shifted* and the stars on the screen were different. They were somewhere new.

Acconcio looked around the simulacrum chamber in awe. In Maria's opinion, it wasn't much different to see the jump from here than anywhere else in the ship with a camera screen, but he seemed taken by the experience.

Xi Wu, on the other hand, looked like she'd been punched in the stomach. That was a relatively normal state of a Mage post-Jump, however, so Maria simply kept an eye on her.

"Jump complete," Wu reported over the intercom to the bridge. "We are at Tau Ceti-Cinnamon Jump Zone One."

"Navigation confirms," Rice told her. "Well done, Mage Wu. Mage Soprano? Next jump?"

"Two hours," Maria confirmed, drifting over to the simulacrum platform and waving for Wu to go get some rest. "ETA in the Cinnamon system just over seventy-two hours."

"Prompt and efficient service," the Captain said with a smile. "Thank you, Mage Soprano. Let me know if there are any concerns."

CHAPTER 10

HOWEVER UNUSUAL and terrifying David's last Ship's Mage had turned out to be, Montgomery had still only been one man. A single Mage could move a ship only so fast.

With four Mages aboard, the speed that *Red Falcon* was moving between systems seemed blisteringly fast to David. In just under three days, they'd traveled over thirty light-years, erupting into regular space about a light-year and a half away from Cinnamon.

Not only could his new ship carry more cargo than most of her competitors, she could also deliver it faster. The economic potential of that was still dizzying to David, though it was also easily offset by the sheer cost of operating *Falcon*.

Mages weren't cheap. A four-hundred-strong crew wasn't cheap. *Antimatter*, for all that most systems had a secured space station where Mage criminals created it, definitely wasn't cheap. *Red Falcon* carried almost seven times as much cargo as *Blue Jay* had, which made it harder to find cargos but cost just over ten times as much to operate.

The solution David was seeing was to move as quickly as possible. It took *Falcon* less time to get from system to system and less time to get in and out of a given system as well. If he could move three or four cargos in the same time it took a ship with a single Mage to move one, then even at a significantly reduced profit per cargo, he was going to come out ahead.

Way ahead.

The Mage-King's gift was a dream come true. David could see why most shipping lines wouldn't want a ship like *Falcon*—finding enough cargo to keep her full and moving was going to be a nightmare, and her initial cost would be insane if you had to actually pay for her—but he could make her work.

"Stop gloating inside your head," Campbell told him sharply, his XO leaning in over the side of his command chair. "I bet you anything the Mage-King thinks he got the better end of this deal."

"Likely," David agreed, shaking the grin he hadn't realized he was wearing off his face. "That's the sign of a good deal."

He glanced around the bridge, busier than he was used to, and lowered his voice.

"Plus, Stealey warned me that some of the fragments of Azure's syndicate may still come after us," he told her. "They're seeing us as bait, which means they're still planning on getting value from giving us *Falcon*."

"Figured something of the sort, especially after I got shot," his XO replied. "Anyone else filled in on that?"

"Kellers and Skavar have guessed, I'm pretty sure," he told her. "I have the feeling Soprano knows more than any of us have told her. Acconcio is paranoid enough that I'm not too worried."

The tactical officer was currently at his station, walking two of his new staff through the scanners. Every member of the gunnery crew had at least some experience with civilian-grade weapons, but *Red Falcon*'s weapon systems were an entirely different animal—and so were the sensors.

"What's that?" one of the gunners asked.

"That's..." Acconcio began brightly and confidently, then trailed off. "I don't know," he admitted. "That's strange."

"What have we got, Tactical?" David interrupted.

"I'm calling it a ghost for now," *Falcon*'s third officer told him. "Focusing the passives, unless you want us to go active?"

"Let's not paint the neighborhood with targeting beams just yet," the Captain replied. "Tell me what you see."

Acconcio was already diving into his controls, the training session reduced to "watch the expert work" for at least a few minutes.

"Contact is between forty and sixty-five light-seconds away," he reeled off. "Blips of thermal signature, some reflected light. If it's a ship, they're being *very* careful to not fire engines where we can see them."

"Someone being sneaky?"

"Or a random rock with some hydrocarbon outgassing," the tactical officer replied. "But...yeah, someone with a heat-absorbing hull trying to be sneaky. Sixty-forty."

"At that that distance, they're not a threat, right?" David asked.

"They could hit us if they had top-tier antimatter missiles, but I don't think they're planning on it," Acconcio said. "I think we're being watched, but I don't think they're picking a fight today."

"Then why are they watching us?" David wondered.

"At a guess?" the ex-Navy warrant officer said softly. "Because they're planning on picking a fight another day and want to know just where we are."

David nodded.

"I never thought I'd miss having to fly without a formal flight plan," he said dryly. "Keep our eyes open, Acconcio. If they move in our direction, I want to know before they do."

"Eyes on, Captain. Eyes are on."

Maria relieved an exhausted Shachar Costa. The Tau Ceti native Jump Mage was probably the weakest link of her little collection of Mages, but he could still make a jump every eight hours. Maria herself could push to five, and she'd be comfortable pushing Xi Wu to the Navy's standard six for emergencies.

The small, gaunt youth couldn't push past eight. It wasn't a mark against the youth, just something his boss had to keep in mind.

"Soprano, it's Rice." The Captain's voice echoed through the intercom as she began to check into the ship's systems. "One of our new gunnery students spotted a ghost and Acconcio can't nail it down. It looks like we've got a stalker. Any suggestions?"

She considered, pulling up the data on the contact on her screens.

"Not much we can do at that distance," she admitted. "This isn't a real amplifier, so there isn't much I can do with magic outside the ship anyway. If I wake up everybody, I could cloak us, but..."

"But they already knew we were here," Rice agreed. "Someone dropped them our flight plan and they're checking to see if we're following it."

He sighed.

"We're keeping an eye on them, but other than making me nervous, they're not doing anything. We *could* get a missile to them, but I imagine they'd be able to jump away or shoot it down, and I'd like to keep the Navy birds close to our chest."

"I suggest we leave it be, sir," Maria told him. This was exactly what Alois had wanted her on Rice's ship for. "If they want to jump us, we've a few ugly surprises for them, but picking fights is only going to get us in trouble."

"My thoughts as well," Rice admitted. "How long till jump?"

Maria poked at her internal reserves and gave her Captain a bright smile.

"Depends on how twitchy you're feeling," she told him. "I was trained to the *Navy* standard, after all. Want to show these guys our heels?"

"Dealing with stalkers, I'd rather punch them out, but I don't have the grounds for it," the Captain said. "Take us away, Mage Soprano. Engines aren't even online."

"Sound the alert and give me a minute to double-check my calculations," she promised. "Then I'll get us the hell out of his sights."

"Carry on, Ship's Mage," Rice replied. "And thank you."

David stayed on the bridge after the early jump, watching the scanners. He was somehow unsurprised when Iovis Acconcio did the same.

He was relatively certain the tactical officer had been scheduled to be doing something else after his training session—potentially sleeping—but instead, the man had remained behind.

Eventually, there were just the two of them on the bridge, waiting out the double-length pause between jumps.

"How long, do you think?" David asked the other man in the silence after they'd been alone, both watching their screens, for at least ten minutes.

He didn't say what he was asking about. He knew the other man understood, or he wouldn't have been there.

"Guessing two Mages," Acconcio grunted. "Call it four hours between jumps, but they were waiting for us. I figure two and a half, maybe three hours."

"We'll pick them up?"

"No question. These are Navy-grade scanners; there's no way we'll miss a jump flare." The gunner shrugged. "If they're *smart*, they'll jump in a light-hour or so off from the normal waypoint. That way, we'll be gone before their light reaches us, but they'll be able to confirm we were here.

"It's not like they can exactly track our jumps, after all."

"I've been chased by people who could," David said quietly. "It wasn't a fun experience."

"That's not possible," the ex-Navy man replied. "Yeah, if you know where someone's coming from and where they're going, you can ambush them, but you can't *chase* people."

"I don't know how," David noted. "But I was chased when I didn't have a course on record anywhere, and people I trust tell me that's how I was followed." He shrugged. "Fortunately, everyone I know can do it is dead."

Unmentioned was that both of the ships he'd known to track him through jumps were dead at the hands of his crew. If Acconcio hadn't realized there was more to LaMonte, for example, than a pretty face, well...he'd have some surprises coming.

"Damn," the man said. "So far as I know, the Navy still thinks that's impossible."

"Well, like I said, I don't know how to do it," David told him with a grin. "The bastards with my flight plan are bad enough."

"We'll deal with them, boss," Acconcio said grimly. "Between me, Skavar, and Soprano, no one coming after this ship has a damn clue what kind of meat-grinder they're running into."

David shook his head.

"Between the three of you, I keep half-expecting to discover this is actually *still* a Navy ship that everyone lets me think is mine out of courtesy."

His three ex-military officers were all recent muster-outs, and they'd all dropped all too neatly into his lap. They'd mostly come to him through Burns—and Burns had Alaura Stealey's trust, which was enough for David Rice. It was still enough to weird him out.

Acconcio laughed.

"If this was a Navy ship, they wouldn't have let Soprano anywhere near it," he pointed out. "And *I'm* here because of her." The ex-warrant officer paused, then chuckled again. "I'll give you Skavar. *He* might still be a Marine, for all I know. He certainly produced a full platoon of ex-Martian Marines at the drop of a dime, from what I heard."

David shared the laugh.

"If that's the case, I guess I can be thankful the Protectorate is watching my back?" he asked. "There's a point when you wonder, though, just how much debt you've racked up and when you're going to be asked to pay it back."

His tactical officer's gaze went serious and dark.

"I know," he admitted. "And sometimes you have to choose just what you're prepared to sacrifice to pay your debts."

Something in Acconcio's tone told David that wasn't something to ask about, not yet, and he let the silence descend again.

"There," the other man suddenly snapped, gesturing at his console. "Not sneaky enough, my friends."

"What have you got?"

"Jump flare at five light-minutes; lit him up like a Christmas tree," *Falcon*'s tactical officer replied. "Pretty sure it's our ghost; the reflection reads like a stealthed hull."

"So, he knew where we were going."

"Oh, yeah," Acconcio confirmed. "Should have jumped even further out. Now I know what we're dealing with."

"And that is?"

"*Caribbean*-class patrol corvette," the dark-skinned man reported. "Hundred thousand tons, fusion engines, fusion missiles, couple of light lasers. Built as an in-system cutter, they only have a jump matrix for delivery to the destination.

"Couple of systems build them, probably eighty, ninety of them scattered around the MidWorlds and the Fringe." He shook his head. "Our friend here had his hull upgraded with heat-scattering tiles, but the jump flare lit him up cleanly."

"All he needed to know to ambush us *and* a stealthy ship," David murmured. "Why am I not feeling loved today?"

"We're forty minutes from the scheduled jump to Cinnamon," his officer pointed out. "He can't intercept us; he's just watching. Stalking."

"Assessing our jump patterns for when he has our *next* flight path," *Red Falcon*'s Captain said grimly. "I hope your people are living up to your expectations, Mr. Acconcio, because I think we're going to have work for them soon."

CHAPTER 11

MARIA CONCEALED a sigh of relief from her junior Mages as they emerged into the Cinnamon system. She hadn't been making the jump, so she'd been watching the sensor data and had seen the ship reappear at the last jump point.

Cinnamon was a MidWorld and a relatively unindustrialized one, so her system defense force was minimal—but the dozen corvettes showing up on *Red Falcon*'s long-range scanners would have made short work of a single ship if it decided to chase the freighter.

"That's our part done," she told the Mages. "Well done, people. Thirty-six light-years in three days sets a fine precedent for the Captain to use when bidding for cargo—if we can deliver the most cargo the fastest, then we'll be the first choice of shipper for a lot of people.

"That keeps the ship busy and us paid," she concluded with a grin. "Go rest, all of you. We're still half a day or so from orbit, and I'll want you all rested when we start the calculations for the next trip. Go!"

Her new subordinates, the oldest of them ten years her junior, drifted out of the simulacrum chamber. Maria was left alone floating amidst the stars, and she studied the Cinnamon system.

The quiet of the system's reputation showed in more ways than one. They'd just left Tau Ceti, a system where human habitation was guarded by massive anti-meteor defenses. Here, nature had provided a shield against the same—the third planet was the habitable world, named

Cinnamon like the system, but the fourth was a massive super-Jovian gas giant named Peppercorn.

Peppercorn had smashed anything in the system that had been farther out than Cinnamon and sucked all of the debris into its own orbit. The gas giant had massive rings of gas and rock—but the star system didn't have an asteroid belt of any kind.

Just two rocky worlds, too hot and small to support life—Ghost and Jalapeno, according to Maria's files—and a third world, slightly larger and less dense than Earth, smack dab in the habitable zone.

Cinnamon had a gravity slightly higher than humanity's homeworld, a day slightly longer than Earth or terraformed Mars, and only a single ocean.

Most of the planet was a single landmass, wrapped around a single contiguous body of deep water that covered just over forty-five percent of Cinnamon's surface. The planet had a low axial tilt, calm seasons, and a climate supportive of Earth-native crops over a vast area.

Its local life hadn't progressed much past plants—but some of those plants were the reason for the system's theme naming. The original survey had found four plants that were edible to humans and made for spectacular exotic spices.

The colonists had found half a dozen food crops among the native plant life and another twenty spices. Cinnamon exported the spices that gave the world its name and vast quantities of food.

What industry the planet had was mostly in orbit, keeping the atmosphere of the world below clean for both the people and the vast farms that occupied it. Eventually, the exports would allow Cinnamon to bootstrap itself up to a higher standard than many worlds, but for now, it was relatively unindustrialized by MidWorld standards.

"Soprano," Rice's voice cut into her thoughts as an intercom screen opened. "Did you check the scan reports for the last jump point?"

"We were still being followed," she confirmed. "That's going to be a headache. Any chance it was the locals?"

"Acconcio says they're using a completely different class of corvette," the Captain told her. One of the two men on the bridge had clearly had the same thought. "Tau Ceti–built."

"What do we do?" she asked.

"For now?" His image shrugged. "We're about ten hours from making orbit at zero relative velocity. We'll deliver the cargo, get paid, and see what we can find to carry on from here."

"And when we leave, we keep our eyes open."

"This ship is heavily armed enough to take out any pirate," Maria noted.

"And they know that, even if they've hopefully underestimated our defenses," her Captain agreed. "So, I worry about just what they'll bring to the party when they decide to play. Are your people up for any kind of assistance in a fight?"

"There's some training in the Jump Mage curriculum," she admitted, "but I wouldn't rely on it. None of our juniors are *that* fresh out of school." She considered the planets on the screens around her for several seconds. "I'll refresh their training," she promised. "We won't add a lot more to *Falcon*'s defenses than the RFLAM turrets do, but every little bit helps."

"It does. Thank you."

"Part of the job, sir. If you'll excuse me, I'll go look up some training books," Maria told Rice. "It's been a while since I had to do missile defense without an amplifier myself!"

Cinnamon Station was a smaller station than many Maria had seen in her years in the Navy, but like most MidWorlds orbitals, it was the central pride of their space presence. A central fat cylinder, two hundred meters across and two hundred meters high, remained motionless to allow for starship docking. Linked to that was a ring, just over fifteen hundred meters across, that spun fast enough to provide a full gravity of centripetal acceleration at its rim.

The hundred-meter-tall exterior of the ring had probably been more than enough space when it was installed, but Cinnamon had expanded beyond the original capacity of the station. At some point, six carefully balanced towers had been added to the outer rim. Each was about two hundred meters wide and extended three hundred meters "up" and "down" from the ring.

Presumably, they'd added extra thrusters or something to the towers to help keep the whole assemblage spinning safely. Maria was simply glad that no one was making *Red Falcon* dock at the rotating towers—not that anything larger than a shuttle *could*.

Red Falcon's sheer size meant they were getting an entire side of the central hub to themselves, docking nose to nose with a space station that wasn't, all things considered, significantly bigger than the AAFHF herself.

As a Navy Mage-Commander, Maria had been fully trained to carry out docking operations for ships of even greater size, but she was still glad that it was Campbell and Rice who were docking *Falcon* today. She didn't even need to be in the simulacrum chamber—she just found it helped her think.

Her wrist-comp pinged as they closed with the station, and she sighed. She'd sent a report in to MISS with the rest of the mail delivery, relayed to the main office in Nutmeg City.

Part of her had hoped that her reports were simply going to disappear into the bureaucracy of a galaxy-wide security agency. In this case, she was reasonably certain that the Protectorate knowing that they were being hunted wasn't going to hurt anyone aboard *Falcon*, but it still felt wrong to betray her shipmates' confidences.

The response was a simple text message that had somehow managed to arrive on her comp without a return contact address.

Situation more critical than expected. Local details an additional complication. Meet me.

No name. Just a time and an address.

Maria sighed. She'd hoped that this job wasn't going to include cloak-and-dagger bullshit. Give her a ship, give her an enemy, she knew what she was doing. Sneaking around sending reports and receiving secret orders?

She'd ask how an honest soldier had come to this, but she *knew* the answer to that one.

"And there we go," Campbell announced with a confident satisfaction in her voice. "Primary connection made; Cinnamon Station is extending umbilicals. We are locked on."

"Thank you, XO," David told her. "How's my message inbox looking?" he continued with a grin.

"You've Cinnamon Station on the line, wanting to chat with you about docking fees and contracts, but that's it for now," she replied. "I can't speak to your actual inbox, but if Nguyen was remotely on the level, there will be people looking for you pretty quick."

"Nguyen's on the level," he confirmed. "I'll go sort out our docking fees. If anyone from the system government or Nguyen's import syndicate calls, feel free to interrupt. You know how much I *love* station control."

"Will do," Campbell promised.

With the magical gravity now laid out, it was barely a twenty-second walk to his office, where David settled down behind the desk and linked his wrist-comp into the office systems, ordering them to bring up the channel to the station administrator.

"Captain Rice," the heavyset man on the screen greeted him. "I am George O'Toole, dock administrator for Cinnamon Station. It's not often we see a ship of your scale dock here. I'll admit I wasn't sure we could link up to your fuel tanks!"

"It's the same fittings, Mr. O'Toole," David replied. "We just have to pump longer. We'll also need to acquire antimatter, which I'm assuming is not in your regular umbilical setup."

The administrator stared at him for a moment.

"I suppose I should have been paying more attention when you burned in," he finally admitted. "Antimatter?"

"*Red Falcon* is an ex-Navy ship; we still run on antimatter main engines," David confirmed. "I'll have to check my systems to be certain, but I think we'll need to restock a couple of hundred kilos."

Several hundred kilograms of antimatter, even with magical transmutation for production, was going to set him back more than the thousands of tons of hydrogen he was going to have to take on to refuel his power plants.

"I'm not certain that we even have that much antimatter on hand," O'Toole said delicately. "I will have to check around."

David carefully did *not* note that Protectorate rules required Cinnamon to maintain a conversion facility and a stockpile of at least five tons of antimatter to refuel any Navy ships that passed through the area. That fuel would be sold to a Navy vessel that arrived and could be sold to anyone. O'Toole might simply not know that, though.

And if they'd screwed that up, well, *Red Falcon* could easily visit three or four more systems before she actually ran out of antimatter, and could function at reduced efficiency entirely on hydrogen.

That wouldn't make him *happy*, but he could do it.

"Let me know," he told the other man. "Do you have a fee sheet for regular fuel and services?"

"Sending it over," O'Toole promised. "I apologize, Captain, but your ship is unknown in this system, so we will require payment for all services in advance. No credit."

No wonder Cinnamon was having problems attracting shippers. That was a problem for a speculative shipper.

"I'm under contract to the Cinnamon government," he pointed out. "They are obligated to cover my docking fees and refueling."

O'Toole coughed.

"They are welcome to reimburse you, of course, but we require immediate payment by electronic transfer," he told David. "If you cannot pay, we will have to seize your ship and cargo to cover the costs."

"You will do no such thing," David snapped. "My contract, Mr. O'Toole, is quite clear: the Cinnamon system government is covering my docking fees. You can contact them for your payment. I can even forward you the contact information I have if you somehow can't get ahold of your own government."

"I—"

David held up a hand.

"And before you bluster further," he told O'Toole quietly, "I remind you that *Red Falcon* was a Navy *armed* auxiliary. You can't take her from me—and if you insist, I will invoke the break clauses in my contract and leave.

"In which case, Mr. O'Toole, *you* would have to explain to your government why they're suddenly out a billion-dollar cargo under the penalty clauses."

He smiled as O'Toole blanched away from the camera.

"Do we have an understanding, administrator?"

David gave himself several minutes after the conversation ended to regain his composure. He'd grown used to dealing with the bureaucracy of the Martian Navy, which had received specific orders from a Hand to cooperate.

He'd forgotten how obstructive normal bureaucrats could be.

A large cup of coffee and a small shot of whisky later, he had calmed enough to actually start reaching out to people. The majority of his cargo belonged to an importer syndicate, one that included the Cinnamon government as a major partner, and they hadn't contacted him yet.

Nguyen had given him contact information for the lead partner in the syndicate and David plugged it in. Given that he owned half the cargo himself, he wanted the wheels moving.

His wallscreen lit up with the image of an attractive woman with graying hair cut short around her shoulders. Like Nguyen in Tau Ceti, she wore a simple black suit and a black bowler hat. She unleashed a bright smile on him when she saw him.

"You must be Captain Rice," she greeted him. "I apologize for the delay in reaching out to you; my wife is currently in an emergency meeting of the partners."

"And you are, ma'am?" he asked delicately.

"Paula Hayashi," she answered. "Atsuko Hayashi should have been your contact—she's my wife. Your ship is fast enough that you arrived well ahead of any news of your arrival, and no one was expecting a shipment of this magnitude."

"That explains the problem with the docking authority," David said dryly.

"Oh, for crying out loud," Hayashi snapped. She sighed. "I apologize, Captain; we don't see very many ships that haven't been here before, and most that are new fly under the Green Seneschal Line, which has pre-existing arrangements with the dock authority."

A hard look settled over her face.

"And you're not the first non-Green Seneschal captain to complain," she noted. "I think I'm going to have to talk to Harry and have him look into just what their arrangements entail."

That sounded promising, though David didn't know who "Harry" was. Hayashi saw his confusion, however, and chuckled.

"Apologies, Harold Hayashi is the Member of Parliament for Cinnamon Station," she explained. "Also, Atsuko's and my husband."

That sounded complicated—and also like the triad basically *ran* Cinnamon Station between them. O'Toole was going to have problems in the near future, a likelihood David couldn't feel sorry for.

"So, if your wife is in this meeting, should I be waiting to sort out what's going on with my cargo?" he asked.

"Sadly, yes," Hayashi admitted. "Harry gets elected, Atsuko runs the import syndicate, I'm 'just' the secretary."

And, unless David missed his mark, the woman who actually *ran* the trio's affairs. Anyone who underestimated Paula Hayashi was going to find themselves in a lot of trouble.

"Am I likely to have any issues?" he asked carefully.

"Ha! No," the older woman replied. "Cinnamon *needs* your cargo, Captain Rice. You let my partners work out how we're paying you for it, but don't worry." The brilliant smile widened.

"We are most *definitely* paying you for it."

CHAPTER 12

THE DIRECTIONS from Maria's contact led her to a bar in a seedy portion of Cinnamon Station's lower-tier residential sectors. There were areas, most of them aboard space stations in general, that managed to be poor but not problematic.

This wasn't one of those areas. The corridor lights had been covered in transparent ceramic armor at some point, a knowing sacrifice of light quality in trade for the lights not needing to be replaced. No one living on a space station would let things get bad enough for there to be actual garbage in the corners, but the walls were dirtier than she was used to, suggesting that whoever ran Cinnamon Station's cleaning robots had programmed them not to come there.

A course of action that, like the armor on the lights, was taken only in response to repeated damage or theft.

The bar itself didn't look much different from Xu's back in Tau Ceti, though the Xu cousins would probably have objected to the comparison. It was brighter-lit and cleaner than the surrounding area, but the patrons were all genteelly ignoring each other as the bartender glowered at them.

The bartender was one of the few obvious cyborgs Maria had ever seen. Cybernetic replacements were reasonably common in the Protectorate, but they were built to resemble the real thing as much as possible. Even combat cyborgs like the Legatan Augments, an extreme rarity in an era of powered exosuit armor and Combat Mages, were hard to tell apart from everyone around them.

The bartender, however, had clearly either lost his arms at some point or had them voluntarily replaced with cybernetics that made no pretense at just being an attempt to restore function. Maria could pick out the distinct lines in the man's shirt of the reinforcing plating wrapped around his chest to support the powerful motors visible in the augments.

He'd have no trouble evicting even the most problematic of customers, and as a bonus, his mechanical limbs were probably even more precise at pouring and mixing than his organic ones.

The bartender spotted her entering, met her gaze, and jerked his chin toward a specific booth. She was clearly expected.

Maria wasn't used to crossing a room without drawing attention, and today was no exception. She was, for once, wearing something that actually covered her cleavage—she wasn't going to try to weaponize her body against an MISS agent, after all—but that didn't seem to reduce the number of eyes on her as she walked over to the booth.

The bartender let the stares continue for several seconds and then cleared his throat loudly and dropped a metallic arm on the table.

"Oi!" he bellowed. "Lady's here for drinks, same as you lot. Keep your damned eyes in your damned heads."

The degree of simultaneity with which the patrons' gazes snapped back to their drinks was enough to keep Maria chuckling as she slid into the booth. The man occupying it shared her amusement and smiled at her.

He was burlier than she'd expected and didn't look at all out of place in a bar that catered to physical laborers. His head was shaved, with a tribal tattoo covering half of his face, but he smiled warmly as he offered her his hand.

"Bruno is much more of a sweetheart than he wants people to think," he murmured as he shook Maria's hand. "Nikora Samuels. You know who I work for."

"The augments probably help," she replied.

"Lost his arms in an accident, insurance fucked him," Samuels said bluntly. "Only way out was mob enforcer, but that got him arms like that." The man grinned. "'Course, Bruno is *much* smarter than he looks, though I don't think he *planned* on marrying a cop to get out of the mob."

Maria shook her head. That would be one way to escape obligations to the mob, yeah.

"Hence, this place," Samuels concluded. "Bruno doesn't turn his old friends into his wife's bosses and keeps a few booths with privacy fields he doesn't ask questions about, and they considered his debt paid."

"And MISS uses the booths too?" she asked.

"We do," he confirmed. "In exchange for *our* deal with Bruno, which is that if his old friends ever change their minds, we protect him."

"Works well for him," the Mage concluded, glancing back at the big bartender. *Much* smarter than he looked. "Married, huh?"

"Happily, three little girls," the MISS agent replied. "And because Bruno is Bruno, if anyone touches his family, every legal and illegal organization on this station is going to rip them to pieces."

Samuels smiled.

"I can only *wish* for that kind of protection."

"I've got *Falcon*," Maria said with a grin. "With Rice's history, I think I'm fine."

"That man?" the burly stranger shook his head. "I read his file this morning, the parts of it I can access, anyway. I'd trust him to have my back. And we're going to have his."

"That's reassuring," she admitted. "Giving reports on my crew makes my spine itch."

"That never goes away," Samuels said. "You just get used to it. Look, I've got your reports on your stalker in my queue to head back to higher up and disseminate. My data doesn't mention anybody out there with a grudge against Rice with access to even pocket warships, but that just leaves me thinking we've missed a Blue Star Syndicate leftover somewhere."

"That's my fear as well."

"So, we'll keep our eyes open," the spy promised. "We've got enough links back into the Navy that if a problem comes up, we can bring the fire down pretty quickly."

"That might be rough on us in the meantime," Maria warned.

"That's why the Hand gave him that ship." Samuels shook his head. "Look, much as you needed the update and assurance that, yes, we are watching your backs, that wasn't why I asked you to meet me."

"I figured," she replied. "Nice office you have."

"MISS has a *gorgeous* office building in downtown Nutmeg City," he told her. "Lovely thing. I've visited, oh, once. I'm a less obvious asset, working specific files. *My* file, Mage Soprano, is the Legatans."

"What about them?" Maria asked.

Legatus was the first and foremost of the UnArcana worlds, a heavily industrialized system that forbade the practice of magic. Since magic was the only way for ships to visit them, they allowed Jump Mages...so long as they only jumped. No other magic allowed.

There were about a dozen more UnArcana worlds, but Legatus was the leader and the one that seemed determined to throw wrenches into Protectorate affairs.

"There's a lot about them," Samuels said with a laugh. "Today, though, I'm tracking what appears to be a black-materials conduit for them. Supplies are moving around, appearing and disappearing at random as they send shipments without official notice. We haven't managed to track anything through the chain of trades; at least some of it's moving legitimately, but—"

"But they're hiding something."

"Exactly. And I want you to see if you can find out what."

Maria hesitated before replying but then shook her head at Samuels.

"My understanding was that my job was much more defensive than that," she pointed out. "I was tasked with working on Rice's ship and watching his back, not being an investigator for MISS."

"You took an Agency salary, Mage Soprano," he argued. "That means you're on call for whatever tasks we need." He sighed. "To be fair, though, yes, that was your job. This would be an additional task, which means I'm not going to order you to take it on. But...the Legatans are up to something, and if they're not stopped, it could threaten the entire Protectorate."

"Surely, it's not that bad," Maria replied. "What are they going to do, declare war on us?"

"I don't know," Samuels admitted. "But there's always been an independence movement in the UnArcana worlds. I can't see a war, but... they could cause a lot of damage.

"And we don't know what their plans are or what they're moving, Soprano. It could well be that bad."

She shook her head again, but the meaning was different now.

"I'd say I swore an oath, but that was pretty thoroughly voided for me," she said quietly. "But...fuck it. I was an officer of the Mage-King of Mars and there are things you cannot take away from me."

"You're an *agent* of the Mage-King of Mars, now," Samuels pointed out. "Same needs, different oaths."

"What do you need me to do?" she asked.

"My information is that there's a company here on Cinnamon that's basically being used to launder funds for this project," he told her. "Money is funneled in from various sources and used to acquire products for export. Those are shipped elsewhere, where they're sold and the money used to acquire the next part of the chain.

"Most of the ships that have come through Cinnamon of late have been Green Seneschal—another point of concern, but nothing I need you to look at!—so they haven't been able to ship as much of their acquisitions as they'd like. They've got a stockpile big enough to justify hiring *Red Falcon,* and MISS thinks they've flagged Rice as a useful ally."

"So, we're going to get an offer for work?" she replied. "And you want us to take it?"

"Silk Star Trade Exports," Samuels told her. "I'm not sure where they're going to ship to, but I need Rice to take that job. You're his first officer, his Ship's Mage. Think you can make it happen?"

"Yeah," Maria admitted. "But if it comes to a choice between the safety of *Red Falcon's* crew and this job—"

"Protect your crew, Ship's Mage," the agent said with a laugh. "That's the first thing we wanted you on that ship for—and nothing has changed.

"We may need to use David Rice as bait, but that doesn't mean we don't owe him and want him *alive.*"

"Good. We'd have a problem if it didn't," Maria warned.

In the end, David ended up meeting Atsuko Hayashi in her office. To his surprise, having spoken with Hayashi's wife, Atsuko was significantly younger than he, a dark-haired woman in her early thirties of clear Old Earth Japanese extraction.

"Captain, come on in, have a seat," Hayashi instructed after David knocked on the door of her office.

The other occupant of the room was a slightly older man with the melting-pot ethnic features of the either Martian-born or Martian-descended. He wore the same simple suit as Paula Hayashi or Factor Nguyen, with a simple golden pin at his collar suggesting some level of importance.

"I'm sure Paula mentioned us both," the woman continued, gesturing to her companion. "I am Atsuko Hayashi, head of Dancing Fox Importers. Harry here is the Member of Parliament for Cinnamon Station. You spoke with our wife."

"I did," he confirmed. "From what she said, I created more of a headache than I expected on my arrival."

Mrs. Hayashi laughed.

"Not your fault, Captain. Harvey Nguyen found an embarrassment of riches and felt he needed to get it home," she told him. "He probably should have given you more of a warning about how things would blow up when you got here, but it also might not have occurred to him."

"Harvey hasn't been home in over a decade," Harry Hayashi interjected. "Things change in that kind of time. We've had new players move in, new needs arise, but..." He shrugged. "Harvey sent us what we needed and then some. He made the right call; Atsuko and I just had to smack some heads together to make sense of it."

"So, I'm getting paid for this delivery, right?" David asked.

"Delivery fee was deposited to your credit as soon as I was out of the meeting," the youngest Hayashi told him. "That much I could do from my own accounts, though I'm quite certain about getting reimbursed for everyone else's portion."

David had seen less predatory grins on sharks.

"Now, as I understand, part of your deal with Factor Nguyen was that you own forty-five percent of the cargo, correct?" Harry Hayashi asked.

"Exactly," David replied. "I helped fund the purchase of the cargo on the expectation I'd be able to sell it on this end."

"That, sadly, is part of what my partners are flipping their damn lids over," the attractive CEO noted. "They're used to being able to triple or quadruple their investment in anything we buy in Tau Ceti; the thought of having to share that profit is hurting their pretty little heads."

"Which, my love, I need to point out is a real concern to the government," Harry told his younger wife. "This syndicate you put together is starting to look more and more like an oligarchic monopoly. Even the government being a major partner isn't going to protect them from charges of profiteering much longer."

She held up a finger.

"I know that and you know that, but convince *them* of that," she replied. "But that isn't Captain Rice's problem. I have a compromise to suggest, Captain. One that I think is of value to all parties."

"I'm listening," David said carefully.

"Given the price that Nguyen acquired this cargo at and the premium he gave you to get his funding, I must be honest: if you take the time to sell it yourself to the right parties, you could easily quadruple your money," Atsuko told him. "*Finding* said parties would require a local partner, but the right local partner—such as, say, Dancing Fox Importers"— she grinned at him—"could probably get that up to five times.

"But it would take weeks. Months, even. While billions could certainly help offset your operating costs for that time, men don't take to the stars because they like sitting around."

That was true—but it was also a lot of money that the Hayashis were suggesting he could make by staying.

"What my dear Atsuko hesitates to point out is that your staying might not be safe," Harry said quietly. "There are reasons I and the government worry about the import syndicate. Between them and certain other corporate parties, Cinnamon politics are more dangerous than they've been in some time—and you'd be sticking yourself right in the middle."

"What's your compromise, then?" David asked. Poking a hornet's nest wasn't his idea of a good time. He'd done enough of that with Damien Montgomery as his Ship's Mage.

"I am prepared to buy your portion of the cargo, today, no questions asked, for a one hundred and fifty percent premium over your investment," she told him. "That will be an entirely separate deal from the syndicate, between just yourself and Dancing Fox.

"We'll offload the cargo with everything else and you'll be a few hundred million or so richer with no major entanglements to a MidWorld you'd be just as happy to never see again," she continued. "*My* share is being backed by the Cinnamon government"—she nodded to her husband—"so you don't need to worry about the payment."

"And if I want to take a day or two to shop around for a better deal?" he asked.

"Feel free," Atsuko replied, smiling at him. "The government's main concern is that the cargo doesn't leave Cinnamon. While I'm certain you could get better prices for portions of the cargo, you're not going to find a single deal in a few days."

"I'll let you know," he promised. The odds were that it was a good deal, but he didn't want to leap on it straight away. His crew would get portions and he had an obligation to them, if no one else these days, to make sure he made the best deal possible.

"I wouldn't expect a decision straight away," Atsuko Hayashi said brightly, though her husband looked disappointed. "You have my contact information. Let me know when you want to deal, Captain Rice.

"The syndicate's cargo, we'll start off-loading tomorrow. Assuming you either take my deal or arrange for storage of your portion, we should have your ship emptied in three days."

She offered her hand across the table.

"Regardless of whether you take my offer, Captain, it's been a pleasure doing business with you. It's not often I get to watch these idiots have to squirm around, admitting they don't want to share profit."

Returning to *Red Falcon*, David called a meeting of his senior staff. The new ship had a lot of officers and crew, more than he was used to, but his core staff was still barely over half a dozen strong.

Falcon, unlike his last ship, actually had a good-sized meeting room in the gravity ring, easily usable for meetings of this size or even larger. The table was cheap Navy-standard issue like most of the furniture aboard the ship, but it was more than big enough for the six of them.

"We're going to have work for you, Nicolas," he told the new First Pilot.

Fulbert Nicolas was cut from much the same short-haired, gaunt mold as Kelzin was, though ten years older than the junior pilot and with a twelve-year stint in the Tau Ceti Orbital Patrol behind him. Primarily a search-and-rescue pilot, he knew both the big and small shuttles *Red Falcon* carried inside and out.

Only Campbell and Kellers were really known quantities among his senior officers, though. They'd been with him for years now, and stuck with him while the Protectorate had taken its time getting him a new ship.

The other four, Nicolas, Skavar, Acconcio and Soprano, were all new faces. He trusted them to a point, but no one—not even them—thought their opinions carried as much weight as his old hands.

"The Importers' Syndicate is going to start offloading their fifty-five percent of the cargo tomorrow," he told the pilot. "We'll want our shuttles to help out, make certain everything goes smoothly."

"Easy enough," Nicolas grunted.

"As for my chunk, I'm in discussions with one of the lead partners of the Syndicate for them to take it off our hands," David continued. "We'll probably start off-loading it as soon as we're done with the Syndicate's share. Selling it ourselves would have us stuck here for weeks, and that doesn't appeal to me."

"Most of the crew is happy so long as they get paid," Skavar said. "But there's always a few with permanently itchy feet. A few days? No problems. A week? A few grouches. *Weeks?* Yeah, we'd have problems."

"I don't expect to stay that long," David noted. "But if we do…"

"That's Security's problem," Skavar agreed. "What's the plan, boss?"

"I'll sort out the fate of our current cargo and then take a look to see what I can find for new cargo. If all goes to plan, I'd expect to be on our way again in a week or so. Crew leave can run on the usual schedule; just make sure we have enough folks on hand for our safety and the cargo work."

"At least with *Falcon,* we don't need to shut down the gravity ring to off-load," Campbell pointed out. "Everyone can stay aboard ship."

Most of the freighters in the galaxy used long "ribs" for their gravity sections. Those rotated outside the cargo attachments, which meant that the ship had to shut down gravity to offload or load cargo. Since *Falcon's* gravity ring was its own section of the ship in front of the cargo, there was no requirement with the new ship.

"And we will," David told them. "I've been warned that our cargo has pulled us into the middle of what looks to be a midsized economic and political clash between the Importers' Syndicate and the elected government of Cinnamon.

"That's not a game we want to play," he concluded dryly. "I've been in too many fights these last few years to want to get dragged into another one."

"Any bites on new cargo yet?" Acconcio asked. "How giant a target will we be painting on ourselves this time?"

"Nothing yet, but hopefully not that big," David told him. "We're going to want to throw ourselves off the standard flight path on our next trip either way. I'm expecting our stalker to show up with friends, and I don't see a reason to get dragged into a fight I don't need to."

"Easy enough to do," Soprano told him. "Pull the jump by a light-month each time the first four or five jumps; we'll be half a light-year from where they're looking for us and they'll never have a chance to catch up."

"Unless we run into another Tracker," Campbell warned, and David winced.

"I'd like to think that's not going to happen," he told her. "Two in one lifetime was enough."

"A Tracker?" Skavar asked.

"Someone who can follow a ship through jump instead of pursuing by guess and course estimates," Soprano told him. "I thought they were a myth."

"So did I, until someone chased me when I didn't *have* a course," David replied. "I know they're out there. It just depends on how much money whoever is chasing us has on the table."

That was a cheery thought. Fortunately, the only man who'd ever been willing to spend that kind of money chasing David Rice was dead.

CHAPTER 13

"HEY, DAVID, I've got that O'Toole fellow on the line for you again," Wiltshire told David, his voice echoing over the intercom into the Captain's office.

Off-loading was still several hours away and David was going over the handful of offers he had received to compete with the Hayashis' offer. Like Atsuko Hayashi had predicted, though, they were for portions of the cargo only. Ten million for the surface container ship here. Two million for a fusion reactor there.

The prices suggested that her estimate of a fourfold return was about bang on, but he'd only received offers for a twentieth or so of the cargo. Selling it all would take some time.

"Put the administrator through," he told Wiltshire. He didn't really want to talk to O'Toole, but regardless of what he thought of the bureaucrat, the man was in charge of Cinnamon Station's docks.

O'Toole's image appeared on his wallscreen, the man somehow even more florid-faced and unhealthy-looking than he had been the first time.

"What can I do for you, Administrator O'Toole?" David asked politely. He'd kicked the man in the ass once. There was no point being *rude*.

"I wanted to get in touch again, Captain, and apologize for my earlier behavior," O'Toole said. "The Cinnamon Government has covered your accounts, as promised, and there have been no problems.

"Our policies are quite specific, Captain, but you were correct that your contract with our government called for an exemption," he continued. "I appreciate your...patience."

"It's not the first time I've run into rules that haven't been fully thought through," David said sweetly. "I hope we won't have any further problems?"

"We shouldn't," the administrator replied carefully. "I also believe I've managed to track down a supplier for antimatter for you. Cinnamon has limited transmutation capability, so the government keeps the Naval stockpile under firm lockdown.

"I've managed to speak to the company that owns our transmutation facility, however, and they're willing to meet with you," O'Toole told him. "Consider it an...apology for my earlier rudeness."

Well, that was something, at least.

"I appreciate your candor and your assistance," David said. "While we do not need to refill our antimatter tanks here, it would certainly make my life a lot easier."

"Of course. Mr. Rhee is available to meet with you at eleven AM Olympus Mons Time. Would that work for you?"

O'Toole shouldn't have been setting up meetings, but if he felt that was the best way to make up for his screw-ups, David wasn't going to argue. And the chance to fully refuel *Red Falcon* couldn't be passed up.

"I'll make it work," he promised. "Send me a location. Thank you, Mr. O'Toole."

"The least I can do." The administrator waved him off.

The location came over the link and the channel cut off, leaving David looking at an address in one of Cinnamon Station's more prestigious office districts.

Nothing was particularly *wrong* about O'Toole's actions, but it didn't feel quite *right*, either.

The solution to that, of course, was easy.

He hit the intercom again.

"Skavar?" he greeted his new Chief of Security. "Can you meet me in my office, please?"

Accompanied by two of his security team, David knocked on the door of the address he'd been given. It swung open immediately, allowing him to enter a plainly decorated front office.

"Captain Rice?" an impeccably turned-out young woman with dark hair asked him. She was sitting behind a desk that, despite its apparent plainness, he recognized as Sherwood oak.

Sherwood was another MidWorld, almost on the exact opposite side of human space. Wood from Earth itself would have been cheaper.

"I am," he told the woman. "I'm here to meet with a Mr. Rhee?"

"Of course," she confirmed. "He's just making some arrangements right now; he'll be available in a moment. Your...friends can wait out here."

David had half-expected that and smiled brightly.

"I'd prefer they came in with me," he noted lightly.

"Mr. Rhee is quite specific about who he meets, Captain Rice," the woman said. "The appointment is only for you."

He nodded his seeming acceptance and gestured the two guards to seats as he took one of his own. Having noted the quality of the desk, he carefully studied the rest of the furniture and fixtures.

It all looked plain and austere, but...the chairs were handmade from Old Earth maple, and David's quiet search on his wrist-comp confirmed the craftsman worked solely on Mars. The two pieces of art on the walls were originals by a famous Tau Ceti artist who'd passed away thirty years earlier.

Everything in the room *appeared* simple, but the pieces he could identify alone would have paid for a heavy cargo shuttle. In many ways, the tastefully austere decoration was an even worse flaunting of wealth than many of the gaudy offices he'd visited in his life.

David waited in silence, his two guards scanning the room with very different eyes from his. Cinnamon Station rules restricted his men to the stunguns they openly wore, but he would have been shocked to discover the ex-Marines weren't carrying something more lethal concealed inside their jackets.

"Mr. Rhee will see you now, Captain Rice," the young woman told him. "Would your friends like coffee or tea while they wait?"

"We're fine," the senior security woman replied instantly. David didn't say anything, but he gave her an approving glance.

He didn't expect Rhee's people to poison his guards, but he didn't trust this meeting as far as he could throw his *Falcon*.

The room the un-introduced receptionist ushered David into was designed to the same style as the outer reception area. The desk and old-fashioned wood paneling were all imported from Sherwood. The electronics came from Mars.

When he realized that the single piece of art on the wall behind the man at the desk, encased in a carefully low-key environmental control system, was an original Van Gogh, he was quite certain what kind of man he was dealing with.

"Please, Captain Rice, have a seat," Rhee told him. "I am Benedict Rhee. Water? Tea?"

"I'm fine," David replied, taking the indicated chair. He was unsurprised when the apparently plain wooden chair quickly adjusted to his posture and size. One particular wooden strut flexed just right to release a knot he hadn't realized he'd been carrying.

Rhee's office fit the man like a glove. He wore a plain white dress shirt without a tie and had short-cropped dark hair, faded brown skin and warm blue eyes. He *looked* the austerely calm type of man this office fit, and David suspected the shirt was as ridiculously sourced as everything else around him.

"I'm glad Mr. O'Toole could arrange this meeting," Rhee finally said. "I have a number of interests here in the Cinnamon System; it is my home, and I'll admit I haven't left as often as I should."

"I was told you could get me antimatter," David replied.

"Yes, I own and operate the Cinnamon Penal Transmutation Facility on behalf of the Mage Guild," the businessmen confirmed. "We don't have a lot of Mage criminals here, so our production is lower than many systems, but we maintain the stockpile the Protectorate requires and some extra."

"Name your price, Mr. Rhee," David told him. "That is why I'm here, isn't it?"

"It is part of why you are here," Rhee told him. "You've also, Captain Rice, tangled yourself up in several of my other interests, and I wanted to make sure that we cleared the air between us as to what is going to happen now."

There was no overt threat in Rhee's tone. He spoke levelly, calmly, as if talking about an order for coffee—but David understood *exactly* what was happening.

"You see, even the presence of your ship here means that my partners in Green Seneschal are going to have to have a conversation with Factor Nguyen," he said genteelly. "It's been our understanding for some time that we are prepared to tolerate only the most minor of cargos being shipped into Cinnamon under other auspices, and yet here you arrive with a megafreighter the likes of which Cinnamon has rarely seen.

"This isn't your pond, Captain, and you don't know the waves you've stirred up. Nguyen had no authority to make the deal he made with you. No shipment of this size should have been sent on a tramp freighter, however large or impressive-looking, and he certainly had no right to sell you any portion of the shipment.

"You now effectively find yourself in possession of stolen goods, Captain Rice," Rhee told David. "That cargo belongs to the Importers' Syndicate, and Nguyen's so-called 'sale' to you was fraudulent."

That was an interesting legal perspective. One that David was quite sure wouldn't hold up in Cinnamon's courts, let alone Tau Ceti's. For the moment, however, he remained silent and let Rhee continue.

"I understand," the businessman said magnanimously, "that you had no way of knowing this. To allow for the misunderstanding and avoid any ill will, we are prepared to reimburse you the money that Nguyen defrauded you of and honor the carriage part of the contract."

Rhee smiled. There was no warmth to the expression.

"Of course, since you got tied up in Nguyen's scheme, it would probably be best if you never came near the Cinnamon system again," he warned. "We will off-load and refuel your ship, but then you need to leave and never come back."

David had to give the man points for delivery and sheer audacity. He wasn't sure of any ship captain who would *buy* the line Rhee was feeding him, but then, most ship captains had a more than passing understanding of interstellar contract law.

It took him a moment to process the sheer insanity of the man's stated position, but once he had, he simply chuckled and shook his head at Rhee.

"That's an interesting fantasy," he told the man. "One that I suppose is reassuring if you're determined not to let a single cent slip through your fingers. It's also legally unenforceable and we both know it, so why don't you tell me your *real* offer?"

From Rhee's taken-aback blink, the mogul wasn't used to being challenged on his interpretation of reality.

"That wasn't an *offer*, Captain Rice," he replied. "It was a statement of what is *going* to happen."

"And if I refuse to go along with this sequence of events?" David asked sweetly.

"Then I'm afraid you will suffer an unfortunate accident on your way back to your ship," Rhee said flatly. "Since even Nguyen was intelligent enough to include a clause where, on your death, we both acquire ownership of the cargo and assume your debt.

"Or, of course, we could simply seize your cargo and ship for your involvement in the transport of stolen goods," he continued. "Believe me, Captain, I can make the argument of a fraudulent purchase of stolen goods hold up *quite* nicely in Cinnamon's courts.

"The accident course is easier for me, however, and I am much enamored of...*efficiencies*. My offer is more generous than you have any right to, Captain Rice. Accept it and get out of my system."

"Why is it that utter scum always think they're in the right?" David asked conversationally. "For your information, Mr. Rhee, I regularly record conversations I expect to involve contract negotiations. In this case, since Mr. O'Toole did not strike me as the type to go out of his way to make an apology, that recording is also being live-streamed to my ship.

"I'm reasonably certain that this conversation is sufficient grounds to see you arrested for a whole list of charges, not least attempted collusion in an attempt by Green Seneschal to monopolize shipping to the Cinnamon System—an attempt your own words have validated."

Rhee smiled.

"Your communicator has been jammed since you arrived, Captain Rice," he pointed out. "Your negotiating position is not as strong as you think."

David returned the man's smile.

"Isn't it? Consider, Mr. Rhee, that my people were *expecting* that transmission."

Cinnamon Station Security didn't even bother to knock. The exosuited trooper who led the way simply walked *through* the door, the bright blue and white paint on his armor emerging through the expensive wood in a spray of splinters and the extended barrel of a multi-function webber/stungun.

"Benedict Rhee, you are under arrest for unlawful detainment," a voice boomed from the two-meter-tall suit's shoulders. "You have the right to remain silent. Anything you say can be used against in a court of law. You have the right to an attorney—"

"Do you know who I am?!" Rhee demanded, lunging to his feet.

The webber coughed once, a ball of sticky strands blasting past David's head and hammering the mogul into the wall.

"Yes, Mr. Rhee, as a matter of fact, my men *do* know who you are," Harold Hayashi said dryly as he stepped up beside the armored cop. "And we've been waiting for an opportunity to have this conversation with you for a *very* long time."

CHAPTER 14

ONCE AGAIN in Atsuko Hayashi's office, this time with both Soprano and Skavar hovering over his shoulder like worried hens, David gladly accepted the glass of scotch the CEO of Dancing Fox pressed upon him.

"CSS checked," she told him. "Someone had inserted a worm into the transfer pod controls. As soon as you got into a pod headed back to the dock, it would have run the power level to three times safe."

The youngest member of the Hayashi triad shook her head.

"Even if you'd survived the gee forces, the pods aren't designed for them. You'd have been flung into space, and those pods have a limited local oxygen reserve. If you weren't crushed, you'd have asphyxiated."

"Even paranoids have real enemies, it seems," Skavar noted. "I'm guessing there wasn't a deactivation code for if the boss took Rhee's deal?"

"Of course not," Harry Hayashi replied. "One way or another, Rhee wanted you dead. Nguyen accidentally threw you into the middle of our growing political crisis with every damn hook he possibly could have."

"Are you really expecting me to buy that it was an *accident*?" David said dryly. "He didn't strike me as the type to be that uninformed."

"It...may not have been," Atsuko told him. "But he didn't have any instructions from us to do anything of the sort."

"What happens now?" David asked.

"Rhee faces a court. The Importers' Syndicate probably comes apart—as, to be honest, it should have a few years ago. That kind of organization is supposed to be temporary, but it helps make some people very rich, so..."

She shrugged. "Even realizing it was a problem, it was hard for me to advocate for its dissolution. It's going to cost me quite a bit of money. While I'd hate for you to feel obligated, Captain Rice, I'd be *very* pleased if you took my deal now."

"You can guess how much better it is than the only *other* deal I've been offered for the whole cargo," he replied dryly. "Send the paperwork to *Red Falcon;* we'll make it happen."

"What about Green Seneschal?" Soprano asked. The ex-Navy officer's voice was hard. "That kind of crap is—"

"Outside Cinnamon's jurisdiction, I'm afraid," Harry Hayashi interrupted. "If the evidence we pull out of Rhee and O'Toole's computers adds up how I expect it to, I'll present a bill to Parliament to have them declared corporate persona non grata here." He shook his head. "That will leave Atsuko and Factor Nguyen scrambling to find new carriers, but I think we'll be better off that way!"

"Too many of the Protectorate's problems are caused by interstellar corporations muscling around system governments," Soprano growled. "Please make sure that the MIS is informed of this."

The Martian Investigation Service handled investigations that passed between system boundaries but didn't justify a Hand's involvement. As Harry Hayashi said, Cinnamon didn't have jurisdiction over Green Seneschal's activity outside their system—the MIS *did*.

"What about O'Toole?" David asked.

"He is also under arrest," Harry Hayashi replied. "Protective custody right now, but we have warrants to rip his personal and work computers to pieces. I expect we'll find some interesting tidbits in there."

"I feel like I was intentionally sent in here as a stalking horse," *Red Falcon's* Captain complained. "I hope you get what you need out of it."

"I think so," the MP replied. "The scale of just what Rhee had set into motion surprised us, but we were pretty sure he and Green Seneschal had their hands dirty. Your recording is enabling us to get warrants across the planet."

He shook his head.

"Some of what he said is *also* making us look quite closely at judges who weren't as helpful as we expected them to be in the past," he noted. "I have some pointed questions to be asking."

"What's a general Member of Parliament doing in the middle of all of this crap?" David asked. "It seems a little out of place."

"Before Atsuko convinced me to go into politics, I was the Deputy Head of Cinnamon Station Security," the male Hayashi replied. "So, when my party became government, I was tapped for the Justice portfolio."

"So, when Atsuko said you were a Member of Parliament..."

"She didn't lie," he said. "She just didn't mention that I'm *also* Cinnamon's Minister of Justice.

"Which makes cleaning up the mess Rhee made—and you have so kindly dragged into the open—my problem."

On their way out of the Hayashis' office, Atsuko Hayashi waved David back to her desk.

"What do you need?" he asked.

"Nothing you haven't already managed," she replied with a throaty chuckle. "But a contact drifted across my radar looking for you, and I figured that after your most recent encounter with our local businessmen, you'd want some reassurance that they were on the up-and-up."

"What kind of contact?" he said carefully.

"One of our bulk exporters has had some problems with finding shipping lately," she told him. "Reading between the lines, Green Seneschal was playing games with them, trying to force them to agree to an exclusive deal.

"Now, however, they have managed to build up an unusually large stockpile of goods they want to ship out, and one of their people reached out to mine to quietly get a figure on your ship's cargo capacity."

"We can carry almost anything," David replied. "Rhee called us a 'megafreighter', which is a bit of exaggeration but not much of one."

The handful of ships that actually met that description were never owner-operated. They were big, thirty megatons or more, vessels that made the short-distance, high-volume routes between the Core Systems. They carried enough Mages to make them quick once they made it far enough out to jump, but their sheer scale meant they didn't accelerate quickly.

"So, I had my people send back to Silk Star," Hayashi told him. "Silk Star Trade Exports—primarily spices and dried food. I won't swear they're innocent as pure-driven snow, but they're not going to screw you and they aren't tied up in Rhee's bullshit!"

"That's good to know. I'll keep an ear out for their call," David promised.

"I certainly can't get you a cargo heading outwards," she warned him. "I owe you, but I'm an importer, Captain, not an exporter. And I did just dissolve the syndicate that allowed me to deal in twenty million-ton cargos," she concluded with a grin.

Given the Hayashis' demonstrated influence and reach, David wasn't entirely surprised to find a recorded message waiting for him when he returned to *Red Falcon*. He left it for a moment while he let Skavar and Soprano take seats in his office.

"So, why exactly did you meet with the guy who wanted to kill you?" his Mage asked sweetly. "If we were so sure this was going to go sideways, why did you meet with him at all?"

"I didn't expect it to go *this* sideways," David admitted. "I expected him to try and gouge us for the antimatter costs—antimatter, I'll note, that we're *not getting*." He shook his head.

"I was recording it and transmitting it because I was feeling paranoid. I was expecting *Skavar* to come save the day, not CSS Special Weapons Teams."

He leveled his gaze on his Chief of Security.

"Just how did that happen?" he asked.

"It's generally considered rude to fire boarding torpedoes into a friendly station," Skavar said calmly. "Short of something that drastic, I wasn't going to get my people to you in less than fifteen minutes—but I could call CSS, and they brag about a five-minute response time."

David thought back to his conversation.

"You called them the moment he started jamming me?" he asked.

"Hell, yes," the ex-Marine confirmed. "If nothing else, military-grade jammers like that are illegal in civilian ownership in the Cinnamon System. Once the dude fired up one of those, I knew we had trouble."

"And they managed to get frigging Harry Hayashi there in five minutes?"

"Reading between the lines, they fired off a raid they'd already been planning on Rhee's office," Skavar told him. "They had warrants and everything. He was already in deep shit; trying to threaten you just put the nail in his coffin."

"And good riddance," Soprano added. "Scum like that create half of the Navy's work."

"And the other half is pirates," David replied. "Hopefully, Cinnamon will make something stick. If they don't, well, we'll be a long ways away."

"Do we have a cargo yet?" she asked.

"Atsuko told me we'd hear from someone," he told them. "I have a message I expect to be from her contact, so as soon as you're done lecturing me over my lack of concern for my own safety..."

Soprano shook her head.

"I've read the unclassified part of your file, Captain Rice," she said. "I'm starting to think it wasn't your *Ship's Mage* who was a magnet for trouble."

The recorded message turned out to be another of Cinnamon's stereotypical tiny Asians, a dark-skinned woman in a tight-fitted dark red dress.

"Captain Rice, I am Hyeon Choi of Silk Star Trade Exports," she greeted him with a bright smile. "We have a large cargo that needs to leave the Cinnamon System as quickly as possible. We have several contracts for delivery that are already due for late fees as we could not find shipping.

"Everything is going to one destination and I am advised by my contacts aboard Cinnamon Station that your ship should be able to carry our cargo.

"I would like to meet with you in person to pass on the details and negotiate a contract," she concluded. "Please reach out to me at the contact information attached to this message."

Choi bowed over her desk.

"I look forward to your response."

CHAPTER 15

CHOI'S OFFICE felt very familiar to David when he and Soprano arrived—it was the exact same style of short-term rental office space he'd been using in Tau Ceti. There was no reception area, just a single open set of cubicles with half a dozen young men and women busily working away and one closed-door office off to one side.

Hyeon Choi met them at the front door, in another tight-fitted dress, this one blue, that managed to both be professional and quite frankly outline an athletically feminine figure.

"Captain Rice, Ship's Mage Soprano, welcome, welcome," Choi said as she led them through to her office. "I heard about your problems with Mr. Rhee, quite a shock! He's always been a difficult man to do business with, but that..."

She trailed off, shaking her head as she closed the office door and gestured them to seats.

"Drinks? We don't have much on hand, just water and tea," she admitted. "This isn't a permanent office for us, as you may have guessed."

"I had," David confirmed. "What brings Silk Star up to Cinnamon Station on a temporary basis?"

"Normally, we hold our cargo on the surface and ship it up as needed," Choi told him. "That means we don't have any office space or storage space up here on the Station.

"Of late, however, we've needed to put more of our goods in long-term storage and, well, vacuum is one of the best preservatives known to man. Approximately seventy-five percent of our inventory is in an orbital storage pod that's also being rented on a short-term basis."

She shook her head.

"Honestly, our inability to ship our cargo out has been causing some problems with our cash flow," she admitted. "Your presence here is a godsend, Captain Rice."

"What kind of cargo are we talking about?" he asked.

"Food and spices, all prepaid by our customers out-system," she told him. "We're prepared to pay standard carriage rates on eighteen point five million ton of cargo for shipment to the New Madagascar System."

"Ah," David exhaled softly. Of course there was a catch. New Madagascar was a Fringe World, with a primarily resource-driven economy—and was an UnArcana world.

"I'm sure you're aware, Miss Choi, that shipping to the UnArcana worlds is rarely done at 'standard carriage rates'," he pointed out gently. "There is a distinct risk and...unpleasantness for our Mages in such a trip."

He studied Soprano out of the corner of his eye. She looked uncomfortable but not unwilling.

"I was afraid of that," Choi said with a sigh of her own. "We have cargo headed to several systems, but New Madagascar is the only one with a large-enough load to justify hiring your ship. Your *Red Falcon* fits our needs perfectly, but I understand the concern.

"What is the normal premium for such a shipment?"

"Anywhere from seventy to a hundred percent," David replied. "Given the number of Mages aboard *Red Falcon* and the speed we can deliver at, I'd expect something at the high end of that range."

"Ah," Choi said softly. "As I said, we are in some degree of financial distress from the holdup on our shipments. I could see us being able to pay a forty percent premium, but any more would require me to touch base with my partners and financers back on the surface."

"Of course," David allowed, letting her set her negotiating position. "Forty percent definitely wouldn't be enough for us to travel to an UnArcana Fringe World," he warned, "so I suggest you do that and get back to us."

The last time he'd gone to an UnArcana Fringe World, a lot of people had died. Plus, before he agreed to that kind of job, he'd want to make sure Soprano was entirely on board.

"I can do that," Choi promised. "I am certain we can come to an agreement, Captain Rice, but I can't commit to higher than a forty percent premium on my own."

"I understand," he told her. "I am certainly interested in the job, Miss Choi, but I must discuss with my senior officers and wait for your next offer."

"I appreciate your patience, Captain Rice."

"It'll be two more days before we're fully off-loaded," he told her with a grin. "I can be patient."

Maria skimmed through the files MISS had provided her on Silk Star Trade Exports and found herself wondering if Green Seneschal had had a clue who they were trying to pressure. The links to Legatan money and Legatan operations were subtle, but they were definitely there. Some she'd have caught on her own; some were pointed out in the analyst commentary in the files.

Silk Star was owned by Cinnamon natives, with its financing secured through private lenders also on Cinnamon. Those lenders' books were closed and their ownership was secret—but MISS had tracked them back to Legatus.

Other things were more visible, if less incriminatory. When a major deal had been negotiated with Legatus for the purchase of spices and food from Cinnamon, Silk Star had led the way—and they'd been a central part of a deal to acquire Legatan farm and industrial machinery a few years before.

It could easily just be a long-term relationship between an export company and one of their customers. Or it could be what MISS thought it was—that Silk Star was being funded by Legatan covert operations as a way to launder money without it obviously coming from Legatus.

Finding out which was why MISS wanted *Red Falcon* to take the job.

The admittance chime on her door sounded, and the Ship's Mage smiled. She'd been waiting for the Captain to drop by.

"Come in," she instructed, watching the door slide open to reveal David Rice. "I have coffee on."

"Am I that predictable to you?" Rice asked, crossing to the pot and pouring himself a cup.

"You'd be a worse Captain than I expect if you didn't check in with the Mages before taking on a shipment to an UnArcana world," she pointed out. "Have they come back with an offer yet?"

"Not yet," he admitted, then shrugged. "Choi will talk to her bankers and partners and come back around a fifty percent premium. I'll counter at eighty. We'll go back and forth a few times, settle around sixty to sixty-five.

"New Madagascar isn't one of the UnArcana worlds where I expect to find frothing fanatics looking for Mages to step out of bounds; it should be relatively safe. That said..." The Captain met her gaze. "It's not my call if we go to an UnArcana world. *I'm* not the one at risk."

"You're the Captain," Maria replied, taken aback by his willingness to toss a major deal on her say-so.

"And part of my job is protecting my crew," Rice said. "If you and your Mages aren't comfortable going to an UnArcana world, I'll kill the deal. I haven't had great experiences going into that sector of space myself, so..."

Under normal circumstances, she'd be tempted to hold him to that. She'd visited UnArcana worlds as a Navy officer, and even then, with the weight of the Mage-King's authority behind her, that had been an unpleasant experience.

But MISS wanted them to take this job—and she could see why. She couldn't tell *Rice* that, though.

"How many cargos big enough to justify *Falcon* are we actually going to see ship out of Cinnamon?" she asked.

"Ha! Not many," he admitted. "But with what I got for funding Nguyen's shipment, we can afford to pick up a speculative cargo on our own dime and haul it back to Tau Ceti. We won't make a lot of money on that, but we'd at least match normal freight rates. And we'd be better off looking for a new cargo in Tau Ceti than in New Madagascar."

"But better the bird in the hand?" Maria asked. "A sixty percent premium on standard rates for eighteen-odd million tons of cargo is nothing to sneer at, boss. *And* it would let you send the money back to Tau Ceti to cover the loan you took out."

He laughed.

"And here I thought it was my job to convince you!"

"You came in here willing to kill the deal if I wasn't convinced," she pointed out. "Well, I'm not convinced that New Madagascar is that much of a threat, boss.

"Let's take the deal. Flying on someone else's dollar is always going to be cheaper for us."

CHAPTER 16

WHILE THE TRIP to Cinnamon hadn't been David's worst visit to a star system—it probably didn't even make the bottom ten—he certainly wasn't feeling particularly sad to see Cinnamon Station fall away behind *Red Falcon* as they moved away under maneuvering thrusters.

"Cinnamon Station confirms fifteen-thousand-kilometer safety radius and wishes us a safe flight," Campbell told him. "We're clear to bring the engines online."

"Let's be a bit more sparing of the antimatter this time," David told her. "New Madagascar had to import their Navy-required stockpile; I sincerely doubt we'll be able to refuel there."

"We have enough fuel to visit two systems after that before needing more AM," his XO pointed out. "Are you planning on swanning us through every UnArcana world you can find?"

"Dear *God*, no," he replied with a laugh. Soprano might have been okay with visiting one, but he wasn't going to drag his Mages through multiple UnArcana worlds in a row. "I don't want a repeat of some of our last trips."

Campbell shook her head.

"So far, boss, since getting this ship, two groups of people have tried to kill you and we've been dragged into one major political crisis," she said. "This all feels far too familiar. Are you *sure* Damien was our bad-luck charm?"

"Never was," he said softly. "I got Damien in trouble first, if you recall. No, I'm pretty sure I'm the trouble magnet around here, Jenna.

Me and my unwillingness to turn down a sob story or a sucker in trouble."

She shook her head at him.

"Which is why we're flying a freighter with the guns of a pocket warship and an entire platoon of Marines aboard," she pointed out. "Your white-knight habit seems to have made you some friends along the way."

"Skipper, you need to take a look at this," Acconcio interrupted. "I just picked up a ghost on the long-range passives."

"Our friend from before?" David asked.

"I can't be sure," the gunner admitted. "She's quite a distance away and, well, it could just be a sensor glitch."

"Intercept course?"

"No," Acconcio said. "She's ballistic along our path, though. Watching for us to jump, I think."

"And then going to follow and ambush us between the stars." David shook his head. "Any sign of friends?"

"Just the one. We could take her."

"*If* she's the same pocket corvette we saw last time," Campbell said. "You said yourself, Iovis, we can't be certain."

"No, she's just going to try and play the same game as last time," the Captain concluded. "She knows where we're going; there's no hiding the kind of deal Silk Star closed with us. So, she'll meet us one or two light-years out, along the standard jump route."

David smiled and opened a channel to the simulacrum chamber.

"Mage Soprano? Do you have that course we discussed set up?" he asked.

"First four jumps are eleven light-months," she confirmed. "That's going to *suck* for some of my Mages, just so you know. I suggest we take at least a twelve-hour rest after the short-jump sequence; it actually takes *more* out of my people."

"I don't argue with experts," David told her. He understood enough of what the Jump Mages were doing that he could review their calculations. Tradition said he *didn't*—that was Soprano's job and he was expected to let the Mages work their magic without supervision—but he knew how.

And he knew she was right.

"We'll be at jump distance in four hours," he continued. "It's going to take them more than twelve hours to work out just what the hell we did. If you're concerned, I suggest we hold for a day in deep space to make sure your people are fully recovered."

"I'd appreciate that," Soprano admitted. "Costa especially will need it."

"We've got almost a week of extra time built into our contract," David told her. "With four Mages aboard, we can take a day.

"Just like we can waste a good chunk of our first four jumps to make sure we're safe."

"They'll never know where we went," she promised.

Eight hours later, Maria kicked Costa out of the simulacrum chamber, sending the jump mage off to sleep. She took one quick glance around to make sure everything in the starship's magical heart was functioning as expected, and then moved into her office.

A Ship's Mage's office was a cross between a flight control center, an administrator's cubicle and a jeweler's workbench. A collection of tools for working with the silver polymer of the runes woven throughout the ship—and each of the Jump Mages' palms—were laid along the workbench at one end of the room, while a multi-monitor structure was set up to allow three-dimensional viewing of the area around the ship.

On a ship like *Red Falcon*, with multiple Mages, each of the Mages also had their own desk with half-height cubicle dividers. There wasn't much administration beyond the jump calculations to be done, but the Mages needed space to do it.

With all of her juniors asleep, Maria tucked herself into the course-plotting station and began the slow, careful process of validating just where the big freighter had ended up. She knew her own jump had been exactly eleven light-months, to within a thousand kilometers.

She was not nearly so certain about any of her subordinates. The exact distances hadn't been a big deal while jumping. Usually, a Mage only had to make one short jump in an entire trip, for the final arrival, a task that Maria had been keeping to herself so far.

The Navy trained its Mages better for variable jumps than civilian Jump Mage training did. It was an exhausting, uncomfortable process, requiring far more fine-tuning of the spell than normal. She'd have been surprised if any of her juniors had actually nailed the jump exactly.

As *Red Falcon*'s computers began to correlate the stars around her against the immensely detailed charts stored in their files, however, she realized she was doing them a disservice. Across four jumps with four different Mages, they had overshot their forty-four-light-month goal by less than a light-second.

That was actually *better* than she would have expected from a Navy crew. She owed her people a beer.

"Got a minute, Maria?" Acconcio's voice asked from the door. She looked up from her calculations, realizing she hadn't closed it behind her.

"We're not jumping for a day," she told him. "I can spare a few. What's up?"

The heavyset ex-warrant officer pulled a chair from one of the desks and looked at the star charts.

"Are we where we expected to be?" he asked.

"Yeah," she confirmed. "Closer than I expected. Still another twenty-three jumps to go to New Madagascar, but we'll be off from the normal route the whole way. May as well be invisible."

Acconcio shook his head.

"Just what did you get me into, Maria?" he asked. "Assassination and blackmail, political crises, stealth ships stalking us... My time in the Navy was quieter!"

"Did you even look at the Captain's history before you signed on?" Maria replied. "Rice basically waged a one-man war on the Blue Star Syndicate—and one of the largest criminal organizations in the galaxy came off the worse out of the equation!"

To Maria's surprise, the man sitting across from her flushed, a bright red that showed even through his dark complexion.

"Honestly?" he half-muttered. "I looked long enough to know you were aboard, and that was about all the research I did. Not many civilian ships needing real gunners—and only one ship out there with Maria Soprano aboard."

That was *not* the response Maria had expected. It implied an interest she hadn't realized was there...an interest that would have been *very* against regulations when she was a tactical officer and Acconcio one of her warrants.

"My poor Iovis," she said softly. "I knew what I was getting into. I didn't mean to drag you into trouble alongside me!"

"No place I'd rather be," he admitted. "Sorry, didn't mean to—"

She put her hand on his, cutting off whatever he was saying.

"No apologies," she ordered. "I didn't know. Give me some time to process, okay?"

He chuckled.

"I ain't going anywhere," he replied. "I may have leapt before I looked, but this is a damned fine ship and I'm on board. To the end."

"Thank you," Maria said. "I'll try not to get us killed first!"

Acconcio laughed.

"My impression, my dear Maria, is that Captain Rice is the one likely to get us all killed!"

The rhythm of the ship seemed to miss a beat when they drifted in deep space for an extended period. The patterns and activity of a starship in motion were calibrated around the jumps. No matter how long they went between them, a ship's crew adapted to that time and everything ended up scheduled around them.

A jump wasn't particularly unpleasant, but no one wanted to be in the middle of things when one happened.

An extended gap between jumps threw that habit entirely to the wind. Everyone knew they'd be back to the every-two-hour metronome soon enough, but there was a chance to do some longer tasks. If they'd been farther along their trip, Maria figured Kellers would have had something for the crew to do, but as it was, there really wasn't anything extra *to* do.

All that was left was a disconcerted, unbalanced feeling that followed her through the ship until she ended up at Captain Rice's office. She hadn't quite realized that was where she was heading, but she shrugged and chimed for admittance.

"Come in!"

She stepped through the door and dropped into the chair across from the Captain. Rice, for his part, suspended whatever file was on his screen and leaned back to look at her in silence for several seconds.

"What can I help you with, Maria?" he finally asked.

"Just feeling out of sorts," she admitted. "New ship, new crew, new rhythms. Brain's all over the place."

He raised a questioning eye at her.

"Has your brain actually *settled* since leaving the Navy?" he asked softly. "It took me two years to get used to all of the changes, and I'd been planning my retirement for a year."

"It wasn't *really* unexpected by the time the court-martial wrapped up," Maria admitted. "It was clear pretty quickly which way the winds were going to blow." She sighed. "Honestly, the surprise was that they didn't throw me in a Navy prison with a dishonorable discharge to boot."

"From second-in-command of a Navy destroyer to first officer on a merchant freighter in ten months," Rice said. "That's quite the shift. Give yourself some time."

"Fair," she allowed with a smile. "I hadn't looked at it that way." She looked around his office. It was surprisingly plain still. She'd half-expected him to fill it with memorabilia from his past—the man certainly had enough of it.

The only pieces of memorabilia, though, were a standing model of a *Venice*-class freighter and a picture of a pale woman with flaming red hair and bright green eyes in a black business suit and visible shoulder holster.

"I have to ask, boss," she finally said, "what's your rules on on-ship relationships? There wasn't anything in the handbook."

Not that *Red Falcon*'s handbook was anything except a copy-paste of the standard Guild rules.

She hadn't made up her mind about Iovis Acconcio yet—she'd been enjoying having her bed to herself far more than she'd expected, given her usual habits—but she was certainly more interested than she would have expected if someone had suggested it a week before.

Rice laughed.

"Rules? What rules?" he asked dryly. "LaMonte seems to make a habit of bedding Ship's Mages and, from what I can tell, had *some* kind of fling with Kelzin that ended with a disturbing degree of amicability."

"What habit?" Maria asked. She didn't know anything about Costa or Lakeland bedding the engineer, but...

"She was dating my last Ship's Mage, the only one aboard," Rice replied. "And she's been spending her time with Xi Wu. I specifically have *not* been paying enough attention to see if the two are doing more than making friends, but the way Kellers framed it to me..."

"That...explains where my best junior Mage keeps disappearing to," Maria said with a smile. "Some ships are strict about that."

"So long as it doesn't cause trouble, I don't care," he told her. "When it comes to junior officers and ratings, I expect their senior officers to yank it up before it becomes a problem. When it comes to senior officers, I expect you to know better than to be a problem.

"Clear-enough rules?"

She laughed, the moment of humor breaking a dark cloud she'd barely realized was settling in on her.

"Clear enough, skipper. Thanks."

"I like a smooth ship. So long as we have a smooth ship, I have no complaints."

CHAPTER 17

LOGICALLY, ONCE *Red Falcon* was avoiding the standard jump coordinates of the route between Cinnamon and New Madagascar, there was no way they could have been intercepted. While David was well aware that Trackers existed, they were thankfully few and far between, hunters available only to the highest levels of the criminal underworld.

Nonetheless, the entire trip had him jumping at shadows, and he greeted their arrival in New Madagascar with a sigh of relief.

"Mr. Acconcio," he said aloud. "Are we clear?"

"Sensors are drinking deep, skipper," the gunner replied. "Looks it so far, but Madagascar isn't quite as clean and pretty as Cinnamon was. More debris out there."

Cinnamon had a notably low level of debris. New Madagascar was more normal. Six rocky inner worlds orbited close to a burning furnace of a massive A-type blue star, only the sixth cool enough to be habitable. A thick asteroid belt sat outside those worlds, with four smaller gas giants orbiting at the edge of the system.

Ten worlds, a planet's worth of asteroids, a few billion comets and meteorites. In theory, almost anything could be hidden out there.

In practice, starship engines were visible from a long way away, and anything that hoped to catch *Red Falcon* without lighting up the entire star system with their engines would need to be close enough to show up regardless.

"I've got one more jump-ship, coming in from the other side of the system," Acconcio reported. "Reading about sixty in-system ships of various types, including an even dozen Legatan-built gunships."

He shook his head.

"Jump-ship is a freighter," he continued. "Not sure of class, but given her heat signature and acceleration, she's running about six million tons loaded. On the small end of midsize.

"Threat board is clear," he concluded. "Our stalker hasn't shown up yet, and once we're in the cover of those gunships, he won't want to play."

"Any chance of someone hiding in the mining platforms or ships?" David asked. New Madagascar paid for its imports by exporting rare earths and heavy metals extracted from that massive asteroid belt. It was wealthier than many Fringe worlds, thanks to the ease of access to those resources.

"It's always *possible*," Acconcio said. "But none of the ships out there are the right size to be our stalker. Most of them are fifty to eighty k-tons—in-system small fry—or multimegaton in-system haulers.

"Pretty sure we're clear."

"Thank you, Iovis," David told him. "Jenna, ping the gunships and the orbital with our bona fides and let them know we're on our way in. Someone down there has the munchies, and we've got twenty million tons of snacks for them!"

Somehow, Maria wasn't surprised to find Acconcio outside the door of her office as *Red Falcon* began her final approach to Darwin Orbital. He wore a broad grin and was carrying a bunch of flowers she had *no* idea how he'd managed to acquire aboard the starship—*Falcon* had a small hydroponics section to help with oxygen recycling and provide fresh vegetables on longer voyages, but it wouldn't normally be growing roses!

"Iovis," she laughed at him. "Where *did* you find roses?"

"Went in with LaMonte on bribing Tech Suero," he said cheerfully. "They worked out *quite* nicely for her and Xi Wu, from ship scuttlebutt."

"I'm not a star-struck twenty-four-year-old who hasn't been surprised with flowers aboard ship before," Maria said, mock-scoldingly. "What do you want, Iovis?"

"Well, I wanted to give you roses," he said reasonably. "And then, as it happens, I've pulled a directory of restaurants aboard Darwin Orbital, and there is a top-ranked North American–style steakhouse aboard which just *happened* to have a reservation free tonight.

"Only for two, of course."

She laughed.

"Do I want to know what *that* cost you?"

"Only if it would make you more likely to come to dinner with me," Acconcio told her. "I'm pretty sure the bribe is transferrable, if tonight doesn't work!"

"That's good," Maria told him seriously. "The Captain and I are meeting with the client in about two hours, which I would expect to overrun when I'd be able to do dinner." She held up a finger on her left hand while her right hand slipped the roses out of the gunner's grip.

In another UnArcana system she might worry about going aboard station, but New Madagascar was supposed to be forgiving so long as she didn't actually *use* magic in front of people.

"So, *if* you, Mr. Iovis Acconcio, can get that reservation shifted to *tomorrow* night, I would be delighted to meet you for dinner—but duty calls tonight!"

He sighed and bowed his head in mock dismay.

"The Captain doesn't *really* need you," he said, but he was grinning as he said it.

"Maybe not," she agreed. "But he's taking me, he's taking Skavar, and he's carrying a goddamn pistol. After the last few trips, Rice isn't going *anywhere* without babysitters." She shook her head. "The man is a magnet for trouble."

"That he is," Acconcio agreed softly. "I'll hold you to that promise," he told her. "I'll get the reservation shifted and be around to pick you up bang on eighteen hundred OMT tomorrow!"

She laughed again and squeezed his hand. His adorable semi-awkwardness had helped make up her mind. It seemed to work for him.

"All right, Iovis," she told him. "I'll be waiting!"

It was assumed whenever someone arrived on a new station that they had no idea where they were going or how to get there. Like most orbital platforms, Darwin Orbital had a very competent intelligent guide map that linked in with wrist-comps and gave directions to your destination.

David let Skavar load the software and lead the way through Darwin. He wasn't entirely certain that he needed the entire ensemble that was accompanying him today—Soprano, Skavar, and two of Skavar's security troops—but they'd had enough troubles, he wasn't arguing.

Darwin was an unmodified spoke-and-wheel design, likely assembled from prefabricated parts shipped from Legatus or another Core World. Easily upgraded, easily modified, the design served across the galaxy.

This one only had two connectors from the hub to the wheel, limiting the places where travelers went from the zero-gravity hub to the outside ring with its centripetal "gravity". The one they followed disgorged them into a brightly decorated market area, the smell of hot food and the colors of vivid clothing just part of a cacophonous assault on the senses.

"Does this actually sell anything to anyone?" Soprano half-whispered in his ear. "It hurts my eyes just looking around."

"I've seen the same kind of setup in at least half a dozen systems," he replied. "So, I'm guessing it works. I know I've bought food in this kind of market."

"This way, Captain," Skavar told him, gesturing for the others to follow him as he made his way through the open marketplace. "Our appointment is, of course, halfway around the ring, and New Madagascar didn't splurge for the internal passenger transit system when they bought this place. I hope everyone feels up to a walk."

At least Darwin Orbital kept their gravity at a relaxing point six gee. A kilometer-long walk in that wouldn't be too bad, even for people mostly confined to a single starship.

Something in how Skavar and his other ex-Marines moved sent a clear message to the crowd around them, a path opening to easily carry them through the marketplace and out into the station's corridors.

"Directions are pretty clear," the security chief said. "Let's keep our eyes open, though. We're all trooping along with the Captain for a reason."

Five minutes into their walk, David began to wonder if perhaps his paranoia was justified.

"Are we sure the address they gave us was through here?" he asked aloud. They'd moved into a section of Darwin Orbital that was clearly unoccupied. All of the doors they passed were still sealed in the manufacturer's wrap. If only part of the orbital was occupied, surely their purchaser wouldn't be on the other side of an empty section?

"This is where the directions are taking me," Skavar replied, but the security chief had unclipped the cover of his holster and had his hand on his gun. "But yeah. We're a lot further away from the inhabited sections than I would have expected a shortcut to take us. Lisa, can you check the directions on your wrist-comp?"

Lisa Ambrose joined her boss, the two comparing the maps on their screens.

"Both of ours are showing the same thing," Skavar concluded. "But... I don't like this, boss. How much of a headache is it going to be if we cancel this meet and reconvene with the client?"

"Not that big of a headache," David replied, making an instant executive decision. They should have turned back earlier. If the client really was headquartered on the wrong side of a construction zone, they could do business electronically!

"Let's get out of here," he ordered. "This doesn't smell right."

No one was arguing with him. All three of the security officers had drawn their guns now. Soprano glanced over at them and shucked her gloves, the silver runes inlaid in her palm glittering in the dim light.

For the first time since meeting the Mage, David actually *looked* at the runes on her hands and breathed a half-concealed sigh of relief. Jump Mages had one rune in the center of each palm, required to interface with a jump matrix.

Soprano had a third rune just beneath her right middle finger, a small whorl of silver that he recognized from the handful of Marine Combat Mages he'd known. That was the projector rune of a fully qualified Protectorate Combat Mage, a step above even Guild enforcers and other civilian Combat Mages.

"You're in the middle, boss, Soprano," Skavar ordered. "At this point, I'm in charge until we're back aboard ship. Anybody arguing?"

David smiled grimly. This was *exactly* what he had a Chief of Security for.

"No, Chief," he replied. "Lead the way."

CHAPTER 18

IF THERE HAD BEEN any question in David's mind about whether or not things were going very, very wrong, it disappeared the moment they hit the first sealed hatch.

"That was open when we went the other way, right?" he asked.

"Yes," Skavar confirmed grimly. "I'm not using the mapping software anymore, just my PC's backtracker. We're going back the exact same way we came."

"Can we get it open?"

"Ambrose!" Skavar snapped.

The security trooper holstered her weapon and stepped up to the control panel for the hatch, poking at its keys for a minute before shaking her head.

"Local control is overridden," she reported. "I can open up the panel and get it open, but that will almost certainly get us written up for vandalism."

"If they fine us, we'll deal with it," David snapped. "The alternative is to have *Maria* open it, and that will get us in even more trouble."

Like most UnArcana worlds, New Madagascar recognized the right of visiting Ship's Mages to use their power in self-defense. Blasting a hole through a sealed security hatch was still going to leave them in a world of headache.

Ambrose didn't even wait for him to finish speaking before producing an electronics kits from inside her jacket and going to work on the casing for the control panel.

"Reyes, with me," Skavar ordered. "Covering positions. Someone wanted to trap us in here, and I doubt it was just to watch us squirm at the door!"

The two security men stepped back and knelt down, watching the open hall behind them with their handguns out. David stayed by Ambrose but checked the safety and ammunition on his own weapon.

If this was someone's idea of a prank, it was going to get very ugly very fast.

Glancing around, he coughed, an acrid taste settling into the back of his throat. He barely had time to notice it, however, before Skavar swore, hitting a sequence of commands on his com.

"Something is being pumped into the air," he warned. "I didn't bring fucking *gas masks.*"

"You brought a Mage, Chief," Soprano reminded him delicately, a soft white glow rippling out from her hands to surround them. She shivered slightly, then shook her head. "Any Ship's Mage can do an air purification spell. They won't have counted on this to work."

"Well, maybe they should have gone for a hardware solution on the door, too," Ambrose pointed out. The security trooper stood up, packing away her electronics kit as the hatch slid open. "We're clear."

"For now," David murmured. "Lead the way, Chief. Maria? Keep that screen up."

If Madagascar wanted to raise hell over them using magic to keep the air around them breathable, they could kiss his ass.

Skavar gestured for Reyes to move up with him and stepped through the door, sweeping the path with his gun.

"Keep your eyes and ears peeled," the ex-Marine told them all. "Everything so far has been chuckle-fuck incompetent, but whoever arranged this hot-wired the station's guidance software to lead us astray. That is *not* easy."

Normally, the presence of atmosphere-containment security hatches was part of the background. They were designed not to impede traffic on the corridors they covered while still being common enough and secure enough to protect the rest of the station from breaches or toxic leaks.

David hadn't even registered the presence of the hatches on their way out from the dock. Now, however, he was realizing that Darwin Orbital was built to the "best practices" standard of a hatch every twenty-five meters on a major accessway.

He was realizing that because they were *all* closed with their local controls overridden. None of the three they'd passed through had impeded Ambrose for more than a few minutes, but each door held them up for a few minutes.

"We're being jammed now," Skavar told him quietly as Ambrose worked on the fourth hatch. "I'm not sure if someone is actually planning on attacking us or if they just intend to drive me crazy from paranoia. This is...bullshit."

"The air is growing more and more toxic," Soprano pointed out. "Someone has to have completely rerouted the environmental controls for this section. There's no oxygen refresh going on, and I think we're getting the entire CO_2 dump from half the station."

"Subtle," David said. "We get lost, trapped, and asphyxiated. Nothing to show there was anything except a systems glitch in an uninhabited area of the station. Sad and preventable, but accidental."

"With Maria here, that plan's a bust," the security chief said. "For which you have my thanks and undying adoration, Mage Soprano."

She laughed, but there was an edge to her tone.

"I can't do this forever," she said softly. "If they'd just cut off the air circulation, I could keep us for days, but they're pumping in a lot of extra CO_2. I can only keep that clean for so long."

"Even at this rate, we should be out of here in twenty minutes," David replied. "Are we good for that long?"

She nodded.

"I'm just not sure I can do anything *else* and keep us safe," she admitted. "I can take out a door anytime you want, but unless we're sure it's the *last* door..."

"Understood," David accepted grimly. "Ambrose?"

"It's not like these doors are *designed* to be locked," she pointed out. "Here we—"

Gunfire echoed down the corridor as the hatch sprang open, and Ambrose spun backward as multiple rounds slammed into her.

"DOWN!" Skavar bellowed, the ex-Marine managing to turn around without ever rising from his kneeling firing position. The fusillade of gunfire continued and there was no cover. Nothing.

Reyes and Skavar returned fire and David joined them, but if the security troopers could see anyone, *he* certainly couldn't. In the time since they'd come the other way, someone had moved several station security barricades into the hallway, providing the bulletproof cover *Red Falcon*'s crew lacked.

Then the bullets flying at them hit *something*, air solidifying into a solid, visible presence between them and their attackers. Gunfire ricocheted from the magical shield, and David glanced back at Soprano.

"I can stop bullets and make air, but I can't do both for long," she warned. "Any chance of calling for help?"

"Still jammed," Skavar replied. Their bullets were also hitting the barrier—magical or not, the barrier was solid enough to stop fire going both ways. "I can't even get a good visual, but those are good guns. Military-grade close-assault weapons."

"How's Ambrose?" David asked grimly, trying to think of a way out of this mess.

His security chief shook his head.

"She's gone," he said flatly. "Three of those rounds took her in the head."

David swallowed hard and glanced at the door they'd just opened. Ambrose might have been able to close it again to give them cover, but she was dead. Soprano could have destroyed it, but that wouldn't have helped them...except that the hatch was designed to be even tougher than most of the structure of the station.

"Maria," he said to his Ship's Mage, "if you could punch out that door, you should be able to go through the walls, shouldn't you?"

She grimaced.

"Stop bullets. Make air. Destroy a wall. We're getting down to 'pick one'," she snapped.

"Get us out of here and the first two are redundant," David told her. "Make me a hole, Mage Soprano!"

She snarled something unintelligible and gestured. The projector rune on her right palm flared, and the defensive shield the Mage had generated crashed away from them, smashing down the hallway to hammer into the barricades and throw their enemies off-balance.

Before anyone, including David, could do anything else, Soprano hammered fire into the deck beneath them. Plating flashed to vapor and heat scaled his skin—and then the acceleration of the spinning station flung the chunk of metal she'd cut free outward toward the next deck, taking them with it.

David hit the deck hard, his breath going out of him as he ended flat on his face. He could already tell he'd scraped and cut himself in half a dozen places in the landing, but it was a vast improvement over being shot at.

"Come on," Skavar snapped gruffly, yanking the Captain to his feet. Soprano was leaning on Reyes, looking shattered.

"How are you doing, Soprano?" David asked.

"Better now the air is working properly around us," she replied. "I'd rather not have to stop bullets for a few minutes if we can manage it—and I don't know how long it will take these bastards to get control of the air and hatches here!"

"We need to move, sir," Skavar told them. "They can come down that hole the same as we did—and if they have half a brain, they'll be leading with grenades."

"Marketplace is that way." David pointed. "You're right. Let's go."

"What about Ambrose?" Reyes asked, glancing back up at the hole behind them.

"We'll come back for her," David promised. "With station security."

Their attackers apparently hadn't allowed for them to go through the floor. The air systems were functioning properly there and the security hatches were open.

That wasn't as reassuring as it could have been, given that they were still in an unoccupied section of the station. Given normal procedures for this kind of orbital, roughly the eighth of the station they were in would be basically abandoned and running on minimum power. The only reason there were light and air at all was because it was cheaper to let everything cycle through on minimum while they were uninhabited than to purge the crap that would build up if they let the air sit.

More expensive stations were designed to either only be assembled as needed or to leave entire sectors of the station in vacuum until occupied. New Madagascar had bought the cheapest, and, as usual, that meant it would cost more in the long run.

They made it through two of the security hatches before the third one slammed shut in their faces.

"I'm not as good at this as Ambrose was," Skavar admitted as he yanked the cover off the control panel. "Anyone see anything to use as cover?"

"Well, since I'm not cleaning the damn air, give me a second," Soprano replied. Magic flared around her and flashed out in neat, perfectly controlled lines of fire.

Ten seconds later, there were some ugly-looking holes in the walls—and a chest-high barricade stretched across the hallway.

"Thanks, Maria," David told her. At this point, if Darwin Orbital's masters weren't going to accept self-defense as an excuse for anything the Mage did, they could continue the discussion with *Red Falcon*'s battle lasers.

This was supposed to be a civilized station. An easy stop. Not a run-and-gun battle against assassins!

"Here they come," Reyes announced, the security man having clipped a single-sided earmuff-like device over one ear. "Doesn't sound like they brought any cover, but...who fucking knows."

Skavar joined David and Reyes at the barricade.

"I think we're out of retreats," he told them. "There's still at least three more doors before we're back in inhabited sections of the station. Why didn't we figure there was something wrong *before* we ended up over a quarter-kilometer into fucking nowhere?"

"Because none of us are used to the station guides lying to us," David replied, leaning against Soprano's barricade and studying the empty corridor in front of them.

He shook his head.

"Out of options, folks," he said quietly. "I *hate* death ground. Let them come to us and hope we have more bullets than they have assholes."

The first people around the curve of the station corridor wore dark gray form-concealing cloaks, presumably over armor of some kind, and carried ballistic shields. Those large black mobile barriers weren't capable of stopping military-grade weapons...but were more than enough against the handguns David and his people were carrying.

When the attackers saw the barricade Soprano had carved out of the station walls, the shields went from "held in front" to "grounded" and their carriers tucked in behind them before opening fire.

From there, David could actually *see* the guns being fired at him. The Martian Armaments Caseless Close Assault Weapon, Nine Millimeter, was basically the big brother of the MAC-6 pistol he was carrying, a close-range bullet-fountain designed for exactly this kind of ugly fight.

If he'd had a MACCAW-9 himself, those ballistic shields wouldn't have counted for much. Fortunately for *him*, Soprano's barricade was several centimeters thick and the high-velocity rounds ricocheted off harmlessly.

So far.

"Any brilliant ideas?" he asked quietly.

"Yeah," Soprano replied. "Don't piss me off."

With a cold smile, the Mage rose up and pointed the projector rune on her right hand directly at the closing attackers. A precisely measured line of flame flickered out, punching straight through one of the ballistic shields and into the face of the attacker behind it.

A second lance followed, clearing the hallway of attackers while Soprano dropped back behind the barricade.

She was breathing heavily but shook away David's concerned look.

"Yes, I'm overdoing it," she said flatly. "But so long as someone is willing to keep everyone off my back while I sleep for a week, I can *do* that. For a while, anyway."

She wasn't bleeding from her eyeballs yet, he noted. That put her ahead of several Mages he'd known who'd lived through their exertions.

"I still need a Ship's Mage when this is over," he warned, glancing over the top of the barricade. "There were more than two. I'd say at least five shooters before. Where are the rest?"

"Coming," Reyes told him—and there was something wrong with the security trooper's voice. David looked over to see that the man's face had gone deathly pale.

"They're in armor."

David turned back over the barricade to confirm what his man had said. Four more troops with ballistic shields and MACCAW-9s were coming around the corner—following two in dark gray unmarked exosuit battle armor.

Nothing they had was even going to scratch that.

"Maria?" David asked, somewhat helplessly, as he ducked behind the magically formed barricade for cover.

His Ship's Mage shook her head.

"I've got the armor on the right if you've got the rest," she told him bluntly.

"Unless someone is packing magic armor-piercing rounds, we're in serious trouble," David replied, glancing over at Skavar. "Chief?"

"I have a monomolecular knife that *might* get through the armor," the gaunt ex-Marine replied. "If they get that close."

David closed his eyes, inhaling deeply and listening to the sound of heavy rifle fire slamming into their cover. Soprano had clearly done more than just move the metal into place in front of them, as the rifles the armored attackers were carrying should have punched clean through the station's interior walls.

"Do what you can," he ordered.

He felt as much as heard Soprano's nod of agreement. As he opened his eyes again, his Mage was rising to her full height, energy flaring into existence around her hands as she drew on her power again.

Lightning crackled in the corridor as Soprano sent a cascading crash of power along the hallway at the two armored soldiers. Mere focused lines of fire like she'd used on the ballistic shields wouldn't suffice against exosuits. Those were *designed* to give mundane soldiers half a fighting chance against Mages.

In an open battle, fresh and prepared, Maria Soprano could have taken an entire squad of exosuited soldiers. Today, at the edge of her reserves, she obliterated just one before she collapsed to the ground.

From the screaming, at least one of the unarmored soldiers had been caught in the blast as well, but Soprano was down too. David crawled over to her and confirmed his worst fears: she'd been hit.

The bad news was that she'd taken a round from one of the exosuits' heavy battle rifles. The good news was that it had been an armor-piercing round and had punched clean through her shoulder blade before continuing on its way.

That wasn't going to save her if she didn't get prompt medical attention, but it meant she wasn't *instantly* dead.

"Skavar! Medkit!"

His Chief of Security threw him the small box before popping up to see what was going on.

"Exosuit down. One of the unarmored guys too, plus they've got at least one wounded," he reported as David pulled a tube of auto-coagulant from the kit.

This wasn't the *healthiest* thing he could do, but anything else was going to take too long. He dumped the entire tube into the hole through his Mage's shoulder, blood clotting fast as the pale green foam filled the wound.

The foam itself hardened after a moment, designed for exactly this kind of emergency use, filling the wound and stopping the flow of blood. It would take a surgeon to remove the block of foam now, but Soprano wasn't bleeding out, either.

"What do we do?" Skavar asked quietly.

"We wait for them to get close," David admitted. "And you get that knife ready. Reyes, how are you holding up?"

The other security man flipped him an unexpected thumbs-up.

"This is a much nicer place to be than the bug-infested mudhole I was pinned down in *last* time I thought I was going to die," the ex-Marine told him. "We'll be fine."

"I'm guessing you had air support that time," David replied. "What do you expect to have this time?"

"No fucking clue," Reyes said cheerfully. "Station Security seems most likely. *Someone* has to be paying attention to all of the explosions and gunfire."

Then David caught the difference. The gunfire peppering their position had stopped. He listened carefully and could hear the heavy thud of exosuit armor approaching.

Apparently, their new friends had decided that penetrators weren't getting through the barricade, and seemed to be short of grenades.

"Get ready," he hissed.

Then something exploded. A series of rapid single shots followed, then a second explosion, and then silence.

"Captain David Rice," a voice called out. "Are you all right?"

"Who the hell are you?" David replied. A rescue sounded hopeful, but he wasn't feeling particularly trusting.

"The name's Leonard Conroy," the speaker said. "You don't know me, but we have a mutual friend: James Niska."

That was...unexpected.

Major James Niska was a Legatan Augment super-soldier, trained as a Mage-killer.

And he worked for Legatan Military Intelligence.

CHAPTER 19

THE HALLWAY was silent for a moment, and then Conroy coughed.

"I hate to rush you, but while there are no cameras back here, you and these idiots made enough noise that *something* is going to have triggered back in security HQ. Now, *your* involvement is fine, but I'd really rather not have someone asking pointed questions about where my penetrator rifles came from," he pointed out.

"Plus, well, New Madagascar is pretty reasonable about magic in self-defense, but it could still take you weeks to extricate your Mage from the mess it would create. I suggest we move."

David carefully rose back to his feet and looked over the barricade. Two people, a heavyset red-headed man he presumed was Conroy and a tall broad-shouldered woman with short-cropped dark hair.

Both carried the same kind of heavy penetrator battle rifle the exosuits had been wielding, a weapon that easily weighed twenty-five kilograms and had enough recoil to put a gorilla on its ass. From the shattered suit of power armor and dead cloaked attackers scattered around them, the two strangers had no problem using the guns.

Which meant David's suspicions were confirmed. He was looking at a pair of Legatan Augments.

"We had to leave one of our crew behind," he said softly. "They killed her."

"Fuckers," Conroy agreed. "Can you show Rihanna?"

"Reyes?"

"Can do," the trooper replied. "What about Soprano?"

"She took a hit," David explained.

Conroy crossed to the barricade and gave Reyes a hand over, gesturing him towards the woman.

"Go fetch your friend," he said gently. "I'll take Soprano."

He lightly leapt the hundred-and-twenty-centimeter-tall barricade, landing like a cat next to David and studying Soprano's unconscious form. He blinked rapidly and then pressed his hand gently against her throat and then her upper arm.

Finally, Conroy looked back up at David.

"She hasn't lost as much blood as I'd feared," he said quietly. "Body temperature and blood pressure depressed, and the blood to her arm is dangerously limited. She'll be fine if we can get her to a doctor."

He glanced at his gun, then back to Soprano.

"If you take my rifle, I can take her. I'm about ninety percent sure Legacy doesn't have any more active direct-action assets on Darwin Orbital, so we should be okay."

"Are you sure?" David asked. "I..." He glanced at the heavy rifle. "I'm not sure I can fire that thing."

Conroy laughed.

"You'd be surprised," he said. "We installed after-market venting to reduce the recoil. It's not perfect, but you should be able to get a shot off before it knocks you to the ground. I, ah, didn't leave the Legacy twits' guns in a useful state, sorry."

Shields, armor, weaponry...the men and women who'd tried to kill David were in pieces across the hallway. Say what you would about Augments—and David had said much of it himself—they were effective.

"Legacy?" he asked. "Who *are* these people?"

"Azure Legacy," Conroy confirmed. "Mikhail Azure's revenge. More than that, I think we'll want to discuss somewhere safer. Let's go."

To David's surprise, the extraction back to the inhabited portions of the station went off without a hitch. Conroy led them through a series of side corridors and then through a rear entrance into what appeared to be a small corporate office.

Before *Red Falcon*'s crew could say anything, however, a pair of white-uniformed EMTs arrived and took Soprano off Conroy's hands.

"We'll get her in and treated," one of them assured Conroy. "Won't even be a ripple."

"You're worth every penny I pay you, Kai," the Augment replied. "Thanks."

As the EMTs shuffled Soprano onto a stretcher, David cleared his throat and gestured for Skavar to go with them.

"I can't leave you on your own," he objected.

"Chief, if Conroy was going to kill me, we'd all be dead already," David pointed out. "Go keep an eye on Maria—she needs you more."

"All right," Skavar conceded. He turned a point look on Conroy. "If you get any ideas, *cyborg*, I have an entire *platoon* of exosuits aboard *Falcon*. Don't fuck with my Captain."

Conroy grinned broadly.

"I believe you, Chief," he replied, "but, sadly, I'd probably still be more concerned with my boss's reaction than yours. He'll be fine. You have my word."

Skavar grunted disbelievingly, but he followed the EMTs out, leaving David alone with Conroy.

The Augment shrugged.

"Marine, I'm guessing?" he asked David.

"Ex, but yes."

"The Royal Marines have assumed for a long time that, sooner or later, they're going to have to fight the Augment Corps," Conroy said softly. "I can live with his rudeness."

"I hope so," David replied. "I wasn't going to make him apologize. I'm still not sure what the hell is going on here, Mr. Conroy."

"Fair enough," the Legatan said with an even wider grin. "Can I get you a drink, Captain? I have some good rum in my office."

"Sure."

Conroy led the way into one of the small offices off from the main cubicle area. A wordless command, presumably from some communicator built into his implants, opened a concealed gun safe. The penetrator rifle went into the middle of it, surrounded by a collection of knives and guns of half a dozen manufacturers and varieties.

"So, while I can guess what a covert Augment is doing in New Madagascar, I'm not sure why you saved me," David admitted.

The Legatan shook his head, pouring two sodas and adding a carefully measured amount of rum and ice to each before sliding one across to David.

"Would it make more sense if I told you that while I wasn't who you were meeting this evening, I was supposed to be there?" he asked. "Miller knows enough of what the fuck happened that he's not going to raise any questions, by the way. He sends his apologies."

"What the *hell* did happen?"

"Azure Legacy saw an opportunity," Conroy said flatly. "I knew they had a cell on the station, but I didn't know what they were doing here. Ground-work and intelligence gathering, from what I could tell—but the moment *you* showed up they went into action."

The Augment shook his head.

"They're not high on my list of priorities, but *you* are on the absolute top of *their* list," he concluded. "And their team here appears to include a damned good hacker. They set you up, tried to eliminate you, and then sent in their direct-action assets when the first attempt failed.

"We didn't even start looking for you until you were five minutes late," Conroy admitted. "The station isn't that big, thankfully, so once we were looking..."

"Okay, so who the hell are Azure Legacy?" David demanded.

"Mikhail Azure's revenge," the spy—because that's what David was quite certain Conroy was—repeated. "He set up a number of closed, numbered accounts before his death to fund them. Their purpose is to remove whoever killed him and...narrow the field for successors for the Blue Star Syndicate."

"What, he set up a death cult to avenge him?"

"Nothing so dramatic." Conroy laughed. "But worse. He arranged for *lawyers* to avenge him. So long as you are alive and the Syndicate is undergoing its continual meltdown, they will fund the Legacy's operations. Once you're dead, half of the remaining funds are released as a bonus. Once the Syndicate establishes a new leader, the rest is released.

"There's enough money in there that's whoever's left of the Legacy at that point will be able to retire rich as a king," the Augment noted. "Mikhail Azure wanted to be *very* sure that whoever killed him got fucked."

"What happened if he died of, I don't know, cancer?" David asked.

"Knowing Azure, the money would go to whoever cured whatever killed him. He was that vindictive."

David shook his head.

"So, the crime lord I spent years running from is *still* chasing me, even though he's dead?"

"Yeah, pretty much," Conroy confirmed. "Fortunately for you, you're flagged in my files as a high-value asset. Niska's notes made it very clear we owed you big-time, though obviously I have no information as to why."

James Niska had dragged David into a situation where he'd lost one of his oldest friends and nearly lost his ship. The Legatus Military Intelligence Directorate *did* owe him, though he hadn't regarded it that way or expected it to be repaid quite so dramatically.

"I'm no one's *asset*," he replied instead.

"In the sense of you're a shipper we can trust so long as we're not asking you to break your own codes, you are," Conroy replied. "I don't need you to ship slaves or illegal drugs, after all, Captain."

"But you do need me to ship something," David realized.

"I do," the Augment agreed. "But for now, I think I should make sure you get back to your ship safely." A grim look crossed his face. "I'm relatively sure the Legacy is out of their own muscle here, but that doesn't mean they can't hire local."

CHAPTER 20

ABSOLUTELY NOTHING about Shayne Miller suggested that the man would have had anything to do with a Legatan covert operation. He was a pudgy man with a noticeable bald spot and a ready smile, showing every sign of having been the baker his company made a big deal of him starting as.

Of course, Shayne Miller had been that baker in his twenties and was now several years into his second century. He'd had time to turn a successful corner bakery into a planetwide food and agricultural empire.

"I have to apologize for the problems you encountered last night," he told David as soon as he'd passed Skavar's security screen at the boarding hatch onto *Red Falcon*. "For my home to play host to such criminality! I am mortified."

"It's everywhere, unfortunately, Mr. Miller," David replied. "We have a meeting room standing by. Could I get you something to eat or drink?"

Miller smiled and rolled the oversized briefcase he'd brought with him around in front.

"This has enough of the finest coffee and breakfast pastries my companies produce for myself and your senior officers," he told David. "A handcart with enough for the rest of your crew—I took the liberty of looking up the company size of an AAFHF in Martian service before I came out—will be arriving in a few minutes.

"Consider it my apology for last night's incident; it's the least I can do!"

David smiled and accepted the case of food. The gesture amused him—it was warm, friendly, impossible to argue with...and neatly undercut any argument for demanding more actual *money* for the delivery.

"It's a pleasure working with you, Mr. Miller," he said with a nod.

Some of the florid cheer faded as Miller stepped into David's office, taking a seat without waiting for it to be offered.

"The coffee is a gift," he reiterated, "but I would be most appreciative if you'd spare a cup."

"Gladly," David told him, carefully pouring two mugs and sliding one across the table. "I was up early, checking on my Mage."

Miller nodded slowly, a flash of discomfort passing over his face but quickly disappearing.

"I've touched base with Cinnamon Station General Hospital One myself," he said. "Officially, Ms. Soprano was in an unfortunate industrial accident and was never anywhere near the godawful mess they discovered in the uninhabited section of the station."

He smiled thinly.

"Conroy refused to elaborate to me on what happened beyond that he saved you from some attack. I don't poke at that man's business as a rule, but I hope that things didn't go too badly..."

"I lost a crewwoman," David said shortly. "I'd call that going pretty badly."

"Damn. So would I. My condolences, Captain." Miller shook his head. "One never believes this kind of incident would happen in one's home. What a mess."

"From what I can tell, I brought my own problems with me," David replied. "You know Conroy, though?"

"As much as anyone knows the Conroys," the New Madagascan businessman confirmed. "Well enough to know that they're not merely the trade factors they officially are. They don't cause problems for my planet, I don't ask too many questions."

He shrugged.

"I keep an ear to the ground on their activities," he admitted, "and if I thought they were a problem, I'd have told the authorities, but they seem quite on the up-and-up for, well, smugglers."

David snorted. There were tiers of ethics and morals among smugglers. He'd classed himself in the category more than once, after all.

"And our business?" he asked delicately.

"Everything I've seen so far says the cargo is intact and delivered well in advance of the expected arrival," Miller agreed. "There are some penalties on the original contract, but those are between myself and Silk Star, not you.

"I'll authorize payment of ninety percent of the balance outstanding, the last ten percent to be released once we've retrieved the cargo and made certain of the lack of damage," he continued. "The contract also calls for a bonus for prompt delivery, which will be released with the holdback.

"Acceptable, Captain?"

"Good enough," David allowed. "Conroy said he was supposed to be at our meeting last night?"

"He was. I had been asked to make introductions," Miller confirmed. "As it seems he ended up making his *own* introductions, my involvement in his affairs can now safely end." The ex-baker grinned widely.

"I regard Leonard Conroy as a personal friend," he noted. "But after eighty years in this game, I can smell when a man's business is something I want to be well clear of."

And that, David suspected, was all the warning he was going to get.

Maria was far too familiar with the standardized room and equipment of the medical suites the Protectorate mass-produced and sold to its member worlds for cheap. The itch in her shoulder was new, though—she'd spent her military career aboard starships and had avoided being shot until today.

When Rice arrived to check in on her, she was still wearing the flimsy hospital gown. Her Captain averted his eyes from her body as she sat up to greet him, which gave her a soft laugh.

"We both made it through the Navy, David," she teased. "I doubt I'm the first woman you've seen in a hospital gown—or less! I saw the picture of your lover in your office, after all."

Rice chuckled.

"I'm just glad you didn't decide to call her my 'mistress' or some such garbage," he replied. "I suspect Keiko might hunt me down and kill me if I allowed someone to call her that."

"Dangerous company you keep," Maria noted. "And attract. What the hell was that, Captain?"

He glanced around the room. Private patient rooms were supposed to be just that: private. Maria wasn't sure she'd trust it that far, but she was also far too impatient to wait to find out what had happened.

"Apparently, my past caught up with us," he murmured. "Fortunately, some old friends did the same and intervened. They may have work for us."

Maria nodded and sighed. There was only one set of old friends that would have work for Rice here, one set whose involvement would explain MISS wanting them to travel to New Madagascar.

"Legatus."

"How did you know?" he demanded.

"Lucky guess," she said. "It was either station security or someone's special ops team that saved us—no one else would have enough firepower." She shook her head. "And station security was clearly ignoring the mess. Plus, they wouldn't have work for you."

"You may be too smart for your own good," Rice told her. "I don't know details yet. We're still off-loading our cargo from Cinnamon, but then I have a meeting with a Legatan 'expat' trade factor.

"If you're up for it, I'd rather have you at my back."

"A Mage might hurt your chance at the deal," she replied.

"I doubt it," Rice said. "But if it did, I wouldn't want to work for them. I prefer to work for the *sane* Legatans."

Maria shook her head at him warningly.

"You know they're the dangerous ones, right?"

"I do," he admitted. "Are you going to be okay?"

"Yeah. They do good work and have good gear," she told him. "I'll be back aboard by night shift, though I'll be going straight to medbay and staying there for another day."

"*Good* first officer," Rice agreed. "Let me know if you need anything. I don't like people getting shot on my behalf."

Maria winced.

"What about Ambrose?" she asked.

"Her will called for her body to be cremated and her ashes and effects shipped to Mars," the Captain told her. "Her family will deal with funeral arrangements there. We'll have a memorial once we're back in space."

"Good plan. Keep things quiet."

"Every minute I spend in the UnArcana worlds makes my skin itch," David replied. "I've been stabbed in the back *way* too often in these systems."

"It must be your incredible ability to make friends," she told him.

He laughed and shook his head at her.

"Get better, Ship's Mage," he ordered. "I don't plan on staying here a single day more than necessary."

Maria was completely unsurprised and quite pleased to find Acconcio waiting for her at the hatch to the ship as the nurse delivered her wheelchair into *Red Falcon*'s spin pseudo-gravity.

"I got her from here," the tactical officer said gruffly. "You need to walk me all the way to the medbay?"

The nurse smiled—but also very clearly looked at Maria for her confirmation that this was okay. Good man.

"Iovis is good," she told him. "I'll be fine. Thank you, Lokosta."

"Part of the service, ma'am," the nurse replied with a head-bob. "If you're in good hands, I'll leave you be. Take care of yourself."

"As much as I can, Nurse Lokosta. As much as I can," Maria promised.

The nurse disappeared back into Darwin Orbital, his task complete and his day, like that of any medical professional in the galaxy, vastly busy and far from over.

"How are you doing?" Acconcio asked softly, taking over pushing the wheelchair along *Falcon*'s corridors.

"I was shot," she pointed out. "I was looking forward to having a nice dinner tonight, not being stuck in the medbay, being poked and prodded by yet another doctor."

He chuckled.

"Well, hopefully, we'll still be on the station for at least *a* day after you're out of Dr. Gupta's skilled hands," he told her. "I can wait if you still want that dinner."

He shook his head.

"I was worried when I heard about last night," he told her. "Didn't expect you to get dragged into the Captain's business *here*."

"I'm the Ship's Mage," Maria replied, leaning back in the wheelchair to rest her head against his chest. "I'm in the ship's business everywhere."

"That's the job, I suppose," Acconcio agreed sadly. "Just wish I was doing a better job of keeping you safe!"

"Hard to protect us aboard the station when your tools are lasers and missiles, Iovis," she reminded him gently. "Leave that to Skavar—and he did a damn fine job."

There was no need to tell everyone the Captain had been saved by Legatan spies. *That* was a complication they could keep to themselves, she figured.

CHAPTER 21

RETURNING TO THE STATION several days later, David made absolutely certain to verify the address they were heading to and the directions with Conroy before they even set foot on Darwin Orbital. He had a hard limit of "once per star system" on being nearly asphyxiated.

This time, however, his escort and Ship's Mage went unchallenged as they returned to the plain offices of the trade brokerage run by Leonard and Rihanna Conroy, expatriate Legatans working on behalf of several of New Madagascar's midsized import and export firms.

He had to wonder how many of them, like Shayne Miller, knew just who they were working with. No one in an UnArcana system was going to complain about working with Legatan covert operatives, after all. So far as he could tell, nothing the Conroys were doing was remotely illegal.

They just hid their active allegiances, and that wasn't a crime, last time he checked.

If it was, he wasn't going to take bets on how many of his crew were guilty of it. The visible and invisible reach of the Mage-King was long, and at least some of his crew were less *ex*-military than his ship was.

His most likely candidate for that status was with him today, however, and Skavar wasn't raising any complaints about them meeting with people he knew were Legatan Augments. He'd brought two full fire teams of security with them, eight troopers, but that was more a reaction to their last trip aboard station as anything else.

And if there *happened* to be the components of several bipod-mounted heavy penetrator rifles hidden under the jackets of David's security detail, he was sure that was entirely an accident, as the weapons required to take down exosuits were *entirely* illegal aboard Darwin Orbital.

The size of his group clearly shocked the young woman holding down the front desk at Conroy & Conroy.

"Can I help you?" she asked slowly.

"I'm Captain David Rice," he told her. "My Ship's Mage and I have an appointment with Leonard Conroy." He smiled. "Everyone else is going to ask you for a recommendation for a nearby café and come back when we're done."

"That won't be necessary, Captain," Conroy's voice boomed from behind the reception desk. "Nellie, Conf Three is open as well, right?"

"Yes, boss."

"Throw some extra chairs in there for Rice's people and get them coffees and sandwiches." The Augment grinned. "Believe me, given the size of the good Captain's ship and what hiring him is going to cost me, I'm not even going to *notice* feeding his security."

The young lady flashed her boss a strained smile but nodded her understanding.

"Of course," she confirmed aloud. "If you ladies and gentlemen will come with me? Captain Rice, Mage Soprano, it seems Mr. Conroy was waiting for you."

"Thank you, Nellie," Conroy told her. "Hold any calls until we're done as well. Anything urgent, send it over to Rihanna. She knows I'm in Conf One."

"Of course, boss."

"Now." Conroy turned back to David and Soprano, offering his hand to the Mage. "Mage Soprano, a pleasure. You were unconscious when we last met."

"David tells me you carried me to safety," she said softly. "Thank you."

"By the time I was carrying you, things were already quite safe," the Augment replied. "But yes, I got you into the hands of Darwin Orbital's capable EMTs. They did good work?"

Soprano shifted her shoulder.

"Bit stiff still," she admitted. "But I think so. I've never been shot before."

"It's an...illuminating experience, isn't it?" Conroy said. "Shall we move into Conference Room One and talk business, Captain, Mage?"

The conference room was a beige space, plain colors and furniture clearly designed to be the opposite of *ostentatious* and do the opposite of *be remembered*. Conroy gestured the two *Red Falcon* officers to seats at the table and poured them coffees.

"Anything stronger in the coffee?" he asked with a raised eyebrow.

"Too early for me, thanks," David replied. Soprano just shook her head, but the Legatan grinned broadly and poured a generous dollop of rum into his own drink.

"Guess it bothers most people more than me," he said brightly, placing the coffees in front of them and sliding a tray of milk and sugar across the table.

David had never met a senior starship officer who put anything in their coffee except occasionally alcohol. Neither he nor Soprano were exceptions, and they sipped their coffee black while Conroy paused to marshal his thoughts.

"We wouldn't be here if I didn't have work for you," he finally said. "I'm sure it's not a shock that we need it done under the radar with a degree of, shall we say, misdirection."

"I'm not overly interested in getting tied up in anything illegal," David replied. He'd had enough of that crap to last him several lifetimes—not to mention Legatan cargos that ended up somewhere other than they were supposed to.

"Nothing illegal, Captain Rice," Conroy said. "I've read your file. I'm not asking you to ship guns or slaves or drugs or anything that's going to hurt *anyone*."

"If you've read my file, you know why I won't ship anything without knowing exactly what it is," *Red Falcon's* Captain replied. He'd made that mistake once—and found himself with a cargo of about ten thousand cryo-frozen teenagers destined for involuntary participation in the sex trade.

They hadn't ended up at their planned destination—and Mikhail Azure's son had ended up dead, resisting arrest. Not asking questions had led to a lot of David's problems.

"Fair enough," Conroy allowed. "For reasons I *won't* go into, I have been stockpiling cargo here that I haven't been able to ship. I actually have more than even you can carry, but twenty million tons will bring my backlog back down to something I can stuff in a few passing regular tramps."

David grunted noncommittedly. He was starting to realize that the biggest disadvantage of *Red Falcon* was that finding twenty million tons going one direction was hard. He had a massive, fast, capable ship...and he was realizing it was hard to turn down a cargo that could actually fit his ship.

"The cargo is pretty rough raw material," the Legatan continued. "Partially refined here in New Madagascar, so you're not hauling straight rock, but..." He shrugged. "Iron, titanium, cerium, gadolinium, about a dozen other -iums. About half is iron and titanium; the other half is rare earth and heavy elements."

"I assume you have the proper containers for your stack of magnets and radioactives?" David asked.

"Of course," Conroy confirmed. "Everything is perfectly safe and contained. That's not the catch."

David sighed.

"And the catch?"

"Officially, this cargo is going to Legatus," the spy replied. "In reality, it needs to go somewhere else. I...can't really say where unless you agree to take the job, but I will promise you that it's not an UnArcana world."

"That's reassuring," David said dryly. "This whole mess *still* sounds like a trap to me, Conroy. Why exactly would I get involved?"

"Because I pay well," the trade broker replied. "I'll pay you a hundred percent premium over standard carriage rates, plus information."

"What information?" Soprano demanded. "This sounds like you're asking us to get involved in Legatan covert operations."

"Nothing so outré, Mage Soprano," he told her. "Officially sanctioned smuggling at worst. How much trouble do you really think we can cause with twenty million tons of metal and magnets?"

"If my math is right, about two cruiser-equivalent warships," she said. "That's not nothing."

"Fair," Conroy allowed. "Assuming we had some secret shipyard where we were building a clandestine fleet for nefarious purposes, this cargo would be most of the construction requirements for several warships. All I can tell you is that we're not building warships.

"And the information, Captain, Mage, is something of mutual interest," he continued. "Azure Legacy will hunt you until you are dead. I don't have the resources or authority to deal with them, but I can put you in touch with a friend who has her own reasons to take them on. I suspect you could find a way to handle them, working together."

"I see," David said, cutting off any further response from Maria. "That's a solid offer, Mr. Conroy, but you're asking us to take on more risk than I think we need."

Finding a cargo in New Madagascar might be a pain, but there were other people moving entire asteroids' worth of raw material out of the system. People who *weren't* running smuggling operations for the Legatus Military Intelligence Directorate.

"I appreciate your help, but I think we're going to have to decline."

Conroy sighed, but nodded.

"I understand," he admitted. "If you change your mind, let me know, Captain. I'm not going anywhere and neither is my pile of metals."

Maria waited until they were well on their way back to the ship, realizing that her own half-instinctive revulsion to working for Legatus had undermined a good chunk of the reason she was aboard Rice's ship—and certainly a good chunk of the reason she was receiving two salaries!

"Okay boss," she finally challenged Rice. "Why exactly are we turning down easy money? And help dealing with the guys who want to kill you?"

"Because *Legatus*," he replied. "The last time I worked for Legatus, people died. Not to mention that I can't help but feel that whatever they're doing isn't in the Protectorate's best interests. And it's not like *you* were seeming enthused."

"Yeah, but I'm a Mage," Maria pointed out. "Nobody expects me to play along with the UnArcana worlds. I was poking at him because I was assuming we *were* taking the job, to make sure everything was as clean as he was claiming."

"It probably is," her Captain admitted. "Just the very idea of working with them makes me twitchy."

Maria shook her head.

"How do you think *I* feel?" she pointed out. "Most of the Protectorate military feels like we've spent the last twenty or thirty years watching Legatus measure our backs for the knife. Sooner or later, their clash with the Mages is going to spill over."

"So long as they need Mages to haul cargo and people, it can only spill over so much," Rice reminded her. "But I know. And I've wandered into the middle of enough of LMID's affairs..."

He shook his head.

"It could take weeks to find another cargo big enough to justify flying *Falcon* anywhere," Maria said. She hated manipulating Rice, even at this level, but this had to be what MISS had wanted them involved in.

"Weeks, I'll point out, that we'll just be sitting here in New Madagascar orbit, collecting dust and angry glares."

"I wouldn't stay that long," he replied. "A few more days, then we'd head back to the Core Worlds. What we'd lose in riding light or empty, we'd make back in actually being able to find cargo."

Maria shook her head back at him.

"A bird in the hand is worth two in the bush," she quoted at him. "Plus, every day we're swanning around the galaxy, this 'Azure Legacy' is detailing the target on your back. On *all* of our backs, really. *Red Falcon* is a big target."

"I know," Rice admitted. "So, what, you think we should take the job?"

"Have you got another cargo on the docket?" Maria asked. "Because if you don't, I think we'd all rather get out of New Madagascar as quickly as possible—and Conroy's job is how we do that."

Rice nodded.

"I guess you're right. Are you able to swing back in with me?"

"No," she admitted. "I promised Acconcio a rain check on a date—a rain check I am determined to honor!"

Her Captain chuckled at her.

"Don't stay out *too* late, first officer."

"Oh, I have no intention of staying *out*," Maria purred.

CHAPTER 22

FROM THE SILLY GRINS on his tactical officer and Ship's Mage's faces, David could only conclude that the dinner the previous night had gone according to everyone's plans.

The rest of the officers gathered for the staff meeting he'd called didn't look quite as pleased with themselves, but everyone was looking accomplished at least. They'd delivered their second cargo, got paid, and survived a full-scale assassination attempt to get there.

"All right, people," he told them. "Maria and I met with our potential client last night. While I have some issues with the job on the table, as Maria pointed out to me, we don't have any other good options at the moment."

He smiled.

"We're working for a private company that handles trade imports to Legatus," he told them. "Officially, at least, they have contracted us to deliver a load of raw materials to Legatus itself.

"What doesn't go beyond the senior officers, at least until we've left this system, is that the import company we're working for is a front for the Legatus Military Intelligence Directorate," David continued. "They arrange for covert smuggling of resources around Protectorate worlds to enable projects that the Legatus government doesn't want becoming public knowledge."

Unless he'd severely mistaken his crew's allegiances, hiring him for those tasks was a mistake. But it wasn't one he could bring himself to

GLYNN STEWART

correct. Soprano was right, after all—*Red Falcon* couldn't sit empty. She cost too much doing so, and that was *before* the opportunity cost of what she could have been doing.

"We are going to make one jump along the regular New Madagascar–Legatus Jump Line," he concluded. "That's our officially declared course, which presumably is where our hunting friends will look for us if they've caught up.

"From there, we are diverting to Svarog. For those of you aren't familiar, Svarog is one of the MidWorlds, colonized by one of the interstellars as, basically, a company town.

"While most of the worst results of that have been corrected since, Svarog remains one of the two or three most industrialized systems outside the Core," he concluded. "Like most systems, they have an asteroid belt they're raiding for raw materials, but refined metals like our new cargo will be gratefully accepted."

"What's our loading cycle?" Kellers asked. "Svarog is a good place to get refits and repairs done. *Falcon* doesn't need much yet, but I wouldn't want to pass up the opportunity while we're there."

"Most of the cargo is already in containers. The Conroys have promised we'll have everything aboard in forty-eight hours, at which point I plan to get the hell out of this system," David told his engineer.

"Jenna, Nicolas," he addressed his XO and first pilot. "I want you to coordinate with Conroy & Conroy's people. The last thing I want at this point is issues in the loading."

"So long as we're being paid," Campbell responded. "Nicolas and I'll make sure everything is clear."

The pilot simply nodded agreement with her.

"Svarog isn't a great place for leave, but I agree with James," David continued. "We'll want to get some minor repairs and refits while we're there. With three trips behind us, we should know what bits are fragile by now!

"Once we announce the course change to the crew, we'll sweeten it with a week's leave while we're getting the work done," he told them. "I'd say Svarog is safe, but...I'd have said the same thing about New Madagascar or Cinnamon.

170

"Our luck hasn't been promising on *safe* of late."

Plus, while he didn't have the details yet, there was apparently enough of a Blue Star Syndicate successor organization in the system for the Conroys to have a contact there.

"We'll be ready for trouble," Skavar told them all grimly. "Time to ratchet the paranoia, people. Before, we were running regular security. Now we *know* the Captain is being hunted—and that makes us *all* targets."

"You write the rules on that," David promised. "But remember, we need to get our work done too."

"I know," the security chief allowed. "But I'm not losing anybody else, Captain. I refuse."

David nodded his agreement in silence.

David was honestly surprised by how long it took after the meeting for Campbell to show up in his office. He'd been expecting her inside of an hour, but it was actually late evening—and well after the cargo had started loading—before his executive officer knocked on his door.

"Come in, Jenna," he instructed. "I've been waiting for you."

"Am I that predictable?" she asked, dropping into the chair across his desk. "Been around that long?"

"No, but you and I have much the same history with LMID," he pointed out, "and since *I* almost turned the job down..."

"You figured I'd be asking what the hell you were thinking," Campbell said. "Because, well, what the hell were you thinking?"

"I laid my thoughts out clearly earlier," he noted. "There weren't a lot of other options. It was take this or fly back to the Core empty. This seemed like a better option, despite the risks."

"Last time we worked for LMID, people died," Campbell replied quietly. "A lot of them, even if only a handful were ours. And we don't have Narveer anymore."

Their last contract with LMID had ended in a boarding operation that had collided head-on with their then first pilot, Narveer Singh. Singh had acquired a suit of exosuit combat armor and had massacred the attackers—but he'd died in the process.

"I know. There are two factors I didn't tell the rest of the staff," David told his oldest remaining friend. "First, Maria is damned convincing. And she was right. Most of what I reeled off was her argument after I walked out on Conroy."

"I'd have figured the damn Mage would have been against working with LMID," his XO replied. "Unless...she's not as *ex*-Navy as she told us."

"Oh, she's ex-Navy," David confirmed. "Cashiered for disobedience to orders. Barely skated out of a ten-year stint in a Navy penitentiary because her intentions, at least, were in line with the traditions of His Majesty's Navy."

He shook his head.

"I have my suspicions," he admitted. "I want you to keep an eye on her. I trust her more than I thought I would, but I'm also quite certain our Ship's Mage has another agenda in play."

"Then why are you taking her advice?"

"Because she was right," he said. "I can't have *Red Falcon* sit around collecting dust or flying empty. Between salaries and reactor fuel, this ship costs something like thirty thousand dollars a day just *sitting* there."

And almost four times that when she was in motion. His profit on the Cinnamon trade was barely enough to keep the ship in motion for a year. A single quarter of *Red Falcon*'s operating expenses would have paid for *Blue Jay* for eighteen months.

"And secondly," he continued, "because Conroy offered us more than just money. He has an ally in Svarog that he's going to give us contact information for. One with their own fight with Azure Legacy."

Campbell shook her head and sighed.

"Boss, from what you said about the Legacy, there's only one other type of person who'd have their own clash with the Legacy," she pointed out. "It was created to do what, again? Avenge Azure and make sure the Syndicate had a single successor, right?"

"Right," David agreed. He knew what conclusion his XO was stretching for.

"So, this contact...is a Blue Star Syndicate member?"

"Or was," he confirmed. "Probably someone who has taken over Blue Star assets and regional operations."

"So, a pirate, a slaver...a criminal."

"Hopefully not a slaver," David replied. "Or a pirate. I'm hoping for a nice 'innocent' smuggling operation."

"Wonderful."

"The problem is that we don't have a choice, Jenna," he told her. "The Navy is already using us as bait; we know that. If we're going to dig our way out of this hole, it's one inch at a time, on our own."

"We don't work for the Protectorate, David," she said. "We're not spies. We're a goddamn merchant ship. Why don't we just...I don't know, run? Opposite side of the Protectorate?"

"We could probably be safe if we stuck to Core System runs," he admitted. "But...most of the big cargos in the Core are locked up by the big shipping lines. *Falcon*'s speed and firepower aren't that much of an edge there. In the MidWorlds, though...our advantages are worth a lot.

"We can make a fortune out here, enough for everyone to retire."

"Or die. We could also die out here, especially if we're being hunted by assassins and pirates."

He nodded.

"But they found us in Tau Ceti," he pointed out. "No, Jenna, I think the only way we're going to survive this is if we throw every resource and ally we can gather at this Azure Legacy—the Navy, the Legatans, whatever remnants of Blue Star will work with us...

"I'll take what allies and work I can get to make sure my people are safe and paid," David concluded. "I have no intentions of being the Protectorate's spy, Jenna, but I didn't pick this damned fight. If Azure's hand wants to reach out from the grave to start it, then I will damned well finish it!"

"You know, you could have just stuck with 'the ship costs too much to leave empty'," Campbell pointed out. "I don't think I needed to know we were about to start a war with Azure's interstellar hit squad."

David smiled grimly.

"You're my XO, Jenna. Whatever I'm digging us into, you do need to know."

"Thanks," she said dryly. "Your confidence enthuses me."

To Maria's pleased surprise, it turned out that Iovis Acconcio, unlike many officers, actually knew how to cook. *Red Falcon* was large enough that the senior officers' quarters each had their own kitchenette, and the heavyset man set to it with a will in preparing her supper on their second "date."

"The ship is almost half-loaded," he observed as he spiced the sauce for the pasta. "We'll be out, what, day and a half?"

"Give or take an hour or so," Maria replied, sitting in a chair she'd leaned against the kitchenette wall as she watched her new lover cook. "I am looking forward to getting out of UnArcana space."

"Even if we're working for Legatus?" Iovis asked. "Goes against the grain a bit, doesn't it?"

She shrugged.

"We're not Navy anymore," she pointed out. "Legatus is just another employer, and it's not like they're asking us to do anything illegal. Deceptive, yes, but not illegal. There's no *legal* requirement to file an accurate interstellar course plan; it's just smart, as it enables search and rescue."

"And unexpected intercepts," he replied. "That's why we were doing the short jumps, wasn't it?"

"Yeah." She shook her head. "Won't need to do that this time, not with the course being off from our declared plot. It's going to be an unpredictable-enough course, leaving towards Legatus and then bouncing to Svarog."

Iovis nodded as he served up spaghetti onto two plates.

"The Captain seems to be dragging us into more politics than I was expecting," he admitted softly. "I worry—especially about you; the Ship's Mage is in the middle of everything!"

"And the man in charge of the guns isn't?" Maria asked with a soft smile, touched by his concern. She sniffed at the pasta and her smile widened. "This smells amazing."

"My mother's secret recipe," Iovis replied with a grin of his own. "Figure it's a good start for buttering you up."

"And just *what* do you think you're buttering me up for, mister?" she purred at him.

"Well?" David asked Conroy as the Legatan's image appeared on his screen. "How are we doing, Mr. Conroy?"

It was late at night, but it wasn't like David kept regular hours or had anything else to distract him. The only contact he had with Keiko Alabaster was occasional messages, mostly sent to wait for him at Tau Ceti, and a promise that she'd make time for him whenever he made his way to Amber.

He envied the couples taking shape on his ship, but it wasn't wise for the Captain to have entanglements aboard, even on a merchant ship. Plus, well, he *liked* his understanding with Keiko.

"We're doing better than I expected," Conroy told him. It wasn't clear to David whether Leonard and Rihanna Conroy were *actually* married, or if that was just their cover there—but they'd been there long enough, he doubted it mattered.

The Augment almost certainly had somewhere warmer and less lonely to be tonight than David did.

"We're about sixty percent loaded already," he continued. "Your pilots have set to with a will; they've been making my people look slow and lazy." Conroy grinned.

"My people don't *like* that, so it's a feedback loop that gets a lot of work done," he concluded. "You'll be good to go in plenty of time."

"And payment?" David asked dryly.

"You're carrying the details in your encrypted databanks," his client promised. "Our partners at your destination will see you paid, I promise."

David shook his head at the phrasing. Secure as the line might be, Conroy still wasn't going to say they were heading anywhere other than Legatus on a communication channel.

"And the rest?"

"Of course," the spy confirmed. "I'll provide you contact information on a chip before you leave, but the contact is a woman named Turquoise. She runs an organization made of Blue Star Syndicate leftovers."

Conroy shook his head.

"Last I heard, she hadn't named her new organization anything in particular, but she controls all of the resources and surviving personnel that were part of Blue Star in six star systems. There are bigger fragments, which makes her a target for the Legacy as they try to force a reunion of the Syndicate."

"A reunion she'd rather have under her control or not at all, I'm guessing?" David asked.

"Exactly. I don't know Turquoise's real name. My understanding is that she was relatively junior in the Syndicate before you and Azure had your final encounter. How she parlayed whatever position she had into ruling the underworld of six systems, I don't know, but she's been a useful asset for us.

"She'll meet with you as a favor to us. Anything after that, you'll have to convince her of mutual interest."

"If nothing else," David said, "we appear to make great bait for anyone hunting the Legacy."

"I refuse to admit if that thought crossed my mind, Captain Rice," Conroy told him with a smile. "Good luck."

CHAPTER 23

DESPITE ALL of the chaos beforehand, the process of loading and leaving New Madagascar went perfectly smoothly. Shuttles holding cargo containers swarmed out from Darwin Orbital, locking onto the long "stem" of *Red Falcon*'s hull and its support struts.

Everything went so according to plan that almost before David knew it, they were on their way. Even with the detour, they were only thirty-six light-years from Svarog, a little over three days' travel at *Red Falcon*'s pace.

The middle of the trip found him alone on the bridge, watching the stars of a random chunk of space a dozen light-years from anywhere. Deep space was reassuring these days, the knowledge that out there, he and his people were safe.

In theory, he was safer in port, but given Legacy's apparent reach, he wasn't as sure about that. When he posted accurate flight paths, he could be intercepted by knowledgeable enemies. *Knowing* he was being hunted, however, he could avoid those threats. There were others, but they were rarer, less predictable threats.

Which made the depths between the stars the best safe haven he had. He couldn't *stay* out there, *Falcon* didn't have the supplies or capacity to be self-sufficient, but while they were out in the void, they were safe. Mostly.

So, David Rice sat on his bridge and sank into the humming rhythm of his ship. Soon enough, he'd be in Svarog and have to decide whether or not he was willing to make common cause with criminals.

Survival was a powerful motivator, and he'd lain down in the muck before. Flight wasn't an option—the Protectorate's gift was a millstone around his neck. To keep *Falcon* flying, he *had* to work, had to carry cargo.

Had to be bait for the Mage-King's enemies.

Maria should have been resting. She'd jumped barely three hours beforehand, and it would be another five before it was her turn to cast the spell that carried the starship through the stars again.

Nonetheless, she'd left Iovis sleeping in his quarters and returned to the simulacrum chamber, surrounded by the screens that showed the stars through which *Red Falcon* drifted.

There was no point to engines there. A few thousand kilometers more or less wasn't going to change anything in the end; they could arrive only so close to Svarog's star.

The big freighter's speed was normal to her, though most of the rest of the crew were impressed by it. The whole point of the AAFHF design, however, had been to keep up with the warships of the Royal Martian Navy.

For all of her mass and speed, *Red Falcon* was no true replacement for the destroyers of Maria's naval service. Her crew worked well together, but they weren't the family she'd known aboard her last ship.

The family she'd convinced to follow her into what had arguably been mutiny.

MISS might think they were giving her a chance to honor her old oath, but they couldn't give her back that belonging, that family. No matter what, she was no longer Navy.

That still hurt.

Maria sighed.

It still hurt, but not as much as it had. Not enough to send her back into a dive bar to drink herself to death again. Brent Alois had done her that much of a favor, and David Rice had welcomed her into his crew.

The Captain treated her as his strong right hand, with more trust than she'd expected.

She was a screw-up who'd been kicked out of the Navy, after all.

And then there was Iovis Acconcio. She had to wonder how long the older warrant officer had nursed his flame. It would have been utterly inappropriate when they served together, but aboard a merchant ship, it wasn't a problem.

She smiled softly. He might even be in love with her, which was a little scary. He was kind and gentle and considerate, but she didn't love him.

She supposed that could change. Certainly, she enjoyed his company enough.

But there were times she needed to be alone, so she floated in an unmarked shipsuit inside the heart of the Mage sanctum aboard *Red Falcon*, relaxing and corralling her loose thoughts.

From the simulacrum chamber, she could see everything going on around the big freighter—which meant she spotted the jump flares.

David was considering setting the ship to automatically alert him of anything changing and heading to bed when the intercom from the simulacrum chamber flipped alive.

"David, check two-forty by sixty-eight," Soprano's voice snapped. "We've got at least one jump flare incoming."

He swallowed hard, pulling up *Falcon*'s scanners and checking the direction she'd provided. The simulacrum chamber's systems could give the Mage a decent view of what was going on, but they weren't designed for detailed sensor display.

The bridge systems were and he swallowed hard as they began to resolve the contacts.

"Not one," he told his Mage quietly. "Six, and I have fusion-engine flares." He waited a moment as the computer tried to analyze it. "I'll need Acconcio up here to be certain," he admitted, "but I think we're looking at an entire strike force of corvettes."

"Damn," Soprano replied. "I make the range forty light-seconds, give or take. Can we touch them from here?"

"We can hit them with the antimatter birds, but..." He shivered. "Those ships have a crew of sixty to a hundred apiece. Five, maybe six hundred people. I can't just blow them away.

"When can we jump?"

His Mage looked ill.

"Costa's next on the roster, but he can't jump early," she admitted. "Wu...could jump in an hour or so, but so could Costa. I could jump in two. They've got us pinned, boss."

"They brought through enough base velocity to halve the range by then," he warned. "They could easily have fusion missiles that could tag us from there, but the flight times would suck."

David hit a series of commands on his controls, lighting up *Red Falcon*'s massive engines. Whether the strange ships had been lucky or extremely well informed, they had a two-thousand-kilometers-a-second velocity toward his ship.

They were burning toward him at ten gravities, so either they had gravity runes aboard or were absolutely *punishing* their crews. He could match that acceleration, but for now, he just activated an automated evasion program.

Those corvettes had lasers, and he wasn't interested in testing the bastards' luck.

"I'm flagging red alert," he told Soprano. "Wake everyone up and poke your Mages. I'd love to jump out of here before I discover if these people are here to kill us."

It was nowhere near as easy to activate the red alert as it would have been to take a warship to general quarters, but despite her weapons and engines, *Red Falcon* remained primarily a cargo hauler. Nothing changed in the bridge or the simulacrum chamber on the intercom screen, but the ship's systems informed him that the klaxons and lights calling everyone to emergency stations were now ringing throughout the ship.

"If they're here to kill us, how did they even *find* us?" Soprano asked. "We're easily ten light-years from where we're supposed to be."

"But we didn't play any games beyond that," he said grimly. "They knew where we were going, Maria. They knew both the deception and the real destination.

"Somebody sold us out."

And much as he wanted to think so, he didn't think it had been any of Conroy's people.

The strangers made no attempt to communicate as they closed with *Red Falcon*, a glaring warning sign to David. Nonetheless, as a civilian in command of an armed ship, Protectorate law was quite clear: if he fired first, he would be guilty of murder.

And regardless of what the law said, he would be guilty in his own mind.

Despite her guns, his ship wasn't a warship, and it took time for crew to report to emergency stations. Acconcio and Campbell arrived almost simultaneously, both of their quarters as near to the bridge as any space on the rotating gravity ring.

Others filtered in over the following few minutes, taking up their stations around the bridge and across the ship. Various sections of the ship flipped from a greenish-yellow—night-shift operations, only one or two people on duty—to the bright orange of emergency stations on his displays.

"These guys should *not* be here," Acconcio said grimly. "Two *Caribbean*-class corvettes. One might be our ghost from earlier; the radar signature is wonky enough for stealth plating. Two *Antioch*-class ships—those are Legatan-built; putting jump matrices into them must have been a *pain*. Last two aren't any class I recognize, custom civvy jobs but basically corvette equivalents."

The gunner shook his head.

"*Those* are pirate ships," he concluded. "And like I said, they should not be here!"

"Someone sold them our course," David replied. "And believe me, Iovis, I intend to find out who. Jenna!"

Campbell looked over at him.

"Yes, boss?"

"Hail them," he ordered. "And put me on."

A small screen in his chair's repeaters showed him the image he was sending out to the other ships, and he carefully adjusted to glare directly at the camera.

"Unidentified vessels, this is the armed merchant freighter *Red Falcon*, Captain David Rice commanding," he barked. "We both know this isn't a regular jump point, which leaves me wondering just why you're here.

"Your approach suggests unkind intentions. I warn you that this ship is armed and we will defend ourselves. If you do not begin to vector away, I will need to regard your approach as threatening and prepare to take necessary actions.

"Clarify your intent and break off," he ordered. "Or I will be forced to defend this ship."

"On the chip," Campbell told him.

"Send it," David replied. "Iovis, do we have them dialed in?"

"Of course," the tactical officer confirmed. "Assuming they're all equivalent to the *Antiochs* and *Carribeans*, though…"

"Finish the thought," David said as the man trailed off.

"At this range, it would take a full salvo to guarantee taking down a ship," Acconcio said. "We could spread our fire out as we thin their numbers, but we could easily burn half our magazines of antimatter birds to take them down."

And while David was authorized to *possess* antimatter missiles, there hadn't been any discussion of him buying new ones. He had the connections to sort that out—if nothing else, Amber had no laws regarding sale of weapons of any kind, and a chance to visit with Keiko wasn't to be passed up—but fifty AM missiles was a lot of money.

"I'm not prepared to fire first," he said softly. "Load all launchers with the fusion-drive kinetics. Target our ghost first, and the *instant* they open fire, you start shooting.

"And you don't stop until they're debris or have surrendered."

Seconds turned to minutes. More than enough time passed for David to be certain that the attackers had received his message and could have responded.

They didn't. The six ships continued on their steady approach, accelerating toward *Red Falcon* at ten gravities. He surrendered control of the ship to Campbell, allowing her to keep up the evasive maneuvers—but they weren't accelerating away from the pirates.

"We're in range of our fusion missiles," Acconcio reported softly. An uneven blue circle appeared on the main display, extending around *Falcon* to show the reach of her lighter missiles. The civilian-grade self-defense weapons could accelerate at two thousand gravities for ten minutes, roughly the capability that David would expect pirate missiles to have.

At five million kilometers, the pirate's velocity would bring them within reach of *Falcon's* missiles, but David still waited.

"No reaction to our message?" he asked.

"None," Campbell confirmed. "Their course didn't even twitch."

"Of course not." *Red Falcon's* Captain considered for several seconds.

"Iovis, bring up Laser One," he ordered. "Warning shot at forty percent power; keep it at least ten thousand kilometers clear."

At two gigawatts—forty percent of their rated firepower—the heavy battle laser would resemble the heaviest weapons David had originally acquired permits for. If the pirates didn't know who they were fighting, it might be enough to scare them off.

If they *did*, it might help them underestimate him. With one ship, however well-armed, versus six, he'd take every advantage he could.

"Jenna, clear the RFLAMs," he continued. "Keep humans in the loop but bring up the automatic defense protocols. I don't want to be waiting on our reflexes to save us if we've missed something."

"Turrets coming online," she replied instantly.

"Warning shot ready," Acconcio reported. "Firing."

All twenty-five of the icons marking *Red Falcon*'s rapid-fire laser anti-missile turrets flipped green, with a red outline marking them as fully active and under computer control.

A moment later, the computers drew in the laser beam as a single white line on the screen. The high-powered beam wasn't operating on any visible wavelength, but the computer picked up the slight scatter of radiation and told the humans where it was.

It sliced directly past the pirate ships, just inside David's ordered ten-thousand-kilometer margin.

"Put me on again," he said softly, then faced the camera once more.

"Unidentified ships, that was a warning shot," he told them. "I will not tolerate any further aggression. Break off *now* or I will have no choice but to open fire."

Letting the message send, he turned back to Acconcio.

"Status?" he asked.

"All laser capacitators at full charge," the ex-Navy man reported instantly. "Launchers one through ten loaded. I have a passive lock on Bogey Alpha, our ghost, but I'd like to get a hard active lock before I fire."

"All RFLAMs are online and clear to fire," Campbell added.

"We're standing by in the simulacrum chamber to add what we can," Soprano reported from her station. "*Falcon* may not have a warship's amplifier, but we were all trained for this. We'll sweep anything the turrets miss."

"Thank you, Ship's Mage," David murmured. "Jenna. Any sign of a response?"

"Negative."

He exhaled heavily, then nodded.

"Third Officer Acconcio," he said formally, "you are authorized to bring up active sensors and acquire hard lock. Stand by to fire on my command."

"Wait!" Campbell snapped. "Incoming transmission!"

"Play it."

A broad-shouldered man in an expensive but ill-fitted suit suddenly appeared on David's screen. At some point, the hair on his scalp appeared to have been permanently lasered off in some kind of pattern that wasn't quite visible from the front.

He smiled broadly, showing sparkling white teeth and warm brown eyes as he turned a grin that David would normally have found reassuring on *Red Falcon*'s crew.

"I don't see any reason for me to give you a name, Captain Rice, but you know who I work for," he said cheerfully. "But let's lay our cards on the table, shall we?

"I am under contract to the Azure Legacy to deliver either you, dead or alive, or proof of your death, to an agent in a system I'm not going to tell you," he continued. "I won't pretend you're likely to survive live delivery, Captain, but I'll be up front with you:

"My contract is for *you* and you alone. Surrender peacefully and I will permit your crew to leave with your ship." The pirate shrugged. "I have six military vessels, Captain Rice. You have one half-armed freighter. Fight me and your crew dies.

"Are you not prepared to sacrifice yourself to spare others?"

The message ended and David swallowed a snarl.

"Iovis."

"Captain?"

"You may fire when ready."

They might have been ignoring most of *Red Falcon*'s attempts at communication, but the pirates didn't ignore it when Acconcio lit up the leader with directed radar. Alongside the weapons systems, the Navy had left behind the targeting scanners to aim them.

Even at fourteen light-seconds, there was no missing it when *those* beams pinged somebody's hull. *Falcon*'s computers easily resolved their target, ignoring his stealth plating, but the corvettes started real evasive maneuvers—in case the next stage was a massed laser strike.

"Holding lasers for now," the third officer said calmly. "First missile salvo away. Reloaders running...estimate fifty seconds to second salvo."

"Thank you."

The new icons joined *Falcon* and her attackers on the screen, ten tiny triangles with their own vector-dating zipping across space toward the pirates.

They were joined in turn by at least thirty triangles around the corvettes.

"They fired first, I take it?" David asked.

"Six seconds after the radar pulse hit them," Acconcio confirmed. "Thirty-two missiles in the mix: the *Antiochs* have six launchers apiece, the rest have five. Accelerating at twenty-two hundred gravities."

"Well, at least we're worth the good stuff," the Captain replied. "Jenna?"

"Missile defenses are tracking," she confirmed. "Estimate nine-minute flight time; RFLAMs will range at sixty seconds from impact, relative velocity at that point will be just over point oh three cee."

"You can handle them?" David asked.

"I've got twenty-five turrets to thirty-two missiles, and sixty seconds to shoot them down," Campbell said confidently. "First salvo is easy. Everything after that depends on their cycle time."

He nodded. He knew the math—better than Campbell did, if he was honest. Her only space combat experience was the trouble she'd got in with him. He'd been *trained* for this. Once. A long time ago.

Acconcio, though...

"Iovis?"

"Salvo running clean and true; second salvo launching...now," the gunner replied. "Seeing if I can herd them into a nice, neat box for the lasers."

"How out of our weight class are we?" David murmured to his third officer.

Acconcio smiled thinly, half-baring his teeth.

"You got the question the wrong way around, boss," he said. "They fucked up. *Hard.* This little squadron could have taken any of the disarmed AAFHFs, sure. But a fully equipped, fully armed Navy auxiliary?"

The screens started to light up as the anti-missile turrets lit up on both sides. All six pirate ships combined had fewer turrets than *Red*

Falcon did, and the turrets of six individual vessels didn't sync up as well as those aboard one ship.

Campbell shredded the pirates' entire first salvo, but the second was close on its heels. Only forty seconds passed between the two missile salvos, cutting her intercept time for each successive salvo.

The *pirates,* on the other hand, stopped only eight missiles. Two missiles hammered into the "ghost" corvette at just under ten thousand kilometers a second. Combined, the ship took the equivalent of twenty megatons of force and simply...came apart.

The other ships had moved to help intercept and evade, and *now* Acconcio unleashed the lasers. Ten five-gigawatt battle lasers, even more powerful than those mounted by Navy destroyers, opened fire. The white lines of the computer interpolation sliced across the screen in wide arcs, covering as much space as possible.

At this range, still over ten light-seconds, even the herding from the missiles couldn't guarantee hits. Luck was as big a factor as anything else—and two of the pirate ships were unlucky. Massive amounts of energy pulsed into their hulls, shattering hull plating and ripping through them like an ax through tissue paper.

With three of the six ships gone, the missiles dove in on the lead survivor, the other *Caribbean,* through a much-reduced defensive perimeter. David wasn't sure if they'd stopped *any* of the missiles at all, because there was nothing left of the corvette after *Falcon*'s fire had swept through.

"We could use—"

Red Falcon rang like a bell, the entire multi-million-ton mass of the ship lurching enough to be felt through the magical gravity runes, as part of the pirates' fourth salvo made it through. Even as the ship began to spin, Acconcio hammered a command on his systems again—and eight of *Falcon*'s battle lasers spoke as one.

Only three hit...but that was one more than the gunner had needed to wipe out the last pirate ships.

David swallowed.

"I was going to say we could use prisoners," he echoed, "but...fair enough, Iovis. LaMonte—get me a damage report! Campbell, keep us maneuvering and keep those turrets spinning—their motherships might be dead but those missiles are still dangerous! Let's not die *after* winning the fight, shall we?"

CHAPTER 24

"THE GOOD NEWS IS that Laser Six and Laser Nine are basically intact," Kellers explained later. "The bad news is that they're effectively no longer attached to the hull. The hit that disabled them went through the radiation cap and severed several key internal structural supports for those weapons."

"What about the cap itself?" David asked.

His engineer shook his head and gestured to LaMonte. The junior engineer tapped several commands, and the air above the conference room table was suddenly filled with a three-dimensional image of *Red Falcon*.

David had already seen the reports on his own systems and heard LaMonte's summary. It was still a shock to see the ship laid out in full, the damaged areas red spikes into the hull of his ship.

Shown like this, the hit that had taken out the two lasers was a clear, straight-through hole, entering the hull on the starboard side of the radiation dome and exiting on the port side—spilling a not-insignificant mass of water along the way.

The radiation dome held far more water than the ship's crew could ever actually use, since the material made a fantastic barrier to radiation, was required for the crew and many of the ship's systems *and* could, in an emergency, be converted into both fuel and air supplies.

"If I'm looking at this right," Campbell said in a slow, somewhat ill, voice, "it missed the habitat ring and the bridge tower by meters."

"It was twenty-three meters away from the bridge module," Kellers replied. "At its closest approach, it was three-point-two away from the gravity ring. The other hits aren't quite as severe-looking, but..."

The engineer shrugged.

"The good news is that the cargo is undamaged, though several containers are in rough shape," he concluded. "The bad news is that the main structural connection between the engine pod and the main portion of the ship is badly damaged. Between that, the engines, and the damage to the radiation cap, I can't recommend accelerating more than half a gravity or reaching a velocity above point oh one cee."

"That'll make for a long trip into Svarog, but we can do it," Campbell pointed out. "We'll be okay, then?"

There was a long pause.

"None of this is reparable out of onboard resources," the engineer said finally. "The structural damage is bad enough, but we're all ignoring the other elephant in the room."

David's gaze was drawn to the glaring red blotch at the rear of the ship where he should have had a fifth antimatter engine pod.

"If we'd been under heavier acceleration when that missile hit, we wouldn't have engines at all," Kellers noted. "We lost engine four. It's *gone*. The others are damaged but functional.

"We don't carry spare antimatter engines. Most star systems don't have them in stock. Unless we visit a Navy base, wherever we go is going to have to rebuild the thing from scratch."

"We'll do what we have to," David said grimly. "Fortunately, Svarog *should* have the facilities to do just that, and our insurance will cover it."

He shook his head.

"And the defenses?"

"We still have every damn laser turret," the engineer said. "For all the good they did us in the end."

"Three hits, James," David reminded him. "*Three*. They fired over three *hundred* missiles at us. I think the turrets did just fine by us."

"We got unlucky," Acconcio concluded. "We had them outclassed from the beginning, but with their velocity, they had no choice but to keep closing once they realized it."

"We're still here, we didn't lose any people, and everything is reparable," David said. "Our cargo is intact, and no one can be truly certain how heavily armed we are. We were lucky enough."

As the officers were leaving, David caught LaMonte's eye and gestured with his chin for the junior engineer to stay. She looked somewhat concerned but held back as everyone else filed out of the meeting room, and waited for David to speak.

Instead, he closed the door to the room and checked the security systems. The room had been built by the military, after all, and it had a quite impressive suite of anti-intrusion measures. Ones he'd never actually turned on before.

They were old enough that he didn't entirely trust their assessment that the room was clean and sealed, but it was all he was going to get.

"Grab a seat, Kelly," he told the currently green-haired LaMonte. "I need a favor."

"You're the Captain," she pointed out cautiously. "While you're *supposed* to go through my boss, I do work for you."

"You work for me as an engineer," David said. "I need a programmer, a security specialist, someone who knows our computers and communications inside and out." He grinned, a moment of amusement spiking through his dread.

"I *need*, Miss LaMonte, the reason why your schedule always lined up with Damien Montgomery's even before everyone knew you were sleeping together and made it happen intentionally," he concluded. "I know James secured his schedules at least half-decently, mostly because *he* knew he'd easily forget what he'd put in originally if anyone changed them."

The young woman flushed, then shook her head.

"I didn't think anyone had ever caught that," she admitted.

"James did," David told her. "Of course, around when he did that, you were busy saving our lives with some of the slickest programming work I've seen yet. How's your hacking, Miss LaMonte?"

"I'm...not certain this is a conversation I should be having without a lawyer, skipper," she said carefully.

"Kelly, the only thing I know you've ever hacked is a department schedule so you could make sure to lunch with your crush," he replied. "I don't think you have anything to worry about."

"It's just a hobby," she admitted. "Never been great, but I have a few tricks. But...what is this about, sir?"

David finally took a seat himself and took over the controls for the holoprojector in the middle of the room. The battered image of *Red Falcon* disappeared, replaced by a local astrographic chart.

"We are here," he told her unnecessarily, pointing at the green icon in the center of the chart. Their course back to New Madagascar was lit up in straight white lines, each exactly one light-year long in reality and four centimeters long in the display.

"We aren't on the jump line from New Madagascar to Legatus," he continued. "That would have put us here." A ghostly gray icon appeared on a direct continuation of the first white line on the hologram. "If we'd gone directly to Svarog, we'd have been here." A second ghostly icon.

"The pirates knew who we were. They knew where we were supposed to be going and where we were going...*and* they knew how we were planning on getting there," David concluded.

"You're here, Kelly, because I know you didn't know that last," he continued. "Even if you did, I trust you as much as I trust Jenna or James, and their computer knowledge is quite specialized."

"Someone sold us out." The young woman's voice was calm and level. She might be adorable, but in one memorable instance, Kelly LaMonte had been directly responsible for the destruction of a bounty hunter warship more powerful than any of the corvettes they'd fought today.

"Someone sold us out," he confirmed. "Someone that I am sadly quite certain is aboard this ship."

"We have a lot of new crew," she said.

"We do. A witch hunt would be disastrous for morale and the proper function of the ship," David agreed. "But. Someone sold us out. Either one of the handful of people who knew our planned course or someone who stole that information from the Mages' computers.

"I need you to find out who, Kelly," he told her. "The only other people on the ship with the right skillset are in the security detail...and they're *all* new."

"And Marines," she reminded him. "They're probably okay."

"Ex-Marines," he said. "And while they all served their terms, we don't know *why* they didn't re-up."

The young woman smiled enigmatically and nodded.

"I'll trust Marines over most spacers," she admitted. "That said, there isn't anyone on this ship I wouldn't trust."

"Twenty-four hours ago, I would have sworn this crew was solid gold," David said sadly. "Now, I know at least one of them set me up. Do you think you can find out who?"

"I don't know," LaMonte warned him. "I'm a talented amateur at best, and odds are whoever sold us out did it sneakily. It might take some time."

"It'll take what it takes," he told her. "I'll make sure James knows what's going on. If you need any help, he can back you up."

"And if I find out who?"

"Tell me," David ordered. "No one else. Not until I know and can make plans."

Best-case scenario, it was one of his new crewmembers. Worst-case scenario, it was one of the Mages or senior officers.

Absolute worst-case scenario...it was Soprano.

"Go rest," Maria told her Mages, her three younger subordinates clustered around her, hoping she had some answers after the meeting with the senior crew.

"But..." Costa objected.

"We're going to take some time to let everyone breathe and for engineering to see if they can patch up the worst of the holes in the engines," she told them. "We won't need to jump until they're done, but we'll want to be ready when they are.

"So, go rest," she ordered.

With various degrees of obedience, Costa, Wu and Anders all drifted out of the workshop slash office of the Mages' main working area. Maria waited calmly until the last of her subordinates had left and the door had closed behind them.

"*FUCK.*"

Her shouted curse word echoed through the confined space, and she crossed to a small section of the compartment where they'd set up a target dummy in front of an armored chunk of wall. Mage combat practice was dangerous, and she took a moment to charge the runes that created a shield around the practice area.

Then she channeled her frustration, conjuring flickering orbs of lighting and fire that smashed into and over the dummy. Fists and feet followed, a flurry of Navy hand-to-hand training and combat magic that the dummy was *supposed* to be able to survive.

It lasted about forty seconds before a particularly vicious strike of fire shattered its protective and grounding runes. The matrix that sustained it interrupted, the dummy came apart under her assault almost instantly.

"Fuck," she repeated, her voice strained with exhaustion now.

They should have stopped the damned missiles. *She* should have stopped those last missiles—but the RFLAMs had been completely effective until that salvo. She'd had a moment of overconfidence...and *Red Falcon* had been nearly crippled by her mistake.

Worse, she'd been the one to craft their course. Their far-too-straightforward-once-anyone-knew-exactly-what-their-plan-was course.

No short jumps. No diversions other than the obvious one. One jump toward Legatus, and then divert to Svarog. It should have been enough, but if someone had sold the Legacy their *true* destination, easy enough to predict.

No one had died, but that wasn't because of *Maria*. That had been pure luck.

She'd failed her crew. Failed her promise to Alois. Almost lost them all.

It was starting to become a pattern, and it wasn't one Maria liked.

At least Rice wasn't likely to fire her the moment they reached Svarog. He seemed a decent-enough Captain, he'd probably let her screw up twice before he kicked her to the curb.

Maria sighed and moved back over to the workshop office's computers. They were *probably* safe now, with their hunters destroyed, but working a few short jumps into the rest of their trip would help keep them that way.

And while she might have screwed up once, she was *not* going to let another crew suffer for her mistakes.

CHAPTER 25

EVERYONE WAS AWAKE and on edge when *Red Falcon* finally jumped into Svarog, two days later than planned and in far worse shape than hoped. The big freighter drifted slowly through the outer system for several minutes as David waited patiently for Kellers to talk to him.

"We should be good," the engineer finally told him. "Half a gravity; don't take us over one percent of lightspeed, like I said. I can't get us any better than that until we can fix the structural damage."

"And the engines?" David asked.

"The ones we have left are as solid as I can make them, but I'd still rather have a proper shipyard go over them."

"Well, you're in luck," *Falcon*'s Captain replied, studying the screens showing Svarog. "Unless I'm misreading this, there are two decent-sized yards in orbit of Dazbog. They should be able to fix us up."

"I'm looking forward to it. Any chance of us not getting shot at here?" David grimaced.

"Given our current luck, I'm not taking bets," he admitted.

"Wonderful. I'll let my people know to be careful."

"Thanks, James."

The engineer shook his head and cut the channel.

David continued to look over the system. Humanity's expansion had generally been undertaken with an eye to preserving the environmental stability of the worlds they moved onto. Repairing Earth and protecting its teeming billions from the legacy of a thousand years of industrialization remained a work in progress—and the Protectorate hadn't wanted to go through that again.

Dazbog, Svarog's habitable planet, was an example of why that thought had been required. Colonized by one of Sol's industrial cartels as a source of raw materials, they had demonstrated just what modern technology could do to a virgin world if unchecked.

The planet's ecosystem had been minimal, mostly bacteria and simple plant life. Enough to support a breathable atmosphere and a small animal kingdom, but nothing that the strip miners had felt guilty over when they'd moved in.

Some of the strip mines were visible from orbit. What was visible even from there, a full week's flight out at *Falcon*'s reduced pace, was the change in the atmosphere. Still, technically, breathable, the spectrographic analysis *Falcon*'s scanners pulled together told a hazardous story, one of trace toxins and dangerous gasses.

Dozens of asteroids had been pulled into orbit as well, and the planet's surface apparently bore the scars of the "mistakes" from that process—the final straw that had broken the camel's back and triggered a violent revolution from the masses of indentured workers.

The Protectorate had returned self-rule to the system in only the last five years, and while the Mage-King's hand had been gentler than the cartel's, the massive industrialization project had continued. Svarog's asteroid belts were being dismantled and moved to the refineries more carefully now, but the process of feeding those raw materials into the refineries and factories that swarmed above the planet continued.

What *had* changed was that the Mage-King had banned any new mining or factories on the surface. The new elected government had reaffirmed that commitment: they were already going to have to functionally terraform the once-habitable world to be safe for most humans again, but they were trying not to make it *worse*.

Svarog would never be a rich MidWorld system. The vast industrial base they commanded was enough to allow them to have many things other MidWorld's couldn't...but so much of the wealth and resources that industry would otherwise have given them was being plowed back into rebuilding their planet so they'd have someplace to live that didn't require space station–level atmosphere systems.

"Any word from Svarog Control yet?" he asked Campbell.

"Nothing so far," she replied. "I've got a few local destroyers and a three-ship Navy picket on the scanners, but no one is saying hi yet."

"Let me know once they do," he told her. "I don't think we're going to need help getting in, but I *know* insurance is going to blow a lid over this." He shook his head. "We'll want to get started on that sooner rather than later!"

Maria waited until Iovis had gone to sleep before slipping out of his quarters and returning to her own. She was spending the night as often as not these days, but she also had work to do—and *not* the job she held aboard *Red Falcon*.

Locked away in her quarters, she ran through the events of the previous several trips as quickly and methodically as she could. Svarog had a Runic Transceiver Array, installed during the period of direct rule to allow the Mage-King to keep up with affairs in the system he'd been forced to take over.

Today, it would allow the local MISS office to relay her report back to authorities on Mars—so long as it was kept very short and sweet. A Runic Transceiver Array could transmit the voice of a Mage standing in the middle of it to another RTA in another star system...but that was it. No artificially created sounds. No datastreams. Just one voice at a time.

So, while she was attaching chunks of sensor data and as much information as she could to the file, the front section of the report was an executive summary that could only be a few minutes long.

"Captain Rice has definitely attracted the attention of the elements MISS expected him to find," she began. "*Red Falcon* was chased and intercepted by what appear to be forces of an organization called Azure Legacy. We were engaged by six corvettes, but the weapon systems left intact aboard *Falcon* were sufficient to carry the day.

"We have also interacted with Legatan agents, who hired us to transport raw material to Svarog while keeping its actual destination secret. Those agents also provided Captain Rice with a contact among organized crime here in Svarog.

"We will be in-system for some time for repairs. I do not know if Captain Rice intends to make contact with the individual the Conroys provided us or not, but I may need to know what resources are available to us to make certain that *Red Falcon* survives being bait."

She shook her head into the camera.

"We promised Captain Rice his safety. If we are to keep that promise, I need more than just myself to turn the tide."

Maria Soprano might have agreed to betray David Rice's trust and keep the Protectorate informed of his movements and activities, but she had every intention of extracting a very specific price for that information.

If *Red Falcon* was going to be bait for the Protectorate's enemies, then the Protectorate needed to provide the rest of the trap.

"Captain, do you have a minute?"

David looked up from the message he was composing to Keiko—to go out through the RTA once they docked—to find Kelly LaMonte standing in the door to his office.

"The door is open, Kelly," he pointed out. If he needed to work in privacy, he'd close the door—though he tried to be available to all of his people. Given what he'd asked LaMonte to do, he'd have time for her even then.

She nodded in response to his comment—and then closed the door behind her as she stepped in and took a seat.

"I've been looking into our coms," she said without preamble. "And, well...we have a problem."

He sighed. While he had hoped that LaMonte would turn up a blank or something pointing back off the ship for evidence, he hadn't really expected it.

"We knew that," he confessed.

"No, you didn't," LaMonte said flatly. "You thought we had *a* spy."

It took him a moment to process just what she meant, and then he sighed again and laid his hands on the table, studying the young, currently green-haired engineer.

"How bad?" he asked.

"I'm still trying to dig into who might have sent data packets off the ship while we were in New Madagascar," she said. "We didn't have anything in place to actively track communications, so it's a longer, more manual process. But..."

"But?"

"Kellers and I had a chat after you and I spoke," she told him. "We figured the most likely method of someone trying to sneak data off the ship right now would be to add it to our encrypted post box."

David nodded.

His ship had a set of databanks that no one aboard was supposed to have any access to. They linked up with the Royal Post Office in each system, which downloaded and uploaded the vast amount of data, mail, financial information, etc., required to run an interstellar society.

Those databanks were heavily secured and encrypted, though he'd had the non-financial portions opened up a few times in the past. Adding something to them, though, would have been much easier than taking something out—and since *Red Falcon* had automatically transmitted their contents in response to a request from the RPO barely two hours after arriving in the system...

"So, you tracked additions?"

"We set up a program to track every change and batch of changes to the encrypted databank," LaMonte confirmed. "We couldn't access them, and the databanks wiped themselves once the local PO had confirmed receipt and the checksums, but we know how *many* additions were made."

David nodded his understanding of the spiel. "And?"

"Four," she said quietly. "Four separate additions, presumably going to four separate destinations from four separate people. This ship is a goddamn mole hill, Captain. Some of those are probably...benign, but..."

"Define 'benign'," David asked. "Because people on my ship who are selling my information to others make me twitchy."

LaMonte sighed.

"Some of the security troopers aren't as good at keeping their mouths shut around a pretty girl as they probably should be," she said dryly. "And at least one was trying to talk Wu and I into his bunk and *really* didn't keep secrets well.

"At least *some*—though I'm not sure how many!—of our security troops aren't *ex*-Marines at all," LaMonte admitted. "We've got at least a squad, and I wouldn't be surprised at the entire platoon, of active-duty Royal Martian Marines aboard."

David put his face in his hands and exhaled sharply. He'd suspected *Skavar* might be more linked to his old employer than he'd thought, but an entire RMMC *platoon* aboard ship?

No wonder they'd had no problems acquiring exosuit battle armor and heavy weapons normally restricted to the military. They'd probably just been issued straight from the Corps' quartermasters!

But...as LaMonte said, having secret Marines aboard was probably benign. The *other* three messages, though...

"Any way to see what they were sending out?" he asked.

"Not easily," she confessed. "James had some thoughts; he's working on them, but he figured he'd keep all of the chatter on this down-low through me. Anyone asks, I'm telling them you're mentoring me for my Mate's certificate."

David chuckled.

"That'll work," he agreed. "Want me to?"

Technically, all of his senior officers were supposed to have Mate's certificates except Soprano—her Jump Mage training was regarded as equivalent. In practice, that was waived in the case of ex-Navy people like Acconcio or long-serving people aboard a given ship, but for LaMonte to move into a chief engineer or other officer role on another ship, she'd need the certificate.

"Kellers is giving me most of the help I need," she told him, though a wicked grin grew over her face as she spoke. "But I do have some questions that would be better asked of a Captain..."

CHAPTER 26

"RED FALCON, this is Mage-Commander Guerra commanding *Dance of Rising Freedom*," the man on David's screen said calmly. He was fair-haired but dark-skinned, though not dark enough to blend into the black uniform of the Royal Martian Navy.

His destroyer was now barely a million kilometers from *Red Falcon*, allowing for a semi-reasonable conversation despite the lightspeed lag.

"We're pleased to see you, Mage-Commander," David told Guerra. "We probably don't need the escort in, but I am not turning it down."

Guerra nodded.

"Neither I nor Commodore Andrews thought you would," he said. "I've reviewed your reports and will be taking close scans of your vessel to validate your damage assessment. That should help with your insurance."

"I appreciate it," David said. "I've had my run-ins with my insurers before. I'm surprised they were willing to insure *Red Falcon* at all!"

"The fact that she's almost as well-armed as my destroyer probably had something to do with it," Guerra said with another chuckle. "If you'll permit it, I'd like to have a team of my engineers come over and go over *Falcon*'s weapon systems. While I'm sure that your people are well trained, my people are specialists in exactly those systems."

"I would appreciate that," the merchant captain replied. "Though a good chunk of my engineering people *were* Navy personnel first. They have experience with weapons."

"Of course," Guerra agreed instantly. "I also must admit to some degree of responsibility with regards to the planet." He coughed delicately. "The Svarog system government has...*requested* that we verify the safeties and containment fields on your antimatter missiles and drives before you approach Dazbog orbit."

Given the writ David carried, he didn't actually have to comply. On the other hand, Svarog didn't actually have to let him in their system. And given that he was carrying a hundred one-gigaton antimatter warheads—*plus* enough fuel to multiply that explosion tenfold—it was a reasonable request.

"Of course, Mage-Commander," he echoed. "I understand their concerns, and while I am quite confident in the stability of my systems, it's a reasonable request—especially given our damage. And like your escort, Mage-Commander Guerra, I'm not going to turn down a second set of expert eyes on my antimatter stockpiles!"

Guerra nodded once more.

"I appreciate your cooperation, Captain Rice," he told David. "His Majesty's Navy will do everything in our power to return that cooperation while you are in the Svarog system. May I invite you and your Ship's Mage to join me for dinner aboard *Dance*?

"From your reports, it's going to be a long flight home."

Maria was half-amused and half-terrified by the fact that no one except her seemed to think that having her aboard a Navy destroyer was a bad idea.

Kelzin was a good pilot and the ride over was as smooth as any she'd ever experienced, the small personnel shuttle from *Red Falcon* passing by a dozen transport shuttles from *Dance of Rising Freedom* carrying maintenance techs and engineers to go over the big freighter's guns.

Approaching the destroyer, it was all she could not to automatically stiffen her spine to attention. *Dance* was a white square-based pyramid, exactly one hundred meters on a side and massing just over one million tons. For all that she was tiny compared to *Red Falcon*, she carried twice as many missile launchers, half again as many defensive lasers and over twice as many heavy battle lasers.

The whole process had a strained familiarity to it. She wasn't approaching this destroyer as a member of its Navy, arriving as one of the senior officers aboard or as a visiting senior officer from a similar ship.

Today, she would be an outsider aboard *Dance*, not part of the extended family. It was a strange feeling.

"You'll be fine," Rice murmured from beside her, and she glanced over at him in surprise. "The first time I was invited aboard a Navy ship as a civilian was weird," he continued, "and I was only a Petty Officer—and I mustered out voluntarily.

"So, it'll be weird. It'll be awkward. And you'll be fine."

She exhaled heavily but nodded.

"Okay, boss," she told him. "I'm going to hold you to that. There will be consequences if you're wrong."

Her joking threat brought the intended chuckle from him, and she found herself relaxing slightly as Kelzin swept the shuttle into *Dance of Rising Freedom*'s shuttle bay. Thrusters flared as she settled onto the floor, the magic of the warship's gravity runes reaching out to grab the shuttle and claim her.

"Come on, Maria," Rice said. "Let's go."

Guerra met them himself, waiting behind the shuttle bay safety shields until the air around the shuttle had cooled and then crossing the bay floor to greet them as they exited the spacecraft.

"Welcome aboard *Dance of Rising Freedom*, Captain Rice, Mage Soprano," he told them. "My XO is currently aboard your ship, so it will just be the three of us for dinner tonight. If you'll come with me?"

Dance of Rising Freedom was a newer ship than *Swords at Dawn* had been, but the bones of the layout were the same. Maria knew within a minute of leaving the shuttle bay that the Mage-Commander was leading them to the Captain's quarters and his personal dining room.

A space that, among its other virtues, was also one of the most secure meeting rooms aboard the warship.

She let the two captains carry the conversation, quickly realizing that neither of them was attempting to make it serious. Like her, Rice was ex-Navy, but he didn't bring that up chatting with Guerra.

Once they finally reached the Mage-Commander's dining room, however, Guerra quickly locked down the security features.

"My steward will be serving us shortly," he assured them, "but we needed a few private moments. I have all of your reports and filings for insurance with regards to the incident, but I am aware of realities, Captain, Mage.

"What *didn't* make it into the reports?" he asked flatly.

Maria exchanged glances with Rice. She'd already told the Martian Interstellar Security Service everything that Guerra might be asking about, but her Captain didn't know that. She wasn't sure what level of secrets he was planning on keeping from the Navy.

"Not all of that is...information I am privy to disclose," Rice finally said slowly. "What I can tell you that I can't tell my insurance is that we knew we were being hunted. A surviving portion of the Blue Star Syndicate has marked me for death for my involvement in Mikhail Azure's death, and they seem *quite* determined to carry through on the threat."

"Damn," Guerra said mildly. "We've warned our superiors that the Blue Star Syndicate isn't as dead in this sector as any of us would like. New names, new leaders, but the entire Syndicate apparatus in Svarog and several surrounding systems survived intact.

"Between the Navy and local authorities, we've convinced them to keep their heads down so far, but the Commodore and I are nervous about just what resources they may have access to."

"How bad are we talking here?" Maria asked. "Blue Star wasn't that powerful, was it?"

"It was the Protectorate's largest crime syndicate," Rice said quietly. "I killed the son of their leader, so he came after us. It didn't end well for him, but an organization that big…"

"Exactly," Guerra confirmed. "The biggest issue *here* is that half a dozen destroyers under contract to Grand Interstellar Foundry went missing when the Protectorate took control of Svarog. They'd be obsolete now, unless they were kept up to date, but we've only ever accounted for one of them."

Maria grimaced. "Accounted for" in this context could only mean that the ship in question had been destroyed in combat with Protectorate or militia forces.

"Our best guess is that they ended up co-opted into pirate organizations and that at least some of them ended up in Blue Star Syndicate hands," he continued. "And we are quite certain that those assets passed on to the new leader of the successor organization here.

"They may be keeping their hands clean as piracy goes so far, but they have the tools for it. Every ship passing through is being warned of the danger. It's less…immediately applicable to you, but you still wouldn't be entirely safe if they jumped you with those destroyers."

"I appreciate the warning," Rice said quietly. "Especially since it seems like Mikhail Azure's heirs specifically have it out for me."

Guerra smiled grimly.

"The reports I've seen of his death are so redacted, they're hard to read," he said. "I have enough to know that it wasn't just you who killed him, Captain Rice, but I doubt the Syndicate has that much information."

"Well, the 'good' news is that I'm going to be hanging out inside your defense envelope for a few weeks while we patch up the *Falcon*. I trust His Majesty's Navy to keep us safe."

Maria said nothing. They knew Turquoise, the woman who ran the very organization Guerra was concerned about, was headquartered there. They also knew the Legacy was hunting the weaker successor factions almost as hard as they were hunting David Rice.

She doubted Dazbog's orbital yards were going to be any safer for them than the rest of the Protectorate.

CHAPTER 27

"THIS IS FOUNDRY YARD ALPHA," a trained contralto voice purred over the voice channel. "We've received your list of damages, and it appears we do have a yard large enough for your vessel, Captain Rice."

The speaker coughed delicately.

"One yard," she emphasized. "You're in luck, as it just came available. We're transmitting you a course to Slip Alpha-Six." She paused. "There is a base charge for the use of the yard that needs to be paid on arrival. Have you sorted affairs out with insurance?"

"I have spoken to my insurers," David told her. Of course, the people he'd spoken to didn't actually work for his Mars-based insurance company. That entity had offices in fifteen systems, but it couldn't be everywhere. They had deals with local insurers in systems like Svarog to handle their affairs.

"While I don't expect to have any problems," he continued, "I'll pay the docking fee up front myself." He studied the chaotic swarm of struts, ships, and EVA suits that made up Foundry Yard Alpha and smiled.

"Would Foundry Alpha prefer to provide a tug?" he asked. "*Falcon* is a very large vessel, and our primary engines are antimatter rockets."

There was a pregnant pause.

"There is normally a fee for that," the controller purred, "but given the circumstances and, as you said, the size of your vessel, we will waive it in this instance. Please proceed to the entry coordinates you were given; a tug will meet you there."

The channel cut off and David glanced over at Campbell.

"You heard the lady," he told his XO. "Take us over to the entry point and let's wait for the tug."

Campbell shook her head.

"That woman's voice is practically a deadly weapon," she observed. "Do you figure they've got a man with just as trained a voice for the female Captains?"

"Probably," he agreed. "And they probably try and dig up any given Captain's preferences before they chat with them—though that is assuming that she's actually a *person* and not a voice-changing program they run whoever's on duty through.

"You'll note she didn't give us a name, after all."

"I also noted that she is *very* aware of just how much money these repairs are going to make them," Campbell replied dryly. "I checked. Bastion Yards—what *used* to be Foundry Yard Bravo and changed the name after being sliced off—has a slip that can fit us, but doesn't have the expertise for an antimatter-engine rebuild.

"They're the only ones who can do the work and they know it."

"I wonder if our friend over there was actually done or if they kicked her out for us?" David asked, highlighting a ship moving out of Slip Alpha-Six. Like *Red Falcon*, she was a big ship. One of the rare jump-capable asteroid miners, often used as anchors for a hundred smaller sublight ships in systems without an inhabited planet.

"I'd guess she's a more regular customer, so she was probably done," Campbell said. "*I* certainly wouldn't want to piss off, what, thirty thousand grumpy asteroid miners? Not for a one-shot windfall, anyway."

David shook his head.

"Neither would I, though that's no guarantee. Can you handle the docking?"

"I'm going to sit here until they attach a ship with one crew member and a million ion thrusters to *Falcon*'s ass and then watch as they shove us into place," his XO replied. "I don't need to do anything. Best kind of docking."

She grinned at him.

"Yeah, I got it under control."

"Good. I need to go call the client and let them know which repair yard they need to pick their cargo up from."

"Bruno, Boots and MacDonald Materials Imports, Margaret Hall speaking," a cheerful white-haired woman on David's office screen boomed out at him. "How may I direct your call?"

"Good morning, Ms. Hall," he greeted her. "I am Captain Rice of the freighter *Red Falcon*. I have a cargo delivery for your company out of New Madagascar. I believe I spoke with Mr. Boots earlier this week?"

Hall took a moment to respond, clearly running through files on a hidden screen in front of her.

"That's correct, Captain Rice," she confirmed. "I have a note here that you were heading into the yards to repair damages but didn't know the slip number yet?"

"Exactly," he said. "Is Mr. Boots available, or should I just give you the information?"

"Mr. Boots is currently off-station, but Mrs. MacDonald is available," Hall told him. "All of the partners keep up with our major affairs like starship shipments. Should I put you through?"

"Of course. Thank you."

Mrs. Charity MacDonald was a heavyset woman, blockily built with sunken eyes that seemed to glare at a spot about eleven centimeters above David's right shoulder.

She coughed indelicately, clearing her throat into a tissue before speaking.

"Captain Rice," she said calmly, her voice rough. David revised his estimate of her age up another ten years. She did not sound well. "How may I assist you?"

"Mrs. MacDonald," he replied politely. "*Red Falcon* is currently on our way to a repair slip at Foundry Yard Alpha. Mr. Boots informed me that you would need to know which slip we ended up in to make arrangements to retrieve our cargo."

She grunted and considered him in silence, her gaze still centered over his shoulder.

"There's only one slip at Alpha that can fit an AAFHF," she observed eventually. "And Alpha are the ones who do the Navy repairs when needed. They're the only ones who can fix up your antimatter drives.

"That means, Captain, that you were only ever going to be at Foundry Yard Alpha's Slip Alpha-Six," she concluded. "Given Wu Tang's notorious lack of tact, I suspect I will have to speak to Executive Kha and soothe troubled feathers."

"Ma'am?" David asked questioningly.

MacDonald laughed, then choked and coughed into another tissue.

"Executive Erikas Kha owns and runs *Big Rock*, the ship that Yardmaster Wu Tang will have displaced to host you," she told him. "*Big Rock* was in for regular maintenance, the kind that doesn't need a yard but is easier in it.

"Shuffling him out will cost him at least two days on his repairs, and with thirty thousand unemployed miners waiting for *Big Rock* to haul them back to the Corvid system...only the greatest of tact could have kept Kha happy.

"And Wu Tang doesn't have that."

"I see, Mrs. MacDonald," David said carefully. That didn't sound like *his* problem, thankfully, unless some of those miners decided to take the delay out on his crew.

"I will speak to Wu Tang as well," she continued, half-ignoring his response. "We will have shuttles moving in to remove your cargo by tomorrow morning. Was there any damage to it in your troubles?"

"Several of the containers are damaged, but our scans show that the cargo is intact," he replied. "There was no radioactive leakage or anything of the sort."

"Good, good. I or one of my partners will be in touch about the loading. Good luck with your insurance and repairs, Captain Rice."

Before David could say anything in response, the channel cut off. MacDonald, it seemed, didn't spare much time for pleasantries.

So long as he got paid, David could live with that.

CHAPTER 28

FOUNDRY YARD ALPHA was centered on one of the Protectorate's near-ubiquitous spinning-ring stations. This one was wrapped around a central spire that protruded roughly two kilometers out from either side of the ring, serving as an anchor point for the collections of gantries and machine-shop pods that made up the working slips.

While it was theoretically possible to access the spire from *Red Falcon*'s dock and travel to the ring station and its amenities without ever going into vacuum, Maria and Acconcio rode aboard a personnel shuttle carrying the first liberty group.

Somehow, once Maria realized that the pilot was Kelzin, she wasn't surprised to find both Xi Wu and Kelly LaMonte aboard the shuttle. There were about twenty members of *Falcon*'s crew on the shuttle all told, and including the three youths, a quarter of the group were officers.

Wu and LaMonte spent the first half of the flight holding hands in the passenger compartment before disappearing into the cockpit, causing Maria to chuckle to herself.

"What?" Acconcio asked.

"From my own experience, you *can* fit three in the cockpit of one of these shuttles," she observed. "But it's a...*cozy* experience."

The big ex-warrant officer glanced at the closed door leading to the cockpit, then chuckled himself.

"I see," he noted. "As a passenger, I have to hope there isn't enough space in there to get *more* than cozy."

"Even if there was"—and, in Maria's own experiments in the area when she'd been LaMonte's age, there most definitely wasn't—"Kelzin is too damned good a pilot to let them distract him—and those two are too damned sensible to try."

"Ah, to be young and in love," Acconcio mused—and then snuck his hand across to take Maria's.

She returned his smile, then paused as her com vibrated.

"Give me a moment, hon," she told her lover, checking the text message.

We need to meet in person. Green Parson's Bar, FYA Central Level 6. 2200 OMT.

She sighed. She *had* been planning on dragging the burly gentleman holding her hand back to a hotel room after dinner, but...if MISS wanted her to meet with them, it was probably important.

"Work calls," she said softly. "Some ship's business I'll need to deal with after dinner."

"Want company?" he asked brightly, but she shook her head.

"Mage affairs," Maria told him gently. "They'll only meet with me."

Green Parson's Bar was in a much nicer location than Maria had been expecting. She'd headed to Level 6 after dinner with Acconcio, expecting to end up back in the same kind of dive bar she'd been recruited in.

Instead, she discovered that the section of Level 6 the bar was in was a subdued semi-residential section. The type of station section with double-wide corridors and carefully manicured trees in the thoroughfares.

The bar was designed in a "neighborhood pub" style, with an open patio surrounded by a handful of real trees for both atmosphere and privacy, and a set-back "indoor" area with faux wooden paneling on the wall. There were probably nicer bars on Central, but not many.

Despite the casual atmosphere, it was clearly not a "seat yourself" location, and she approached the front desk, where a pair of young women in matching jeans and dark blue T-shirts, clearly a uniform, were waiting.

"My name is Maria Soprano," she told them. "I'm meeting someone here; I'm guessing there's a reservation?"

They checked and the right-hand girl nodded.

"Of course, Mage Soprano," she said after a quick glance at the medallion at Maria's throat. "If you'll follow me, please?"

Maria nodded and followed the waitress into the "indoor" portion of the restaurant. *Through* the restaurant, in fact, as the girl led her to a side door and into a private room.

"Ms. Choi, your guest is here," she announced as she led Maria in. "Your server will be with you shortly."

The waitress paused.

"She'll knock before entering," she added before disappearing back out the door and closing it behind Maria.

The woman waiting at the table was a tall and elegant woman with shadowy skin and a pronounced fold to her eyes. Not, Maria noted absently, the ethnic mix of the Martian-born and Mages, but the coloring of a purer extract from Old Earth's Asian regions.

"Ms. Soprano, please, sit," the woman told her. She wore a long, tight sheath dress that drew attention to her legs and athleticism.

Maria was all too familiar with using sexuality as a weapon and could recognize a fellow mistress of the art at this range.

"Ms. Choi," she returned the greeting as she took the seat. "You'll forgive me bluntness but, given the circumstances around my ship I need to be clear. Who do you work for?"

Choi laughed.

"I am System Coordinator Bluma Choi of the Martian Interstellar Security Agency," she replied brightly, slipping an ID hologram out of her cleavage and onto the table. It flashed to light for a moment, showing a three-dimensional image of the woman along with the rank and name she'd given.

The microprojector vanished back into Choi's cleavage, and the agent smiled at Maria.

"I am responsible for all MISS operations in the Svarog system," she noted. "I find Foundry Yard Alpha Central to be a convenient base of communications—the main MISS office is on the surface, but I and my senior analytical team are up here.

"Where no one looks for us," she finished with a grin.

"I wouldn't have expected to find the system coordinator up here, I'll admit," Maria agreed. "You wanted to meet with me?"

"I did. I reviewed your report and forwarded the summary on via the RTA," Choi confirmed. "It took you long enough to get into the station that we actually managed to get a response—and Hand Stealey was no-where near Mars."

"Wait. *Hand Stealey?*" Maria demanded.

"Yes. Hand of the Mage-King Alaura Stealey appears to have taken a personal interest in your ship, and she sent a message via the RTA for you, specifically," the MISS agent confirmed. "Before we continue this discussion, you need to hear it."

There was a knock on the door, and Choi smiled.

"While I suspect you've already eaten, we can also get drinks while we're here. Green Parson's has an excellent bar."

Once the waitress had returned with their drinks order and they were relatively certain of a stretch of uninterrupted time, Choi tapped a few commands into the comp on her wrist.

"This message is for Mage Maria Soprano aboard *Red Falcon*," the voice of an unfamiliar woman said into thin air. "It is to be relayed through the MISS local office under security protocol six."

Maria wasn't familiar with the security protocols of the Mage Guild's Transceiver Mages. She only knew that they were sworn to a level of secrecy and confidentiality that lawyers and accountants only aspired to.

Every message that came into an RTA was recorded, categorized and classified before being distributed. It was theoretically possible to have a block of unrecorded time for a direct conversation, but that required both parties to be Mages and a lot of either money or authority.

There was a pause, enough to allow the routing information to be collected without requiring the transceiver Mages to listen to the entire message, and then the speaker continued.

"This is Alaura Stealey, Hand of the Mage-King of Mars. Mage Soprano, you are not aware of my involvement, but I have made *Red Falcon* and her crew something of a personal project. I owe—the *Protectorate* owes—Captain Rice a greater debt than he realizes.

"It was as partial payment of that debt that he received *Red Falcon* and that you were encouraged to take service aboard his ship.

"We also, however, expected him to attract the exact attention he has attracted," Stealey noted grimly. "I'll admit, however, that the scale of the operation that appears to have been deployed against Captain Rice surprised me. I suppose we should have expected Azure to be the vindictive type and anticipated such an action, but this Azure Legacy is a new type of threat for us.

"We do not wish them to succeed in *either* of their stated objectives. While many of the Blue Star successor organizations are dangerous in their own right, even the aggregate of their efforts is a far lesser threat to humanity than the Syndicate itself was.

"I have no choice, Mage Soprano. You *must* convince Captain Rice to continue on the course these Legatans have set him on. You must make contact with the individual they sent you to and see what you can drag out of the shadows."

That was a big ask. A potentially suicidal one, in Maria's opinion. But...the Hand might well be right. Rice might well be the only wedge they had to break open the entire Legacy and, through it, keep the Blue Star Syndicate from re-forming.

"I am not prepared to lose Captain Rice in this pursuit, however," Stealey noted. "Nor am I prepared to lose you or his ship. These are *your* instructions. Director Choi has received instructions of her own through regular channels.

"More importantly, Commodore Andrews has also received instructions through...less regular channels. His resources are not what I might prefer them to be in this situation, but anything he can put at your disposal, he will."

The Hand paused.

"I am also making arrangements for the Commodore to be reinforced and..." She sighed. "I am *attempting* to get myself out there. Sadly, I don't expect to be free of my current affairs until this situation is resolved.

"So, I have no choice but to leave it in your and Captain Rice's capable hands. Commodore Andrews and Director Choi will support you, but you and Rice are at the center of it all."

Maria was staring at the comp on Choi's wrist in horror.

"This Legacy is an active danger to the safety of the Protectorate, Mage Soprano. We need you to stop them."

The small private dining room was silent for a while, Maria considering the bombshell that had just been dropped on her from every angle she could fit into her mind. The mission she'd been dragged into had a *Hand* at the core of it?

"So, what do we do?" she finally asked Choi.

"From what the Hand said, you need to talk Rice into meeting with this Turquoise, which I leave entirely up to you," the MISS director told her. "For my own purposes, I'd like you to get me every piece of information you can on who and where *Falcon*'s cargo is being delivered to.

"If there's a Legatan covert op running through my region of authority, I want to track it down."

"That's fair," Maria agreed. "I don't know how much danger a giant pile of raw materials can be, but the fact that they're trying to move it around without our knowing about it is a warning sign all on its own."

"I agree completely," Choi said. "Those materials can be turned into a lot of things, Mage Soprano. And the factories and foundries of Svarog would be a good place to turn them into things without being noticed.

"There's very little they can't make here, but there's less attention on the MidWorlds than on the Core. Or, perhaps more important for this question, there is much less attention on Svarog than on Legatus. Svarog isn't even an UnArcana world."

"We're delivering to a specific factor, but they're just a middleman," Maria warned her. "Bruno, Boots and MacDonald."

"I'm familiar with them," Choi confirmed. "And you're right. They're a middleman, nothing more. One renowned for their discretion and confidentiality. We could get answers from them with a warrant, but I'd need more support to get a warrant out of local authorities."

"What do you need?" Maria asked.

"I need to know where that cargo ends up, Mage Soprano. We'll do our best to follow it, but there are ways to make it easier."

Maria sighed.

"I'm presuming that you *have* trackers I can plant in the containers?" she asked dryly.

"I have several varieties, including some that are stealthy enough that I don't think the Legatans will ever know they were there," Choi said with a smile. "We'll have a case delivered to you in the morning. Will you need assistance?"

"I was a Navy Mage, Director Choi," Maria replied. "I'm relatively sure I can float some trackers into the cargo containers without help."

"Of course. I appreciate your assistance, Mage Soprano."

"Last time I checked, we work for the same boss," Maria said. "I'm not even really sure how my chain of command through MISS works, but I took the job. We'll find them, Director."

"I know we will," Choi confirmed. "And we'll keep Captain Rice safe. A few of my people have already started watching his movements. If something like the bullshit on New Madagascar goes down, he'll have backup fast.

"I promise you that!"

Maria finished her drink and stepped out into the restaurant, only casually surveying the space as she exited. She'd made it out the door before the familiarity of one of the faces at the bar struck home, and sheer surprise propelled her the rest of the way.

A moment of panic familiar to any woman on any planet followed, and she quickly moved out of sight from the open patio, stepping into a coffee shop on the corner of several corridors a good fifty meters away while she looked back.

"Can I help you, ma'am?" the woman behind the counter asked.

"No, I'm fine," Maria replied, looking back to see if she could catch another glimpse of Iovis Acconcio.

It was possible she'd made a mistake and it had been some other heavyset, olive-skinned man wearing the same dark gray outfit. She didn't judge it likely, however, which meant that her lover had ended up in the same restaurant as her.

She hadn't told him where she was going, and her blithe earlier comments would have suggested she was heading to the Mage Guild's office.

Had he followed her? She liked Acconcio well enough, but that was a glaring red warning sign.

"Are you *sure*, ma'am?" the barista asked. "You don't look like you need coffee."

"Sorry, just realized my boyfriend might have been stalking me," Maria admitted in a rush, relying on the sisterhood of shared experience.

"I see." The other woman glanced out the window, then gestured Maria closer to her.

"If you go down that hallway," she pointed, "there's a staff-only door past the washrooms. Go straight through, turn left. The door there exits out onto a completely different corridor."

For half a second, Maria wondered if she was doing Acconcio a disservice or if she was being too paranoid...but even as a Mage-Commander in His Majesty's service, she'd encountered enough throwbacks not to take her safety with that much certainty.

She could confront him, but that was unlikely to end well. For now, discretion was the better part of valor.

"Thank you."

CHAPTER 29

"SO?"

"So what?" David asked Campbell as their shuttle crossed the void toward Anvil, Dazbog's primary orbital station. Like the central hub of Foundry Yard Alpha, it was one of the many ring stations in the galaxy, but in Anvil's case, the ring itself was easily a kilometer wide.

The station was a transfer hub for the vast edifice of the orbital industry and the planet below. Since living on the planet now required filtration systems and air masks, over a million people lived on the massive platform.

Like most sensible importers, BB&M operated out of a set of offices and warehouses in orbit. An even dozen heavy transport shuttles accompanied the personnel shuttle that the two officers rode in, each of them hauling a ten-thousand-ton cargo container: the first of many flights that would slowly move *Falcon*'s cargo over to Anvil for repackaging and transfer.

"So," his XO echoed, glancing around the passenger compartment, empty except for them and two security troopers, "are you going to make contact with Turquoise?"

"That is the question, isn't it?" he replied softly.

If he trusted the Legatans, their referral would at least get him in the door with the crime boss. *If* he and Turquoise could come to a deal, they could combine their assets against a common enemy—*if* Turquoise wasn't feeling vindictive about her old boss's death.

Too many *ifs*.

"It seems like the best way to put an end to us being hunted across the galaxy," Campbell said. "At the price of walking right back into the dens of snakes I thought we were trying to stay out of."

"Exactly," he agreed. "I've got a good ship and a good crew. All I want is to run cargo, make money and be left the hell alone."

He'd include "not having my crew sell all my information" in "left the hell alone" too, but he could live with that part if everyone else would stop shooting at him.

"So, yeah, we could poke at it," he said. "We could talk to this Turquoise, draw the Legacy out, smash Azure's little leftover gift to the universe.

"*Or*, I can find the biggest cargo here that's going as far as possible and run off to the other end of the Protectorate. We have a faster ship than most who might chase us. We can't quite outrun the news of our existence, but we can keep one jump ahead of whoever wants to cause us trouble."

David shook his head.

"That has its own flaws, of course," he admitted. "But on reflection, I'm starting to like it better than walking into the middle of an underworld war. I owe our people better than that."

"That's certainly an argument," Campbell said unconvincingly. "Do you *really* have it in you to walk away, boss?"

He shook his head with a small laugh.

"I don't know," he said. "But I owe our people. None of them signed up to be dragged into a war with a bunch of assassins. Self-defense is one thing, Jenna, but we're talking about actively going to war."

He shook his head again.

"No, Jenna, that's outside our scope," he told her. He was quite certain everything he'd learned had already ended up in the hands of the Protectorate, or he'd plan to pass the information on. "We got tied up in this Legatan mess because we needed to, but we can get repairs and anti-matter here in Svarog. And a cargo big enough for *Falcon*.

"There's no reason to start a war, not when leaving is much safer for *everybody*."

His XO grunted. She didn't sound convinced, but she let it go for now. "And this 'Legatan mess'?" she asked quietly.

"We're meeting with BB&M; we'll pass on the cargo," he told her. "We'll *quietly* let the Protectorate know, and then we will get the hell out of everyone's affairs. I've had enough cloak-and-dagger for one lifetime!"

Melvin Boots was waiting for David and his people at the shuttle bay as they boarded Anvil, the delicately featured businessman clearly perfectly comfortable in the zero-gravity docking area. His black suit was the latest fashion from Mars, carefully tailored to stay in place despite the lack of gravity, and he offered David a cheerful smile and an extended hand.

Shaking hands in zero gravity was an exercise in acrobatics, but Boots was clearly as experienced in the dance as David was.

"Welcome aboard the Anvil, Captain Rice, Officer Campbell," Boots told them. His gaze flicked over the two security guards with them, but he didn't comment. "I have a transport pod laid on once we reach the ring. Anvil is quite large; you don't want to walk all the way to our offices."

"I appreciate the courtesy, Mr. Boots," David said. "Shall we?"

"Of course. And no business on the way," the small man ordered with a smile. "It spoils the trip—and sadly, Anvil's walls are known to have ears."

"If you don't mind, Captain," Boots began as they finally dropped into the automated transit pod, "I have to ask: just how does a merchant captain end up with one of the Navy's armed fast freighters? I didn't think there were many of those left!"

"There aren't," David confirmed. "I think once we took possession of *Red Falcon*, there were...two left in mothballs? I'm not sure. Jenna?"

"Three, according to the conversations I had with the yard people in Tau Ceti," his XO confirmed. "One in Tau Ceti, two in Sol. None of them are active, but the Navy apparently wants to have them around in case they ever have to deploy the battleships for extended duty."

Boots laughed nervously.

"They don't expect to ever *do* that, do they?" he asked.

"Who knows?" David replied. "They did build them, after all. And sometimes I imagine it's more convenient to send one absolutely massive ship than a cruiser squadron."

He grinned.

"If nothing else, His Majesty's battleships are *impressive*." He'd seen one of them at Tau Ceti. Massive spikes in space carrying enough weaponry to sterilize half a planet, it was reassuring to know they were on his side...and even more reassuring, in many ways, to know there were only twelve of them!

"But to answer your question," he continued, "you get an AAFHF by doing a Hand a very large favor. I can't tell you *what* I did, but by the time it was done, I didn't have a ship anymore, and the Protectorate felt they owed me."

That the Protectorate also felt he'd painted a giant target on his back and wanted him to have some surprises in his pocket wasn't Boots's business.

The importer laughed, somewhat less nervously.

"I've never even *met* a Hand," he admitted. "Most people don't. I'm impressed, Captain Rice; you're not what I expected to be delivering this cargo."

"I've made a lot of strange friends over the years," David agreed. "People from all walks who trust my sense of honor." He smiled. "As the saying goes, it's not what you know or what you do that matters—it's who knows what you know and what you do."

"I think the saying might be simpler than that," Boots noted. "But I understand your point. I looked over the specs for your ship. With a full suite of Mages and no damage, there isn't much that can outpace you."

"And that's the way I like it," David said. "It'll be a few weeks before we can leave Svarog, sadly. I really do prefer *not* getting jumped by pirates."

"I heard." Boots shook his head. "No one likes having pirates in the area of their home. You did us all a favor blowing those bastards to hell."

"The alternative was dying quietly. I didn't like that option."

Boots laughed dryly again, glancing out the window and pausing uncomfortably.

"What the hell?" he said softly, as the pod began to slow to a halt.

"Mr. Boots?" David asked, looking out the window himself. They were in one of Anvil's warehousing sectors, the pod trundling along its designated path amidst doors labeled with company names and nothing else.

This was the personnel accessway. The massive doors for cargo would either open to space or to the massive cargo pathways that ringed Anvil. They weren't needed for humans.

"This isn't right. We're in the wrong district," Boots told him. "Officer Campbell, hit the emergency stop!"

Campbell obeyed, but the pod ignored her, continuing on its way—but also continuing to slow down.

"Sir," one of the guards snapped. "The pod is setting itself up as an easy target. We need to get *out*."

The other security trooper hit the door release, which ignored him. Reyes clearly hadn't been expecting it to work, however, as he was already removing a large knife from inside his coat with his other hand.

"Stand back," he told the others, and hit a switch on the knife's hilt. The edge of the blade lit up in glittering blue as a plasma arc flashed into existence around it.

David hadn't even been aware there were any plasma-arc blades aboard his ship. They weren't even restricted to the military. The anti-armor hand weapons were outright *illegal*.

The superheated blade made short work of the light metal frame of the pod, and the trooper kicked the wreckage of the door out of the moving vehicle.

"Go!" he barked, disabling the arc on the knife but continuing to hold it. The metal *steamed* as David dove past the trooper, rolling to absorb the impact as he hit the floor.

Boots followed, half-thrown from the vehicle by David's men, with Campbell right behind him.

The security guards jumped clear a moment later, seconds before the pod turned a corner at a much slower pace—a pace that left it suspended in the corner, near-motionless for a fraction of a second.

The explosion of the rocket that slammed into it left afterimages in David's retina and he inhaled sharply.

Apparently, his security people were just paranoid enough to keep up with his enemies.

"Move back," the senior security trooper ordered. Corporal Nour Nejem had already produced several blocks of nondescript metal and plastic from inside his jacket as he waved the officers back.

As David watched, those components rapidly assembled into a MACCAW-9. He was relatively certain the gun wasn't *supposed* to be concealable in that fashion, but given that the ex-Marine assembled the weapon in under ten seconds, he suspected Nejem could do several things with the gun that weren't in the design manual.

"I hate space stations," Reyes noted quietly, the second security trooper having produced a more easily concealed MAC-6 pistol from inside his own gear. "No cover, no friendlies, no backup."

"Anvil Security should be on their way!" Boots insisted. "There's no way that explosion went unnoticed."

"Someone reprogrammed your pod," David pointed out. "I wouldn't put it past them to have reprogrammed the cameras, too."

Boots looked terrified.

"What do I do?" he demanded. "I'm a businessman, not a soldier!"

"You listen to me," Nejem told him harshly. "And you move back with the Captain and the XO while Reyes and I watch for the bad guys."

David grabbed his client's shoulder before Boots could object, pulling the delicately built man along with him as they retreated back along the pod track. It was remotely possible their attackers were going to write them off as "dead in the explosion", but...

Nope.

Six men—in the uniforms, light armor and face-concealing riot helmets of Anvil Station Police!—came around the corner. Five carried carbines, the sixth a magazine-fed multi-launcher. Unless the heavy gunner was incompetent, he'd already switched from rockets to fragmentation grenades.

"Stop right there!" one of them snapped. "What the hell did you do to the pod? You're under arrest!"

"Not a chance in *jahīm*," Nejem replied bluntly. "Not with you holding the damn rocket launcher that just blew up our pod!"

The man with the multi-launcher clearly decided that was all the conversation that was needed. He lifted his weapon to fire—and then went flying backward as everyone confirmed what David had suspected: even theoretically *ex*-Marines had *far* better reflexes than any corrupt cop in the galaxy.

Reyes put four six-millimeter high-velocity rounds into the gunner's chest, two into his gun, and one into his head before the man had finished raising his weapon.

Nejem opened fire in the same moment, a neatly controlled spray of bullets that put two of the attackers down before the others opened fire, retreating as they tried to cover themselves.

The initial flash of violence was over in seconds, and the man David was dragging was clearly hyperventilating. Mr. Boots, it seemed, had no exposure to violence at all.

Unlike David's crew.

"Jenna, take him," David ordered, passing their client over to his XO. He produced his own sidearm and glanced over at the two security troopers.

"Your call, Nejem," he said quietly. "I know who the experts are right now."

"We've got a clean straight line until we're out of the warehouse district," Nejem replied. "We can move back, but we can't get out of their line of fire." The heavily tanned ex-Marine shook his head. "I checked. We're jammed. No coms, no way forward."

"So, we fall back and hope we see them first," David interpreted.

"Oh, I'm quite certain we'll see them first," Nejem said with a dangerous smile.

To David's surprise, they made it most of the way down the hall without interruption. Their original attackers seemed to have been scared off, but the continued jamming suggested that the Legacy wasn't done with them yet.

The sound of an approaching transit pod was the only warning they received of the second string to the attackers' bow.

"Off the tracks!" Nejem ordered as the sound reached them.

David followed the security troopers to the side of the hall, helping Campbell haul the still-in-shock Boots with them. His troopers might have better gear than he'd expected on them, but he doubted they had anything that could stop a several-hundred-kilo transit pod.

The emergency brake in this pod clearly *was* working, as it came slamming to a halt barely ten meters from them and the door sprang open. Before David or his people could sound any kind of challenge, however, four small cylinders flipped out simultaneously.

The gaps between the grenades were perfect, one landing every three meters and leaving David staring at them in horror—until they started spewing smoke, at least.

His people might not be instantly dead from smoke grenades, but they also couldn't *see* anything—and he heard motion from the pod. Heavy feet slammed into the ground as someone—multiple someones, clearly able to see through the smoke—charged out of the track-linked vehicle.

Nejem's MACCAW barked, short controlled bursts firing at *something*. Then the gun went silent as the distinctive *hiss-crack* of a stungun firing its SmartDarts cut through the smoke.

A shadow moved through the smoke, not coming from any of the directions he knew his people were in, and he opened fire. He landed at least three hits on the figure, but it ignored the bullets, lunging through the smoke to rip the pistol from his hand with impossibly strong fingers.

The smoke began to clear and David found himself pinned, his hand held in an iron-hard grip that forced him to his knees as he looked at a completely nondescript man wearing long black leather gloves over his hands and forearms.

"Uh-uh." The stranger shook his head, holding David's pistol in his free hand. With a cold smile, he *crushed* the gun like it was a toy. "No tricks, no clever games. It's over."

The movement, the strength—the man was a cyborg. But his accent was distinctly local and his eyes lacked the distinctive square pupils of non-covert Legatan Augments. Not an Augment, then. "Just" a thug with upgrades.

As the cyborg used his grip on David's one hand to twist the burly Captain around to see the rest of his people, he realized there was no "just" about it. These men were going to kill him.

Nejem and Reyes were down. Both appeared to be alive, the only guns the cyborgs were carrying were stunguns—an odd mercy for rent-a-thugs.

"Contract says you die," the cyborg holding David told him. "We don't get paid for nobody else, so nobody else dies."

Campbell and Boots were in much the same shape as the security guards. Shot with SmartDarts, they were almost certainly going to live. David, it seemed, wasn't going to get the mercy of such unconsciousness.

"Stop toying with him," another of the thugs snapped. Instead of the gun David had expected, he produced a metal box of...syringes?

"Blue are MemErase," the leader snapped to his minions. "Red isn't."

Passing the blue-marked syringes to his men, the leader knelt down by David with the red one.

"Could've told them bad cops ain't efficient," he said conversationally. "But that's the breaks. Pod accident, Captain. Your friends won't remember anything different. If it helps"—he tapped the syringe—"they swear this shit is painless."

The man who'd first grabbed David now grabbed his free arm, pinning the big Captain down as the leader approached with the syringe.

"It ain't personal," the man said as he knelt by David. "Just business." And then his head exploded.

However subtle the new players' approach might have been—and David didn't think *anyone* had seen them coming—there was no subtlety in their actions. Military-grade heavy penetrator rifles barked at point-blank range as three exosuited soldiers appeared out of nowhere.

One of the cyborgs managed to avoid the opening fusillade, dodging sideways at superhuman speed and producing a knife from somewhere. What he was planning on doing with said knife against exosuit armor would be a question for the interrogators, as the cyborg froze in place, barely visible bonds of force slapping down on his arms as the *fourth* member of the rescue party, the reason they'd approached unseen, gestured.

The Royal Martian Marine Corps Combat Mage was in full uniform but had eschewed the heavy exosuit armor of her companions. She stepped between them, her hand still outstretched and the projector rune on her palm glowing to David's eyes.

"My name," she said calmly as she approached the cyborg, "is Mage-Lieutenant Jeanette Williams—and you are under arrest. Now, are you going to be a good boy and cooperate, or do I need to *float* you down to Navy country?"

All Williams's magic was doing was holding the cyborg's limbs in place. He could speak but instead chose to snarl wordlessly.

"Very well," the Marine said crisply, gesturing. The thug lifted off the ground, floating helplessly over to her, where he looked down at the relatively petite woman. Williams started to open her mouth to say something else...and then the cyborg's head exploded, spraying blood over the officer's face in a manner that David completely sympathized with right now.

"Down!" One of Williams's exosuited troopers was suddenly on top of her, interposing the several centimeters of metal and ceramic that protected his suit between the Mage and the incoming fire.

Heavy slugs smashed into the armor, but they weren't the saboted penetrators needed to go through it. The Mage was protected—and the other two Marines returned fire.

There was a scream, and a shooter David hadn't seen went down. More gunfire echoed for several seconds afterwards, a slug ricocheted off the wall near him...and then it was silent.

"They're gone," one of the Marines said gruffly. "Scanners show clear. Sorry, ma'am, we should have seen them coming."

"Retrieve the bodies," Williams snapped. "See what kind of ID you can sort out."

She glanced over the unconscious forms of David's companions and sighed.

"Well, that is going to make my life easier, isn't it?" she asked rhetorically. "We got a ping from an MISS team that had you under observation, but my impression is that *everybody* will be happier if nobody realizes the Protectorate is covering your ass."

She checked her com.

"Anvil Police are being informed as we speak. *Vetted* officers," she noted, the emphasis clear. She knew who at least some of the people who'd attacked Rice were. "These gentlemen"—she gestured at the cyborgs her Marines were scooping up—"were never here."

She smiled, a brilliant green sparkle lighting up her eyes.

"And so far as anyone else is concerned, Captain Rice, neither were we. Understood?"

David blinked, wiping another man's blood from his face and coughing.

"Yeah, sure," he agreed. "What the *hell* is going on, Lieutenant?"

"These were all guns for hire, Captain," she told him. "Not bounty hunters—someone directly offered them real cash to come after you. That someone cleaned up their loose ends and is almost certainly still in play. Watch your back."

He finished wiping the blood off his face and looked at her wryly. "I intend to," he said, "but it's nice to know someone *else* is too."

CHAPTER 30

MARIA FLOATED cross-legged in the middle of the simulacrum chamber. It would look to anyone around her, she was sure, that she was simply meditating surrounded by stars. While she'd started with that, she was also moving the tiny trackers that MISS had given her into the cargo containers.

Just attaching the trackers to the containers themselves wasn't enough. She actually had to open each container, drop the tiny finger-nail-sized devices into the contents, then close the container up.

It was a slow, painstaking process. Thankfully, access to the simu-lacrum made it significantly easier. The jump matrix wouldn't amplify the minor spell she was using the way a military amplifier would, but it would let her see the outside of the ship with perfect detail and fidelity.

It was also enough of a distraction that she wasn't thinking of the un-pleasant surprise at the end of the previous evening. She hadn't spoken to Acconcio since she'd seen him in the Green Parson's Bar and was still sorting through her reactions.

Unfortunately, she'd come to the conclusion that there was no good reason for him to have been there. Either he'd been following her be-cause he didn't trust her reasons for going to a meeting after their din-ner, or he'd been following her because he was keeping tabs on her.

For any one of a number of reasons. Most of those reasons were even innocent...but the action wasn't. And it wasn't something she could permit.

She was going to have to talk to him. Cut things off before it got too deep, too dangerous. Stalking was a red flag she'd ignored only once in her life, and that hadn't ended well for anyone.

A cough at the door interrupted her resolute thoughts, and she unleashed a tiny drag of magic to turn herself. She'd hidden over seventy of the trackers, and while she had thirty more, that was probably enough.

She was surprised to find Xi Wu standing just outside the doorway, where there was still magical gravity. The young Mage looked shaky, worried.

"Xi, what's going on?" Maria asked gently. "Are LaMonte and Kelzin okay?"

"They're fine," Wu said quickly, a soft flush crossing her cheeks. The mild embarrassment seemed to calm her. "We just got a ping from Anvil Station Police—Captain Rice and Officer Campbell are in a station emergency room. So are the troopers who went with them."

A sharp chill ran down Maria's spine.

"ASP wants to talk to whoever's in charge," Wu noted. "That's... you, ma'am. Until one or both of those two is conscious, you're in command."

"I understand," Maria said calmly. "Thank you, Xi. Can you let whoever is holding down the communication watch know I'll be on the bridge in a few moments?

"I'll talk to Anvil there."

She couldn't quite bring herself to take David's chair, so Maria took over Jenna Campbell's navigation station and quickly double-checked the cameras.

"Link them through," she told the tech holding down the com watch. The young woman gave her a grateful nod and hit a key.

"This is Mage Maria Soprano, first officer of the merchant ship *Red Falcon*," she said sharply into the camera. "I'm informed my Captain and executive officer are in a station emergency room. What happened?"

"I was hoping you'd have some idea yourself, Mage Soprano," the pale dark-haired woman on the other end replied. "I am Sector Captain Alicia Nguyen of the Anvil Station Police. I'm not entirely sure what the hell went down, but three of *my* men are dead."

"It's your station, Sector Captain," Maria pointed out. "Don't you have surveillance systems?"

"They were disabled, Mage Soprano. And while they were disabled, someone shot three ASP officers to death and stun-darted your crew members. Any information you have would be appreciated."

The cop's tone made it clear she suspected that Maria's crew had something to do with her officers being shot.

"Captain Nguyen, there are groups with long-standing grudges against Captain Rice," Maria told her. "While those grudges have rarely ended well for those bearing them, this ship was nearly destroyed by pirates on our way to this system.

"I would not put it past those behind that piracy to attempt another attack here," she concluded. "You should be proud of your officers. In the absence of any communication, they clearly attempted to save civilians and paid a high price for doing so.

"I, and I'm sure my Captain, once he's awake, can only extend our thanks for their service and our deepest condolences to their families."

Nguyen didn't look like she quite bought it. Maria wasn't entirely sure she bought it herself—but she was quite certain that if David and his bodyguards had shot Anvil Station Police, it had been in self-defense.

"I will be aboard Anvil shortly to collect my Captain and crew," Maria continued. "Assuming your doctors think he can be transferred?"

Nguyen looked like she was going to argue for a moment, but she picked up on the unspoken comment—that Maria wasn't going to *not* collect her Captain for anything short of a doctor's opinion or an arrest order.

And the combat-mage swords on her Mage medallion warned that getting in her way would be unwise.

"Skavar, you're with me," Maria snapped at the Marine as she walked into the armory. "Captain and Campbell got stunned and are in a station ER; ASP is being...difficult."

"How difficult are we talking?" the gaunt officer replied, the pieces of the weapon he had dissembled in front of him clicking back together with practiced speed.

"I'm not sure yet," she admitted. "Several of their officers ended up dead and they seem to think the Captain might have been involved."

The security chief was on his feet, strapping the MACCAW into a harness she hadn't seen him wearing. He was thoughtfully silent for a moment, gesturing at several of the troopers in the room to get prepped as he pulled an armor vest out of a locker.

"If the Captain shot somebody, they started it," he concluded.

"I agree. I'm willing to let ASP save face by officially assuming their officers died protecting the Captain and his client, but we are getting our people back aboard and into Dr. Gupta's capable hands ASAP."

"No argument there," Skavar said grimly. Four of his men and women were suddenly standing with him and Maria, all wearing armor vests and carrying SMGs.

"Kelzin and Wu are waiting for us at the shuttle," she told the suddenly assembled squad. "Let's go get our Captain, shall we?"

"Somehow, I'm not surprised that we're having to rescue him from the police," Skavar replied with a grin. "I've seen his file."

Maria glared at him for a moment, looking at the men around them.

"And how, *exactly*, did an *ex*-Marine get access to the Captain's confidential file?" she asked sweetly.

Skavar coughed.

"Maybe we should talk about that after we rescue him?"

Two Mages, five blatantly armed security guards, and one obviously armed pilot made for a surprisingly large bubble of clear space as Maria and the crew stalked through the corridors of Anvil Station.

Neither the Mages nor Kelzin carried the deadly-looking close as-sault weapons Skavar and his people were packing, but Kelzin's hol-stered pistol was obvious, as were the Mage medallions on the two women.

Wu might not have been a trained Combat Mage, but she'd passed the self-defense portion of the Jump Mage curriculum with flying colors and had impressed Maria in practice. She'd *rather* have a Marine Combat Mage or another Navy Mage with her, but in the absence of those op-tions, Wu was a solid second choice.

Maria was well aware that her little party looked ready for war, and she didn't mind in the slightest. If the Station Police decided they were going to be trouble, she wanted to have all the firepower, both literal and figurative, to hand that she could.

The receptionist at the front desk of the ER looked up as she walked in, and visibly swallowed.

"How may I assist you, Mage?" he asked carefully.

"I'm here to collect Captain Rice and his crew," she told him. "I understand they are in rough shape but should be dischargeable to our doctor's care."

"I will check," the receptionist said. He skimmed over his system and then looked up at her awkwardly. "I have them marked as persons of in-terest in a police case," he admitted. "I am not able to release them with-out ASP permission, Mage."

"I see," Maria said calmly. "And is there someone on site who can give that permission?"

The receptionist swallowed.

"I believe they're under guard," he said slowly. "I don't think they have authority to release them without speaking to senior officers. You'll have to speak to Sector Captain Nguyen."

"I *did*," she told him. "And I was not aware that my people were under arrest."

"Not arrest," a voice said from behind her. "Locked down as persons of interest. In case someone decides to try and break them free before I can ask them questions."

Maria turned very precisely on her heel and found Captain Nguyen standing behind her. The Asian cop wasn't armed *herself,* but the pair of looming ASP exosuit troopers were mute testimony to her authority.

"And given that our ship currently can't fly, what exactly gives you the idea we're going to disappear before you can ask your questions?" she asked. "On the other hand, given that someone appears to have actively shot at and stunned my Captain, I would far rather have him on our ship than in an unsecured ER."

"As you can see," Nguyen said calmly, "this is *not* unsecured."

"And if the same people who killed three of your officers and blew giant holes in *Red Falcon* came for him in force?" Maria replied. "How much collateral damage can you accept, Sector Captain?"

"My job is to avoid collateral damage, Mage Soprano. Collateral damage appears to follow your Captain around. I'd rather keep him contained," she said. "This is my decision and my authority, Mage Soprano. You may visit with your Captain and crew, but both they and Mr. Boots are remaining in protective custody at *least* until I've had a chance to interview them.

"Understood?"

There were ways Maria could override Nguyen, but they would take time and she'd laid her position out pretty clearly. Force was an option but probably a bad idea.

There were, of course, still compromises available.

"Skavar?" she said.

"Ma'am?"

"You'll join Sector Captain Nguyen's people in securing the Captain and our people," she ordered. "We'll cooperate, Captain, but we need to be *very* certain of Captain Rice's safety."

Nguyen nodded grudgingly.

"That is acceptable," she allowed. "I don't expect to have to detain your people for long, Mage Soprano—but my men are dead and I *will* have some goddamn answers."

CHAPTER 31

DAVID HAD ARRIVED at the ER conscious but had fallen asleep while the nurses went over the bruises, scrapes and minor injuries he'd acquired along the way. He'd avoided the SmartDarts that had taken down the others, but the cyborgs had handled him roughly enough to leave him the worse for wear.

When he went to sleep, he'd been in the same room as Campbell, at least, but when he woke, he was alone. Heavy security dividers had been moved in around his bed, not just curtains, and the only exit was through a clearly locked door.

That was...not a good sign.

He caught a moment of unclear argument through that door, and then it slid open to reveal Maria Soprano and an unfamiliar pale woman in an Anvil Station Police uniform. They stood slightly off-angle from each other, both women unconsciously giving themselves space to defend themselves against the other.

That wasn't a good sign either.

"Maria, Officer," he greeted them. "What's going on?"

"I am Sector Captain Alicia Nguyen," the cop introduced herself. "You were found near the wreckage of a crashed transit pod, with your companions shot and stunned and several dead ASP officers in the area."

She grimaced.

"Three of my men are dead, Captain Rice, and you're the first conscious person who was there," she told him. "Would you care to tell me what the *hell* happened?"

David leaned back in his bed and studied the two women.

"Do you want the truth or the answer that will make you feel better, Sector Captain?" he asked bluntly. "I can spin a story of brave heroics and grand sacrifice on the part of your men, but it won't be consistent with anyone else's story, will it?"

"I am an officer of the law, Captain Rice," she ground out. "*What happened?*"

He sighed.

"Six of your men were dirty," he said flatly. "I don't know who paid them or why they allowed themselves to be bought, but they set up an ambush. Recoded the transit pod that Boots reserved to take us to somewhere they knew there would be no witnesses.

"The pod was then disabled with a rocket launcher, but my guards were paranoid enough to get us all out of the vehicle before they shot it. They came to finish the job; my people defended themselves."

He shook his head grimly.

"Not, perhaps, as effectively as we'd hope, since most of us ended up wounded or unconscious, but enough that we survived. As did our client, not that we were being paid to see to his safety," David concluded dryly.

Nguyen sat still as a statue, processing his words.

"You *admit* that you killed three Anvil Station Police officers?" she asked softly.

"Honestly, I don't know for certain if they were actually ASP officers," David pointed out. "I know they were wearing ASP uniforms and had access to heavy weapons I wouldn't have expected to be in anyone's hands aboard a main orbital station."

"I see." The cop was silent, then shook her head.

"For your information, Captain Rice, all of the dead men were Anvil Station Police officers," she confirmed. "None, however, were on duty. Can you be more specific as to what heavy weapon you saw?"

She was giving him more benefit of the doubt than he'd expected and he stretched his memory.

"It was a multi-launcher, capable of launching both rockets and grenades," he concluded. "I wasn't exactly catching the brand, but I only know two companies that make systems like that: Legatus Arms and Martian Armaments."

Nguyen sighed.

"We have four Martian Armaments fifty-five-millimeter multi-launchers in our inventory," she said quietly. "I'm not going to believe you without question, Captain, but I *am* going to see just where my multi-launchers were last night.

"But I *will* get to the bottom of this," she promised him. "If you're lying to me, I owe it to my men who died to see justice done. If you're not...there are least three dirty cops still under my command, and I owe it to the *rest* of my men to see justice done.

"Do you understand me, Captain?"

The cop left, leaving Soprano and David alone.

"That is going to be a giant disaster," he admitted.

"She has a stick up her ass, but it's a *police-issue* stick," Soprano told him. "If her people are dirty, she'll burn it out."

"We can hope," David said. History wasn't quite as assured on cops removing their bad apples as Soprano sounded. "The whole mess was a disaster. Is Boots okay?"

"Yeah, he's two rooms down, sleeping off a SmartDart," she told him. "Same with Campbell, Reyes and Nejem. Everyone is fine."

"Good." He glanced around the room. Unless Nguyen was less competent than he expected, they were bugged. That meant there was an entire aspect of the fight that he *needed* to talk to Soprano about that he couldn't.

He wasn't sure he trusted her. There were too many missing pieces on too many of his officers—but at the same time, MISS seemed to be watching his back and that meant they almost certainly had someone on his crew.

"It doesn't look like Nguyen's going to let you out," his Mage concluded. "I've got the off-loading continuing as planned. I'll be in touch with Bruno and MacDonald next to make sure everything is still on the level..."

She shook her head.

"What *else* do you need me to do?"

"Until I'm out of here, you're in charge," he told her. "I'm sure the clinic will let you talk to me if you have questions, but I have full faith in your ability to run a ship. While she's in dock. Cut open by repair teams."

His Ship's Mage laughed at him. Despite his concerns, he *liked* Soprano. He couldn't help hoping she wasn't one of the several spies his ship had clearly acquired.

"You're right, I can probably do that," she admitted. "Is there anything...else?"

He looked around the room as obviously as he could, driving home the point that they were being listened to.

"Watch our people," he ordered quietly. "The Legacy is not done with us yet and this stunt was all rental thugs. If they have their own team or teams here, they aren't playing yet."

"Understood."

"But get the ship off-loaded and fixed up as a priority," he continued. "I want to be the hell and gone away from this place as soon as possible."

At this point, he wanted to be as far away from any involvement in the underworld as possible. Turquoise and the Legatans could go hang— he needed to keep his people safe!

She nodded her agreement.

"I'll make it happen, boss," she promised. "We'll be on our way."

CHAPTER 32

CHARITY MACDONALD looked perfectly calm, despite the fact that one of her business partners was in the ER, a carrier under contract to her company had been shot at, and station police were asking a *lot* of questions.

Walton Bruno, on the other hand, did not look calm. The third and most senior partner of Bruno, Boots and MacDonald was an unusually tall man with only the sparsest wisps of white hair remaining on his liver-spotted scalp.

His eyes were ice-blue and level, but he was pacing back and forth in the meeting room and his hands were visibly trembling.

"Just what, Mage Soprano...has your Captain...dragged us into?" he asked, pausing repeatedly to breathe heavily. "This whole business...risks our positive...relationships with ASP... which are...essential for our business."

Maria managed not to visibly shake her head. She doubted the old man had any illusions about just where *Red Falcon's* cargo was coming from. Given that his company was intimately involved in a Legatan covert smuggling operation, to complain about *Rice's* problems was hypocritical.

"My Captain didn't choose to be attacked by dirty cops," she pointed out. "That's not in *anyone's* desired schedule."

MacDonald laughed.

"She's right, boss," she told Bruno. "Besides, given our delivery delays, the client would be *furious* if we turned away *Falcon's* cargo."

Bruno growled.

"That's fair, and true," he allowed. "I apologize, Mage Soprano. I worry...for our people."

"We all worry for our own," Maria allowed. She, for example, currently wasn't being allowed off the ship without a two-person armed guard. She *could*, as acting Captain, override Skavar. She wasn't going to.

"Is there anything I should know about this client?" she asked politely. She presumed the main one in question was Legatus, but if they would just tell who the cargo was being delivered to...

"Our stock...in trade, Mage Soprano...is our...confidentiality," Bruno said, still breathing heavily as he paced. "We give no more...information...than we must. You must be...content with...your money."

The old man turned to face her and smiled.

"It is, after all, quite a bit of money," he concluded. "Charity?"

"I presume, Mage Soprano, that you are authorized to sign the releases and paperwork in Captain Rice's stead?" the heavyset woman demanded.

"I am *Red Falcon*'s first officer," Maria confirmed instantly. "As first officer, Ship's Mage, and acting Captain, I am authorized to sign on the ship corporation's behalf."

"Good, that does make this simpler," MacDonald told her, producing a datapad from somewhere on her person. "Shall we?"

The downside to being accompanied everywhere by armed guards, regardless of whose side those guards were on, was that it made it difficult to do things in secret.

Maria trusted Skavar's people, but there was a vast gap between trusting her crew and admitting she was an MISS plant to the same crew. She needed to check in on the status of her trackers, but she couldn't drop down in a quiet hallway and run the tracing program.

"Come on, ladies," she told the two guards with her. "Let's grab a coffee. I don't need to be back on the ship just yet, and I could use the break from paperwork."

"We just got paid," Corporal Campo pointed out. "No one's going to argue with coffee on the multi-million-dollar trip!"

Maria chuckled. Interstellar carriage rates would have read like highway robbery to Old Earth surface shippers—rarely exceeding single-digit Martian dollars per ton—but twenty million tons of cargo made for a lot of money.

Of course, most of that money was almost immediately consumed by the operating costs of a ship of that scale, and a good chunk of what was left would be eaten by the deductible on *Red Falcon*'s repairs. She wasn't entirely sure what the net profit that Rice would claim on the trip would be, but she suspected it wouldn't be very much.

Pirates were murder on the bottom line.

Walking into one of Anvil Station's local coffee store chains, Maria ordered three expensive coffees. Passing two on to her guards, she settled down into a corner and opened up her wrist computer's systems, linking into her tracer program.

They'd moved over half of the cargo off of *Red Falcon* toward Anvil Station, and sixty of her seventy trackers had gone with it. At the coffee shop, she was close enough to ping the ones that had moved over, activating their microsecond pulse.

In theory, the responding pulse was too quick to trigger any sensors looking for bugs. She wasn't going to rely on that and made sure to save the map of the responses.

Forty of the trackers were together in one spot, a spot her map quickly confirmed to be Bruno, Boots and MacDonald's storage warehouse. Ten didn't respond at all—that wasn't a surprise; the downside of the trackers being stealthy was that they were also fragile.

The last ten were also together but not on the station. They were in open space, heading away from Anvil Station.

"Crap," she murmured.

"Ma'am?" Corporal Campo asked over her latte.

"Nothing," Maria replied. She had a single location pulse. No vector, no velocity. There wasn't much she could do with that...but hopefully, MISS had access to the station sensors. Director Choi should be able to identify which ship had been at that location at that time.

She hit a command to forward the tracker results to Choi, then shut down her PC and drained her coffee.

"That's probably enough hanging about," she told her guards. "Let's get back to the *Falcon*."

Maria was unsurprised to find an encrypted message waiting for her when she returned to her office aboard *Red Falcon*. It was easily an hour to get from Anvil Station through the chaos of Foundry Yard Alpha to *Red Falcon*'s repair slip—more than enough time for MISS to dig through the sensor scans and see where the ship she'd picked up was going.

To her surprise, however, the message wasn't a recording or even a long text message. It was simply a com code and an encryption key.

Shaking her head, the Mage plugged both into her wrist-comp and activated its holographic display. There was no need for this conversation to go through *Falcon*'s computers.

The first thing to appear was a floating and gently spinning hourglass, the ancient symbol for "please wait."

That suddenly expanded into a holographic cascade of sand that formed into a request for the encryption key.

Shaking her head, Maria entered the key again. The cascade turned back into an hourglass for a moment—and then the hourglass exploded back into sand that resolved into Director Choi's face.

MISS apparently went for fancy hold graphics.

"Mage Soprano, I'm glad you could reach out," Choi told her immediately. It appeared the woman in charge of all MISS operations in Svarog had been waiting for her call.

That...probably wasn't a good sign.

"Until *Falcon* is repaired and Captain Rice is released, I'm surprisingly underemployed for an acting Captain," Maria replied. "What do you need?"

"A few things," Choi admitted. "But for now, I need to update you quickly. First, we've already put words in the right ears at ASP. While we don't have any evidence that Nguyen can use to nail her dirty laundry to the wall, we *did* feed her enough data that she should be releasing your crew shortly—and she knows where to look to find her problem."

"Why didn't you give her this before?" Maria asked. "Surely, it's in MISS's interest to put dirty cops behind bars."

"Because we didn't have it before," Choi told her. "We pulled it together following up on the attack on Rice. We have significantly more reach without a warrant than Sector Captain Nguyen, but as I said, much of that evidence isn't admissible in a court of law."

The Director smiled thinly.

"But what we can give her should give Nguyen enough of a direction that I'm not worried about those cops staying *out* of jail."

"Good," Maria said flatly after a moment. "Did you track those cargo containers?"

"We did," Choi confirmed. "And now I have big ugly questions I don't have answers to. Your Captain has a talent, you know that?"

"For trouble?" Maria asked. "I've been figuring that. Where did it go?"

"All of the cargo is heading for a company called Red Dragon Astrophysics," the intelligence agent replied. "If it doesn't sound like they need twenty million tons of rare earths and radioactives, I'll note that RDA is *the* primary producer of particle accelerators and similar high-energy experimental systems in the MidWorlds."

"That doesn't seem like something the MidWorlds would use much of," Maria said.

"Yeah, but across fifty-odd worlds, you're looking at at least three or four major high-energy projects in a year," Choi said. "That's enough to consume a *lot* of these materials. And GDA has been needing a lot more raw materials of late."

Maria winced.

"Why?" she asked carefully.

"Their shipments, both in-system and out-system, have been seeing a rash of thefts," the MISS Director told her. "What I find interesting is what one of my analysts just pointed out."

"Which is?"

"The thefts over the last year or so add up to about forty million tons of components. With your shipment, the supplies they've received via BB&M add up to just under forty million tons of raw materials.

"Given that Legatus is involved in those shipments, I'm not sure that is coincidence."

"No. Neither am I," Maria admitted. "What do we know about these thefts?"

Choi sighed.

"You're not going to like it."

"Director?" Maria demanded.

"We haven't identified all of them, but the ones we have identified were all carried by Silent Ocean ships.

"Silent Ocean is the organization Turquoise runs. Your contact, Mage Soprano, is more deeply involved in Legatan operations that our worst fears. We *need* to know what they're doing."

"Damn."

Maria sighed, studying the panels of the ship around her.

"I'll talk to Rice," she admitted. "But you realize I'm going to have to tell him everything, right? I can't bring him in on this blind; he deserves better than that!"

"Hand Stealey made it very clear, Mage Soprano, that you are in charge of this operation," Choi told her. "As it happens, I agree with you—but it's your call."

Maria exhaled again.

"I'll see what I can do. Thank you, Director."

CHAPTER 33

DAVID RETURNED to his ship with an unexaggerated sigh of relief. He hadn't been *worried*, exactly, but given that he and his people had shot and killed multiple Anvil Station Police officers, there were all kinds of potential complications and problems that could have arisen in custody.

Instead, they'd all been released. He had his suspicions as to why, but he wasn't complaining about anything that got him back to *Red Falcon*.

He was somewhat surprised, however, to exit the shuttle into the magical gravity of the shuttle bay to find only one person waiting for him. He'd half-expected to be met by at least all of the senior officers, but instead, only Maria Soprano was waiting for him.

The dark-haired Mage was holding a perfect Navy-style salute as he exited the shuttle with Campbell and the two security people in trail, which he awkwardly returned. It might have been over twenty years since he'd been in the Navy, but muscle memory lasted a long time.

"Captain, we need to talk," she said instantly, before he could say a word.

"I was hoping you could update me on my ship," David said dryly.

"I can do that. You, me, and Jenna in the Captain's briefing room?" Maria replied crisply.

He considered asking if he was allowed to take a shower in his own quarters first, but something in her stance and voice told him he didn't want to wait. Plus, well, he wanted to know exactly what his ship's status was.

He was a starship captain first and foremost, and his starship was his baby.

Plus, despite everything, he realized he trusted Soprano's judgment, and if she said he needed to hear what she had to say, he needed to hear what she had to say.

"Lead on, Ship's Mage," he replied. "Reyes, Nejem—you go crash. I'm sure Skavar will have one hell of a debrief for you, but tell him *I* said you get a shower and eight hours in the rack first, clear?"

"Yes, sir."

"What about me?" Campbell asked. "Do I get a shower and eight hours?"

"Nah. *You're* my second officer." David grinned at her. "You get to join me in finding out just what Mage Soprano has done to my ship!"

Entering his briefing room, David took a seat at the head of the table. Campbell followed suit, collapsing into a chair with the exhaustion of someone who'd had a *really* bad few days. David, at least, hadn't been stunned—and she wasn't fully recovered from having been shot a few weeks before.

"How's the ship?" he asked Maria without further preamble.

"Coming together," she told him. "If you want details, you'll need to pin Kellers down, but I've got the high-level. Damage to the engines is repaired and our replacement engine is almost finished being fabricated. The lasers are remounted and the structural beams in the middle of the ship are repaired.

"We've got about two days' worth of work in the bow dome to get the radiation cap structure finished, sealed up and ready to go, and then we need to install the new antimatter drive unit." She shrugged. "If I'm reading the reports correctly, we're about four days away from being ready to go to space.

"Our cargo is all off-loaded, we've been paid, and our deductible has been covered," she concluded. "We probably don't want to try and load cargo until we're out of the yards, but we can probably start sourcing it."

"Good." David rose, grabbed a glass of water from the sideboard and took a swallow. "I want to be the hell out of this system ASAP. The biggest cargo going the farthest away. I want fifty light-years between us and the Legacy."

Maria sighed and he made a checkmark in his mental list of bets while taking another drink of water.

"And you're about to try and argue me into making contact with this Turquoise," he concluded. "And yes, I'm sure we could make some solid coin with another pseudo-smuggling job, and we'd probably get some intel that the Protectorate would love, but I need to remind you that we *don't work for the Protectorate*."

He turned around to face his two senior officers.

"You work for me," he reminded them. "*I* am in this to make money. I also have a moral obligation to our crew to make sure they get their shares at the end of the year and that they live to spend them.

"That's it," he said. "That's all. That's our job. We ship cargo for money, we pay ourselves, we pay the crew."

The room was silent for several seconds.

"Well?" he asked. "Am I wrong?"

"At least hear her out, David," Campbell told him with a tired look. "We sit in a ship that the Protectorate gave us because we *didn't* walk away from things that weren't our problem."

"Fine."

Soprano looked just as tired as Campbell did. Maybe more so.

"You were rescued by Protectorate agents on Anvil Station," she said quietly. "Did you wonder *why* you were being watched? Why there was a *Marine strike force* standing by to rescue you?"

"Everywhere I turn, *someone* seems to be watching me," David snapped. He had wondered that. Perhaps more importantly, however, he hadn't told anyone about that and everyone else had been unconscious when the Marines had arrived.

"Because I told them to," Soprano told him. "Because Alaura Stealey left orders that you were to be protected, even as she handed you a ship that she knew was going to paint a target on you for all of your enemies.

"I work for you," she continued. "I *also* work for the Martian Interstellar Security Service. My main role is to keep you safe and advise MISS when people like the Legacy came after you or the Conroys recruited you."

David took another drink of water before he said anything, buying himself time to think. So, apparently Soprano was the second mole, another "benign" one, as LaMonte had put it. He wasn't even surprised, not really.

"All right," he said. "Now, assuming I don't regard that alone as sufficient reason to kick you off my ship, why the *hell* would we make contact with Turquoise?"

"MISS tracked our last cargo," she replied. "It was delivered to a company that builds particle accelerators and similar high-energy scientific equipment, on a massive scale. That company has seen forty million tons of raw material delivered from the Conroys over the last two years...and has had forty million tons of particle accelerator components 'stolen' over the same time frame.

"Now, I don't know what you could *do* with forty million tons of particle accelerator bits, but I can't imagine it's something we want the Legatans to be doing," she concluded. "The Navy might have dismissed particle accelerators as weapons, but that doesn't mean someone hasn't come up with a solution."

David shook his head.

"No," he admitted, his brain running ahead of him and coming to a terrifying conclusion. "Legatus wouldn't be sourcing particle accelerators for weapons. You know what the Centurion Ring is, don't you?"

Both of the women inhaled sharply.

"The Centurion Accelerator Ring," Campbell echoed. "That... that would be a hell of a lot more than forty million tons."

The Centurion Accelerator Ring was a single massive particular accelerator that encircled the gas giant Centurion in the Legatus system. Its sole purpose was to produce enough antimatter to run a modern industrialized society without needing Mages.

A ring space station with a two-hundred-thousand-kilometer diameter, the Centurion Ring was probably closer to forty *billion* tons than forty million, though most of that wouldn't be the particle accelerator itself.

"They're building a secret antimatter production facility," Soprano concluded. "Fuck me."

"All of the Protectorate's calculations over whether or not the Legatans would risk a civil war factor in their known fuel supplies," David continued woodenly. "Another major facility, without the consumption of an entire system's industry...would change the balance of power."

He sighed.

"Damn you, Soprano," he snapped. "And just what can *we* do about this?"

"The people stealing the cargos appear to work for Turquoise," she told him. "Learning what she wants and needs could give the Protectorate an edge in working out what the hell is going on."

"And we still share an enemy with her," Campbell said. "Throwing our enemies' resources at each other sounds...useful."

David sighed and finished the water, setting the glass aside.

"You realize that, regardless of whether the *Legatans* trust us, this Turquoise will see us as expendable assets who know too much, right?"

"Yes," Soprano agreed. "Which is why we'll need a backup plan...and as it happens, I *also* have a contact number for Commodore Andrews."

He sighed.

"Get Skavar in here," he ordered. "If we're going to do this, let's at least get the cards I *know* about on the damn table."

The security chief entered the room and looked at the gathering of senior officers with a visible degree of alarm.

"Why do I feel like I just walked into a court-martial?" he asked dryly.

"Close the door, Ivan," David ordered. "Then take a seat."

The big man took a careful seat, perched on the edge of the chair like he was ready to spring into action. The room was small enough that it felt cramped with all four of them in it, though it could in theory fit another four people for a meeting.

"Jenna, check the security systems," David continued. He waited while his XO checked the panel, locking down the room from any surveillance.

"I won't swear by these systems," he observed to the others, "but they are better than anything I've ever had before. Our discussion *should* remain private."

"Private," Skavar echoed. "I'm feeling even more court-martialed here, Captain."

"That's not a bad comparison," Soprano said with a chuckle. "But don't worry; you're not the one in the most trouble here, Chief."

"Somehow, that's not reassuring," he replied.

"It's not intended to be," David told him. "Ivan. Be honest with me. How many of your security troops are active-duty Marines?"

There was a long silence.

"All of them," Skavar finally replied. "Drawn from ten different companies so it wasn't obvious to anyone watching. Gear was issued by the RMMC logistics team in Tau Ceti."

"I'd guessed that part from the fact that you had all of the gear of an actual Marine platoon," David observed. "Though I'll admit that Miss LaMonte was the one who broke the illusion for me in the end."

The Chief of Security looked confused, then sighed.

"Fuck. One of my idiots tried to get the lesbian couple into bed, didn't he?"

"Bingo," David confirmed. "So, all things considered, Chief Skavar, would you like to explain just who you actually are and how you got a Marine platoon aboard my ship?"

Skavar sighed and relaxed back into his chair, his bulk sliding back to allowing him to lean against the back.

"I told you I was retired and was asked for a favor, the call coming down from on high," he reminded David. "What I didn't mention was that it wasn't really a favor: I was Active Reserve and they recalled me.

"And *commissioned* me," Skavar continued. "I'm technically a Lieutenant in Royal Martian Marine Corps Forward Combat Intelligence, on special assignment under the authority of General George Bracken, as requested by Hand Alaura Stealey."

"I see that Stealey wasn't exactly trying to leave well enough alone," David observed. "Does anyone on this ship *actually* work for me?"

Soprano coughed.

"It was made quite clear to me," she said softly, "that I *did* work for you. I just also worked for MISS."

Skavar looked at her in surprise.

"You're MISS, ma'am?" he asked.

"It's an all-cards-on-the-table kind of meeting, Ivan," Maria told him. "I believe we've convinced the Captain to take some risks on his own part and the part of this ship in the name of the Protectorate, which means that those of us the Protectorate planted on his ship to keep him safe have a job to do."

The Marine nodded, squaring his shoulders.

"Wilco, ma'am," he confirmed brightly, then turned back to David. "We may still be Marines, sir, but there was no question in my orders. We report to you. No one else."

"But you're sending reports home, right? Both of you?" David asked.

They nodded.

"All right. So, here's where things get ugly," he told them. "I had LaMonte look for people burying covert transmissions off-ship. Assuming each of you is responsible for one set of communications, we *still* have two spies aboard ship."

He sighed.

"And I have *no* idea who, so nothing we're discussing leaves this room. Understood?"

CHAPTER 34

THE IMAGE on the wallscreen in David's office didn't resolve into a person once the call connected. The general "call holding" sign dissolved into a large rotating turquoise gemstone, glittering with an inner blue fire.

"Captain Rice," a melodious female voice greeted him. "I'll admit I'm surprised to see you contacting me with this code. I wasn't aware that you had connections to LMID."

"I'd believe that, ma'am, except that I'd be surprised if you didn't know exactly whose cargo I arrived with," David pointed out with a chuckle. "The Legatans tell me we share an enemy."

The gemstone giggled in turn.

"Well done, Captain," she murmured. "I was aware you'd arrived with a cargo being run through LMID's little smuggling project. I'm still surprised they'd provide the man who killed Mikhail Azure a secure identification code to contact me."

"As I said, they think we share an enemy in the Azure Legacy. They're hunting me quite specifically, and my understanding is that as the leader of one of the organizations to fragment off the Blue Star Syndicate, you're on their list as well."

Turquoise giggled.

"Call me Turquoise, Captain," she told him. "And yes, I am on Azure Legacy's hit list as well. We do share an enemy. But I doubt a man of your reputation would reach out to me without more reason than *that*."

"The bodies I've been sending home are a damned good reason," David said quietly. "So long as the Legacy hunts me, my *crew* are at risk. If we can work together to end the bastards, we both benefit."

"There is that," she replied. "Plus, well, if you hadn't killed Mikhail Azure, my own boss wouldn't have been vulnerable and Silent Ocean wouldn't exist. You could say I owe you. I don't suppose you have a plan?"

"Inklings of one," he told her. "I'd be delighted to share them with you."

She giggled again.

"In person, I think, Captain Rice. Unless you *want* to negotiate with a glowing gemstone?"

"I've done worse," he said levelly.

"I'm sure you have," she replied. "You're still at Foundry Yard Alpha, yes?"

Of course the woman knew more about his ship than he was comfortable with. David concealed a sigh.

"We are," he confirmed.

"Go to the Salty Dragon Wench in the central station at twenty-two hundred OMT," she ordered. "Tell them you're on Oceanic business, and they'll deliver you to me. Bring one escort, no more.

"We will make the Legacy suffer," she concluded.

The Salty Dragon Wench was...even worse than what David had been expecting given the name. He and Soprano made their way through one of the seedier sections of the Foundry Yard Alpha Central station. They weren't—quite—into the areas where brothels had signs openly advertising their business, but David suspected that was only a few corridors over. Certainly, they were already into sections with stereotypical neon-style signs declaring GIRLS GIRLS GIRLS or BOYS BOYS BOYS, depending on the establishment.

The Salty Dragon Wench's sign didn't leave much doubt as to the nature of the establishment, either. The text announcing the bar's name was beneath an anthropomorphized dragon with exposed breasts. Loud music leaked out each time the door opened, and David managed to not *actively* look uncomfortable as he followed his Ship's Mage under the sign.

Soprano, to his amusement, was utterly unbothered by the neighborhood. She led the way up to the door and rapped on it calmly.

It popped open and a massive man loomed over them.

"Cover is ten," he growled at them.

"We're on Oceanic business," David replied calmly.

The human mountain growled wordlessly at the back of his throat, then gestured for them to follow him.

He led the pair of officers into a dimly lit space. The only brightly lit areas were the stages, where David was unsurprised to see mostly naked women cavorting around poles.

Most places in the Protectorate, he'd be sure they'd chosen to be there. Knowing this bar was tied to a Blue Star Syndicate offshoot, though...

Soprano's hand settled onto his shoulder.

"You can't tell the difference between the volunteers and the trafficked at a glance," she murmured in his ear. "Leave it. For now."

He coughed but caught the meaning of both her restraint and her addendum. They had the connections to let a few people know about the Wench and let *them* poke into it without it getting attached to his name.

He didn't have to screw up today's meeting to make certain that any of the kids flashing their bodies across the stage unwillingly were taken care of.

Calming himself with plans of future vengeance, he allowed Soprano to gently pull him after their immense guide.

He had work to do.

The room the bouncer led them to was clearly a private party room, a slightly larger version of the closed booths where a certain class of patrons could pay for lap dances and such.

There was only one occupant, a young woman who looked about nineteen, with a face and body whose proportions and lines were just on the wrong side of too perfect to be natural. She was facing them, wearing a tiny pair of dark blue shorts and a similarly sized crop top.

Carefully keeping his eyes on her face, David inclined his head.

"Turquoise, I presume."

She giggled...and then moved. If he'd doubted his assessment for even a moment before, he had no doubt when he saw her move. Turquoise was built like a stripper, but she *moved* like an assassin.

The miniscule outfit would easily draw attention away from the holster nestled into her mid-back with the small-but-deadly needler pistol tucked into it, and something in how she moved suggested her muscles were as natural as her breasts.

As she leapt down from the stage, her hair flickered in color, changing from a glittering fiery red to a shimmering, gem-like blue.

"Well done, Captain Rice," she told him, offering her hand. "You'd be surprised how many people, even in this day and age, assume the pretty girl is a bonus."

She *had* to be older than she looked, David presumed, but given the amount of surgery and upgrades she'd clearly had, he wasn't going to hazard a guess as to how old.

"When meeting the underworld boss of ten systems, it pays to err on the side of caution," he replied after he'd shaken her hand.

Turquoise giggled.

"Six systems, Captain. Flattery will get you my amusement, but it won't change the deal," she warned. "Sit. Khaleesi—bring us drinks."

The last was directed at a similarly built woman with long blond hair, clad in a thin blue robe. Tucked against the wall and invisible from the entrance, Khaleesi was about six inches shorter than Turquoise but otherwise had clearly been pressed into the same bodysculpted too-perfect mold.

Her eyes were downcast and her posture submissive as she produced three glasses of soda...but translucent as her long robe appeared, David's practiced eye also picked out the two areas where it was concealing weapons. The blonde had the same less-visible "upgrades" as her boss, too.

"Somehow, I get the feeling that it's no accident that someone's idea of 'sexy assassins' ended up running the show," he observed.

Turquoise smiled. There was no humor in it.

"Khaleesi, myself, some others," she said simply. "We were Conner Maroon's bodyguards and private assassins. Once *he* was dead, it took surprisingly few fatalities to bring the rest of the sector in line."

David managed to conceal a shiver. Maroon had, apparently, underestimated his bodyguards—and David could guess why the oversexualized assassins he was sharing a room with had turned on their employer.

"And the Azure Legacy regards you as trouble, I take it?" David asked.

"More, I'm not one of the ones they've decided are the 'most likely heirs'," she replied. "Not least because I have no interest in anything beyond my six star systems. So, I am an impediment to their 'duty' to reunify the Syndicate."

The humorless smile returned.

"They would rather see me broken and brought to heel than destroyed, but I *refuse to kneel again.*"

"So, as Legatus presumed, we share an enemy," David agreed. He wasn't sure this bitter, enraged, probably-ex-slave assassin-turned-crimelord was a better option than Mikhail Azure had been, but she was the ally he had to hand.

"Indeed," she said. "I understand you clashed with a squadron of Legacy warships on your way here. How many survived?"

"None," he told her shortly. "They underestimated my ship."

"That's an error they won't repeat," Turquoise warned. "They will now *over*estimate you, to be certain you are destroyed. Do not underestimate the resources that can be mobilized in this age by the application of vast quantities of money."

"Your old boss had a Navy *cruiser*," David said. "I don't underestimate *anything* he set in motion."

She shook her head.

"You took down *Azure Gauntlet*," she said aloud. "I'm impressed. And I must thank you, Captain Rice. You made all this"—she gestured around—"possible. If Azure had lived, I would have remained an assassin.

"Now I am a queen, and I have no intentions of becoming a slave again. Together, we can break the Legacy."

"They already see me as a threat and are trying to take me out," he pointed out. "If we can arrange for them to 'accidentally' learn my next destination, then you can ambush them with whatever ships you have."

"Clever, if somewhat obvious," Turquoise told him. "No, let them overestimate you. Let them overestimate *us*. If we are to be allies, let them *see* that we are allies—so they do not see the sucker punch we are preparing with our other hand.

"I have a cargo that needs to go to a covert staging area," she continued. "It's part of the Legatan business you're already tied up in. They will expect it to be escorted—so you will be met at the first jump point by my own ships.

"They will expect that, and once they see the force, they will bring everything they have in the sector to intercept you. And then *I* will intercept *them*."

"Surely, they know how many ships you have," David said. This didn't sound safe, though he could see ways to make it work in his favor once he involved the Navy.

"I have many ships scattered across my systems, but I have toys they do not believe fell into my hands," Turquoise told him. "I will keep my secrets, Captain, but don't you worry.

"I will guarantee you that whatever the Legacy brings, my ships *will* be victorious and your ship will be safely delivered to my station.

"We will crush our shared enemy and your ship will be on its way, free of pursuit and heading far away from *my* systems." Her eyes flashed dangerously.

"Are we understood? Do we have a deal?"

He glanced at Soprano. From the look in her eyes, she'd caught some of Turquoise's very specific phrasing as well, but she nodded slowly. He knew from past experience that he could only run so long.

Sooner or later, it was time to turn and fight.

CHAPTER 35

MARIA WATCHED from a viewing gallery as the massive assembly that made up one of *Red Falcon*'s main antimatter rocket pods swam delicately through space, guided by a trio of small tugs and more men and women in rocket-equipped EVA exosuits than Maria could count.

If Foundry Yard Alpha's crews were half as competent as she figured they were, at least two of those EVA suits contained Mages, using their magic to help guide the ten-thousand-ton engine into place.

"Hey," Acconcio's voice said quietly behind her. "May I join you?"

She sighed.

She'd been avoiding him for three days, since she'd spotted him in a restaurant he had no reason to be in. But they were about to go back to space, and she couldn't go into the void with the man without letting him know where they stood.

"Sure," she replied, her voice dull. She stepped over to one side, continuing to watch the shipyard at work as Acconcio stepped up to join her at the window.

"It's always amazing to watch this kind of shit, isn't it?" he asked. "Those engines are huge and we have five of them." She felt him shake his head. "It's an incredible amount of power."

"And nothing without the magic to carry them between the stars," she reminded him. "The eternal irony of modern man: our technological prowess is only meaningful when linked to an arcane gift we barely understand and hate the source of."

It wasn't something she thought about much, but Maria Soprano was a Mage by Blood. One of her ancestors had been MGS-276, one of the late-stage experimental subjects of Project Olympus, freed by the first Mage-King of Mars.

Her ancestry couldn't be traced any further back than that. All she could be certain of was that the nameless and unmarked graves on Olympus Mons included *dozens* of her forebears.

"I feel like I stepped in something," the ex-warrant said quietly. "I'm not even sure *what* I did, but..."

"It's pretty obvious, I would think," Maria told him. "Were you or weren't you in Green Parson's Bar the other night?"

Silence.

"Yes," he admitted. "I was."

"You followed me."

"Yes."

"What do you *think* you stepped in?" she snarled. "You fucking *followed me*, and you're wondering why I'm pissed?"

"I wanted to be sure you were safe," he protested.

She spun, power flaring around her hands and encasing her in a glowing shield of force.

"If I'd needed your help, Acconcio, I would have told you," she told him. "If you'd wanted to help, you would have offered.

"Instead, you *stalked* me to see what I was doing." Power collapsed, leaving her cold and alone as she stared at the man a meter away from her. "We're done. There are lines you don't get to cross, Acconcio, and that's pretty high on the damned list."

"You lied to me about where you were going," he pointed out.

"And?" she asked. "Where I was, who I was meeting, it *was* ship's business—and it *wasn't* yours. But you couldn't accept that, and that's a glaring red sign *I* won't accept."

"So, that's it, then?" he asked. "One strike, I'm out?"

"Fuck, yes," she agreed. "Never met a man yet who didn't fuck it up eventually if given a second chance. We're done." She shook her head. "I'm not going to get you kicked off the ship or anything stupid like that, Acconcio. We worked together before; we can still do so. Right?"

He was silent again but sighed.

"Yeah, sure," he agreed.

Through the window, the mass of the engine slid home and dozens of welding torches lit up like tiny fireflies circling *Red Falcon*'s bulk.

"Well, James?" David asked.

"They do good work," the engineer replied calmly, studying the screens in the control station in engineering. "Physical connection of the engine is complete. We're setting up the feeder lines and control runs right now."

He shrugged expressively.

"Give me twenty-four hours and we'll be ready for engine tests," he promised. "Barring unexpected issues, we'll be out into space in thirty-six hours and looking for cargo, boss."

"We got cargo sorted out already," David told him. He glanced around, making sure they were alone. Kellers's people were backing up the yard staff, with LaMonte and the other junior engineering officers managing to somehow be *everywhere*.

"Any luck tracking down those transmissions?" he asked softly.

"Not much," the engineer admitted. "I've got a program running and crunching cycles in the background, but it's a slow, bloody-minded process to get anything useful."

"If it'll help, I can tell you who two of them were from," David said with a sigh. "One is from Soprano and another is from Skavar. Those are...now known and 'benign', as LaMonte put it."

Kellers choked, then shook his head.

"Is there anyone on this ship who actually works for you?" he asked.

"Both of them assure me they work for me as well, at least," the Captain said. "Surprisingly...I trust them."

"Those two are good people," Kellers agreed after a moment. "So... Protectorate agents?"

"Marines and MISS," David confirmed. "Keep that to yourself. *Maybe* to LaMonte, if you think she can keep it out of her bunk."

The engineer laughed.

"Boss, it took me *three weeks* to realize she was dating Xi Wu—I almost missed it until after they started being obvious about it—and another two to realize why Kelzin was okay with it," he replied. "That one can keep her mouth shut when she chooses to—and she's a better programmer than I am, though don't tell *her* I said that.

"If we want to track down our remaining moles, we need her."

"Then fill her in on that," David told him. He shook his head.

"We're working with crooks again," he warned his engineer. "Dragging our coat to see if we can lure Legacy out for the local Blue Star leftovers to take a shot at. This, of course, means that *we* are going to get shot at."

Kellers coughed again.

"Yeah, probably by *both* those groups," he pointed out. "I just got this ship *fixed*, boss."

"And hopefully, Acconcio will stop them putting more holes in her this time," David replied. "But yeah, I'm not expecting Silent Ocean to stay on our side, even if we *are* carrying cargo for them."

The engineer nodded.

"Speaking of *on our side*, boss," he said, even more quietly than before, "look at this."

He brought up an image on his screen, gesturing for David to follow. It was a familiar set of data from David's Navy days, the datastream for an RFLAM defensive turret. His gaze automatically picked up the timestamp.

It was one of their rear turrets, during the battle with the Legacy corvettes. He studied the data as it went by, a visual representation appearing on the other screen.

"Wait, that missile hit us," he said as a targeting package crossed the feed.

"Yeah, that's the one that took out our engine pod," Kellers confirmed. "Bridge passed down targeting instructions for three turrets to take it on. It wasn't missed. It didn't sneak through our perimeter. Three turrets took a total of fourteen shots at it."

That was...unlikely. The chance of the antimissile lasers hitting varied based on a million factors, but fourteen beams should have killed a missile.

"What happened?" he asked.

"What happened is that someone fucked the code on our rear defensive systems," the engineer said flatly. "Any missile that looked like it was going to hit the engines acquired a new code tag I've never seen before, which activating a sequence that misaligned any laser firing at it by point zero three degrees."

That wasn't a big misalignment. Not one that they'd even notice in a review of the action. But it was enough of one that the missiles wouldn't be hit except by pure dumb luck.

"Please tell me this code has been removed."

"It's out," Kellers confirmed. "I have a copy of it; I'm going over it for signatures and such in my spare time, but not having any luck. But... while it wouldn't take a lot of command authority to insert that code, it was in the unlinked firmware."

"What do you mean?" David asked.

"The targeting computer on the RFLAM turrets has an 'input-only' data connection," his engineer replied. "You can't modify the software on the turret via its datalinks. To change that software, you need physical access to the turret.

"Someone rigged our aft defenses to specifically allow a disabling strike through...and that someone is aboard this damn ship."

David studied the datastream again for several long seconds. He'd known he had a mole, but a *saboteur*?

That was a new level of problem.

CHAPTER 36

RED FALCON **LEAPT** toward the outer reaches of the Svarog system like a prime thoroughbred finally unleashed. Five antimatter engines lit up with their characteristic bright white flare, pushing the ship away from Dazbog at a full ten gravities.

The magical gravity negated that acceleration inside the runes' effect, allowing David to sit comfortably on his bridge and survey the reports and stats for his ship.

All five engines were purring along perfectly, new-built and repaired alike. They weren't burning at full power, as *Falcon* was only carrying a three-quarters load this time. Turquoise's load was only eleven million tons, and he'd put out a call for partial containers for his official destination of Amber.

The four hundred ten-thousand-ton containers he'd acquired in response to that call would be all that he had aboard when he actually reached that system, but that was fine. He'd be rid of the cargo of high-energy components and power sources he was carrying for the criminals and have a cargo to justify visiting his girlfriend's home planet.

And if he was very lucky, he'd gut the organization determined to kill him off along the way.

"Time to jump?" he asked Campbell and Soprano.

"Two hours," Campbell confirmed. "Soprano?"

"I make the same," the Ship's Mage replied. "Initial jump is six light-months to the designated rendezvous point."

David nodded and turned to look at Acconcio. *Falcon*'s third officer had been out of sorts for several days now, but that wasn't unusual for a man who'd just been dumped. David wasn't going to ask questions, but he was relying on the man not to be a *completely* useless weight.

"Iovis," he said to the man. "I don't trust Silent Ocean as far as I can throw this ship. We're supposed to be meeting a trio of Amber-built armed jump-ships."

Amber had been founded by North American libertarians. The system had exactly enough laws and government to fulfill the Protectorate's requirements for law enforcement and healthcare, and not one sentence or person more.

That meant that a lot of the illegal armed ships in the Protectorate came from there, as did a lot of gray-area bounty hunter ships and the like.

"Those ships aren't built to any standard specification," he warned the gunner. "We don't know how capable they are, but it's likely we have them outgunned. That said, *watch them.* Like a hawk. If they twitch a muscle without a reason, be ready to blow them to hell."

"They probably won't risk it if they're in laser range," Acconcio replied, confidence in his skills and ship dragging him out of his funk. "We put two or three five-gigawatt lasers into each of them, the game is over. They know that. We know that. They'll behave."

"That's what I'm relying on," David agreed, "but once things start getting hot, I want you to *keep* watching them. We're vulnerable with potentially hostile armed ships that close to us."

He shook his head.

"Make sure you've got a solid cycle of rest with your deputies," he ordered. "We're going to be on high alert until we make the final rendezvous. This whole situation makes my skin crawl."

"Someone will be on duty, watching the scanners and the guns the whole way," Acconcio promised. "No one is going to sneak up on us, and we'll blow away anyone that tries."

David nodded and glanced over at Campbell. He didn't say anything. She knew what he was asking and gave him a clear nod.

So far, everything was proceeding according to plan.

"Jump in five. Four. Three. Two. One. *JUMP*."

Power flared around Shachar Costa as Maria watched, the young Tau Ceti native's pale skin glowing in the light from the simulacrum as he cast the spell that tore them through half a light-year.

The young man was still her weakest Mage, but he'd demonstrated an unusual affinity for the short jumps despite that. Or perhaps because of it; she wasn't sure. It wasn't like a short jump required that much less energy, but apparently it was enough that Costa could focus more and manage the spell in ways that were difficult for most Mages.

Even the short jump left him looking like he'd been run over by a garbage truck with spiked tires, trembling and wavering even he floated in zero gee.

"Go rest," she told him gently as she checked their position. "We're bang on. Well done."

"Thanks, ma'am."

The youth left, leaving Maria alone in the simulacrum chamber as she ran over the sensor data *Falcon*'s systems were feeding her. The big ship sat in deep space, in the section of the void that astrophysicists argued over whether it should be considered part of a star system or not.

She was alone.

"Correct me if I'm wrong, boss," she said over the link to the bridge, "but weren't we supposed to be meeting an escort here?"

"We were," Rice confirmed. "We're two hours from jumping, according to the schedule we gave Turquoise, right?"

"Yep. Want me to step it up?" she asked.

"No. We'll give our erstwhile allies those two hours," he told her. "Then we'll do them the courtesy of leaving a beacon and continue on our way."

Risky, but then, neither Maria nor Rice apparently figured their escorts were going to be helpful.

"Wait!" Acconcio's voice cut in. "Jump flares—multiple jump flares. Bringing up the defense suite and charging the lasers."

"Initiating evasive maneuvers," Campbell added. "I have no ID, no transponder codes."

Maria grimaced. It was *probably* their escort. Probably. But there were enough people out here looking for them...

She drifted to the simulacrum, putting the runes on her palms in the blank spaces on the semi-liquid silver model intended for them, and linking into the ship. She couldn't do much with just a jump matrix, but it let her see more than just the screens would give her.

"All three ships are a quarter-million tons, fusion thrusters, moving towards us at one gravity," Acconcio reported. "Visual makes them out as Amber design, but nothing is pinging as a distinct class."

"Have they hailed us?" Rice demanded.

"Nothing so far," Campbell said.

"I can move us out on your word," Maria told the Captain. "What's your call?"

There was silence.

"Stand by to jump," Rice said. "And, Campbell? Try and open a channel. Let's see if they're friends being *stupid*."

Somehow, David wasn't surprised that they got a response the instant they pinged the incoming ships.

"*Red Falcon*, this is *Silent Atlantic*," the lead ship replied. They were transmitting a visual, but it was just a distorted view of an open sea, waves crashing across it. The voice was male and unfamiliar.

"You'll forgive me if I'm not giving you a name past the ship's," he continued. "We're allies of convenience for the now, but I know your opinion of us."

"My opinion of you almost got you shot," David told the speaker. "Your ships are out of their weight class here, *Silent Atlantic*. Irritating me is a bad idea."

"You underestimate us," the pirate replied. "But our job is to keep you alive. You were Navy, right?"

"Right."

"We'll assume escort formation Delta-Six," *Silent Atlantic* informed him. "Try to not accidentally shoot any of us as we move in, eh?"

The thought was surprisingly tempting but, as the pirate had pointed out, they were allies today. Delta-Six had the three escort ships forming a triangle on a single plane around *Red Falcon* with one ship, presumably not *Silent Atlantic* since most of *Falcon*'s guns faced forward, in front.

They'd all be about thirty thousand kilometers apart. Knife range if anyone decided to open fire.

"We'll be jumping in just under two hours," David finally told them. "Will you be able to follow?"

"Aye. We'll be with you the whole way, *Falcon*."

David nodded and killed the channel, leaning back in his chair and glancing over at Campbell.

So, either the pirate ships each had at least three Mages aboard—far more than he'd expect pirates to be able to recruit...or they didn't expect the trip to be nearly as long as David did.

It took most of the two hours for the pirate ships to match velocities at their intended locations, but then the four ships were left to drift gently through space.

The tension on *Red Falcon*'s bridge was thick enough to cut. Acconcio had done everything short of pulsing the pirate ships with active radar to lock them in for his weapons, and David was all too aware that Delta-Six put two thirds of their "allies" out of the line of fire of *Falcon*'s heavy lasers.

If he was lucky, their bridge crews were feeling just as twitchy as his. *Red Falcon* didn't have much of a reputation yet, but she'd killed six Legacy corvettes so far—and David knew *his* reputation with the Blue Star Syndicate.

Much of the body count they'd racked up the previous year had been due to his Ship's Mage, but since that part of the story was classified, he knew he was a personal bogeyman to many of the Syndicate's survivors.

He couldn't bring himself to be bothered by that.

"We're ready to go, sir," Soprano reported from the simulacrum chamber. "Course is laid in; we're standing by to jump."

"Send the course to them," he ordered. "Give them a second or so to complete the jump, then follow them through."

"Understood. Transmitting."

A few seconds later, jump flares flickered on his screens, then Campbell flashed him a thumbs-up.

"Mage Soprano?"

Any response she made was lost in the eerie sensation of the teleport.

Despite his paranoia, the next jump point was clear. David's estimate of how many Mages the pirates had was now at a minimum of two each, which was what he would have expected to be their maximum normally.

But no one from *Silent Atlantic* or the other ships raised a peep when they sent out the next jump path two hours later.

"Let them jump first again," he told Soprano quietly. "They're making me twitchy."

"They knew how fast we moved," she reminded him. "They would have made sure they could keep up."

"That's fair," he agreed. "But I dislike that my escorts are pirate ships."

"We don't know they're pirates for certain," Soprano replied.

"No. But we can be pretty sure, can't we?"

She didn't argue the point.

"Jump initiation in twenty seconds," she reported instead. "We'll let them lead and then be on our way."

The jump tore through David in its usual ripple of discomfort, and he sighed.

"Report," he ordered as his guts tried to settle.

"We're alone," Acconcio said instantly. "What the hell? Our escorts are MIA; there's no one else here."

"Maria?" he asked. "Please tell me we got our jump wrong somehow."

"No," she said calmly, exhaustion layering her voice. "Nav suite says we're eleven hundred kilometers from the target point. We're bang on."

"And our 'friends' are missing." David sighed. "Acconcio, full active sensor sweep. Take the ship to battle stations."

"It could be nothing," the gunner noted.

"It could be," David agreed. "But I'm not taking that bet. Battle stations, everyone."

He looked at the exhausted image of his Ship's Mage.

"Go rest, Maria," he ordered. "There's nothing close to us; we'll wake you up if there's trouble."

"Don't forget," she told him. "You may still need me."

"I won't. Go."

He waited long enough for Xi Wu to relieve Soprano, taking over the station in the simulacrum chamber, and then pinged Skavar.

"Chief?"

"Yes, sir?"

"Get your men and women in their exosuits," David ordered. "I don't know what's going on, but I want your people standing by to repel boarders."

"We were born ready," Skavar replied. "We'll be in our suits in three minutes."

"Good."

David studied the imposingly blank hologram in the center of his bridge. Something was wrong. If it was a trap, he'd have expected it to be sprung already.

What was he missing?

CHAPTER 37

SECONDS TICKED BY. Slowly, painfully slowly, they turned to minutes. The emptiness of the void was making David even twitchier, but it also meant his ship was safe. For now.

"There they are!" Acconcio suddenly snapped. "They missed their jump, I've got three jump flares at fifteen light-minutes at exactly the time I'd expect."

Fifteen light-minutes on a one-light-year jump wasn't that bad when you thought about it, but it was enough to throw any kind of escort or formation completely out of whack.

"Are we sure it's them?" he asked. If someone knew their course plot—and it was *supposed* to have been leaked this time—faking being their escort would be an effective way to sneak up on them in plain sight.

"Incoming transmission," Campbell reported. "They must have pulsed it toward our expected emergence just after they jumped."

"Play it."

The same distorted ocean scene appeared on the screen.

"*Red Falcon,* this is *Silent Atlantic.*" The speaker didn't sound particularly happy. "I'm pretty sure you sent us the right coordinates, but they got glitched out in our systems. *All* of our systems.

"I don't need to tell you that's unlikely. We're en route to your expected emergence, but our ETA sucks and there is no way we can jump in less than two hours. We'll plan to rendezvous at the next jump, but...

watch your ass, Captain Rice. From a quarter-billion kilometers away, I sure as hell can't."

"Send an acknowledgement," he ordered. "Keep us at maximum alert. Acconcio, anything on that sensor sweep?"

"Nothing," the gunner replied, leaning against his console in a half-exhausted slump. "We're clear for twenty light-seconds in every direction, at least. That's as far as the active sweep is going to get us."

He shrugged.

"Beyond that, passives are clear except for the *Silent Ocean* ships. No thermal signatures. No EM radiation, nothing. It's dead as the graveyard out there."

David nodded slowly. It didn't feel right, but he couldn't keep his crew at top readiness forever. He trusted the scanners enough to relax a bit—unless someone jumped in right on top of them, which would require more information than he'd left behind in Svarog, they'd have plenty of warning when the other shoe dropped.

"All right, stand us down to alert two," he ordered. "All of you"—he glanced around his bridge—"switch off for your backups and go get some rest. You've been going since we left Svarog, and if we're going to get intercepted on the next jump, I want you all with at least a nap under your belts.

"Go."

"What about you?" Campbell asked, staying at her console.

"I'm the Captain," he told her. "Holding the watch while I send everyone else to rest is my prerogative."

She looked ready to argue, but he shook his head at her and she finally, slowly, nodded.

Campbell rose, joining Acconcio and the others in trooping off the bridge, leaving David behind with his backup crew.

His nerves said he should keep them, but logic said they were clear—and he'd need them rested when they weren't clear anymore!

Maria wasn't sure how long she'd been asleep—it couldn't have been more than fifteen, maybe twenty minutes—before the admittance buzzer on her quarters went off.

The Captain had an emergency link to her wrist-comp. Everybody else should have known better than to harass a Jump Mage right after jumping. She hadn't even taken the time to undress before falling into her bed—though given the circumstances, she'd probably have stayed in her shipsuit with its emergency pressurization and oxygen-supply capabilities anyway.

She ignored the buzzer and tried to go back to sleep—only for it to, unsurprisingly, sound again.

And again.

Grumbling, she got up and crossed to her door. She even managed to suppress the ball of *probably* non-lethal lightning she conjured on the way. Waking her up wasn't really punishable, much as she'd like to hurt whoever had done it.

That urge accelerated when she saw that it was Acconcio standing at her door. He didn't try and come into her room at least, he just stood there, looking even worse than he had on the bridge. His eyes were bloodshot and he looked completely exhausted.

"What the hell is this, Officer Acconcio?" she demanded carefully.

"I was thinking about what you said," he half-slurred. Was he *drunk*? "About...men and second chances."

"Then you damn well have a good reason to be at my door," Maria pointed out dryly.

To her surprise, he shook his head.

"Ain't about us," he told her. "I fucked up, your call, your choice, ain't gonna argue. But I already *gots* a second chance, see? A second chance to go to space. A second chance to fly."

His words were swinging from coherent to slurred at random, and what he was *saying* didn't make sense.

"Iovis," she said gently. "You probably need to go lie down. You're drunk and you're exhausted. Whatever you want to say we can talk about another time."

"No!" he snapped. "Can't. I fucked it up, Maria. I fucked *all of it up*."

His second chance was aboard *Red Falcon*, she realized. If he'd fucked that up... her blood ran cold.

"I sold us out," he admitted. "They said they wouldn't hurt you, that I'd get the ship, make it easy so long as the Captain died. Weren't supposed to jump us in space, were just supposed to kill the engines. They lied, told me it was a mistake.

"But it weren't, were it?" He was staring at her, desperately looking for something even as Maria drew back from him.

She was preparing another self-defense spell. She'd shock him, take him into custody, get him to repeat what he was saying to the Captain. It would give them some of their answers.

"Tried to get you out of the way at Madagascah," he slurred. "Needed their money but didn't want you to get hurt. Kept going wrong. Fucked it all up. Again. And again."

Now he was crying and Maria wasn't quite sure *what* to do anymore. She was half-tempted to hug him and half-tempted to shock him unconscious.

"You rigged the rear turrets," she said, stretching for some kind of logic.

"Yeah," he admitted. "They gave me the code, more than I could put together, but I checked it to be sure it was what they said it was. It was money, Maria, always just money...and they said you'd be *safe*."

"We can still fix this," she told him. "We can change courses, run, hide. Whatever you sold them, we can make it right."

"No, we can't," he gasped out past choking sobs. "*I fucked it all up*, Maria. The ships aren't the—"

Bullets ricocheted off Maria's door, several slamming into her bedroom and one searing a fiery line across her shoulder—but *all* of them went through the big ex-Navy man standing in front of her.

Iovis Acconcio's blood sprayed across her and the big man fell to his knees, blood filling his mouth as he tried to speak, tried to finish his warning.

Then he collapsed forward, revealing the slim, pale-skinned form of Shachar Costa standing behind him—with the ugly form of the MAC-6 pistol in his hand now pointed directly at Maria.

"Drunk and in love, damn, what an idiot," Costa said calmly. "I don't suppose you'd believe me if I told you he was a traitor to the ship and that's why I shot him?"

Maria had already conjured a shield of force between her and her erstwhile subordinate.

"Not really, no."

"Didn't think so."

The gun fired again, bullets smashing into the shield with bone-shattering force. The shield held and Costa shrugged.

"Didn't think that would work," he admitted. Almost casually, he holstered the gun and grinned at her. "Well, 'boss'? Got a plan? A backup spell? Some grand magical trick the Navy taught you that us poor weak civvies couldn't match?"

She'd just jumped. She was exhausted—it was all she could do to keep the shield up. Her lack of response seemed to embolden Costa and he gestured, conjuring a blast of lightning that hammered her defenses, forcing her to step back from Acconcio's body into her room.

"You're crazy," she gasped out. "Every alarm on the ship has to have gone off by now!"

"That, Mage Soprano, would require the internal sensors to be working," the younger Mage told her, a second hammer of lightning flickering across Maria's shield. "And believe me, I am *quite* certain they aren't."

"What have you done?"

"Oh, it's *quite* the list and we don't have time for it," he replied. "I'd *love* to test those Navy-trained skills of yours, but I had *such* a better plan. Iovis fucked it up by opening your door—but hey! He isn't a problem anymore.

"Night-night, 'boss.'"

Costa didn't do anything visible, but the door to Maria's quarters slammed shut between them. Acconcio's outstretched arm had been in the track of the door, but the heavy security shutter severed it with a heart-wrenching *snap*.

She stared at her door for several long seconds, then slammed the open button. She wasn't surprised when it refused to listen to her.

Then she tried to raise the bridge. Her wrist-comp informed her that it was no longer connected to the ship's internal network. Two attempts to send direct transmissions confirmed her worst fears.

She was being jammed. Costa had taken control of the ship's internal systems, blinding Captain Rice to any internal threat.

What kind of threat would require that? They were expecting an attack from outside, but unless Costa had help, he couldn't take the ship on his own...

Except they'd loaded fourteen million tons of cargo. Fourteen hundred ten-thousand-ton containers. They'd scanned the secondary loads carefully, though. So, if there were infiltrators, they'd either had some top-of-the-line concealment gear or...

Or Turquoise had betrayed them from the beginning, and every piece of this was another jaw of the trap.

She made it as far as the access panel for the manual override before she started to find herself short of breath and realized the problem. Costa didn't just have control of the sensors. The bastard had at least partial control of the life support systems—and he'd stopped oxygen circulating into her room.

Maria wove a spell around herself quickly, almost unconsciously, and then slumped against the wall. Just keeping herself alive was going to take everything she had. She forced herself to grab the panel and try to pull it open, but the unused machinery resisted her.

Her fingers slipped free and she collapsed to the floor, relying on her purification spell as she gasped for breath.

This...was not going well.

CHAPTER 38

THE SENSORS were still quiet. The single trio of Silent Ocean ships continued to progress toward *Red Falcon* as the big ship floated through space, and nothing else, threatening or otherwise, marked David's displays.

Somehow, that was only making him more nervous. He checked all of the scans himself, to be sure. Nothing.

Everything across the ship was green and calm, but the hairs on the back of his neck kept itching.

"James, how's everything in Engineering?" he asked Kellers. His chief engineer appeared on the screen, leaning back in his own chair and supervising affairs in his cavernous domain.

"Sleepy," the engineer told him. "Like the calm before the storm."

David laughed humorlessly. His engineer had the nerves as well.

"Anything we need to be keeping an eye on?"

"Engines are green. Guns are green. Missiles are green." Kellers shook his head. "Everything *looks* right."

"But the hairs on the back of your neck are standing up, huh?"

"You too?"

"Yeah." David considered. "Indulge my paranoia, James. Check that arms locker we didn't tell anyone we'd installed, and be ready to arm your people."

"You're expecting boarders?"

"I don't know *what* I'm expecting. It's just too quiet, and I can't shake the feeling that the mis-jump wasn't an accident. And if it wasn't...there should be *something* going down."

"Warn Xi Wu and Skavar," Kellers suggested. "I'll keep Engineering in hand." He paused. "Want me to scrub the sensor data? Make sure we don't have any unexpected viruses in the processing centers?"

David shivered.

"Is that possible?" he asked.

"It isn't *easy*, but given what someone did to our rear turrets..."

"Scrub the data," David ordered. "If our eyes have been blinded, let me know."

Nodding, Kellers turned away, dropping the line.

David then pinged the simulacrum chamber. Soprano had gone to rest, but the schedule said Xi Wu had the watch. There was silence for several moments, to his surprise, so he pinged the chamber again.

Finally, the image of the room popped up, along with the cheerful young Asian Mage.

"Everything's fine here," she chirped. "What can I help you with?"

"Mage Wu, Chief Kellers and I are having a paranoid moment," he told her. "I want you to lock down the simulacrum chamber. Don't let anyone in until Soprano or I give you the okay."

"Sure, whatever you need," Wu said cheerfully, and David froze.

That was *not* the response he would have expected.

"Xi...are you all right?" he asked.

"Everything's fine here," she chirped cheerfully again. It wasn't just an echo. Same words. Same facial expression.

"Of course it is," he said slowly. "Like I said, lock down the chamber and wait for myself or Soprano to tell you to open."

"Sure, whatever you need."

David cut the channel and wordlessly snarled at the screen that had been showing him a computer simulation of one of his better junior Mages—which meant that *someone else* had control of the simulacrum chamber.

He slammed a different sequence into his chair controls, trying to link down to the security barracks.

No response. A chill ran down his spine and he grabbed his wrist-comp, ordering it to disconnect from the ship's com network and try to reach Skavar directly.

"We're being jammed," he said aloud. "And someone is in our computers."

"Sir?" David looked up at LaMonte sitting at the engineering remote panel and remembered that the young woman on his bridge was dating the Mage who was supposed to be in the simulacrum chamber.

"That was a simulation of Xi," he told her. "We're being blinded inside our own ship—can you fix it?"

The young woman swallowed, yanking on a loose curl of currently black hair.

"I'll try. But...what about Xi?" she asked.

"I don't know," David admitted. "But if whoever this is thought they could lock me out of communications on my own ship, I have some surprises they need to learn about!"

With the other shoe at least identified, if not exactly dropped, David pinged Kellers again.

"What?" his engineer demanded grumpily.

"We've lost the simulacrum chamber," the Captain snapped. "Tried to talk to Xi Wu and only got a computer simulation. Not a very good one, either."

"We're busy down here; that's not my problem," Kellers replied. "We've got a critical flux in one of the engines; didn't the ship's system advise you?"

"No," David said slowly, studying the man. "Did you get the arms locker open?"

"What?" his engineer replied. "We're busy down here!"

David cut the channel before the program pretending to be his engineer—*poorly*—managed to make him scream.

"LaMonte?" he asked quietly.

"Everything we send into the main network is getting redirected," she said grimly. "I don't *think* they physically redirected the wires, but the software switched us over the moment you reached out to the simulacrum chamber."

She shook her head.

"It's code, but it's damned sophisticated code. I have admin access, I can get around it...but it's going to take me *time*."

"Then take the time," David ordered grimly. He rose from his chair and crossed to an undistinguished panel near the exit from the bridge. Pushing at the bottom of it popped out a palm reader, and he slapped his hand on it.

The panel popped open, revealing a small-arms locker. It wasn't huge, only big enough for a half-dozen carbines, but it contained a half-dozen carbines no one else knew was there.

"Arm yourselves," he ordered his bridge crew. "Gaspar, do we have external coms?"

Cohen Gaspar was one of the chiefs working under Campbell, and the Old Earth native was the man currently on the communications console. He was already poking at his displays before David asked.

"Clever, clever," he murmured, then looked up. "It's set up to *look* like we do, but it's running into the same datastream trap LaMonte found," he admitted. "Probably won't try to fake a response this time, just leave us silent."

"I am getting *very* sick of discovering my ship doesn't work for me," David growled. "Fortunately, I'm a paranoid bastard."

"Sir?"

"Type in *James Campbell is the biggest idiot that Mars did ever see*," he told Gaspar. "When it asks you why, type in *because I'm his sister*."

The sheer incongruity of the inputs got a chuckle from the chief even with the tension on the bridge.

"It's giving me a whole new menu for short-range coms?" he replied.

"That's because there's an auxiliary com array that's hard-linked to that panel," David said. "Now, I want you to pulse the entire ship with a code I'm transferring to you. It's a high-alert code—both Kellers and Skavar will recognize it."

And assuming he hadn't been speaking to a simulation when he'd ordered both men to prepare their teams for battle, that was going to turn the tide in short order.

CHAPTER 39

NO MATTER HOW tired she was. No matter how drained. No matter if she'd just seen her most recent lover shot to death in front of her. There was no way that Maria Isabella Soprano was going to lie down and die.

Slowly, she pushed herself back up onto her knees, letting her anger fuel the spell letting her breathe. She didn't have much left, but she was moving on pure determination as she levered herself back up the wall, forcing her limbs to cooperate.

The secured panel covering the manual override mocked her. Now that she was looking at it, she could see that *someone*—no prizes for guessing who at this point—had used either magic or some *very* specialized tools to solder the panel shut from the inside.

Physical force wasn't going to open the panel to let her at the lever. Fortunately, however tired she might have been, she wasn't limited to physical force.

She activated her shipsuit's helmet. Its automatic protocols would have triggered in the absence of pressure, but given that the room itself had its own emergency oxygen supply, the designers hadn't added a safety protocol for low oxygen.

The suit wrapped around her and its microcapsules began to release their oxygen supply for her. She let the filtering spell drop—the shipsuit only had fifteen minutes of air, enough to get to a locker with real space suits, but it was enough for what she needed to do.

Taking a deep breath of the fresh-air supply, she channeled energy into her projector rune, conjuring a thin blade of pure force. Four quick slashes later, the soldered-shut panel went spinning off into her room—and she found herself staring at the empty gap that *should* have held an emergency release lever.

Someone had been *very* thorough. Not thorough enough, in the end, but if she'd been asleep, the air would have killed her. If she'd been mostly gone by the time she'd managed to open up the panel, the lack of lever might have been enough to trap her.

But she was a *Mage*—and had served in the Royal Martian Navy as one. Her hand slid in to where the lever would have been, and air solidified in her grip, linking the mechanism buried in the wall to her hand.

She yanked hard, once, and the mechanism engaged. The lock holding the door retracted and half a dozen powerful electromagnets switched off. The top half of the door didn't move—but the bottom half dropped into its slot in the floor with a resounding crash.

Maria dove under the half-closed door before she could let herself hesitate, rolling and coming up with her hands out, ready to unleash magic against whoever was in the hallway.

Which was empty. She exhaled and tapped the command to retract the shipsuit. She breathed the ship's air for several moments, assessing her options.

The internal com network was compromised. Her coms were jammed. She was exhausted, but Acconcio was dead and Costa was on the loose somewhere in the ship—and she doubted that the Mage had set loose this level of catastrophe in the ship's systems without some of follow-through planned.

Her wrist-comp buzzed for a moment and she glanced down at it. She was still jammed, but a single code had made it through by simple virtue of being a more powerful signal. Far more powerful than would normally be directed inside the ship.

It was just a string of letters and numbers, but she recognized one of *Falcon*'s alert codes when she saw it. Rice was ordering everyone to find weapons and fall back to key areas, digging in to hold the key sections of the ship.

Those were the bridge, the simulacrum chamber, and Engineering. She was grimly certain the bridge was cut off and the simulacrum chamber had already fallen. That meant she needed to retake it, and she couldn't do that alone while half-exhausted.

She needed the Marines.

Maria was halfway to the security barracks at the other side of the gravity ring when she first heard gunfire. It wasn't the single shots of pistol fire, either, but the repeated crashes of automatic weapons. *Heavy* automatic weapons.

She did what any good Navy officer would have done: she changed course toward the sound of the guns. That took her around a corner and down a level from where she'd been headed, but the exchange of fire grew louder as she approached.

Part of her, both the sensible part and the tired part, suggested caution. The rest of her realized that hesitation was only likely to get people killed. She mustered the tired shreds of her energy and barreled around the corner.

She wasn't entirely sure what she'd expected to find, but Kelzin and three of the other pilots holding an impromptu barricade assembled from someone's bed didn't surprise her. The two dead men sprawled behind the barricade sadly fit her expectations as well.

But she'd had no idea what they were facing, and the attack force was something out of her worst nightmares. Three exosuited attackers led the way, pushing slowly forward in spite of the hail of fire the pilots' carbines were spitting out.

A six-man squad of lighter-armored troopers had fallen in behind them, hanging back and letting their heavily protected compatriots lead the way.

How an entire assault team had made it aboard *Red Falcon* without anyone knowing was beyond her, but what to do about it was not.

She intentionally crumpled, sliding under the fire from the leading attackers as she crashed into the barricade past Mike Kelzin—using her momentum to flip herself back up as she met three fully armored soldiers at point-blank range.

If they'd been Marines, she would have died. Marines would have made sure to have ID files on the Ship's Mages and would have emptied everything they had as soon as they saw her.

These were not Marines. Mercenaries, probably. Mercenaries who'd never faced a Combat Mage before.

They twisted their weapons toward her but not fast enough to prevent her reaching them. Short-ranged blades of white-hot plasma erupted from each of her hands, burning ugly holes through the two closest soldiers despite their heavy armor.

Years-old combat training reflexes took over, dropping her to the ground as a hail of flechettes, designed to take down unarmed crew *without* wrecking starship hulls, flashed over her head. Still on the ground, she gestured at the last exosuited soldier and conjured fire again.

As the attacker crumpled, the sound of gunfire redoubled as Kelzin and his fellows charged over the barricade. The non-exosuited soldiers didn't stand a chance, though another of the pilots fell before Kelzin knelt next to Maria.

"Mage Soprano, are you okay?" he demanded.

"I am fucking shattered," she admitted. "But since someone seems to have boarded us, I'm going to call that okay."

"Where the hell did these guys come from?" one of the other pilots asked. "For that matter, Mike, why did you have a crate of Legatus Arms carbines in your locker?"

"Souvenirs of my last tour with Captain Rice," the pilot snapped. "Soprano? Any idea what happened to Xi?"

"She should be on duty in the chamber," Maria said grimly. "But Costa has betrayed us, and he seemed to think we weren't jumping anywhere. I'm afraid of the worst...and we need to retake the simulacrum."

"*Fuck*," Kelzin growled. "I'm not trained for this, ma'am. What do we do?"

"We find Skavar," Maria replied. "I'm not entirely sure where these assholes came from, but I can guess."

The security troopers found them first. A pair of exosuited troopers, anonymous behind the faceless plates of their armor but with *Red Falcon*'s ship patch emblazoned brightly on the front of the suits, were sweeping down a corridor, searching for threats.

"Hold position," one of them ordered. "Identify yourselves!"

"Reyes, you bloody well know who I am," Maria snapped, recognizing the voice and stepping forward. "We need to talk to Skavar. We have boarders aboard."

"Damn," the security man replied. "We were sweeping for the possibility, but we have no confirmed encounters yet."

"We ran into a damned assault team heading for the shuttle bays," Kelzin told him. "Thanks to Mage Soprano, they're no longer a threat, but where there's one..."

"There's more," Reyes agreed. "Hold on a moment."

The external speaker on his suit went silent, the trooper presumably linking back to Skavar.

"Chief says to bring you back to the barracks; another fire team is going to take over our sweep," he told them after a moment.

"You guys have coms?" Maria asked. "We're being jammed."

"Personal coms are out, but the exosuits are designed for a combat environment," Reyes replied, gesturing for her and the pilots to follow him. "We have micropulse communicators operating on rotating frequencies, designed to cut through almost any jamming."

That was not civilian-issue gear—but it was gear that Maria knew *Marines* had. She hadn't thought through just what Skavar's people having actual RMMC equipment would mean.

"I don't think anyone was expecting that," she said quietly, going back to leaning on Kelzin.

"That, Mage Soprano, was the point."

By the time Maria reached the security barracks, it was very clear that *Red Falcon*'s security detachment was giving up pretending they *weren't* actually Marines at this point. Orderly fire teams moved down the hallways in perfect rotations, every corner swept, every door checked.

Armored guards had the entrance locked down, checking the suit ID chips for Reyes and his companion before they let anyone through.

Inside, the main lounge area had been converted into a mobile command post. Portable screens and high-powered communicators had materialized out of nowhere to fill the space, giving Skavar a view of his people overlaid on a map of the ship.

The security chief wore an exosuit, but his helmet was off, laid on the table next to him as he studied the ship. He looked up as she came in.

"Mage Soprano, you're all right," he greeted her with relief. "Damn. I'm feeling half-blind and worried that *everyone* is gone."

"Captain Rice is still with us," she replied. "You got the alert, same as I did."

"Captain Rice was still with us ten minutes ago," Skavar said grimly. "I have no communications with anyone except my own fire teams. Internal sensors *appear* to be up, but they're lying to me, which makes them useless."

He gestured at the screens. Green dots marked a growing area in the gravity ring and the magical gravity section of the ship where the Marines had swept. Toward the bridge, however, at the top of the magical-gravity area, the green dots had stopped moving and a set of fuzzy red markers had been added.

"I can't trust anything beyond the cameras of my people," he told her. "We hadn't run into hostiles when Reyes met up with you, but that didn't last. We now have a running firefight in the bridge tower. Exosuits and Augments, plus at least one Mage."

"A Mage?" Maria demanded. "And *Augments*?"

"Not Legatan, I don't think, but bad enough," he said grimly. "I have no idea where the hell these people came from."

"Costa and Acconcio snuck them aboard," she told him.

"*Fuck.*"

"Acconcio had second thoughts," Maria continued. "So, Costa killed him. He's...not a fully trained Combat Mage, but he's a lot stronger than he was pretending. He tried to trap me in my quarters and gas me."

She closed her eyes and sighed.

"We need to check on Anders," she told him. "And anyone else who was sleeping, but I'm most worried about Anders."

Skavar nodded and tapped something on the screens.

"Antonov," he said crisply. "Check out Mage Anders's quarters; they tried to contain and gas Mage Soprano, so he may be in danger. You're closest."

He turned back to Maria. "That'll take a few minutes. What about the simulacrum chamber?"

Maria spared a glance for Kelzin, who was still providing a shoulder to keep her upright, and sighed.

"Wu was holding it down, but...Costa seemed to think we weren't going anywhere. I don't know what happened to her," she said softly, "but I'm afraid she may be dead."

The young man she was leaning on winced.

"I need to check out the chamber," she continued. "And I need an escort; we'll want to punch out whatever force they have holding it. You'll also want to send a team to sweep to Engineering—Kellers will have armed his people, but they won't have the gear to stop exosuits!"

"You can barely stand!" Skavar objected. "We're sweeping backwards along the ship; we'll get there, but you can't do anything."

"Ivan, they were in the cargo containers," she told him gently. "They're already at the chamber and probably at Engineering. There isn't *time* to be methodical. You need a Mage-led assault, and there's only one Mage available with the skillset."

"You still can't stand," he replied.

"You have the standard Marine portable med-suite, don't you?" she asked.

He caught what she meant and started shaking his head.

"It has three doses of Exalt in it," she told him. "Get them for me."

"No," Skavar snapped. "I will *not* let you poison yourself with that shit."

"Chief Skavar," Maria said grimly, "whether we're going by *Red Falcon*'s chain of command or the Protectorate's, you answer to me. Get me the damn Exalt."

Exalt was a mix of drugs and thaumaturgically modified chemicals designed for exactly her current condition. The primary ingredient was a powerful amphetamine, and even the Mages who'd put it together weren't sure why some of the other ingredients worked as they did.

Each dose would give her roughly an hour of full strength. Then the come-down would suck.

If she took three, the final come-down would probably kill her.

CHAPTER 40

AN HOUR. It had only been an hour since *Red Falcon* had jumped into this godforsaken piece of interstellar wasteland.

David's scanners still showed that the space around *Falcon* was clear, but given that his computers *also* told him that his ship was fully in the green, functional and not infested with hostiles, he wasn't sure he trusted them.

"They're still closing," Cohen noted. "No further communication from *Silent Atlantic*, but all three ships are on their way."

"That would be more reassuring if I was certain they were on our side," David told the chief. "Rogers. How's the guns?"

"They seem to be responding so far," Acconcio's deputy replied. "LaMonte? Does it look like I'm being fed bullshit?"

"Not yet," the engineer replied. "You're about to lose everything for seventy seconds, though—I'm resetting the weapons firmware to factory settings."

She glanced over at David.

"I figured we wanted guns before anything else," she said apologetically.

"Go for it," he ordered. "But I'd love internal sensors."

"Someone's coming," one of the support techs said from the door. The young woman had grabbed one of the carbines and was standing guard. David had minimal faith in her ability to hit anything with the gun, but he couldn't fault her enthusiasm.

Or her intelligence. She'd linked the carbine's gun-cam to her wrist-comp and was watching around the corner with the barrel instead of exposing herself.

"That's not right," she murmured. "Boss, I got three black-as-night exosuits heading our way. Weren't ours..."

"Gray," David said quietly. "Gray with the ship crest. Show me."

Internal sensors and cameras showed the corridor as completely empty, but the gun-cam told him everything he needed to know. Three exosuited troopers carrying heavy auto-shotguns were advancing down the hallway.

The exosuits were the wrong color and the guns weren't a weapon Skavar's men had in their stockpile.

"We've been boarded," he told his people. He'd been pretty sure before, but seeing it confirmed was still heart-wrenching. "Cohen?"

"Boss?"

"The carbines won't do crap against exosuits, but there's a couple of black cylinders in the arms locker. About forty-five centimeters long, with clips on top?"

"Found them."

"Bring them to me."

Cohen handed David the first of the under-barrel weapons, looking at the one he still held like it was a venomous snake.

"Do I want to know what I'm holding?" he asked.

"No."

David locked the single-shot tube onto his own carbine, linking the gun-cam up with his own PC and activating a secondary program in the gun's systems.

Then he stepped around the half-closed hatch, lined up the carbine and pressed the trigger on the under-barrel tube. The gun nearly kicked itself out of his hands with recoil as the over-compressed chemical charge lit off, barely managing to not disintegrate the tube as it fired its single massive projectile.

The sabot was discarded before the round had traveled two meters, stabilizing fins popping out as a secondary rocket ignited, adding even more velocity to the penetrator rocket.

It slammed into the chest of the lead exosuit, punched clean through the first layer of armor, and then detonated inside the man's chest.

The suit of armor just...stopped, frozen in place as it held its occupant's corpse upright.

David dodged back into the bridge as a hail of return fire echoed down the corridor.

"Next," he ordered grimly. "Give me a distance?"

"Ten meters and closing," the tech told him. "There's no time."

"There's *just* enough time," David replied. He clamped the second disposable penetrator onto his carbine and repeated the stunt.

This time, the attackers were waiting for him, and flechettes ricocheted off the walls around him. Even as several of them tore into him, he resisted the pain long enough to aim carefully before firing the second rocket.

He didn't wait to see if he'd hit. He let himself fall through the door and raised his voice so *Falcon*'s computers could hear him.

"Bridge lockdown alpha," he snapped. "Voice authenticate. Seal *now*."

It was easy to forget that *Red Falcon* had been built as a military ship. So much of her design and functionality—outside of her weapons and engines, at least—was shaped by her core identity as a freighter. One easily ended up thinking of her as a freighter with guns bolted on.

She was no such thing.

At David's verbal command, thick blast shutters, rated to withstand a point-blank nuclear explosion, slammed shut over the exterior of the bridge access. Secondary accesses for maintenance had smaller but equally tough shutters close over them. A miniature isolated life-support system came online.

"Damn it, sir, you've been shot!" Cohen barked. "Medkit!"

David let his people urge him back to his chair, but shook his head.

"Just a flesh wound," he told them. "Bandage it; I'll be fine. LaMonte!"

"Sir?"

"Progress?" he demanded, wincing as Cohen went at his injuries with rough-and-ready first aid.

"Weapons systems are all reset, rekeyed and secured," she promised. "Short of physically taking control of the weapons stations away from the on-mount crews, there's no way they can stop us engaging."

"Good. Sensors?"

"Still working on it." She glanced back at her screen and visibly winced. "Damn. We just lost external sensors. I've got the targeting arrays on the weapon mounts, but the main sensors are now feeding into the same damn black box that's eating our internal scans."

"What's the box showing us?" David asked, then hissed as the antiseptic spray went into his wounds.

"Just the three *Silent Ocean* ships closing, same pace as before," she told him. "The targeting arrays aren't as clear, but..."

"But?" he asked after she trailed off.

"There are at least two more clusters of signatures now," LaMonte reported. "Not sure of range, probably still around eight to ten million klicks. Well outside of fusion missile range but in range of our antimatter birds."

"Without the main arrays, we're firing half-blind at that range," David pointed out. "We don't know who's out there."

It had been eighty minutes since jump. There was no way these were friendlies.

The Legacy had arrived.

"At that range, they aren't a threat yet," he admitted. "Get me internal sensors first, Kelly—and *then* get me the scanners I need to shoot those bastards down."

CHAPTER 41

EXALT *GLOWED*.

It also moved on its own. It was hard to see that in the vial, as Exalt was a clear, transparent liquid, but the glowing made it possible to see the unending wave in the liquid in the prepackaged hypodermic.

The combat drug was probably the creepiest technically inanimate thing Maria had ever seen, but she'd been injected with it before. Once.

Exalt didn't make a Mage more powerful. It simply "borrowed" energy from your future self, giving you a short-term surge of power and strength in trade for long-term hell.

"Are you sure about this?" Skavar asked after one of his people had passed Maria the case with the three glowing syringes. "All I really know about this stuff is that I'm—roughly—better off shooting myself than injecting it."

"Assuming you shot yourself competently, it would be a far less painful way to die as a mundane, yes," she agreed, selecting one of the syringes at random. Exalt interacted directly with a Mage's power. There was no counteragent. It was a deadly poison in a non-Mage.

"That said, I've used it before and I know what I'm doing," she assured the security chief. "And you need me."

"That's true enough," he admitted. "But..."

"We can't make contact with the bridge or engineering," Maria reminded him. "We're starting to run into hostiles every way we go. We *know* we've lost the simulacrum chamber, which means we can't jump."

Before she could argue with him more—or let the soft voice in the back of her mind talk her out of what she knew was actually a really bad idea—she bent her head back and slammed the syringe into her carotid artery.

That hurt. A *lot*. As the auto-injector fed the drug into her system, though, the pain eased. Her exhaustion went with it and new energy filled her. She smiled grimly as she withdrew the needle, laying the empty syringe down in the case and gently placing a patch over the tiny wound on her throat.

The drug didn't give her enough energy to, say, jump the ship, but it put her back in fighting trim and meant she wouldn't need to be carried through the ship.

"All right," she breathed. "Do we have a team for the pushback?"

"We do," Skavar confirmed. "I'm coming with you too, leaving Reyes in charge here." He paused, visibly swallowing as he picked his helmet up.

"Antonov got back to me," he told her gently. "Anders was sealed in his quarters and the airflow cut off. He wasn't wearing a shipsuit." He shook his head. "He didn't make it."

"Damn." She shook her head. "Let's get moving. I've definitely lost one Mage today, and I plan to make it at least two before this mess is over."

"Only if you get to Costa first," Skavar said flatly. "Otherwise, I don't plan on leaving enough of him for you to identify, let alone kill."

Eighteen exosuited security troopers, three armed pilots and one angry Mage stormed their way back along the central stem of *Red Falcon*'s hull. The rest of Skavar's people were sweeping the gravity decks and pushing toward the bridge.

"Are we going to be able to relieve the bridge?" Maria asked him softly.

In response, Skavar finally put on his helmet and was silent for several seconds.

"I don't know," he murmured, his speakers pitched so only she could hear him. "Rice has *probably* gone into lockdown, which means the bastards are stuck between an anvil and a hammer, but they quite likely have more people than I do.

"It could get ugly," he admitted. "But I'm as worried about the next step as anything else."

She nodded.

"Ships."

"Exactly. We need to be able to run," Skavar told her. "Which is up to you."

"If Wu is dead, we're still fucked," Maria warned him. "Taking Exalt means I can fight, but it fucks me for jumping for at least twenty hours."

"I know."

She shook her head, continuing to follow the exosuits down the corridor.

"What happens if this all goes to shit?" she asked conversationally.

"Then we fall back on what Marines hope to never do," he told her. "We pray the Navy gets here in time."

Maria was surprised by how far they made it along the ship's core before they ran into any resistance at all. According to her mental map, they'd almost made it to the simulacrum chamber before gunfire started to echo down the hallway ahead of them.

"Report," Skavar barked, then paused to listen.

"You need to stay back here," he ordered Maria a moment later. "Someone was expecting us, sooner or later, and they've set up barricades and dug in. They don't have much in terms of anti-exosuit gear, but those big auto-shotguns will be hell on those of you *without* suits."

"How many?" she asked calmly.

"Maria..."

"That's *Mage Soprano*," she snapped. "And I asked how many, Chief."

He sighed.

"Two portable heavy barricades, half a dozen men in exosuits, at least four mounted heavy weapons," he reeled off. "The exosuits are carrying anti-personnel guns, but those heavy weapons can take down my men. We need to move up carefully, control the situation."

"We don't have time," Maria reminded him, biting off her words carefully and testing the warm buzz of the Exalt in her blood. "Keep them distracted."

"Distracted?" Skavar said. "What are you going to *do*?"

"My job."

Leaving the security chief behind her, she charged forward, letting the Exalt fill her limbs with energy as she drew on her power. She didn't make it far before she reached the forward position, *Red Falcon*'s people using a half-closed hatch as cover while they tried to take out the heavy weapons.

"We're your covering fire, ma'am," Nejem's familiar voice said from inside one of the suits of armor. "What's the plan?"

"You keep them distracted. I kill them."

"Oorah," Nejem said after a moment of silence. "All people, we have *Mage* support now. Target those heavy weapons; keep the bastards' heads down!"

She gave him a firm nod.

"Good luck."

She didn't respond, channeling magic around her to create her own personal gravity field. It was easier in the magical gravity of *Red Falcon*'s interior than it would have been on a planet—if nothing else, she knew the gravity spells on her ship inside and out now.

Maria leapt delicately into the air as the troopers opened fire. Her magic wrapped around her, sending her plunging feet first toward the barricade. She made it well over halfway across the impromptu no man's land before the boarders saw her coming.

They were smart, though. The moment they saw her, they changed the focus of their fire, and streams of high-speed bullets from the tri-pod-mounted penetrator rifles slammed into the shield she'd conjured in front of her.

It wouldn't hold forever, but it held for long enough for her to reach the position and land on the opposite side of the barricade—and drain the power from the gravity runes beneath her feet.

One moment, they didn't need to secure themselves. Tripods and exosuits alike were braced against the floor but not locked onto it with magnets or the other zero-gravity tools built into the systems.

The next, recoil scattered the entire position as the gravity went away. One of the mounted penetrator rifle crews walked their fire across one of their armored friends, ripping him in half despite the suit.

For a handful of seconds, the entire defensive position was chaos. That might have been enough for Skavar's totally-not-Marines to sweep the barricade, but Maria Soprano wanted her damn ship back.

The boarders spun away from her uncontrollably but not unpredictably. Precisely aimed and calibrated blasts of fire flickered from her hands, burning through exosuit weak points and exposed flesh alike.

By the time Nejem's team reached the barricade, she'd restored the gravity and was calmly waiting for them amidst the bodies.

"Let's move," she said briskly. "We need to take the simulacrum chamber. Wu may still be alive."

She could be sick later. She was quite sure now that she would have been sick later even without the Exalt.

"I think that's far enough," a mockingly familiar voice said a few seconds later as she tried to head down the corridor.

"I'm going to kill you, Costa," Maria said conversationally. It appeared that the young Mage had more access to the sensors than they did, which made sense. *Someone* had to have hacked into *Red Falcon*'s systems, and she'd freely admit that most people, mundane and Mage alike, would assume a Mage didn't have the technical skills.

"You *want* to kill me," he corrected over the speakers. "But if you and your armored friends keep coming down that hallway, who you're *going* to kill is poor little Xi Wu. She's a dear, a pretty little thing who never harmed anyone, and I'd *rather* not put a bullet in her brainpan, but if you don't stop right there, I *will*."

Maria slowed.

"You know if you hurt her, there isn't a hole in the galaxy deep enough to save you," she said conversationally.

"*Stop*, Mage Soprano. Not slow," he snapped. "And you *already* want to kill me. What difference would blowing Wu's brains out make to that?"

He chuckled grimly.

"Besides, if *hurting* her was the line, I'm already fucked, aren't I?" he pointed out.

"You know the game's already over," Maria said. "We're retaking this ship and you can't stop us at this point."

"That's...sixty-forty," Costa said. "Our favor. And that's assuming my friends outside don't get too involved. And since I'm sitting on the simulacrum, I can make sure any friends you'd arranged to show up can't catch us.

"So, I agree, the game is over—but not in your favor. Legacy's only after Rice, though," he pointed out. "I can make a deal if you want to play."

"*You're* Legacy?" Maria demanded.

"I'm as much Legacy as you're MISS," he replied. "More, arguably, since I was part before I joined this ship, where you were a convenience to them. Whatever you think Rice is worth, you're lowballing it. You want *Falcon* itself? I can arrange that. Money? I can make every member of this crew who yields rich beyond their wildest dreams."

"Can you bring Anders back to life?" she snapped.

Silence.

"No," Costa admitted. "Had to be sure the only Mage aboard who could jump was me. There's no going back. I can make you rich or you can all end up dead. It doesn't seem like much of a choice to me."

Maria waved the exosuited security people back, taking several steps forward.

"Is that why Turquoise betrayed us?" she asked. "Money?"

"Oh, I made her a *much* better offer than mere money," the young Mage said with a laugh. "You could get the Legacy off her back. The Legacy...we can make her a *queen*."

So much for Turquoise's assurances she didn't want to take over the Blue Star Syndicate. When it had been waved in front of her as a bribe, she must have leapt at it regardless.

Maria shuffled forward.

"Stop it, Mage Soprano," Costa said quietly. "I can see everything you do. Every step you take brings Wu one step closer to a bullet in the—"

His voice cut off in mid-sentence. Maria hesitated for a moment, and then a new voice came over the PA.

"I have control," Kelly LaMonte announced. "Internal networks back up in proper mode and I've locked Costa out. Maria—*GO!*"

That was all she needed. Knowing that Costa wasn't watching her, power flared around Maria and she charged the simulacrum chamber.

Forty meters. With magic speeding her steps, turning each movement into an arcing leap as she turned gravity into her own personal toy, she crossed them in four seconds.

The longest four seconds of her life. If Costa leapt to conclusions and pulled the trigger, Wu would be dead before she made it into the chamber. Her only hope was that the young Mage didn't realize immediately that LaMonte had cut him off—or was holding off for her inevitable arrival.

The door to the simulacrum chamber yielded cooperatively to her magic, flinging open as she threw herself into the zero-gravity room.

Costa was on the platform next to the simulacrum, one leg hooked around it with an ease of long practice that he'd never shown before. Xi Wu floated next to him, tied to the platform with a length of utility cabling.

The traitor had his gun trained on her head as she floated, and the young woman was clearly unconscious. Blood was visibly leaking down her forehead from a head wound. She was definitely alive, but from the look of her injuries, Maria wasn't sure how long that would last.

"Stop!" Costa bellowed, swinging to press the gun directly against Wu's bloody temple. "Stop it, Soprano, or she dies!"

"If you were going to shoot her, you already would have," Maria pointed out. "Put the gun down, Costa. I'm sure you'd rather come in alive than in pieces."

"You'd like that," he spat at her. "Another chance for the Navy to prove how much better they are than the rest of us, huh? You didn't even realize we'd given you a fake destination. You have no idea where we're *actually* going."

"I figured we had a fake location, actually," Maria pointed out. "And wanting to know the real place is the only reason you're still breathing. Put the gun down, Costa."

They hung like that for several moments and she realized the younger Mage's hand was trembling.

"Acconcio was the first person you'd actually shot, wasn't he?" she said softly. "It was always hacks and tricks and ships blown apart on a screen before, wasn't it? I doubt he was the first you killed, but he was the first whose blood you had to smell."

She could still smell his blood. She'd had no chance to wipe it off, and her shipsuit was covered in it. The thought did not make her any more inclined to let Costa live, but she needed what he knew. One interrogation session with the brat could break open Turquoise's entire operation for the Navy and MISS.

"Put the gun down," she told him, drifting closer. "I'm not going to pretend I *want* to let you live, Costa, but if you put the gun down, I'll make sure you do. Your life for Xi's. You both get to live."

"Go *fuck* yourself!" he bellowed, and yanked the trigger—but he'd let Maria get too close. A wall of force slammed into the tip of the gun, cutting off the barrel and blocking the bullet before it reached Wu.

The gun backfired, exploding in Costa's hand and searing the flesh away from his runes.

Before Maria could do or say anything more, he lashed out. A baseball-sized ball of flame flashed across the empty room toward her, but she batted it aside. *Another* fireball flickered at Wu from point-blank range, but she held the shield.

Defending two people was hard, but for the first time in a while, Maria faced an opponent while fully, if artificially, refreshed. She wasn't holding an air filtration spell or a barrier that needed to stop massed gunfire. The Exalt made up for having jumped. She was as close to full power as she'd ever entered a fight.

And Shachar Costa, whoever he actually was, was not a Combat Mage.

His fireballs were fast and dangerous, but they were brute force and unskilled. He had power to burn, far more than he'd ever shown her, but she had skill and training.

She shielded herself and Wu, and then forced those shields in toward Costa, containing his fireballs again and again as she closed her magic around him, locking *him* inside a bubble of solidified air that defied his spells.

Maria drifted over to him, doing her best to make her suppression of his desperate attempts to escape even more casual, and looked through the bubble.

"The shield isn't letting oxygen in," she pointed out conversationally. "Those fireballs are burning it up fast."

He was already starting to visibly choke.

"You might have burnt it up faster than you can replenish it...if you even have the energy left."

Costa coughed, trying to conjure an air filtration spell himself now. It fizzled. Now she could see that the runes in his right hand were mangled. He wasn't jumping again until someone did a new inlay—and most of his complex magics like the filtration spell interfaced through the runes.

"Fuck you," he gasped out.

"It seems poetic," she replied. "This was how you killed Anders. How you planned to kill me. How does it feel, Costa? Knowing you're going to die?"

He was trying to hold his breath now, and Maria shook her head.

"Unfortunately, I still need you," she told his slumping body. The shield collapsed around his half-conscious form, bands of iron force slamming into place around his wrists and ankles.

"Skavar, get in here," she ordered loudly. "I need Mage-cuffs and a medkit, *now!*"

CHAPTER 42

THE SENSORS CAME UP as Kelly crowed in victory—and then grabbed a microphone to talk to Soprano as the young engineer swept the area of the simulacrum chamber.

David glanced at that, saw enough to hope that Soprano had it under control, and then focused on more immediate concerns.

The lockdown was keeping the attackers out of his bridge, but there was an entire *platoon* of troops outside the heavy blast doors. Thankfully, only half a dozen of the forty or so boarders were in exosuits, but at least that many were sporting visible cybernetic augmentations. Two of those were manhandling a massive plasma cutter into place.

The industrial machine was designed to cut the armor plates used for warships—the same material used for the blast shield. It wouldn't necessarily get through the door quickly, but it was going to get through sooner rather than later.

An even dozen exosuited security men and women were sweeping the living quarters and the rest of the command tower, while the rest of the armored suits were following Maria toward the simulacrum chamber and Engineering.

There were both more boarders aboard than he'd thought possible and fewer than he'd feared. With the guards around the simulacrum chamber down, there were only two forces left: the forty or so boarders trying to break into his bridge, and a similarly sized force heading toward Engineering.

"Do we have coms?" he asked Kelly.

"We have everything except external sensors," she said crisply. "And we'll have those...soon. Ish."

"Keep working," he told her. "You've already saved half the day; no point in leaving the job unfinished, is there?!"

He gave her a grin as she flashed him a pained smile, and then turned his attention to his coms.

"James, come in," he barked. "You should have sensors back up, but you have incoming. Report!"

"I read you," the engineer replied after a painfully long few seconds. "Linking up the sensors now. I shut down the control modules for the engines and life support when I lost contact with you. Rebooted from factory settings, but they've been running on default state since."

He paused.

"There's definitely been some localized overrides on life support," he said quietly. "I don't know who we lost, but at least some people are dead in their beds. I could only make sure the main halls were safe." He swallowed audibly.

"We got sensors," he continued after a moment. "That's...not good, boss. I've got exactly one penetrator rifle down here. Ten exosuits and twenty support troops, plus what looks like someone's chop-shop assault-cyborg squad? We can't stop that."

"Skavar is at the simulacrum chamber," David told him. "He's coming up right behind them. All you have to do is keep them out until he gets there."

"Right. Hold off forty killers with a dozen engineers with guns." He didn't have visual, but David could *hear* his engineer's head shaking. "I'll do what I can."

"Hunker down and wait for the Marines. It's all either of us can do right now," David admitted. "We have new friends outside, too, but I don't have clear eyes yet."

Kellers paused.

"I don't suppose there's any chance of them *actually* being friends?" he asked.

"I didn't expect to be jumped from *inside*," David replied. "Any actual friends are still an hour away."

"That's closer than I'd expect."

David laughed.

"What I can say, James? I'm paranoid and I never trust pirates!"

The hissing sound from the blast door was the warning he'd been waiting for. The plasma cutter's white-hot beam lit up the upper-right corner of the door as the team outside went to work.

"Reyes," David reached out to the security trooper. "The residential and work areas are clear. We have an assault team trying to burn through the door of the bridge, though, which I would quite like some help dealing with."

"Roger," the man replied. "It's going to take me time to reconsolidate the sweep teams, Captain. Five minutes, maybe more. Any faster and we're just feeding men into the woodchipper."

"I know," David acknowledged. "But...I had two one-shot armor rockets, Reyes. And they're both gone. As soon as that door is open, we're *fucked*—and there are hostile ships closing."

The security man sighed.

"I'll do what I can," he promised.

"LaMonte?" David asked.

"I've got into the sensors and have forced a system reboot," she told him. "Three minutes and counting."

"And the on-mount controls?"

"We're in touch with everybody," Cohen reported. "None of them even saw boarders, though they were all smart enough to lock down the modules when communications went down."

He paused.

"Campbell just reported in," he told David. "She and Dr. Gupta are pulling people out of the living quarters and dragging them down to medical." He shivered. "Not all of them made it. Not all of them are *going* to make it."

"Damn," David said. At least Campbell was alive. He'd been worried.

The plasma cutter had made it down about forty centimeters of the door. It would be a while before they were through...but it would be well before Reyes's five minutes.

"Everybody except LaMonte take cover," he ordered. "And then cover LaMonte. Right now, her work is the most important thing happening on this ship."

Not least because while she'd got him back *most* of his control, the boarders still had more worms in his systems than he liked—and he had only the vaguest idea how they'd got there!

He stood from his chair, carefully kneeling behind it as he winced against his injuries. The chair was armored enough to stand up to regular fire, though it wouldn't stop penetrator rounds.

"I make it about ninety seconds before they're through," Cohen noted, most of the bridge crew fixated on the slowly moving red-hot lines in the door. "Any chance of distracting them before that?"

"Wait until it opens, then fill that hole with fire," David ordered. "We don't need to take them out, just keep them out!"

Seconds ticked away and the entire chaotic situation narrowed down to one room, one gun, and one door that was about to be ripped open.

Tunnel vision was dangerous, but it was also the only thing that would get him through the next few minutes. He watched the plasma cutter work its way along, and just as the man-sized hole finished, he opened fire.

The first few rounds slammed into the heavy hull metal, setting the mostly detached chunk of door to vibrating...and then it fell outward and David's bullets hammered into the plasma cutter itself.

It was a heavy-duty industrial tool—but it wasn't designed to be shot at. David wasn't sure what he'd hit, but it was certainly effective. An explosion backlit the new opening in the bridge door, and he and his crew poured gunfire through the hole.

The detonating plasma cutter delayed return fire by several seconds, but that was all. Clouds of high-velocity flechettes flickered into the bridge, ricocheting off the armored chairs and tearing into consoles and people alike.

All that was visible through the door were fire and explosions, and David focused on putting bullets down the hallway, trying not to be distracted by the cries of pain around him.

"Sir!" LaMonte suddenly snapped over the chaos. "We have a problem."

He emptied his carbine's magazine into the hole and dropped to the floor to reload.

"That's a bit of an understatement!" he replied. "What now?"

"We have four destroyers headed our way and they definitely aren't Navy!"

David somehow managed to stay focused even as the ground tried to fall out from beneath him. *Red Falcon* was heavily armed for a civilian ship, but she didn't have the firepower to go toe-to-toe with even *one* destroyer, even an old export-built one without an amplifier or antimatter missiles.

Four, plus whatever other ships were out there, were a death sentence if they couldn't run—and they couldn't run *or* fight with the bridge being actively invaded.

He gave himself a moment to think by popping up over his chair and emptying a quarter of his magazine into an exosuited soldier trying to push his way through the door. The bullets ricocheted uselessly off the armor, and a blast of flechettes ripped up the back of his chair in response.

David couldn't see that side of his command chair, but he suspected the illusion that it *wasn't* a chest-high barricade of hull armor was long gone now. Despite everything they could do, the first exosuited trooper was now *in* the bridge, the armor visibly damaged but unbroken by the fire pouring into it.

And now the bullets weren't even reaching the suit, as a field of magically solidified air locked around the opening, the Mage with the assault team finally acting to protect the members of the team they apparently valued.

For several eternal seconds, David realized it was over. There was nothing he could do to stop the pirates taking the bridge. He'd failed...

And then the shield flickered and disappeared as the incoming fire from behind the exosuit seemed to stutter. A single carefully targeted penetrator round flashed through the hole in the security door and punched through the helmet of the pirate who'd made it in.

They slumped forward, and suddenly no gunfire was making it in—even as the gunfire outside rose to a sharp crescendo...and cut off.

"Sir?" Reyes voice projected through the hole. "I'm sorry, I didn't manage to take any prisoners—but the bridge access is secure."

David swallowed and carefully levered himself to his feet. He hadn't even noticed that he'd been shot again. Several times, he now realized as the adrenaline wore off and he half-collapsed against his chair. Nothing serious, but he was bleeding.

"Mr. Reyes," he said as seriously as he could. "No prisoners? Really? I may have to dock some of the raise that comes with the promotion I now owe you!"

The crew forced a laugh, and he looked around. His bridge was a mess. Gaspar Cohen was dead and he wasn't the only one. The sheer intensity of the fight outside suggested he'd lost security troops, too. The butcher's toll was already too high, but they weren't done yet.

David carefully lowered himself into his chair and turned to look at LaMonte.

"We have external sensors?" he asked.

"We do," she said, her gaze focused on him so she didn't have to look at dead friends.

"Put it up," he ordered. "Then take over tactical. We've made it this far. I'm not giving up now!"

She nodded, swallowing as she took over control of the primary screens from her station.

As the tactical display of this particular chunk of empty space lit up on the screen, David noted the time.

It had been two hours since they'd jumped in.

CHAPTER 43

THE SMELL OF BLOOD and burnt wires lingered in the air, but David Rice was now fully in control of his bridge and his ship. Releasing the lockdown allowed Reyes and the other security people to haul his casualties to Dr. Gupta's medbay, which meant that at least the dead weren't lying around, distracting the living.

"Engineering is secure," Kellers reported. He sounded exhausted. "We lost six of Skavar's people and as many of mine."

"Gupta is up and running," David told him. "Get your wounded to the medbay; make sure the rest of your people are awake and on duty."

He checked the screens.

"We have a few minutes to play with here," he concluded, "so let's use them to take care of our people."

"What happens when those minutes are up?" Kellers asked.

"We fight. So, be ready for it."

"Against these assholes? I'm always ready."

Switching channels, David cut to the simulacrum chamber.

"Maria, report," he ordered, his voice gentler now.

"Anders is dead," she told him, her voice wooden. "Xi Wu is badly injured; I had Kelzin rush her to the medbay. I think she'll live, but Costa smashed her across the head with a stun baton hard enough that the discharge wasn't even necessary."

"Costa?"

"Costa," she confirmed. "He's with the Legacy. He helped sneak an entire company of boarding troops aboard in Turquoise's containers, then shot Iovis when he had a freak-out of conscience and tried to warn me."

"Damn." The curse escaped David before he could stop it. "Acconcio too?"

"Acconcio was an idiot and in it for money." Soprano's voice was toneless. "Costa's more complicated, I think. He's unconscious and in Magecuffs in Skavar's brig. He'll have some answers for us—or for the Navy, as the case may be. He knows where Turquoise's base actually is."

"Understood," he said calmly. He paused, looking at the approaching warships. "Can you jump?"

"I'm hitting the come-down from a dose of Exalt," she told him. "I'm fucked for at least twelve hours. Costa's jump runes are wrecked, even if I was willing to trust him near the simulacrum. Wu's wounded and Anders is dead.

"We're not jumping anywhere," she concluded. "So, I hope you have a plan to fight these bastards."

"You know the plan," he said quietly. "Survive. We'll make it work, Soprano."

"I'll do what I can," she promised. "But...it won't be much. I'm about one wrong twist away from covering the chamber in vomit."

"Stay with me, Maria," David urged. "But remember: I need you alive."

"I get that," she said. "Keep the bastards from blowing us all up?"

"Wilco, Ship's Mage."

Even David's worst-case imaginings had fallen short of the reality of what Azure Legacy and Silent Ocean had brought to the party to take him down.

The farthest of the four groups of approaching ships was *Silent Atlantic* and her two sister corvettes, a small squadron that *Red Falcon* could handle with her backup fusion missiles if needed. Their probably-intentional mis-jump had put them well outside the coming combat arena.

Closer, inside not merely antimatter missile range but fusion missile range, were the three groups that had jumped in after Costa had crippled their sensors. Two groups consisted of a single destroyer and four corvettes, and the third was two destroyers and two corvettes.

There were four destroyers and nine corvettes, a total of just under five million tons of pirate ships, inside their weapons range of *Red Falcon*.

But no one was firing yet.

"What are they doing?" Campbell asked. David hadn't realized his XO had joined them and he looked up in surprise.

"You all right?" he asked.

"I'm fine," she said shortly. Her eyes were haunted and he knew she was lying, but she also appeared physically unhurt. "Shouldn't those bastards be shooting at us by now?"

"Five light-seconds," David replied. "We could tag any one group with the lasers, but the other two would rip us to pieces. We haven't moved or fired off active sensors. They may still think we're crippled."

"So, what do we do?" LaMonte asked. "I've got them dialed in as best as I can, but...the lasers aren't lined up on any of them. I can hit anyone you want with missiles, but we'll have to turn the ship to hit anyone with the beams."

"And ten missiles won't be enough to threaten anyone out there," David concluded. "Are the launchers loaded with the antimatter rounds?"

"No," the young woman replied. "The automatic reloader can change its cycle, but removing the loaded missile has to be done manually by the on-mount crew. Or we could fire them to clear the launchers..."

"That would be too obvious," David said quietly as a plan began to take shape in his brain. "The launcher crews are all in place?"

"They're undermanned, but they're there," LaMonte confirmed.

David caught Campbell's wince out of the corner of his eye. She'd been pulling asphyxiated bodies out of people's quarters and knew bone-deep why they were undermanned. They were going to need to find some *good* counselors in Amber.

"Have them disarm and remove the fusion missiles," he ordered. "If they think we're dead, they may get close enough for us to pull off a Sunday punch."

"Thirteen warships," Campbell reminded him. "*Red Falcon* isn't a warship, David. She's got guns and armor, but..."

"So, it's a Hail Mary; I know," he told her. "But we sure as hell can't *fight* them head on, so we need to tilt the odds in our favor."

"Get the antimatter missiles up, make sure the RFLAMs are fully online and have no more tricks loaded into them, and charge the laser capacitors," he concluded. "Let them close."

"How close?" Campbell asked. "You're right, it's the only plan we've got, but..."

"Kelly—the moment they twitch wrong, light them up with everything we've got," David told the engineer now acting as his tactical officer. "Otherwise...let them close to a light-second. How long will that take?"

"Ten minutes, give or take," Campbell replied.

David checked the time. Two hours, fifteen minutes since jump. Ten more minutes...if they survived this, they'd have friends pretty quickly.

"You and Kelly have the call, Jenna," he told his XO. "Line us up on the pair of destroyers and light them up with all of the lasers. Dump five AM birds apiece into the other two and keep shooting at whatever's left standing. Surprise *might* just get a clean sweep on the destroyers and we can fight the corvettes."

And either way, the biggest hope they had was that the Navy would get there early.

For the first time since losing internal communications and sensors, David was finally certain that time was on his side. A Navy squadron had been shadowing *Red Falcon* since they left Svarog. They would have arrived fifteen light-minutes from the last jump point thirty minutes after *Falcon* left, and scanned the beacon they'd left behind for the jump calculation.

They'd arrive at this jump point half an hour after *Falcon* should have left. The *plan* had been that they'd jump back to the squadron if ambushed, but Costa had wrecked that plan handily. Now, they just had to stay alive long enough for the Navy to arrive and rescue them.

Of course, David had no objection to rescuing himself, and if the pirates continued to figure his ship was either in their own hands or torn by internal conflict, he had a chance at that.

"Did Costa send any communications out?" he asked.

"Nothing from our systems," LaMonte told him. "They may have had a transmitter aboard the container they boarded from, but they haven't transmitted since we regained external sensors, if so."

"Can we add a bit of spin to the ship?" he asked Campbell. "Make it look accidental, but rotate us closer to the line of the destroyers?"

"We should be able to," his XO confirmed. "Nice and slow, with the maneuvering thrusters at low power."

"Exactly. Give Kelly a clean shot straight at them with the least possible warning."

The engineer nodded, busily entering code and studying her screens.

Carefully, wincing at his hastily bandaged wounds, David rose from his chair and crossed to LaMonte's console, looking over the tactical displays she had up.

"You got this, Kelly?" he asked quietly. "The only people actually qualified for this are dead or on the weapon mounts, but..."

"I've got this," she said levelly. "It's just code in the end. I *know* code." She smiled grimly. "And it's not the first time I've written code I knew would kill people, either. I'm fine." She looked up from her screen at him and her smile flattened.

"*You*, skipper, have holes in you," she continued. "Go sit your commanding ass down before you fall over."

David chuckled. It was just as forced as LaMonte's joke, but it was there.

"I'll do that," he promised. "Any change on our bogeys?"

"They've got evasive patterns running, just in case we're awake," she replied. "They're not stupid, just fat and happy. Of course, they could be running *better* evasive patterns."

"As opposed to?"

"As opposed to the standard type three, type six, and type nine evasion programs taught in the last year of flight school," LaMonte said sweetly. "Which are perfectly effective...if you cycle them up and don't let the person you're sneaking up on watch your movements for ten minutes."

"You can hit them?"

"Eighty-twenty," she told him cautiously. "I mock them, but those are standard evasive patterns for a reason."

"Time?" David asked, glancing over at Campbell.

"Five minutes to one light-second," she told him. "Ten until the Navy will arrive in the zone." She paused. "I have no idea how long it will take them to intervene."

He nodded.

Commodore Andrews's force would emerge fifteen light-minutes away from everything going on. Hopefully, they'd have Mages standing by for emergency jumps.

Because if they didn't, the Royal Martian Navy might well only arrive in time to watch *Red Falcon* die.

CHAPTER 44

"THEY'RE ADJUSTING COURSE," Campbell reported. "Nothing major, just enough to keep them at least half a million klicks from us as they start to slow down."

"Damn," David murmured. "Are they trying to contact us at all?"

"No... Wait, I'm getting an encrypted transmission," his XO told him. "Nothing coherent. I'm guessing they're trying to ping Costa, though."

"And if he doesn't respond, they're going to start shooting," he said grimly. "Range?"

"Seven hundred thousand kilometers. They'll close for another three minutes, but they're vectoring away from us and they won't approach closer than five hundred thousand."

"And they're going to expect a response."

It wasn't a question. They were out of time. If the pirates didn't hear back from Costa...

"LaMonte."

"Sir?"

"When our spin brings us to the closest point, line us up and take the shot."

David waited. He realized he was holding his breath, but there was no time to change anything now. The rotation Campbell had built into their "immobile" course was taking place over a twenty-six-second cycle.

Those seconds counted down...and then LaMonte pushed a single flashing button on her screen.

The engineer had linked her own console into the tactical systems, and that button did several things.

First, it brought the main engines online, turning the big armed freighter the last few degrees of arc to line her forward battery of ten heavy lasers up on the approaching pair of destroyers.

Second, the battle lasers fired. Ten five-gigawatt high-energy lasers flashed into space, five on each of the two destroyers.

Third, the missiles fired. Ten antimatter-drive missiles blazed into space at ten thousand gravities, splitting into two groups of five to charge at the other two destroyers.

Last, to David's surprise, every one of *Red Falcon's* twenty-five RFLAM turrets rotated and opened fire as well. They fired shorter, less-intense bursts than the main guns, unable to penetrate warship armor...and then David realized LaMonte had targeted them on the *corvettes*.

The corvettes didn't have warship armor.

The two destroyers now directly ahead of *Falcon* never stood a chance. They never saw the lightspeed weapons approaching. One moment, they were charging at the freighter, attempting to contact their agent aboard.

The next, twenty-five gigawatts of coherent energy slammed into each of them. LaMonte had dialed in their cursory evasive maneuvers perfectly and hit with every beam.

The effect was similar to jumping into a pit of spikes...only even more energetic. Both ships came apart as the hammerblows struck home, shattering hull and systems alike.

The corvettes were luckier. Only five of the six close enough to be hit were targeted, and the beams that hit them were lighter, less effective—except that the "RF" in RFLAM stood for "Rapid-Fire".

All five targeted corvettes survived the first salvo, but the lasers kept cycling, working their way along the hulls of the pocket warships. One of the ships managed to break contact, dodging behind the destroyer it was escorting.

Four disintegrated—but the surviving ships were launching missiles of their own, and the RFLAMs went back to their real job of protecting *Falcon*.

"Group Bravo is a hard kill," LaMonte chanted. "Charlie is down to just the destroyer, missiles inbound. Delta is still mostly intact, missiles inbound. Alpha is out of range."

"Bring us to bear on Delta," David ordered Campbell. "Keep those missiles away from us and press them, *hard*. They've got more missiles—but we have better lasers. Take them out!"

Return fire was flickering out from the pirates' lasers now, but Campbell wasn't using academy-standard evasive patterns. She twisted the big ship through a series of pirouettes that would have done the smaller corvettes proud, and lined LaMonte's lasers up again.

This time, all ten lasers flashed at a single target. Two thirds of them missed—but the three that *did* hit left the destroyer spinning and leaking atmosphere, unable to evade as the antimatter missiles slammed home.

"Delta-one is gone," the engineer-turned-gunner announced. "Charlie-one took a hit and is leaking atmo, but her lasers and missiles are still in the fight."

"How long till Alpha sees the fight?" David asked. *Silent Atlantic* and her consorts were group Alpha, the first group of ships on the scene. He was reasonably certain they were hostile as well, but they were also a long way away.

"Ten minutes at least, maybe more," Campbell told him.

"Second missile salvo is all on Charlie-one, focusing lasers on the Delta corvettes!" LaMonte was making her announcements at least half to herself, chanting aloud as her hands flew over her console.

"We're hit!" the XO snapped. "Delta-two landed a laser strike on the rad dome. We're leaking water; systems are intact."

And Delta-two wasn't going to be doing *that* again. Delta-three was undamaged and managed to twist out of LaMonte's pattern of coherent energy. Delta-two, already hammered by the RFLAM salvo, didn't. Small and unarmored as she was, two five-gigawatt lasers were more than enough to vaporize the pocket warship.

"Missiles incoming," Campbell reported. "RFLAMs engaging."

There were a lot of missiles in space. The destroyers were old ships, likely the missing ships from Grand Interstellar Foundry's local mercenary fleet, but they'd been updated to carry a *lot* of fusion missile launchers.

The four ships that had lived long enough to launch had sent a salvo of eighty missiles at *Red Falcon*. The RFLAM turrets flared to life, lasers cutting through space. The weapons weren't a lot of use against warships, but they were designed for this job.

"Delta-three is gone," LaMonte announced grimly. "Rotate us to bear on Charlie-one!"

Red Falcon lurched. The previous hits hadn't been felt on the bridge, with the magical gravity in play, but *that* one had.

"That's not happening," Kellers said grimly over the engineering link. "The bugger just tagged us with his main lasers. Engines are down and I don't know when they'll be back up—if I guess wrong, we blow the fuck up!"

"Kelly?"

"I've got twenty missiles in the air at the bastard, but he knows the game as well as we—*holy shit!*"

A brilliant flash lit up the screen and an immense white spike appeared in space between *Red Falcon* and the remaining destroyer. It took a few seconds for the multi-megaton Martian cruiser's sensor to sweep the battlespace for hostiles—and less than a second for its massive *ten*-gigawatt lasers to shred the remaining destroyer.

"Jump flare," Campbell said weakly. "Multiple jump flares. Two cruisers, two destroyers, in escort formation around where we were fifteen minutes ago. Close enough."

"Close enough indeed," David replied. "Hail them!"

The speed the link opened with suggested the Navy had already hailed *Red Falcon*, and the image of a tiny red-haired man with the slanted eyes and dark skin of a Martian native bowed slightly in his screen.

"Captain Rice, the necessity of secrecy denied us the pleasure of meeting in person," the man told him. "I am Commodore Victor Andrews. Captains Laurentian and Vilbur happened to arrive just after you left, and it seemed a shame to turn down their services.

"I hope *Glorious Shield of Justice* didn't cause too much trouble emerging as close to you as we did," he said, his tone halfway between apologetic and amused. "Our location data for everyone was fifteen minutes out of date. I..." Andrews sighed.

"I half-expected to be avenging you, Captain Rice. I can't say how pleased I am that that is not the case!"

CHAPTER 45

TIRED AND INJURED as he was, there was no way that David wasn't going to meet the Navy teams when they came aboard his ship. The space between *Glorious Shield of Justice* and *Red Falcon* swarmed with Navy small craft carrying engineers, doctors, security teams—everything a ship that had just been boarded and shot up needed.

The first shuttle came into a landing in Kelzin's Bay Bravo with the practiced skill of an experienced pilot. The spacecraft touched down on one side of the bay, leaving a clear space for the chain of shuttles following it in.

"How many shuttles are they sending?" Campbell asked from beside him.

"*Glorious Shield* carries twenty assault shuttles, twenty personnel shuttles, and twenty modular work craft," Kelzin reeled off. "They're sending all of them, with the modular birds set up for exterior repairs and most of the assault shuttles carrying the same engineers and doctors as the personnel shuttles."

"The assault shuttles also have small but efficient med stations," David said quietly. "Dr. Gupta will have all of the hands he needs."

They had a disturbingly small number of wounded, roughly half injured in the fighting and the rest only *partially* asphyxiated in their quarters.

Costa had a *lot* to answer for.

The first shuttle lowered its ramp and, to David's surprise, disgorged a small honor guard of uniformed Marines—followed almost instantly by Commodore Andrews himself.

"Captain Rice," the officer greeted David, offering his hand. "Officer Campbell. Officer Kelzin. My people are coordinating as best they can to get aboard quickly. What are the priorities?"

"What we said before," David said quietly. "Doctors and medical gear. We've more dead than wounded, sadly, but our doctor is overloaded."

A tall, fair-haired woman followed the Commodore out and inclined her head to David.

"Surgeon-Commander Ziegler," she introduced herself briskly. "I am *Shield*'s senior physician. Where is your medbay? It sounds like I need to get to work."

"Jenna?" David asked.

"If you'll follow me, Commander," his XO said promptly.

The two women headed off deeper into the ship, and Andrews shook his head sadly.

"I'm sorry we didn't get here sooner."

"That wasn't the plan," David pointed out. "We were supposed to fall back on you. None of us anticipated Costa and Acconcio betraying us."

"It always hurts to be betrayed," the Commodore told him. "As I understand the situation, welcome to covert ops."

David shook his head.

"This is a one-off," he protested. "We got dragged into because we were available and the factions involved trusted us. No one is going to do that after this! They'll know we called the Navy in on them."

"Perhaps...not," Andrews replied.

"Three corvettes escaped," David said.

Andrews coughed delicately.

"No, they didn't," he admitted. "I sent three destroyers to demand their surrender, but they panicked and opened fire on my people. There were no survivors."

David sighed.

"That's probably for the best, though I hate to say that about more dead people."

"Agreed," Andrews replied. "But the point that must be considered, Captain, is that right now, the only people who have any idea how you survived this mess are mine, yours, and Costa and Acconcio."

"Just Costa. He killed Acconcio himself," David explained. There were possibilities in that, but they weren't ones he wanted to poke at. Not yet. "Along with half of the people sleeping in their quarters."

Andrews winced.

"And he's still alive? I congratulate your self-control," the Commodore said. "I'm not sure I would have been so merciful."

"That was Mage Soprano," David admitted. "I'm not sure *I* would have been so merciful."

The Commodore nodded.

"Do you have the coordinates for the base you were delivering to?" he asked. "Turquoise is a problem for this region, and it's not in my nature to leave a job half-done."

"We do, but I'm pretty sure they're garbage," David told him. "Costa implied as much, told Soprano he knew where the base actually was."

"Ah," Andrews sighed. "Then it seems, my dear Captain, that I need to have my intelligence people talk to him. May I request that he turned over to our custody?"

"That..." David sighed himself. "That is probably wise. I'm not sure how long he would stay alive here."

Maria stepped into *Red Falcon*'s tiny brig. She'd managed to grab a few hours of sleep to take the edge off the worst of the come-down from the Exalt, but movement was still a cautious, careful thing.

Shachar Costa sat in a small glass cubicle, his hands locked in front of him inside rune-encrusted manacles—the Mage-cuffs that restrained his powers. One of the security people had done a rough-and-ready first aid job on his ruined hand, coating it in instant cast to minimize infection or further damage.

"Come to gloat?" he asked once he saw her.

"Basically," she agreed. "You failed. The Legacy's little fleet has been destroyed, as has Turquoise's. I'm going to suggest that we make the official story that you sold out the ambush to the Navy, setting your own people up for clemency."

"The Navy?" Costa asked slowly.

"Is here," she confirmed. "We're turning you over to them shortly. They *really* want to talk to you about Turquoise's little base. You might even be able to talk your way out of the death penalty if you're a really helpful little bird."

"Or you'll tell my bosses I betrayed them and leave me out to swing?"

"Or the Navy will shoot you," Maria said flatly. "Active involvement in a major act of piracy? We've more than enough evidence for the Navy Captains to convene an acceptable Admiralty Court and sentence you to death."

She smiled.

"Please, try to not cooperate," she told him sweetly. "Iovis may have betrayed us all, but damn it, I liked the big idiot. I *definitely* liked Anders, and there's a stack of other bodies in the morgue that are all your fault.

"I really, really, *really* want the Navy to shoot you."

He was silent, facing her wordlessly, for twenty seconds. Thirty.

"Did Xi make it?" he finally asked.

"Why do you care?"

"I'm a paid hacker, a murderer and arguably a monster," Costa replied. "That doesn't mean I don't care, Soprano. It just means I'm very good at not listening to that part of me."

She snorted.

"Xi will live. No thanks to you."

He closed his eyes.

"I know you don't believe me," he murmured, "but I'm glad to hear that."

"You're right: I don't believe you," Maria agreed. "So, I suggest you start thinking of ways to make yourself valuable to the Navy, because no one on this ship is going to beg for your pathetic life."

David found Soprano leaning against the wall outside the brig, looking utterly exhausted.

"Maria?" he asked softly.

"I'm okay," she whispered. "Just exhausted. It's been a hell of a few days, and that...*bastard* in there was the cause of most of it.

"And he had the nerve to ask how Xi was doing."

"There's a Marine squad coming to collect him now," David told her. "The Navy will interrogate him. They'll find out what he knows."

"Good." She shook herself. "I had a suggestion, boss. How to make him really sweat."

"I'm listening."

"We have the Navy officially announce that *he* was the one who sold out the ambush," Maria told him. "Only Andrews knows *why* they were following us; we kept it pretty low-key."

"So, Andrews can tell everyone that Costa sold out the Legacy," David agreed. That was *nasty*. "I love it.

"But won't people wonder why he ended up in a cell?"

"I'm sure Andrews and his intelligence people can come up with a reason for that," she pointed out. "We just want him off this damn ship."

"Agreed. I'll pass the suggestion on." David paused. He could hear the Marines approaching. "Now, I understand they've brought Combat Mages, but..."

"You want me to keep watch until he's off the ship," Maria finished for him.

"Exactly."

"Wilco, skipper. How long until we need to jump?"

"We'll be able to fly in about twelve hours, according to Andrews's people," he told her. "We'll *jump*, however, when you and Wu are ready.

We're heading to Amber from here." He shook his head. "Our part in this mess is over; *Red Falcon* has no place in the assault on a pirate base!"

"Agreed." She shook her head. "I can't deny I'd love to see one of those go *right*, but that's the Navy's job now."

Her sadness over that was obvious for a moment.

"Amber is as close to home as I've got," David reminded her. "We'll find a bar for you to get drunk in if you want."

That broke some of her mood and she shook her head at him.

"Given where MISS found me, I think I'm going to avoid bars for the next while," she told him. "Lessons learned and all that."

Further conversation was interrupted by the squad of Marines arriving, two Combat Mages in the lead.

"Commander Soprano, Captain Rice," the leading Mage greeted with a prompt salute. "Mage-Lieutenant Mies Vance, RMMC. We're here for Costa."

"I'm not a Commander anymore, Vance," Soprano pointed out. From the way the Marine Mage saluted her, they'd met before.

"I was on *Swords at Dawn*," Vance said quietly. "You're still the Commander to everyone who was."

"Thank you," she said softly, "but I'm okay with what happened, Lieutenant. My choices had to have consequences." She glanced over at David. "I'm mostly okay with where I ended up, too."

"Good to hear, ma'am." Vance stepped up to the door. "Costa's in here?"

"Yes," David replied. "Mage Soprano and I will accompany you out. I want to make *sure* this son of bitch is off my ship."

Vance smiled thinly.

"From what I understand this...*individual* got up to, I doubt his mother would admit to having him."

CHAPTER 46

KEIKO ALABASTER was richer than David liked to think about, and money very directly equaled power under Amber's special sets of rules and laws. They'd mostly spent time together before in her apartment on Amber's main orbital, but this time she'd invited him, Campbell and Soprano to her home on the surface.

He sat on the patio of the sprawling ranch house and looked out over a vast expanse of open plain. The house sat on the edge of an immense park funded by several dozen of Amber's richest citizens, zoned to never be developed or adjusted from its original native state.

"I'm glad to have you here," Keiko murmured in his ear, leaning against him. "It sounds like you had a rough few weeks."

He shook his head and leaned back against her.

"This business with the Legacy is frustrating," he admitted. "I think we've probably shattered most of their starship assets, which is mind-boggling all on its own, but from the sound of it, they'll just recruit more."

"You know I can protect you here," she offered.

He smiled and nodded.

"A ship in harbor is safe, but that isn't what ships were built for," he quoted back at her. "I'm no better than my ship. I'm out of sorts on the ground, relaxing as it is sometimes."

"*Red Falcon* is good for you," Keiko agreed. "And damn, your new Ship's Mage."

He felt the elegantly tall woman smile against his ear.

"I know you, and I still had a flash of jealousy when I saw her," she said with a giggle. "She's had a rough time too, though. You can see it in her eyes."

"She dodged a dishonorable discharge by the skin of her teeth," David told his lover. "*Red Falcon* is her second chance."

Keiko didn't need to know the oddities of his crew situation. He trusted her, but that he had both an MISS agent and an entire Marine platoon aboard wasn't something she needed to know.

"How long until you're ready to fly?"

"Most of our repairs were taken care of before we made it here," he admitted. "Selling off the cargo we ended up with might take a while, depending on the skill of my local broker, but I need to give my crew a bit of a break."

His "local broker" bit his ear, just hard enough to hurt.

"The 'skill of your local broker,' my ass," she told him. "You know I could have it off your hands tomorrow, but if I *don't* get it sold, I get to keep you, is that what you're saying?"

David laughed and tickled her. That distraction lasted a moment or so, but she turned a level gaze on him again soon enough.

"We'll stay at least two weeks either way," he told her. "My crew needs the rest and I need to hire replacements."

He shook his head.

"Too many dead on this trip," he admitted. "Amber's a decent place to replace crew, but..."

"No one wants to replace crew," Keiko agreed. "There are no reasons to have to replace crew that make up for the hassle, but them getting killed is about as bad as it gets."

He leaned against her and closed his eyes, letting the sun sink into his skin as he forced himself to begin to relax.

"Yeah. And revenge isn't in the cards. It costs too much."

She giggled and ran her hands over his shoulder. "My dear Captain, you need to *relax*." She turned him around and smiled wickedly at him as she met his gaze.

"I'm sure we can arrange something."

He'd spotted the familiar destroyer *Tides of Justice* as their shuttle arced back towards Heinlein Station, so David wasn't entirely surprised when they found a quartet of black-suited Protectorate Secret Service agents waiting for them in the dock.

"Captain Rice, Officer Campbell, Mage Soprano," a soft-spoken young man with a Mage medallion greeted them. "I am Mage-Agent El-Ghazzawy, senior member of Hand Alaura Stealey's security detail. Could the three of you come with us, please?"

"When a Hand invites you, is declining even an option?" David asked dryly.

El-Ghazzawy looked uncomfortable.

"I suppose you could," he admitted. "This is only an invitation, after all."

"It's all right, Agent," David told him. "If the Hand has come all this way, we may as well meet with her, right, ladies?"

Soprano calmly nodded her agreement. Campbell was looking at them both like they were insane.

"A *Hand*?"

"She has business with you three, yes," El-Ghazzawy confirmed. "We have arranged a confidential meeting."

That was when David realized that the docking bay was empty except for them. The Secret Service was trying to keep the Hand's appointments, if not her presence, under wraps.

"Hands don't show up at random," he said quietly to Campbell. "We need to meet with her, whatever this is about."

The Secret Service agent bowed his head.

"If you'll follow me, please?"

Stealey hadn't changed much since the last time David had met her. She was still a stocky, nondescript gray-haired woman. Today she wore a plain black suit and leaned against a window looking out from the edge of Heinlein Station's ring.

The Station was angled to avoid the view being completely dizzying, but the planet outside was visibly moving. The Hand's gaze was focused on it, and she held a glass of whisky in her hand.

"Would you three like a drink?" she asked without looking at them. "El-Ghazzawy knows where the people we rented this from hid the booze."

"Water, please," David told the agent. His officers nodded agreement, and the Secret Service agent produced three glasses in a few moments—and then bowed himself out of the room.

"While I'm quite certain you would have been happier never to see me again, Captain Rice, the truth of the matter is that I always knew we would end up like this," Stealey told him. "Commodore Andrews's report makes for fascinating reading. If we were being honest about what happened to anyone, the crime lords of the galaxy would start to fear your name."

"I'd rather they just forgot it," he admitted. "I don't need them to think I'm useful to hire."

"I do," the Hand said flatly. "That both the Legatans and the underworld seem to regard you as a useful tool is of immense potential value to me, David Rice. I can *use* that."

"And if I just want to fly cargo and be forgotten?" he asked. "Is that an option?"

"Do you think the Legacy will let you disappear?" Stealey asked. "They've been explicitly charged to see you dead. You've destroyed Turquoise. She might escape herself, but with the lost ships and lost base, she's done.

"The Legacy will hunt you until they are destroyed. Underworld faction leaders like Turquoise will find you useful just for that." She shrugged. "The *Legatans*, however, trust you. That has an entirely different scale of value."

He sighed.

"Do you know what they're planning?" he asked.

"No. That's the problem, isn't it?" Stealey said. "The components you were hauling suggest they're building an antimatter production facility somewhere, but there's so many cutouts and layers of deception involved here... You helped peel back some of the layers for us, but... Andrews didn't learn anything new at Turquoise's base."

"I'm surprised," David admitted. "She was definitely working with them."

"Oh, yes," the Hand agreed. "I'm relatively sure *her* people didn't fit the station with an antimatter suicide charge."

David winced.

"They blew themselves up?"

"I'm relatively sure someone *else* blew them up," Stealey said dryly. She tapped a button on her wrist-comp, and a holographic display appeared in the middle of the room.

The space station in the center had started life as a prefabbed ring station. Even a quick glance told David that at least half of it was uninhabitable, open to space or otherwise wrecked. That still left a massive amount of real estate to be sitting in deep space.

A single destroyer of the same type they'd fought orbited the station, with a surprisingly strong fleet of two dozen corvettes...

"What is *that*?" he asked, gesturing at the unfamiliar cigar-like ship hovering behind the station from his viewpoint.

"We don't know," Stealey told him. She turned away from the view of Amber and stepped over to the hologram of the ship. "The Navy has no records of any ship like it. Fifteen million tons, clearly built around internal rotational gravity, *heavily* armed.

"Andrews brought two cruisers and six destroyers to the party—and that cruiser almost fought his fleet to a standstill on its own. No communications. No attempt to run. And when it died, well..."

The hologram moved. Andrews's squadron appeared in it, in the middle of an attack run. The strange vessel came apart as David watched, a swarm of Navy antimatter missiles vaporizing her in a single final blow.

And then the station ignited. It wasn't one antimatter charge—it was six, and by the time they were done, the entire ring station was gone.

"Six corvettes managed to run. Another ten surrendered," Stealey told them. "Interrogations were continuing when Andrews detached a destroyer to courier me his report, but it sounds like the crews we took know nothing about a deal with Legatus or the Legacy."

"So, we know nothing," David said.

"We know nothing new that *you* didn't find out for us," she replied. "You almost *accidentally* shredded a Legatan materials supply chain they'd spent years building—and you did it in a such a way that they don't even think it's your fault."

Stealey smiled.

"I want you to do it again," she told him. "I need you three to be agents-provocateurs, to slide back into the Legatans' covert supply chains and track down where these components were going.

"I can only assume that ship was theirs. So, they're building a secret fleet and a secret logistics base. There's only one reason for Legatus to do that."

"They're preparing for a civil war," David said softly.

"Exactly. And *we* don't plan on starting one," Stealey replied. "The Protectorate needs you, Captain Rice. Will you answer the call?"

He didn't want to. He wanted to take his ship and go back to hauling cargo that didn't have strange questions and traps attached to it. He wanted to keep his people safe and live in peace.

But his gaze kept going back to the explosion of the space station.

"Aye," he finally said. "Aye, Hand Stealey, I will answer."

ABOUT THE AUTHOR

GLYNN STEWART is the author of Starship's Mage, a bestselling science fiction and fantasy series where faster-than-light travel is possible—but only because of magic. His other works include science fiction series Duchy of Terra, Castle Federation and Vigilante, as well as the urban fantasy series ONSET and Changeling Blood.

Writing managed to liberate Glynn from a bleak future as an accountant. With his personality and hope for a high-tech future intact, he lives in Kitchener, Ontario with his partner, their cats, and an unstoppable writing habit.

OTHER BOOKS
BY GLYNN STEWART

For release announcements join the
mailing list or visit **GlynnStewart.com**

STARSHIP'S MAGE
Starship's Mage
Hand of Mars
Voice of Mars
Alien Arcana
Judgment of Mars
UnArcana Stars
Sword of Mars
Mountain of Mars
The Service of Mars
A Darker Magic
Mage-Commander (upcoming)

Starship's Mage: Red Falcon
Interstellar Mage
Mage-Provocateur
Agents of Mars

Pulsar Race: A Starship's Mage Universe Novella

DUCHY OF TERRA
The Terran Privateer
Duchess of Terra
Terra and Imperium
Darkness Beyond
Shield of Terra
Imperium Defiant
Relics of Eternity
Shadows of the Fall
Eyes of Tomorrow

SCATTERED STARS
Scattered Stars: Conviction
Conviction
Deception
Equilibrium
Fortitude (upcoming)

PEACEKEEPERS OF SOL
Raven's Peace
The Peacekeeper Initiative
Raven's Course
Drifter's Folly (upcoming)

EXILE
Exile
Refuge
Crusade
Ashen Stars: An Exile Novella

CASTLE FEDERATION
Space Carrier Avalon
Stellar Fox
Battle Group Avalon
Q-Ship Chameleon
Rimward Stars
Operation Medusa
A Question of Faith: A Castle Federation Novella

SCIENCE FICTION STAND ALONE NOVELLA
Excalibur Lost

VIGILANTE
(WITH TERRY MIXON)
Heart of Vengeance
Oath of Vengeance

**Bound By Stars: A Vigilante Series
(With Terry Mixon)**
Bound By Law
Bound by Honor
Bound by Blood

TEER AND KARD
Wardtown
Blood Ward

CHANGELING BLOOD
Changeling's Fealty
Hunter's Oath
Noble's Honor
Fae, Flames & Fedoras: A Changeling Blood Novella

ONSET
ONSET: To Serve and Protect
ONSET: My Enemy's Enemy
ONSET: Blood of the Innocent
ONSET: Stay of Execution
Murder by Magic: An ONSET Novella

FANTASY STAND ALONE NOVELS
Children of Prophecy
City in the Sky

Made in United States
Troutdale, OR
09/23/2024

23078891R00213